From Rona Jaffe Award-winner Fowzia Karimi, a highly anticipated, lushly illustrated debut novel about a young family forced to flee their war-ravaged homeland of Afghanistan, leaving behind everything and everyone beloved and familiar. The novel's structure is built around the alphabet, twenty-six pieces written in the first person that sketch a through-line of memory for the lives of the five daughters, mother, and father. Ghost stories and fairytales are woven with old family photographs and medieval-style watercolor illuminations to create an origin story of loss and remembrance.

Above Us the Milky Way is a story about war, immigration, and the remarkable human capacity to create beauty out of horror. As a young family attempts to reconstruct their lives in a new and peaceful country, they are daily drawn back to the first land through remembrance and longing, by news of the continued suffering and loss of loved ones, and by the war dead, who have immigrated and reside with them, haunting their days and illuminating the small joys and wonders offered them by the new land.

Praise for *Above Us the Milky Way*

"A sharply etched treatise on the objects of memory . . . powerful in both its beauty and its uncompromising horror whose themes are as sadly timely as they are eternal." —Starred review, *Kirkus Reviews*

"A skilled technician whose prose flows like intuition, Karimi parses the beats of her paragraphs with the attention of a poet. Rich with images and imagery, the book is beautiful, both illuminated and illuminating." —Starred review, *Foreword Reviews*

"Karimi's inventive, allegorical debut renders a family's wartime emigration through a polyphonic mix of voices and genres along with evocative color illustrations and photographs . . . Fans of *Lost Children Archive* will love this." —*Publishers Weekly*

"An ambitious abecedary of family, trauma, and life, and a love letter to the universe with many moments of power and resplendence."
—Jennifer Croft, *Homesick*,
translator of Man Booker International Prize-winner *Flights*

ABOVE US
THE
MILKY WAY

AN ILLUMINATED
ALPHABET

Fowzia Karimi

Deep Vellum Publishing
Dallas, Texas

Deep Vellum
3000 Commerce St., Dallas, Texas 75226
deepvellum.org · @deepvellum

Deep Vellum is a 501c3 nonprofit literary arts organization
founded in 2013 with the mission to bring the world into
conversation through literature.

First printing, April 2020

ISBN: 978-1-64605-002-4 | eISBN: 978-1-64605-003-1

Support for this publication has been provided in part by grants from the
National Endowment for the Arts, the Texas Commission on the Arts, the City
of Dallas Office of Arts and Culture's ArtsActivate program, and the Moody
Fund for the Arts:

LIBRARY OF CONGRESS CATALOGING IN PUBLICATION DATA
Names: Karimi, Fowzia, author.
Title: Above us the Milky Way : an illuminated alphabet / Fowzia Karimi.
Description: Dallas, Texas : Deep Vellum Publishing, 2020.
Identifiers: LCCN 2019054603 (print) | LCCN 2019054604 (ebook) | ISBN
9781646050024 (hardcover) | ISBN 9781646050031 (ebook)
Subjects: LCSH: Refugee families--Fiction.
Classification: LCC PS3611.A78337 A63 2020 (print) | LCC PS3611.A78337
(ebook) | DDC 813/.6--dc23
LC record available at https://lccn.loc.gov/2019054603
LC ebook record available at https://lccn.loc.gov/2019054604

Design by Fowzia Karimi | fowziakarimi.com

Interior Layout and Typesetting by Kirby Gann

Text set in Baskerville, a typeface designed in the 1750s by John Baskerville
(1706–1775) in Birmingham, England.

Printed in the United States of America on acid-free paper

For my mother, my father, my sisters.

Acknowledgments

My gratitude to the book, that perfect and abiding form, and to its devotees, among them: Will Evans, Kate Johnson, Kirby Gann, The Rona Jaffe Foundation, Sebald, Kepler, Christian, Micheline, Meilan, Renee, Muthoni, Allison, Lorraine, Dan, Jodi, Jeana, Merritt, Kendra, Kim.

Preface

Where memory is housed and where it is experienced are two distinct places in the mind. The first is orderly and immense, holding countless and myriad recollections. The air here is cool, still. Where memory is played for the viewing, the space is warm and close. It is furnished with a single chair and the screen takes up the entire wall. During the curious and all-consuming act of calling up the past, consciousness narrows down, excluding the external and the immediate, to focus on a single and earlier moment. And all biological systems join in the act. Is nostalgia not a somatic experience? Does the body in this closed space, in this act of narrowly viewing the past, not heat up? Do the pulse, the breath not quicken? Do the eyes not shuttle left to right, scan top to bottom? The act of remembering requires the participation of skin, nerve, bile and blood, as well as mind. It draws emotion from the body up into the mind, into that intimate screening room, even as it requests one or another recording from memory's extensive vaults over the mind's expedient pathways. My own nostalgic nature and urgings, and my Eastern upbringing in a Western land have pushed memory back and forth across these pathways from one center to the other, from where it is stored, to where it is re-viewed and re-lived. Growing up, I was at once memory's cataloguer, deliberate and careful, and its instrument, playing and replaying what I had gathered and stored, regularly wistful to the point of tears.

If there is a place in the mind where memory is housed and a place where it is experienced, and if there are pathways of travel between the two, then this book comes not from memory's cat-acombs or from its screening room, but from the networks over which memory passes. In my life, memory has passed so often across these networks that they have drawn to themselves the ghosts of my recollections, which coat them as ice in winter, or dew in summer, will coat an electric line. And these ghosts, which are not memories entire or lucid but their residue or their shad-ows, have in places crystallized and in places condensed on these lines. The stories in this book are not autobiographical in the true sense; they relate my history as well as ice, coating a telephone line, might relate the conversations that have passed through that line. The stories here are memory condensed, not whole or linear, but distilled over the many years of my nostalgic life. And as water crystallizes around dust, so my stories would be nothing without many grains of untruth embedded within them. In the end, these are works of fancy born of remembrance.

The work in this book has little to do with the realities of the moment and neither does it desire to be placed in too close a proximity to today's cultural or political landscapes. As it does not espouse or aim to teach some particular moral or to explain the state of affairs in one or another part of the world, it is best to pry it, difficult as that may be for the reader, from the jaws of today's ever-hungry information machine, and to read it in the spirit in which it was written: as a tale. If there is a reality to be found here, then it is the truth of the interior, where story is born and brewed.

I left the land of my birth at a young age. It is an enchanted place, occupying the heart of an old continent, traversed by ancient roads that have conveyed commerce, culture, and conflict over the millennia. The life I was born into was vibrant with story and legend, and warm with family and communion. Not long into my childhood, the country was devastated by war. Though I lived there only a handful of years, I gathered and absorbed much, as children do. I brought the specters and the ruins of my native land to this one, America, the land of few shadows and much sunlight. And it is these ghosts and these ruins, from another place and an earlier time, swallowed whole to protect them from the glaring light, that have informed my life. The pieces in this book are a collection of remembrances, dirges for the dead, and fairy tales—life experienced early and brought forth only after many years of distillation. Let me remember.

Prologue

Inside the house, five sisters, a mother, a father, and always a cat, occasionally two, with one coming, the other leaving, and the two for a moment indistinguishable, the same. Outside, in the yard, always a tree, resplendent, regal, the tallest on the block, whichever block the house was on in that particular year. And he, the tree, a grandfather to the five sisters, in place of the one none but the eldest had met years before in another country. And in the dry soil of that first country, their first grandfather remains buried in a tomb of marble—which some, but not all, of the sisters can remember—in a cemetery of dirt and stone and a handful of slender leaning trees that afford the ancestors a dappled shade at the noon hour and make his tombstone cool to the touch. Five girls and a cat hiding in the tree's evergreen canopy, year-round hanging from its limbs amid the buzzing of bees, beneath a shifting sky of clouds wispy and clouds swollen, scoring into the tree's trunk names and symbols that hold meaning, with depth of score to depth of meaning in perfect proportion, in golden ratio. And the girls peeling off layer after layer of bark to lick the tree's white living bones underneath. Hours spent playing hide-and-seek or magician, tying one another to the tree's trunk using rope from the garage and knee-high socks to cover the bound sister's eyes. Hand-feeding the prisoner salted cucumbers or pink strawberries (because we had too much heart or maybe just stubborn Eastern hospitality that refused to be bred out of us). And celebration all around when the magician finally loosened the rope knots and stood up to shake bits of bark or leaves from her hair.

Outside, the undoing of things. Beneath the grandfather tree, always grass, endless and forgiving of pounding feet and poking fingers and prying faces. In the grass: the tree's knobby knees coming up through dirt. Exiting the grass: a parade of ants that march and march and climb and climb up and around the tree's waist and continue up its many arms, to its very fingertips. The tree: a deity; the grass: a prayer rug; the sisters: joyfully oblivious. Among the blades of grass: bugs, the true kind with two sets of wings and red markings on black. Beneath the green carpet: glistening worms, cold and dry to the touch, and moist, brown earth, which packs beneath digging fingernails and there remains for the day.

Outside, the undoing of things: of hair ties, of shoelaces; of ripe grapes or plums or pears off vines and tree branches; the unraveling of rules and conventions; the unwinding of tongues that release laughter and disparate languages, mixed and broken, and which only the girls and the cat, the same one/many, understand; the unfolding of arms and legs, which gracefully taking to climbing and jumping and hanging, erase millions of years of evolution in a second or show that it too is fixed in time, like the house and the tree and the cat that remain always the same though the neighborhood or the city shifts every few years.

Inside the house, the doing of things: of homework, math and science and reading; of drawings of flowers or mountains or boats on far-off seas; the cutting of vegetables and of fat off the legs of dead lambs and chickens; the rinsing of rice; the stewing and baking of these things and afterward the consuming of them with Father and Mother, now home in the evening; the drinking of tea, always the sharing of tea; the washing of dishes at night while the television sings;

the drawing down of lids over tired eyes; the drawing up of blankets over cold shoulders; the splashing of water over slumberous faces in the morning; the tying of braids and ponytails; the pulling closed of backpack zippers; the shutting behind of doors.

Inside, the family always building a fire, not real but not imagined either. A center, a hearth, and the family around it, its members creating not a circle but a spiral of movement, of heat, at once chaotic, at once bound, burning with friction and love. An upward curling fire always pulsing, pushing always upward. A whorl of voices, of things said and things unsaid—which weigh more—of things whispered and things understood, of laughter which is light, and laughter which is heavy with the burden of remembering and the toil of forgetting. Inside the house and in its center, always a fire, a spiral, like an upside-down cone, shifting, turning, and buzzing with seven voices, six female, one male, and the purring of the cat/s.

ABOVE US
THE
MILKY WAY

The alphabet. A set of letters arranged in a particular order. A set of letters that combine endlessly to form words on the page. What books are made of. What the sisters are made of.

And these letters are set in their particular order as if a strong force runs through the alphabet, locking the symbols in place. And yet, the letters rearrange in inexhaustible combinations to write the words that give positive form to the formless. Like little magicians, the letters are forever in two places at once: bound in their fixed positions—for who could reorder the sequence of an alphabet?—and leaving their posts to form this or that word. The five sisters are also lined up in a precise order, oldest to youngest, held in place by a logic and a force born of nature and chance. And like the letters of the alphabet, the sisters arrange and rearrange themselves in endless amalgamations to give form to what is unspoken, and meaning to the ordinary.

A, the land where I was born.
A, the shore upon which I landed.

A, for ALL: for a story in its entirety. For how it begins, for how into it chaos or pain or desire enters, for what ensues within it, for where it takes us, for how all falls into place at its conclusion, and for the state in which it afterward leaves us. I too am a reader and I understand the need to consume all. I have this appetite. Moreover, I respect the boundaries set up by the two covers. And yet here, in this book, they are no more than lids, no more than two soft curtains opening on a scene. Yes, I too crave the arc. But you will not find one here. The only way forward is through the alphabet.

airplane

When they left the old land, the sisters kissed their grandmother's
spotted hands and did not pull away their faces from her moist,
uneven breath. They hugged their many-aunts, kissing three times
their warm cheeks; they bowed the crowns of their heads to their
many-uncles' hands and lips, nodding respectfully as the uncles
listed the do's and do-not's; and they spoke timidly and in whispers
with the cousins they knew as intimately as they did each other,
avoiding their eyes and their questions, secretly holding the same
unanswerable questions in their own minds. The flight of stairs to
the mouth of the waiting airplane was steep, the metal cold, and the
lofty view it afforded them indifferent to their many-questions: why,
where, how long, and what for? The sisters looked down silently yet
intently at the gathered tribe who stood twelve long and three deep,
in heels and in coats, lipsticked and combed, smiling awkwardly

with relief or with confusion, collectively willing back tears. When waving goodbye from the platform at the top of the stairs to the neatly assembled relatives standing down below, the sisters did not neglect their own reflected images: five small girls dressed in clothes and wearing expressions identical to their own. The mirror-sisters stood inside the terminal and looked back out onto the airstrip from behind ten-foot high windows, not knowing to question, not understanding the airplane, the overpacked suitcases, the flowers in the departing-sisters' arms. The sisters leaving waved and waved again from atop the stairs at the mouth of the airplane, blew kisses and shouted promises to the family who would remain and endure, shouted over the noise of the airplane's roaring engines, and waved again from the belly of the airplane, their small faces plastered two and three to a small window. But the sisters behind the glass within the terminal stood with arms immobile, chins tilted, and did not know what to make of the strange assembly on the tarmac

neat tribe

They were a neat tribe, standing neatly on the tarmac, their backs parallel with the windows of the terminal. Their hands were tidily tucked in their pockets, or clasped behind their backs, or dabbing handkerchiefs daintily at their eyes, or forming small fists beneath compactly folded arms. They did not cry too loudly, show too much relief or confusion, or bounce too exuberantly with excitement or to get a better view of the airplane. Even as the country around them folded in and prepared—and how tidily the visiting forces prepared the country—for the implosion, the tribe neatly stood smiling, waving at the departing family.

tidy forces

How cleanly the visiting forces sever tongues at right angles, remove eyeballs whole, arrange extracted teeth and fingernails in order. How smartly the soldiers line the streets of the occupied city, rifles at their sides, standing tall in their smart matching uniforms, with clear blue eyes, combed blonde hair shining beneath polished helmets. How nimbly their colossal tanks maneuver through the narrow streets of the old city and effortlessly climb and descend its hills. And how smoothly the rich blood flows down those sloping streets! No neighborhood is too inaccessible, too remote, for the humming vehicles of the visiting forces. No walls too high or doors too thick to dull the efficient knock of visitors who do not take no for an answer, irrespective of time of day or night. How neatly the visiting forces prepare the school children, the radio technicians, the hairdressers, the dentists, and the politicians. With great organization and proficiency do they compel the people of the country to follow their program, to emulate their smart ways. And with such soft quiet methods do they dispose of those who will not. The capability with which they dig into the rocky soil of the arid land is wondrous; how tidily they cover the mass graves afterward: not a limb protrudes; not a groan filters through. And those who insist, those who speak, are allowed to do so in orderly and suitable fashion. They are proficiently dismembered, packaged in compact boxes or sacks, and in a timely manner delivered home to their families, who hear them clearly upon arrival. How tidily the visiting forces prepare the country.

the Milky Way

Onto the softly lit stage they step, the cast—not players, not practiced; unknowing.

The stage—world-renowned, and called by various names: The
Silver River, The Straw Road, The Bird's Path.

The cast:
Mother
Father
the five sisters/the girls
grandparents
aunts
uncles
cousins
neighbors
tanks
soldiers
balloon peddlers
the scribe
the stars
farmers
the groom
the bride/the widow
the laundress
the moon
the taxi driver
prisoners
government officials
engineers

mothers
teachers
the cat
the grandfather tree
hands
eyes
ears
fingernails/claws
the book
the rose/the oracle
the mountain pass/the oracle
gods
grocers
policemen
the sun
guests
ghosts
the sea
the dead
the astronomers
the dreamer
birds
dust
and water

the alphabet

And what called the alphabet forth, gave it rise? What basic need gave the letters form—their spoken form, their line-drawn form? Were their shapes not embedded into the fabric of the planet from the beginning days? Were the letters not forged alongside the mountains and the valleys, by the winds and the tides? Did the same elements that animated the cell and the synapse not also give breath to the letters? Do you not see the S curled up in the shadow of the rock? The V as it flies through the air? Look at the I on the milky surface of the pond. Hear the Z's as they hover in and stick to the still summer air. Do we not share a history, we and the letters of the alphabet? Did they not evolve from their rudimentary beginnings, multiply, and beget as we begot? Shift in ways subtle and substantial over the millennia alongside us? And do the letters not have eyes, necks, shoulders, arms, spines, legs, and feet? Were we or they born first? Did we call them forth out of a primal need, shape them with our hands, with our tools—bone, bronze, clay, feather, and fur—in order to set down the unknowable? Or did the alphabet give rise to us in an effort to fathom that same vast deep? See how our ears are shaped, our mouths: the vowels slide in, the vowels slip out. Our tongues click, turn, and tuck to do the bidding of the consonants. Are the letters of the alphabet more fundamental than we, more ancient than our planet? There, an X twinkling in the inky sky over your head!

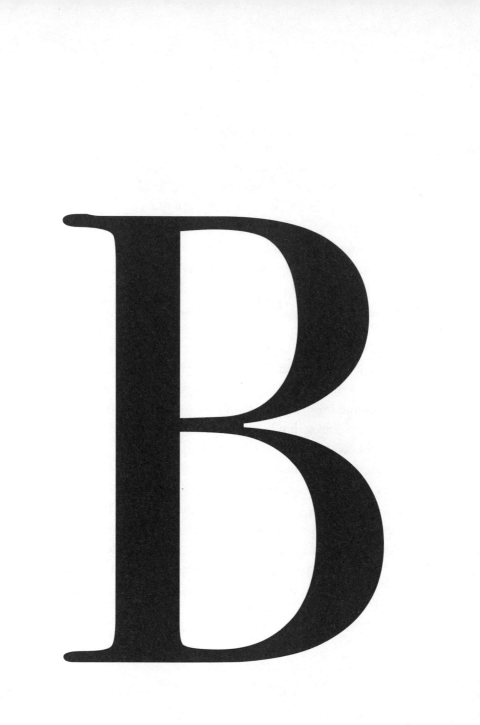

Before. All that happened and existed before the war, in the land that birthed the seven of us. In the beginning, there was life, simple. Then the war arrived. In an instant, much happened and, suddenly, we found ourselves upon a new shore, and looked about us: at the sand, the waves, the bright star overhead. But what was there, before, in the first land, in the beginning? Bood, nabood . . . There was, there was not . . . in the beginning, a family. A great and an ever-growing family composed of: a matriarch,

our grandmother, my mother's mother, the only grandparent living when I came into the world; many aunts and uncles, mostly on my mother's side; and many, many cousins of all ages and heights, with myriad interests and manners, ensuring that we each had a friend of our own when we went visiting. And there was much visiting! There was much food and feasting. Tea served endlessly, sweets set out in great cascading hills, pillows piled on cushions laid over limitless red rugs. There was the regular celebrating and commemoration of births and birthdays, circumcisions and graduations, holidays and anniversaries, of life, great and small, of loss, great and small. There were many stories, those told and those unfolding . . . Bood, nabood . . . Much talk and sharing. Gossip and soothsaying. There was laughter and joy and life spread and interweaved across an entire country. We had my mother's grand family in the city and my father's small family of simple farmers who lived in a village hundreds of miles and a winding mountain pass away. There was travel between the two. And always adventure and play. Wagon rides and tree swings. Carrots tugged out of the ground. Corn twisted off tall whispering stalks. Goats, chickens, cows, and dogs to feed, chase, and climb. A gurgling brook and the strawberries that grew on its banks. Hills covered with dwellings, dwellings bursting with life, streets filled with the traffic of pedestrians, vendors, cars, buses, and bicycles. Connecting all were neighbors, grocers, barbers, midwives, tailors, each like kin. There were markets and movies, street peddlers and their singular calls accompanying a rainbow of balloons or mounds of blood-red beets, which bobbed and peaked over the garden wall. There were rivers and picnics, and the bright-colored, soft-curved automobiles that delivered us there. Parades and television shows. School and friends and painted pictures of sweet ripe watermelon or sailboats crossing bright blue seas. And then there was war. In an instant, much happened and suddenly.

And war, on entering, obliterated everything and all. War, on entering the peaceful scene, turned it upside down and inside out. It shattered, severed, distorted, erased, violated, obliterated life, great and small, harmony, great and small, feeling, great and small, wonder, great and small. What was a flower to war, a child to war, a culture, a melody, a river, a picnic, a ritual, a statue, a farmer, a fairy tale, a people, a memory, a taxi driver, to war? So the buildings and farmlands and mountain passes were bombed; so the people

were disappeared, raped, tortured, dismembered, swallowed whole;
so the children's senses became keener, the adults' minds numbed,
their skin crawled; so the horror straddled and settled over the land.

In   the   beginning,   there   was   war.
Before the war, there was family, there was life, simple.

See how little patience I have for the orderly telling of things?

the soothsayer

The soothsayer looks at Mother, looks at the stones he has cast,
and consults his book. "Her path is yet in this world. In time, her
house will receive her children. No, your cousin shall not die." He
writes a prayer for the sick young woman on a miniature, narrow
scroll. He folds the long piece of paper at angles to make a compressed, triangular, paper jewel. He hands Mother the talisman
and an onion with instructions to take to her dying cousin who
lies in bed at home amid preparations for her imminent funeral:
cushions, china, and food set out for eighty. But the soothsayer
does not let Mother leave without reading her her own fortune.
"In four years' time, you will leave your country, you will go to
one city, then another, then a third, and you will not return here
again." Mother takes the talisman and the onion to her aunt's
house. Her aunt slices the onion in two and places the two halves
on her daughter's chest as instructed. She burns the talisman and
wafts the smoke around her sick daughter's face and shoulders.
Around midnight, the fading young woman sneezes once, twice,

then a third time, and opens her eyes. Mother returns home to
tell Father her cousin lives again and tells him about the seer's
prophecy. Father is vexed; he is not persuaded by the divining
arts, and contests he will ever go elsewhere, will ever take a step
off his own soil.

Much happens, and surreptitiously, in four short years. Mother
and Father, aunts and uncles, teachers and barbers, laundresses
and goatherds, silk traders and dentists do not know, cannot know
what brews and swells beneath the surface. Above it, birthdays
and anniversaries are celebrated, weddings and street parades
attended, newborns delivered and received by homes and bosoms
eagerly awaiting them, roads laid and leveled, fields planted and
harvested. Then one day, Mother and her in-laws step outside to
hail a taxi to visit her father's grave in a cemetery across the city.
A taxi passes, but does not stop for her. A second taxi speeds by. A
third pulls up and asks where it is she wants to go. "Turn around,
turn around, get back inside your house!" the taxi driver yells
at her. "Do you not know what is happening?" Mother and her
guests rush inside, lock the doors and, with the girls, hurry up to
the rooftop. They watch the planes fly over the city below. Night
falls and bombs with it. Night falls and the city quakes. Night falls
yet no one eats, sleeps, breathes. When day breaks, the streets are
lined with soldiers and heavy tanks. When day breaks, neighbors
eye passersby, grocers eye customers, brothers turn on brothers,
nephews turn in uncles, village women preach the new politics of
the new leaders to lifelong neighbors, politicians and engineers,
medical students and bakers vanish. A strange hush falls across
the land. A bewilderment and a terror rises. Tanks rumble and
bombs fall; families gather and huddle and wonder at what is
amiss and who is absent from their midst; individuals are gathered

up and not returned, kept behind doors and bars, prodded, pried, snapped, and unceremoniously pushed into the ground.

The ancient land is tilled up and under once again.

clock

And the moon rotates and revolves and presents the same steady countenance.

the talisman

Mother attends the funeral of her neighbor's son, a young student killed by rockets on his university campus. Her neighbor has three grown sons: the young student killed by the new government; the official high up in the new government responsible for the overthrow of the old government and the dropping of bombs and rockets; the middle son caught in between. The middle son eyes Mother, cautiously whispers to his own grieving mother over the grave of her youngest son. After the funeral, the neighbor woman, carefully, furtively, covered in shrouds from head to foot, stops in to see Mother at home. She tells Mother that her eldest son has received an official document demanding Father's arrest. And as Father and Mother helped arrange his marriage two years prior, the government official has torn up the document and asked his cautious brother to relay the news and the warning to Mother and Father. The neighbor woman warns Mother that there will be other documents delivered to other officials, that time and luck run thin.

Father does not need further evidence. The space about him has contracted even as it has emptied in recent months, as his colleagues and his friends have disappeared in the night and reappeared in morgues and on roadsides in the morning. They are whole one minute and in pieces the next. At their desks one minute, on the television screen denouncing others the next. Father applies for visas for his family and is denied. He pays a colleague a large sum of money in exchange for passports for his family. The man takes the money quietly, he shakes and nods his head in sympathy, he makes the promises in hushed tones, and when Father next approaches him, the man threatens to turn him in.

Mother begs Father to leave on his own, to traverse the winding dusty roads on foot and on truck bed, to cross the borders as others have before him. But Father will not leave Mother and the girls: he knows what will happen to them should he leave and they stay. He is afraid and aware—all eyes and ears, day and night. He does not sleep, does not eat, does not leave the house without looking before and behind, above and about, his person. He asks her to visit the soothsayer again.

Mother returns to the seer and reminds him of the prediction he cast four years prior, in another time and in a different landscape. The seer gazes at Mother, he casts his stones, and consults his book. "By next Friday you will have left your country. By next Friday, you will have flown away." Mother says they have no passports, no documents. Mother says there is no way her five small girls can make the journey on foot, unnoticed, unharmed. He assures her, "You will not be here next Friday." He writes down a prayer for her, hands her the talisman and instructs her on its use: When next you leave your house, burn the talisman before you and pass through its white smoke as you cross the threshold of your front door.

in the beginning: questions

And, in a very short time, the sisters became accustomed to asking questions in silence and expecting answers from sources singular—flowers, ceiling, shoes—knowing that when questions were asked of an adult, the adult sometimes disappeared. In the weeks before their departure, when Mother and Father did not sleep and the sisters lay in bed not-sleeping, many questions filled the sisters' minds. *Why do the adults smile even as they wring their hands even as they speak in the even tone even as their eyes flit from side to side and floor to ceiling? And what happened to the old tones, the warm tones, the rise-and-fall tones of their many voices, which now, by day, speak in a single pitch across the hills and in the streets of the city, and by night, whisper and sigh?* In that time before their departure, the sisters came to see clearly that day had turned into night. And had done so surreptitiously, had done so without the sun's blessing. In the day, in the streets and in the markets, the adults walked as though asleep: silent, unseeing. Yet theirs was a strange trance, the sisters saw but did not remark. Unlike the gliding somnambulist, the unseeing adults moved ever so cautiously, so as not to run into anyone on the street or in the marketplace, know them though they might, so as not to disturb the dust on the dish vendor's ware. And the sisters saw clearly that light, however dimmed, flickered in the adults' eyes only in the late hours of the night, and even then intermittently, and only when the overworked, arching, twitching ears settled back into place on the sides of their heads. The observant girls saw that the adults' ears had in a very short time grown in size and capability, and in that same short time the adults' eyes had diminished in size and sheen. And yet the girls were unaware of their own large eyes and small mouths. The five sisters, ever so watchful, cautiously observed the adults, but they asked their questions quietly of the soup ladle and the spider. The sisters wondered: *Have all the fathers stopped lifting their daughters on their shoulders, stopped singing the folk songs that make the daughters laugh? Do all the mothers sort linens and china, socks and trousers in the dead hours of the night? Some have left; will we go, when will we go, why do we go, where are we going? For how long? And what about everyone else? Will we be back in time to celebrate my birthday with the many-cousins, to open the many-gifts, to eat the three-tiered cake, to choose the biggest brightest balloon from the street peddler's bouquet, to blindfold the giggling cousin, to hide ungiggling behind grandmother's chicken coop with the little sister, to beg and plead to have the beloved cousins-like-sisters sleep over to tell the stories and share the sweets to celebrate my birthday?* While Father paced the living room and looked out the window every five minutes, the sisters questioned the clock and the living room curtains: *who goes there this time of night, when will the sun rise again?* And while Mother, not-sleeping, packed and sighed, they questioned the zipper on the suitcase: *what do you carry, do you have room enough for my green dress, for my dearest doll, for my schoolbooks?*

the scribe

The old man sits on a cushion before a wooden box, cross-legged
and bent over a tidy stack of forms, various official stamps, a jar
of black ink, and nibs of different sizes. Beside him on the ground
is a thermos of black cardamom tea and warm bread wrapped
in a scarf. He sits in front of the government office buildings
that open daily like clockwork, sits beneath ancient trees, and
among others like himself. The scribes arrive at sunrise, and set
up before the offices open for official business. Mother arrives
soon after and approaches the old man. She kneels on the ground
beside him. She has practiced a small lie to get the documents
she needs. Mother tells the scribe, "I cannot write, uncle dear,
no one at home can write, will you please take down an official
request for me?" She has not told Father what she has planned to
do. It is their last chance and she does not want to raise his hopes.
The old man finds the proper form with the proper letterhead
and chooses a nib for his pen. Mother watches him and gauges
whether he can be trusted with more. As he prepares to write, she
puts her hand on his. She tells him her husband's life is in danger,
her children are many and young. She whispers that she will give
him a substantial sum of money, her own and her children's saved
over many years, if he will leave room in the script to add family
members, after she has obtained the signatures she needs from the
government officials in the buildings behind him. He shakes his
head and murmurs. They will both be caught, times are strange,
and strangers treacherous; how can he trust her? He cannot risk
his life, he has a family too. In hushed tones, she pleads with him,
tells him this is her only hope, assures him if she is caught, no
one will know it was he who helped her. She begs and pleads and
promises. So the scribe, in his beautiful hand, writes: *My daughter*

*and I need to leave the country, need to travel to I____ for medical treatment.
We need passports.*

Mother enters the government building, climbs the stairs, and
takes the petition to the office that provides the signatures for her
documents. The upright guard at the door tells her the official is
out, come back tomorrow. She leaves and returns the following
day, forms in hand. The guard at the door tells her, the official is
busy, he is in an important meeting with so-and-so, come back in
the afternoon. Mother is angry, she is frightened. She has burned
the talisman and passed through its smoke. She does not have
much time. She rushes down the hall, past guards and rifles, and
down the stairs, upset. On her way down, she runs into a slight,
frail man coming up the stairs, accompanied by a guard. She
nearly knocks the man over. She wants to apologize, she tries to
avoid eye contact, she looks down. He says, "Excuse me, sister, I
am sorry. I was careless." Mother is taken aback by his kindness;
she watches him go up the stairs. At the top of the stairs, the other
guards salute him and part to let him pass. Mother thinks, *this is
someone, this is an important man.*

She follows him upstairs, sees him enter an office and inquires of
the guard at the door who the man is, and is informed that he is
the head of the department but is not seeing anyone. The official
overhears this through the half-open door. He calls Mother in and
asks her to sit, asks her what it is she needs. Mother gives him the
petition and tells him, untruthfully, her daughter is gravely ill and
daily getting weaker. She tells him they need to leave the country
for treatment. The official looks at her, seems to look through her.
All the while, he himself is disappearing into his overlarge jacket,
his loose collar, his imposing desk chair. He slouches into the

chair, rests his elbows on the desktop, props his head on his knuck-les, and, sighing, asks her a question. Why does your husband not accompany the child? Why is he not here now? She draws out another practiced lie and tells him her husband is a simple, unschooled shopkeeper. "He has a small grocery; he sells this and that. Without his earnings we cannot feed our children. Without him, I cannot run the shop." The official looks at her petition, he looks at her, smiles faintly, fumbles for a pen in his shirt pocket, and signs the petition. He says, "You must not tell anyone I have done this for you, dear sister." He tells her he is only recently released from prison; he is unwell. He tells her the latest coup has bought him his freedom, but his freedom and his position are not assured. He says to Mother, "Wherever you need to go, go, and get yourself out of here by Friday. Now go with God."

Mother returns to the street scribe. He makes the necessary addi-tions to the petition. He writes: *My five daughters, my husband, and I need to leave the country, need to travel to I____ for medical treatment. We need passports.* The old man administers the requisite official stamps. Mother pays him well for his aid. He nods and sways; he says to her, "May God keep you. May God keep us."

Mother visits other offices, pays fees and turns in forms. On Monday, she receives the seven passports. On Thursday, the seven climb the cold metal steps, file into the airplane, and lift up into the sky.

company

Dear reader, we've only recently met, but how comforting it is to have you here. Did I not tell you that I too am a reader? I understand the need to understand all. And yet here, I stumble, eyes closed, I run into this and that, lights dimmed, I search and return, examine and reminisce, as I work to unravel this circuitous tale. How good it is to have your company.

bird, tree, man

Before the war, Father was many-legged. Not spider, not beetle, but capable nonetheless of accomplishing and orchestrating many things with many arms, scrambling here, scuttling there, always active.

No, before the war, Father was a little wren, hopping from place to place and activity to activity, one moment in his tiny rooftop office at his desk over his notes, the next teasing Mother in the living room in front of her guests, and, soon after, high up in a tree with a saw in his hand, clearing dead branches. Father, always cheerful, always flitting. Always tuneful, he sang to his girls the arrhythmic village songs he'd learned as a boy. Sang them out of the blue, after a meal, on long car drives, in the midst of clearing a garden bed. He worked tirelessly and spiritedly. And when he rested, he was instantly drawn back to the farm, and to the first river, the small river on his parents' land, which birthed and bathed him, the river that still drew his gaze, now inward, and soothed him.

Father rose early, dressed early, was from home and at work with the sun, proud. He returned for lunch and for dinner with stories and jests for Mother, and with new ideas and strange objects, unwieldy words and curious customs garnered from his foreign coworkers to share with the girls. Mother, Queen of Stories, lent Father, otherwise timid, her ears and her heart. And the girls, audience to all they did and did not understand, laughed with Mother and delighted in Father's antics when he replayed a scene for their comprehension.

No, before the war, Father was a poplar tree, slender and upright, his leaves always turning, always twinkling: active then nostalgic, timid then jesting, man then boy.

readers

The youngest sisters, the ones still illiterate, marvel at the grown women's ability to read the leaves. Mother and Grandmother, aunts and married cousins, seamstress and spinster neighbor, all pour and sip and interpret the tea leaves expertly. And the older sisters and cousins over the many years and the many pots of tea are steadily initiated. They are taught to study the steeped letters and to decode them by their shapes, shades, and by where they float or rest in the teacup. And the little ones look over shoulders and under arms and listen attentively, record assiduously in their little minds the shapes, colors, and behavior of each leaf and twig, as well as the blessing, the omen, or the story associated with every type.

Their ordinarily reserved aunt squeals and nearly spills her cup of tea before she is able set it down to show them all: *A marriage! A marriage, look! My eldest! Must be. See how the small, dark leaf tucks itself so modestly behind the broader, green one up against the side of the cup where the sunlight shines so brightly on both? Ten yards of silk; two of lace; ten kilos of almonds, fifteen sugar, muslin too!; the photographer's son, such a handsome boy!; four sacks of rice, two lambs, five cars, three hundred plates...* And counting, adjusting her headscarf, checking her purse for bus fare, slipping on her shoes, she trips out of the gathering to head home with the good news.

Mother looks into her daughter's cup and teaches her: *Here, look at how this twig floats and bobs, just beneath the surface; a guest is coming, a man, a tall man, a serious man; your uncle will be here in two days' time.*

Grandmother gathers her guests about her, stares deeply into her cup and deeply into the eyes of the women and girls about her: *Haven't I been warning you all? Another loss, another disappearance; who this time? Look at how the listless leaf floats at an angle. She is not so young, but a virgin still. Someone near to us all. Poor, helpless one. Such a shame!* And all who are present cough and shift, the family pour more tea and press more sweets on their guests.

in the beginning: tea

Dear reader, it is early. We have not left the old land yet. Pull off your shoes, lean back into the cushions. I have poured you a cup. Stay awhile and read with me. Or, if you'd prefer, I can read you in these leaves.

in the beginning: wonder

The ancient land—mountainous, arid, landlocked—had many
rivers coursing through it, and lakes like sapphires set in gray,
impervious rock mounts. The deepest of these lakes lay where no
human lived. But a dirt road ran along its length and when the
family drove beside the blue abyss, Mother would say, *this is where
they bring the sick to heal. Those who are fearless will submerge themselves
beneath its still surface, suppress many breaths, and rise again healed, whole.*
And the girls knew the land was wondrous.

best man

Father, a village native, has the one dear friend in the city. He is a
school friend, a friend like a brother, a man like Father himself: a
builder and an engineer, guided by numbers and rulers, and drawn
to line and form. He shares Father's industrious nature and playful
humor, and Mother's ready ebullience and charm. He is Father's
only representative at his engagement to Mother, and stands beside
him through his wedding and the births of his five girls. He is like
an uncle to the girls, who see both parents reflected in the single
man. He delights them with laughter and love and gifts, and lifts
them high into the air and onto his strong shoulders. The engineer
visits often, leaves and returns with Father regularly so that the
girls come to see him as Father's bright shadow, as Father's steady
but more jovial mirror image. He is a single man, without Father's
familial responsibilities, and he looks to Father and his family as
models for the ideal life, which he has worked long and hard to
earn for himself. And when he has completed his studies, been

offered the job, and found his bride, he brings Father and Mother
to ask for her hand in marriage. It is Mother who decorates and
fills the silver platters with sweets and almonds to offer the future
bride's family. Mother who befriends the bride and sister-to-be.
And it is Father who sits beside the now-shy engineer and speaks
the humble words to, asks the important questions of, the bride's
parents. And her parents are welcoming: her mother nods and
smiles and keeps the teacups filled; her father laughs and boasts and
heartily shakes the engineers' hands. Now he is a joyful man, the
groom-to-be! He has the new job and the beloved betrothed and a
forthcoming wedding celebration to dream about. It is not war he
sees descending. It is not in his nature to sense darkness. He is all
cheer, all light. And with his cheer and his light he drives himself
forward through space and time toward the eve of his wedding.

He is an engineer and leaves the city early with four other
engineers to travel to a neighboring town to draw up the
blueprints for a new school. The five work all day and into the
night, the night before his wedding day. On their drive back to
the city, they are stopped along the highway by the new forces,
omnipresent now in the cities, towns, and villages, and along the
winding lean roads connecting them.

The engineer's brother is a doctor in the city hospital. In the
morning, a colleague from the hospital morgue finds and says to
him, "Five bodies have been brought in and one has your face."

In the morning, Father drinks his tea; he is elated, he is restless, he
readies to leave for work, but thinks only of his friend's wedding
and his joy. Mother has set out her dress and Father's suit for the
celebration. She dries her hair and dresses to leave for the salon

where she will have it styled for the evening. Father answers the door when the bell rings. Mother can see him from where she sits at her vanity in the bedroom, but cannot hear what the unfamiliar man at the door says to him. But she sees Father diminish in stature, she sees his head fall forward and to the side, she sees him tremble and lean into the door. And she feels her own wrists twist and freeze, her hands become rigid and paralyzed in midair, her fingers clamp about the handles of her brush and her hair dryer. Here is the old news, fresh again.

The five have been cut into six each. Their heads, arms, and legs have been neatly removed from their torsos, and thus they arrive at the hospital, a collection of thirty parts. And the engineer's brother, the doctor, cannot reassemble him. And Father, the engineer, cannot buttress his heart or tie his own nerves back together after receiving the news.

It is a day of funerals in the city of many hills. To get to the engineer's house, Father and Mother have to make their way through a city choked with mourners. The masses, young and old, wail and scream in the streets as they follow the casket of the country's beloved King of Music, recently killed by the new forces. Father and Mother have to drive past the house of another of the five dismembered engineers, past his shrouded body carried by his father and his uncles from car to front door. Funerals for the young daily draw and collect mourners still unaccustomed to their ubiquity. The frequency of the ritual dazes the people of this ancient land and energizes its new government and the foreign forces that steer them. The frequency does not dull Father's ache or Mother's terror. They arrive and are received by the bride at her betrothed's house. She is in her wedding gown, her face and hair made up.

She takes Mother's hand and leads her to the bedroom she has spent months decorating with photographs and posters, with garlands and bouquets of flowers, with hand-sewn and embroidered curtains, pillows, bedspread, and bedsheets, all in her favorite colors, pink and cream. She tells Mother it is her wedding day. She grabs a hold of Mother's wrists and says, *my heart is bursting*. As mourners arrive, she takes them to the room so intimate to her senses. And each time she enters the room, she enters as a bride, at once proud and bashful. When she leaves to attend to another knock at the front door, she leaves as a widow in deep mourning, carried out on the arms of those she escorted in.

the disappeared

In the beginning, the taking and the killing was not particular, not honed. They took those who did not look right, who walked askew, who spoke the wrong words in the wrong place to the wrong individuals—individuals with a keen interest in all that was said and done in the streets and in the marketplace, behind every wall, door, and curtain in the cities, towns, and villages of the country. They took those who would be a threat: the grocer comparing his cabbage to the new leader, the bicyclist asking directions to the theater showing the foreign film, the student returning home late from a meeting, the teacher too learned, the banker too well-connected, the athlete unnaturally youthful, the mechanic overly assiduous. Later, they had names, they had addresses. And the names and the addresses were acquired through strange methods by avid hands wielding specialized tools, and purloined from the mouths of the captured grocers and teachers and bankers too much of a threat to the state to ever see their families or their freedom again.

blood

In the beginning: blood.

confidant

Mother loves easily, she loves many and deeply—her girls, her husband, her mother and her many siblings, her neighbors and her myriad friends near and scattered about the city and the country. She loves devotedly and protectively and she does not tell those she loves and whom she must leave behind that she is going. She does not tell them that she leaves for good or will travel far. She cannot tell them where it is she and her family will fly to. But her heart is full and she cannot leave without saying goodbye to those dearest to her. She takes two of her girls, takes a taxi to the far end of the valley, to the base of a newly developed hill. She and her girls climb the steep and narrow streets of the neighborhood on the hill. They climb past houses-like-boxes, like-teeth, past boulders and children playing, women sweeping, men leaning in doorways, to the hilltop where her dear friend, who calls her sister, lives with her two small sons. While the girls and the boys play, Mother tells her friend she must leave, and soon. They are coming for her husband. Her friend, an old friend, a dearer-than-blood friend, does not take her hand, or kiss her cheek, or circle Mother with her arms. She rises, she stares at Mother, she crinkles her lips and furrows her brow, "You are leaving your motherland! You betray our new leader, the beloved father! I can, I will report you!" Mother collects her girls, descends the hill, and returns home. She cannot tell Father, she will not amplify his silence or his fear. Here is the world turned inside out, here new leaders sprouting, savage forces proliferating, flowers and trees fading, old friends wearing new faces, strange declarations spilling from familiar mouths, ancient prisons overflowing, modern ones rising, the earth reluctantly swallowing, life shifted and unrecognizable.

monster

Before the war, the monster the sisters feared was Old Man
Thunder. He arrived with the dark, towering storm clouds to chase
lightning over the city and across the sky. He roared and roared and
the sisters quaked and peered out of the second-story windows of
their house on the hill. The girls were safe as long as they stayed
indoors, Mother said. But if they absolutely must go out, to deliver
Mother's jam to Grandmother's house, or run to the baker's up the
street to pick up the morning bread, or make it down to school in
time to take the test, they would be safe as long as they did not wear
the color red. It was the only color the thunder man could see from
his elevated perch in the storm clouds. And his favorite meal, before
clouds and even before lightning, was children: soft, warm, delicious
children. Mother and the aunts told the sisters many stories of small,
red-garbed children being lifted from the ground and suctioned up
into the dark clouds, into the beast's mouth, never to be seen again.
Families diminished in size. Children lost siblings and playmates.
But life went on, said Mother, because there was nothing the adults
could do once a child was swept up into the storm clouds by the
angry, hungry beast. There was no official or department in the
government they could go to for recourse, no ladder tall enough to
retrieve the children, the aunts said.

And each sister had a favorite article of red clothing, and each was
tempted to test the grumbling sky monster, to draw him out of the
clouds so that they might see him, might finally fix a face to that
roar and rumble they feared and knew so well. The frightened-
curious sisters regularly sat at the upstairs window during thun-
derstorms to look out for children who may have forgotten or
never been taught the rule and may require warning or aid. When

feeling especially bored and brave, they even dressed in the dangerous color and ran out into the yard or down the hill waving a red scarf or lifting pant legs to reveal red socks, while sticking out tongues or wagging fingers at the sky. But they never saw the terrible visage of Old Man Thunder, though each imagined that she had seen an elbow, a fist, or the end of a beard protruding from the clouds, terrifying images that made them race back home to change and hide. Though the sisters were five, not one of their number was lifted into the air by the mysterious beast. It was an airplane, quietly humming and evenly cool inside, that finally lifted all of them into the sky and through the clouds.

denouncer

They take the man into a room, a windowless and unfurnished
room, save a single metal table. They close the door and remove
his crumpled clothes and whip him. They whip him across his
back, across his arms, across his legs. They are careful not to mark
his face. They whip him expertly and tirelessly. He does not know
how long for. It is a long time. Then they leave and the guards
return with a rag to wipe him, and return him to his small cell.
They let him rest and when again they come for him, they arrive
with his clothes, ironed, and a necktie and a suit jacket, which they
tie around his collar and put about his raw, blood-caked shoulders.
They shave his face, comb his hair, give him a glass of water to
drink, and take him by car to the television news studio. *Here is a
list, read it carefully. Here are the names of other betrayers like you. Learn it
well.* They seat him in a chair, at a table. They aim the lights and
adjust the height of the microphone. But I do not know these
people, he tells them. They point to names. *If your tongue does not
flap, we will take your toenails.* He tells them so-and-so has left the
city, returned to his people in the foothills of the northern mountains, he is no longer here. So-and-so crossed the border and left
the country last month. This woman here, she has disappeared,
no one knows how, why, or where to. He tells them I do not know
these other people. I do not recognize these names. Beneath the
table someone with sturdy pliers and a firm grip is at the ready.
Beneath the table his feet are bare and one by one they pull out his
toenails. They recite to him the names of his children and his wife,
his mother and his aunts, of his brother and his nieces, his sisters
and their husbands. They shine the lights, zoom the camera in,
and roll the film. And he reads from the list before him. His teeth
chatter, his tongue thickens and his eyes water, his hands tremble

and he reads the names off the list. Father's name is on the list. It is one of many.

midmorning

Before the war, there was Mother, and the leaning midmorning light she cast across the cushions and the rug in the second floor living room of the house. In her light, the moisture rising from teapot and teacup curled, swayed, and spread. In her light, air's emissaries, dust, like flecks of gold, attended Mother's breath, which sent them spiraling and rising, tumbling and returning. Her ruby ring, illuminated, was a window onto a distant cosmos. And the sister not in school, not napping, looked deeply into this red starry night or with somnolent eyes followed the pink dancing light it cast upon wall and ceiling as Mother sipped from her cup. All was silent, eternal.

Dog and Jackal

Long, long ago, in the beginning . . . *Bood, nabood* . . . There was, there was not, before our time in this city, before your grandparents' time, a pact made between Dog and Jackal. Dog lived in the barren wilderness and Jackal lived here in the city, among us, as a companion and a protector. One day, Dog called across the borderlands to Jackal and said, "Let us switch places for ten days.

You come out and live in the wilderness, where it is fresh and open and where none will bother you, and I will come to the city and live with the humans to see what they are like. When the ten days are up, I'll come back to the wilderness and you can return to your home in the city." The two animals switched places. Dog came to the city. He lived among people and experienced their kind ways. They invited him into their homes, they fed him, and their walls sheltered him from the cold wind and the scorching sun. Jackal roamed the desolate wilderness, chased the swift birds and the nimble hares, picked withered flesh off of dry bones, and shivered in the moon's cool light. The ten days passed, yet Dog remained in the city. The ten days passed, but he did not answer Jackal's call across the borderlands. To this day, Jackal raises his muzzle skyward and howls. From the desolate edges of the city, he calls to Dog in the twilight hour, asks him when he is returning to the wilderness, begs him to remember their pact.

C is for Color. Life in the first country was saturated with color. It was as if life there, before the war, was made up not of events or people or places, but of yellow and blue and green and orange. Of blushing ripe fruit hanging from taxed tree limbs and verdant eager vegetables bursting from the earth. Of crisp blue skies framing our mother's black hair and her coral lips. Of rose-covered skirts and poppy-covered hills. (It is still with me, will not dissipate: a scene of hilltops covered in tens of thousands of papery red poppies. And the scene is at once still, as in a photograph, and stirring. There is a breeze, the clouds sail, the flowers on their tall stems sway, then freeze. There is the sound of a hundred thousand bees in spring. Then silence. I am within the scene, then without. But even then, the four white borders only frame the vividness of color in the first life.) I believe it happened this way: color escaped first.

When the war arrived, *it* disappeared. Thinking of it now, color was gone long before. Where was it during those strange, silent months before the armies began lining the streets, filling the squares, entering the houses? In those months when husbands and wives, fathers and sons and sisters whispered behind doors and curtains, and in the back seats of taxicabs, when everyone eyed the dressmaker, the school teacher, the young neighbor back from his studies abroad, color was nowhere to be found. It was as though color had divined our lot, drawing the information out of the solid ground or from the trembling air, and had simply faded, slowly leaching from road signs, mittens, and potted flowers. It was as though color, long friendly with our people, could not remain to be witness to what would soon befall us. And now I see that of course the two, war and color, cannot coincide. But for red, that most vital of colors, which endures despite, and perhaps informs, war.

Afterward, there were only the brown of the earth and the dull greens and grays of uniforms and tanks and rifles. The pale blue of the soldiers' eyes beneath their helmets. The red of their flags.

In a land without color, we, the sisters, could not dwell. We filed into an airplane and lifted and landed, lifted and landed, again, then again, in search of what we had lost. We did not choose our new home, but it promised us a return of color. When we arrived at the airport of the new country, were the walls of the terminal not painted with a rainbow to welcome us? In the new land, the land of the sun, color reigned.

friends

The five sisters alighted from the airplane tentatively. They felt
the ground beneath their feet, smelled the air, listened to sounds
strange and distorted, sensed an eager heat upon their skin,
and looked about them: at the sand, the waves, the bright star
overhead.

It did not take the new land long to befriend the sisters. It
approached them warmly, artlessly, without judgment or inquiry.
The sisters fell out of the sky and though it knew not whence
they'd come, the new land asked no questions and nothing of
them. It simply wished to play. It was all-innocent and all-gener-
ous, bringing the many gifts and dropping them at the sisters' feet
daily. Here were flowers, seedpods and beetles, here were dresses
to share, dolls to dress, here a cat to chase, a tree to climb, friends
of all ages arriving on bicycles and skateboards, sugary bright
candy and popsicles delivered by musical trucks, sky-skimming
swings and seesaws, an endless lawn to spin and spin and tumble
upon, a sky that turned and turned and showed the same bright
smiling sun, a sun that warmed and caressed their dark tresses,
baked their small hand-shaped earthenware, and drew them to a
blue sea, which kissed and cooled their feet and shared its riches—
seashells and anemones, shorebirds and beach balls, breadth
and a horizon to rest their eyes and dreams upon. The new land
gifted them what they had lost and wanted returned above all:
childhood.

The sisters were not innocent; they had seen and felt too great a
deal too early, lost much and many that would never be returned.
Still, they welcomed the play, the beaming friends arriving, the

strange sounds congealing in their ears, the many-sided words forming on their tongues, the silent library, the playground din, the uncharted neighborhood, the bush-hopping, yard-hopping finches, the flowers like great white saucers and small red lanterns, the light forever golden, the eternally emerald trees, the blue reflective sea.

movable

You have observed, esteemed reader, that the sisters/the girls are nameless. When they arrived in the new land, did their residency cards not identify each of them with the designation, "NO 'GIVEN' NAME?" And what a peculiar way for the new land to label the newcomers! Who does not understand the importance of a name? First and last, a name! We are born into it, answer to it eagerly, wear it proudly our lives through; our greatest hope is to leave it behind us when we pass. And yet, what is a name? A set of letters organized in a specific pattern to label an individual, not according to vocation or nature or form, but based on a whim, a preference for a sound: someone else's whim and preference. The sisters' vocation is sisterhood. They are girls. They are multiform. This is all you need to know about them, dear reader.

The sisters are five, the letters are 26, the numbers are infinite; all are movable. Move the numbers around, they shift, they transform: 26 is not 62; 2 + 6 = 8; 2 - 6 = -4. Multiply them, and the numbers proliferate, exponentially. They are mystical, variable. The numerals move here, move there, shrink and expand, multiply and divide, repeat and transform, infinitely. This is because what is movable is also infinite. But the numbers do not alone claim this attribute. The movable type, the 26 characters, can be organized in innumerable ways to tell innumerable tales, truths and fictions, to fill file cabinets, books, and heads innumerable. Yes, the letters, the type, are movable, have always been so, before and since the printing press (though that great invention gave them a new stage, allowing them to broadcast their tales farther and wider, and gave them new audiences, readers multiplying, infinitely, everywhere). The movable type, like the numbers, endlessly transform, arrange and rearrange to tell ever new, ever different tales. And they are playful, they are players, ever donning new faces, new forms. See the letters of the alphabet say, *we are letters, we are numbers, we are twenty-six, we are 26! We are bears, we are stars, we are joyful, we are anguished, we are fixed, we are movable, have always been so.* And the sisters too are movable, changeable. They shrink and grow; they are one, then they are five, then they are 26, then 1000! The playful sisters move here, move there, climb into trees, travel underground, into and out of the past, into and back from the distant future, into and out of one another, any other, anywhere (they are readers, after all). They infinitely transform, arrange and rearrange themselves into other selves, donning new faces, new forms. The sisters are movable. Their imaginations make them so. Their numbers make them so. The letters of the alphabet, the books on the library shelves, the worms underground, and the stars overhead make them so. If you need to identify them by a name, you may call them the Movable Sisters. According to nature, form, and vocation, they are simply sisters, girls. And they wear the designations proudly.

the recordkeepers

Daily, the sisters walked over the red rugs that covered the floors of nearly every room in the house. The rugs were generations old and had comforted the bare feet of multitudes, those living, and the many long dead. They had been in attendance at weddings, births, and funerals, and had cushioned and absorbed all that fell or spilled or was generated at such gatherings. The rugs had been daily swept by girls who were now old women or lie buried in distant lands. They had been rolled up and carried on the shoulders of men to new homes, over bridges or peaks, as dowry or in exchange for dried goods or fine linens. Through marriage or after death, the rugs had changed hands. War and commerce had driven them across borders.

Recently, the rugs had traveled with the family over continents and oceans to the new country. The family, hopeful and loyal, would not take the new land into its heart because it knew loss and evaded it at the cost of comfort and joy. The family could not acknowledge that it had come to settle in the new land, and yearned still for a return to the before. But the rugs accepted migration as a basic fact, knowing this most recent one was not their last. So, while the girls' feet stepped gingerly, tentatively across the rugs' pile, the rugs themselves settled and released onto the new substrate, letting go the old, letting gravity work the weight of their natural fibers and dyes into the floor. And sensing the tidiness of that immediate subterranean land beneath the floorboards—the pipes and wires of precisely measured diameters, the homogeneous composition of the machine-expelled substrate, the meticulous lines drawn at right angles—the rugs too resolved to reverberate with the hum of neat living that coursed through all houses, cars, and concrete highways in the new country.

The rugs recorded all that went on above ground with the family and in the house over the many years. They shifted the lines of their woven floral and geometric patterns, ever so slightly, across the generations to accommodate the living and to make room for the old histories, which over time became embedded in their patterns, as new stars become embedded in the fabric of the ever-shifting cosmos. The red rugs took in what was girl and what was cat, what was woman and man, guest and ghost, the old sorrows, the fresh humor, the sun's leaning warm rays, the moon's particulate light. The rugs recorded all that passed over their surfaces, and they listened with a keen but wry curiosity to the underground workings of the new land, which pulsed with a rhythm different from any they'd previously known.

two

A sister could laugh at a cartoon playing on the television *and* recite the prayers for the dead, the disappeared, and the imprisoned with the same mouth. She could push a new friend on the playground swing with one arm, and cradle memories of a best cousin with the other. She could look out through the same pair of eyes that looked in. She could look onto the bright and friendly land she stood upon and look back onto the one recently scorched and left behind. *Where have we come? Why have we come? For how long?*

And what about everyone else? From the beginning, the sisters were two as a result of being cleaved.

They were separated from:
- the first—the first self and the first life and the first parents, who all were more carefree, more innocent, more whole than what they'd now become;
- the first land, that ancient and hospitable cradle, now turned fallow, now harboring mines in the ground instead of beets and potatoes;
- their great and grand family, now continuously diminished as bombs fell, as limbs were pulled from trunks, as terror, paralyzing bodies, minds, and tongues, silenced the first land;
- the first culture, that wondrous mix of hospitality, daily bread and bountiful gatherings, story, gossip, mysticism, melody, and kinship;
- the first future, the first dreams, *which must be unfolding somewhere, where?*

They each were split into two by:
- distance and space: unfathomable;
- time, now also two: before and since;
- knowledge and guilt, which competed with curiosity and joy;
- what rose and rose from below;
- what was showered on them from above.

In the land of the sun, the sisters played and flourished. In the land of the sun, they received and cherished the gifts with one heart and buried the dead with the other. In the land of the sun, the sisters learned to divide and multiply.

in the land of the sun

And though the family held back, its members each existing with one foot, one ear, two chambers of their hearts in each of the two lands, Father nevertheless planted the seeds he had snuck into the new country in the ready soil of their small suburban yard. And up rose proud leeks, poppies and tulips, while carrots and turnips nestled in the warm earth, and mint eagerly crawled over it in many directions. Here was earth, here was the sun, and both were wondrous and giving in the new land.

the hand

The sisters had a knack for numbers. They were five but pretended to be three when their landlord arrived. One sister or another, looking out a window or pitching and bobbing above the garden wall on the tree swing, seeing the old man approaching up the walkway, would in feverish haste run to the others and, in the first tongue, yell and shout to warn them of the imminent deep knock on the front door. Father, who had rented the house under the guise of having three, not five, children, had instructed the girls that two of the five must hide any time the landlord came by. And he came by often to: fix a faucet or pick up the rent check or warn the family that the keeping and slaughtering of a sheep in the backyard was not permitted, even if the animal was prepared with prayer and its body aligned with the heavens. But Father was not specific in his instructions to the girls. Each time the landlord arrived, two sisters disappeared, and in the rush and frenzy to subtract two from five, it was a different pair who hid: sometimes the oldest two, sometimes the youngest, or a mix of older and younger, and often the middle girl, who hid because she loved the adventure of hiding and not being found. The sisters dove into closets, slid under beds, clambered up tree limbs, or tucked neatly behind a large bush or a trash can. The old man visited for minutes or for hours, for he liked talking to Father. And if his visits ran endless, the hiding sisters snuck out to grab a snack or the cat or a book to take back to the hiding place, or switched one spot for a better, or swapped identities with an unhiding sister, who either merrily or resentfully took her place. And the landlord never asked how it was the girls, across his visits, suddenly grew or diminished in size, were sometimes friendly and on other occasions timid.

The sisters were five and learned to live in and share two bedrooms between them. But they were sisters, and not paper dolls, so they swapped beds and partners seasonally to accommodate moods, dispositions, and alliances, which formed or fissured overnight. The first room, with two twin beds, lodged two sisters, while the second room, with a twin and a bunk, took in three but not always the same three, so that the legs that climbed the ladder to the top bunk at bedtime were not always the same pair that climbed down in the morning. The movable sisters did not comprehend stillness; movement was in their blood: wars, fickle regimes, and capricious kings had chased the many generations of their ancestors back and forth across borders as far back as their tattered collective memory could paste together. In a similar fashion, every few months, the sisters moved back and forth between the two bedrooms, dragging behind them their precious loads, traveling down the hallway in a lonely caravan of one, occasionally bumping into the other sister, traveling in the opposite direction,

who had been gracious enough or angry enough to trade bedrooms. While desks and beds remained stationary, bed sheets and
pillows, jeans, socks and t-shirts, dolls and posters, schoolbooks and
crayon sets moved with the sisters, and not always without a fight,
from one bedroom to the other.

The sisters were five and related without difficulty to the hand,
that humble yet deft appendage, which accomplished the many
chores set to them by Mother and Father, by teachers, by their own
dreaming, scheming whims. With the five fingers of the hand, they
washed, picked, plucked, scrubbed, rolled, knit, pried, pruned,
gathered, colored, tallied, tailored, climbed, scratched, tickled,
dug, tore, petted, and preened. They clipped the ends of green
beans, scoured the rice for pebbles, kneaded dough for Mother's
biscuits, stitched a collar to a blouse, traced out the lines of a turtle
or a ship, rubbed paint into a hated sister's jacket sleeve, stroked
the cat's unruly fur, pulled the younger sister's hair, stacked the toys
and books neatly, cupped the hands in prayer, and drew closed the
dead beetle's wings.

The sisters knew five and understood and loved the hand, which
also knew five. And so even before they learned the curious words
in the new tongue, they easily adopted the gestures practiced with
the versatile hand in the new land: the wave to say hello *and* say
goodbye from a distance; from near, the handshake, which lasted
too long or was too fleeting, too rigid or too limp, and rarely right
in temperature; the middle finger raised to make their friends
laugh and squeal (the sisters added effect by adding height to the
middle finger, balancing sticks or pencils in place of or against that
finger) and to make passing motorists and bewildered neighbors
shake their heads and turn their backs; the thumb lifted to indicate

approval or, at an angle, to stop a car in the street (the sisters were in awe of this particular ability, and equally scared of it, running away from the car as soon as the thumb had achieved its desired effect); the ringing slap of one open palm against another to share a victory, however small, with a friend; the tapping of knuckles against a hard surface to ward off evil.

In the new land it was the modest but artful hand that completed the old chores and practiced the novel gestures.

whole

And the sisters understood that they were a prime number: 5

And their family of 5 girls plus 1 mother plus 1 father was also a prime number: 7

And they were all divisible only by themselves and by the number 1, a number which they all knew was the only whole number despite what they were taught in school.

numbers

Count, multiply, and subtract. But this way through the alphabet, dear reader.

sea, tree, sky

The sisters turned and turned and looked all about them: at the earth, the sky, the sea, the light, the life, at all that was strange and new. They looked and absorbed, as children do. They gathered and shifted, as children do. And soon they were one with it all. They who were five fell in love with the new land each herself. And each loved with the ardor of five. And the love, which at first rose tentatively, precariously, grew quickly and to great proportions. They stretched out their arms and lengthened the vowels in their proclamations of love . . . *as much as a forest of swaying trees, greater than a mountain of purring cats, bigger than the great green earth, brighter than the dazzling golden sun, deeper than the star-filled sky.*

Father, Mother

In the new land, Father and Mother look about them: at their neighbors who enter and exit their homes, at the occupants of the cars that move to and fro along the streets and highways of their city, at the shoppers who push carts up and down the aisles of the grocery market, at the sun, which rises and sets daily though the war still rages on in the first land. Mother and Father look about them and quickly become wage-earners themselves.

After the girls file away to school, their books, lunches, and a few practiced words tucked under their arms and tongues, Father opens the newspapers and, in his small notebook, neatly puts down the job titles, the addresses, and the phone numbers of

the companies and employers within a thirty-mile radius. He
neatly writes down his own qualifications assiduously earned
over the many years in the first land. He diligently calls to set up
appointments and interviews. He asks Mother to iron his shirt, tie,
trousers, and jacket. He gathers his papers and clicks closed his
briefcase. Father travels the miles on foot and by bus to the companies, waits his turn in the lobbies and vestibules of buildings grand
and modest. He proficiently uses the language of the new land
that he learned as a boy, still a farmer, by the light of the moon
alone, in the first land. And in his notebook he ticks off the names
of the companies and the jobs offered, efficiently sets down the
responses he has and has not received, and his own impressions as
he goes, then returns to take tea with Mother and the girls, now
home from school, pigtails and braids and shoelaces undone.

Father gets his first job in the new land and it is not the one he left
behind in the old land, not the one his experience and schooling
earned him. But it is a job and it allows him to buy his first used
car: a car with a back seat big enough to accommodate five slender
girls, all arms and legs; a car with tires filled and tread deep enough
to drive his family from the valley to the beachside on the weekend,
where the spray of the sea will wake him from his dream. Father
and Mother buy their first house in the new land, a house just up
the street from the one they rented, a house not so different from the
first, not so different from the next, a house with: a tree and a lawn,
a cat, a kitchen, three bedrooms, and a garage. Father plants his
roses and his grapes, tends to the lawn and the shingles, reinforces
a leaning door frame and pours concrete for a patio. He is farmer
and engineer and it is to these occupations he returns each day after
work, and he tends and builds well into the dinner hour, well into
the night, well into the weekend.

Mother, who has always kept the house, herself and her girls pristine, who has cooked the beautiful meals and made her husband
and daughters the matching bright outfits, who has looked after
them in ways remarkable and subtle, and looked after her own
mother and sisters and brothers in need, Mother too now finds a
job, attends school at night to study the new language, and learns
to drive a car. Her first job *is* that of a driver. She chauffeurs an
aging widow about town, to hair appointments and lunch dates,
to department stores and the marina. Mother, who fears nothing
and welcomes all experiences, all people, embraces her new life
and her new friends even as she mourns the loss of her first life
and agonizes over loved ones left behind. She practices the new
language with her daughters. She traverses the busiest highways
and narrowest byways to search out and find immigrated old
acquaintances. She makes new connections with people young
and old, those established and those recently arrived, as she crosses
paths with them, wherever she goes, at work and on the street.
Mother brings home unfamiliar foods and curious flavors she discovers to share with her family, and delights in or is disturbed by
them alongside the others. She learns to cook the rich and varied
cuisines of her newfound friends, friends from around the globe
and down the street, adjusting their dishes to suit her taste. And
she embraces and indulges in the new life's charms: swimming
and barbecues, beauty pageants and horror films. Unlike Father,
she, the storyteller, speaks to others of the horror she herself has
escaped, though neither of them suffers openly in the new land.

Mother moves from job to job as the family moves from house to
house. And to each job she takes her enthusiasm, her strength, her
warmth, and her great heart. At each job she is a beloved and a
bright star. She chauffeurs, she sells used clothing and furniture,

she works with the homeless, makes donuts and computer parts, files papers and manages coworkers, opens her own restaurant and runs others' businesses. And she brings all her experiences home to share with her family: stories about her day and her discoveries; boxes of warm donuts or cold meat sandwiches; piles of old clothes, toys, and jewelry, which her girls rummage through and find rare treasures among; women she's befriended at night school, with their families, cakes, and stews in tow; men recently off the street and off of drugs; youth recently arrived from elsewhere, motherless, penniless, or dying.

Mother works the long hours and welcomes the weekends and her myriad friends, always growing in number. She hosts the festive parties and, with her small army of girls, cooks and bakes, feeds and entertains masses in her small home on secondhand sofas recently purchased and on the fine china she managed to bring over from the first land. She laughs and converses, speaks highly and lovingly of her daughters' many accomplishments to her various guests as the girls serve tea and sweets; she plays the new songs on the radio, or applauds the live musicians she has gathered to sing the old songs about the old land; she tells her varied tales and avidly listens to her guests' tragedies and humorous anecdotes late into the night. On Sunday, she launders and irons piles of her and Father's work clothes for the week. She puts her tapes—deeply cherished and found with great difficulty in small and hidden shops in bustling corners of the city—into the player and listens to and watches the old film songs she grew up with as she irons blouses, trousers, scarves, and jackets. She listens to the melodies to commune with loved ones missing or killed, and with the old days and the keen memories always rising. She listens and she hums along or tells stories of her childhood and her youth to her

daughters fortunate enough to be sitting near among the warm
laundered clothes, folding or hanging them for her. She listens to
the music and is transported and, when she thinks she is alone, she
sheds tears that hiss when they hit the iron or are run over by it.
On Monday, Mother rises before the others and before the sun to
go to work. She is tireless and fearless and all heart. And it is her
with whom the new land has fallen in love in return. She shares
with the land of the sun a common spirit. Mother is all life, she is
luminous, she is a bright star.

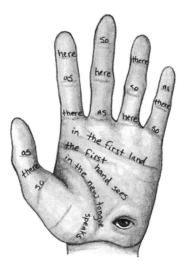

five

The sisters were five. They were five fingers on the same hand,
a hand which knew of itself and knew also that another like it
existed; over there somewhere was another hand that was a mirror image of itself, and as such was imperfect, awkward, and
wrong. The arm, to which the hand was attached, was servant

to it: moved, lifted, and tensed to do the hand's bidding. The body knew of two hands and used them, though not always to similar ends. And the mind knew of the body and of its coarse ways; it knew of the hands and of their unspoken contract with each other; it knew of the fingers, the five in front of the mirror and the five behind, which were like the ghosts or shadows of the first fingers on the first hand. And so the sisters lived two lives on two continents simultaneously, in a present-that-is and in a past-that-might-have-been.

art

The family moved through space, from country to country, city to city, and house to house, a sovereign and a self-sufficient body, a renegade solar system that refused or was forced by circumstance to reject the design, laws, and limits of the universe that was its stage. The family planted peach pits and leek seeds, watered lawns and tended grape arbors wherever it went, yet found it impossible to set its own roots into any soil, even as it dug the earth beneath its fourteen feet with picks and shovels, with fingernails and teeth, in a false attempt to give the appearance of stillness. At the center of this roaming solar system was Mother, like a star, whose density of bone, voice, and will were enough to propel the family on its irregular and unruly course through spaces dark and spaces twinkling, through regions vast and regions close. About her, Father and the girls, like six celestial bodies, were held in orbit by the star's attraction, by Mother's immense gravitational pull. Because each had different requirements for length of day and diversity of seasons, because some needed more time or space alone than others, each body practiced her or his own spin and tilt, and chose elliptical orbits of varying lengths. But none could deny the warmth of that always-regular revolution around Mother, their central fire. The small system, unconscious of its course, was well aware of its size in the ever-burgeoning universe.

When Mother was taken to hospital for surgery, whichever surgery she underwent in that particular year, the sisters keenly felt her absence. The sisters imagined that they might be thrown asunder and out of their orbits into deep and cold space without Mother's central pull on their outlying bodies. But when away, Mother left behind a hole in her place and, instead of the astronaut's weight-lessness, the girls experienced the crowding in of walls, the caving in of the roof. For days, the sisters labored beneath the weight of their mother's absence. The nothingness that replaced her in the center of their home tugged at each girl and drew small objects into its dark void through the air and from all the rooms in the house, swallowing these things up forever: Father's house keys, cubes of sugar, spoons and matchboxes, the sisters' bangles, hairpins and socks. Even the guavas on the tree outside the open kitchen window were not secure. The sisters began to cover fruit bowls with heavy silver platters and to tie down photographs, houseplants, or Father's slippers with bits of string or shoelaces. They locked away teacups, bottles of nail polish, toy cars, and baby dolls in the china cabinet, and when the cat came in from its neighborhood wanderings, they held it firmly on their laps or to their chests. A constant vibration ran through the house, making the windows buzz and the furniture hobble along the walls and across the rugs; the sisters used their own weight to silence the house, leaning against walls or windows, trying to occupy as many

chairs, tables, and sofas as they could with their slight bodies, their
extended limbs.

What troubled the girls most when Mother was away at the hospital were the walls and the roof. Each set out to engineer or craft
her own contraption with which she hoped to battle the impending collapse of the house. One sister brought out her knitting
needles and plastic grocery bag filled with yarn of myriad textures,
thicknesses, and colors, both natural and synthetic, whole skeins,
small, tightly bound balls, and bits not three feet long. And when
she was sure that none of the others were looking, she also pulled
out an oblong wooden box from its hiding place in the large bottom drawer of the end table, behind a stack of old magazines, past
the matchboxes and ashtrays-kept-for-guests, beneath the tar-
nished bronze elephant statue, in the dusty far back corner of that
drawer. Inside the box: her gum collection. She planted herself on
the loveseat, her feet on the coffee table, and went to work knitting
and chewing. She worked earnestly, stitch by stitch, line by line,
her needles clicking, her jaws smacking, and her tongue pushing
out sugary pink, green, or blue bubbles. The other sisters moved
about her, the television flared and went out again, the room dark-
ened, the curtains were drawn and the lamps lit. Hot food, which
was set before her on the coffee table, turned cold. Hours passed,
her creation grew longer, took form, developed feet and arms as
she continued to smack and blow bubbles ever bigger, ever tighter,
her fingers moving ever more feverishly. The multicolored, woolly
tree that sprang from between her needles stretched its arms up
toward the ceiling, while its roots wrapped around the table legs
and inched along the rug in several directions, securing notebooks,
pencils and crayons, coins and flip-flops in its weave as it went.
The tree's trunk thickened between the knitter's legs, warming her

bare kneecaps, enveloping her feet, her toes. With woolly pressure, it leaned against the living room wall and lifted the sagging corner of the ceiling above the television set.

Looking at the upward-reaching branches of the knit-tree, the other sisters were inspired. The eldest dropped the telephone handset, which continued to transmit the tiny voice of her best friend into a hungry room that shortly consumed the voice, then the dial tone, then the telephone itself. She ran into the kitchen where, opening and slamming cupboards, drawers, and the doors of the refrigerator, she pulled out knives, pans, eggs and flour, onions and potatoes, mint leaves and chicken thighs, rice and mung beans, peas and winter squash. She peeled and chopped, rinsed and skinned, lit all four burners on the stove and filled four pots and the oven with stews, soup, dumplings, rice, and sweet bread. The steam and heat that rose reddened her cheeks and lips, plastered her hair to her forehead, coated the windows with a greasy, protective glaze, and softened and expanded the plaster in the kitchen walls, which had been chipping and forming fissures.

The dark and greedy hole that had replaced Mother raged coldly in the very center of the house, halfway between the front and back doors, halfway between the bathroom and the kitchen, in that cold and rugless space between the dining and the living rooms. The sisters dared not approach this drafty space. The two youngest, warmed by the heat streaming from the kitchen, found the courage to face the thing that was not their mother and was, in truth, the absence of their mother. Dressed in their pajamas and armed with nothing but lengths of silver hair ribbon in their hands, the two danced a frenzied circle around the nothingness, weaving a silvery web around the void. Soon the nothingness

had a shape that all had sensed and now could see: it was a great
pulsing, many-fingered orb that floated three feet from the floor,
at times ballooning to great proportions, at others collapsing
and disappearing entirely. Its cold fingers licked the air and continued to charm stray almonds and pennies to it through that
resigned air. But now the objects stuck to the net of ribbon and
went no farther.

The sisters continued their resistance and all the while each saw—
though she tried desperately not to—in the bark of her tree or in
her bubbling pot of meat and vegetables, visions of latex gloves,
of blue-markered flesh, the clean bloodless opening, the parts that
once were Mother, still warm, still pulsing with her blood, pulled
out and taken away by nurses in white uniforms.

The second sister, regardless of the problem, always had one solution to everything: the shoebox diorama. She marched to Father's
closet and pulled out his dress shoes from the last unbroken box.
She ran around the house collecting markers, scissors, tweezers,
paper, glue, cardboard, and foam. From the garden, she collected
twigs, leaves, grass, berries, and soil. She worked quietly, diligently,
always with a secret, giving smile on her lips, in the barely lit corner of the dining room. The others heard the snip-snip of the
scissors, the crunch of paper and the recurrent sigh of her cyclical
smile, which came and went with her focus. In no time she had
built a model of the house, perfect to its finest detail. She called
the others to her. They took turns looking into the sealed shoebox, that beautiful universe in miniature, through a hole in one
end of the box while the second sister shone a flashlight into the
box through another hole in its lid. *Ohhh*, they each said in turn,
and *Yes*. Through the viewfinder, they finally saw the remarkable

thing that ended their struggle and at last quenched the void. Like five small gods, the girls stood in a circle, passing the simulacrum from hand to hand, from eye to eye, no longer anxiously awaiting Father's call from the hospital.

tidy

The sisters were tidy and worked diligently to keep themselves and the house in order. They were neat in appearance, soft in manner, lithe in their gestures. They completed their many daily and weekly chores on time and without complaint. They took turns dusting and vacuuming, cooking meals, setting and clearing the table, washing dishes, watering Father's trees, flowers, and herbs, mowing the lawn, raking leaves, washing windows, scrubbing showers and toilets, buffing Mother's silver teapots and serving platters, taking out the trash, sweeping the floors, doing laundry, ironing shirts and skirts and jackets, serving the guests, feeding the cat.

Everyone who saw them, thought, "What hardworking children," or "How well-mannered," or "How delicate, how gentle these girls are!" All who came to visit or were paid visits by the family praised Mother on her "well-brought-up daughters." When neighbors stopped to speak with Father in the driveway, they complimented him on his dense green lawn or the health and beauty of his roses. On the subject of his daughters, they said little but always were surprised to learn that he had five. "How quiet they are! Five girls, you say? Not two? I would have guessed not more than three from this house. Five! And all girls?"

untidy

The sisters were not fastidious by nature, but by upbringing. They were neither tidy nor demure, though they played the part well and fooled all who saw them. When they were not being watched, the sisters:

- belched, slurped their food, and chewed with their mouths open and their eyes gaping at the television.
- spilled tea, soda, candle-wax, and rubber cement glue on the floor, happy in their assurance that the many-colored, densely-patterned Eastern rugs would not divulge their messy ways.
- proudly wore clothes that were stained green with grass and yellow with turmeric.
- scratched, bit, kicked, and pushed until knees and elbows were covered in scabs loose and scabs obstinate.
- skipped many showers and let their hair became heavy with grease to closely frame their thin, sullen faces, like the veils Mother wore to the many funerals she and Father attended. Fingernails became packed underneath with dirt, leaves, chalk, and the zest of oranges. Mouths turned green or purple with popsicle dye.
- put their chores off until the last possible minute, quickly stuffing laundry, leaves, or silverware into drawers, into jean pockets, beneath rugs, and behind bushes just before Mother and Father came home in the afternoon. They dusted tables wearing Father's socks over their hands, then returned the socks to their drawer.
- peed in bed in the night and simply pulled the covers over the wet, stained sheets in the morning; out of clean underwear, they went to school not wearing any.

- gave away each other's secrets and blackmailed one another for candy or deliverance from a hated chore.
- cursed in two tongues and used the first to confuse or tease their single-tongued friends and neighbors who came to visit, curious and trusting, but unequipped, like visitors from a distant land.
- and, despite what Mother and Father said about stray children . . . *only children without parents, children loose and foul roam the streets to make a show of their deprived upbringing . . .* played barefoot in the front yard, kicking up leaves and skirts, or sat indolently, slouching and sucking a lollipop on the front porch, glaring at neighbors as they passed by.
- rode their bicycles with eyes blindfolded and arms stretched out in the alleyway behind the house, ramming into parked cars and closed gates, laughing at the dogs they vexed.
- made great orange or black or gray arcs in the air as they swung the cat by its back legs.
- hunted garden slugs, following their silvery trails in the early morning, salt shaker behind their backs.
- picked and ate unripe pears, plums, and apricots from Father's beloved trees, and threw the pits at a bird in the same tree or over the fence at the dozing dog next door.
- made elaborate forts and dens using the sofa cushions and Mother's elegant, guest-only tablecloths and bedsheets.
- lied to Mother, to Father, to each other, to guests, to neighbors, to teachers and librarians, and prided themselves on the reach of their lies, which was far and wide and spread their great reputation.

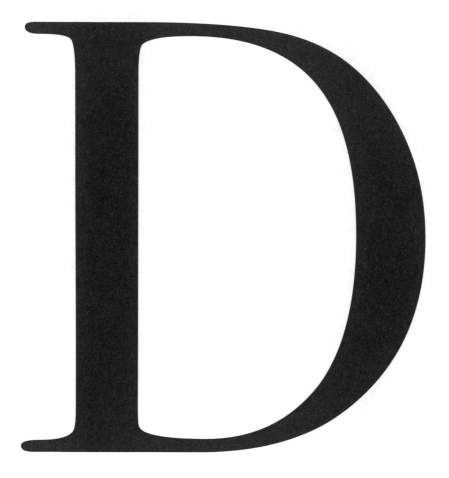

The Dead. And there are many that will file through this book. They are loved ones, family, friends, and some are strangers. They are comfortable here, perhaps not uninvited. I was born into a culture whose first law is hospitality. I have observed this trait in members of my family, near and distant; we all open the door, set out the tea, live with the dead.

My father's family was modestly sized next to my mother's burgeoning clan of city-dwellers. The suffering on both sides was tremendous. But in my father's small family of farmers, the losses seem remarkable. His family was cleaved, and then cleaved again to an excessive degree and in brutal ways by the war. My aunt, my father's only sister, had five children and lost all five, in one or another manner. My father lost all three of his brothers. It is strange, whether chance or fate, that his own life was not taken. In the beginning, when the forces first arrived, disappearances were common. My father would have been labeled as extremely dangerous to the new and occupying government: he worked, after all, for the embassy of their foremost enemy. And his friends, his coworkers, those he was acquainted with and those he cherished, were picked up one by one, imprisoned, tortured, murdered. The week after we left the country, my father's name was read off a list of enemy sympathizers; he was one of many who needed to be brought in and silenced. If they knew my father, they would have known he is silent by nature and would not harm the smallest of creatures. They would know he thinks of family and land, but little of politics. When they came to silence him, we were already gone. They missed us. But just.

We did not leave intact. The knowledge of death, the wisdom you gain from the understanding that a beloved uncle is tortured, then buried alive, a cousin decapitated, that women are raped, have their fingernails pulled out, their breasts cut off, this wisdom you carry with you across borders and over the years of your life. This wisdom circles the nuclei within your cells and ensures you metabolize all suffering, great and small. And this wisdom reshapes the young in ways unknowable to those fully grown. This knowledge remakes the children into something else.

Yes, it was strange to arrive in a peaceful land, to share a classroom and a schoolyard with children who still had their innocence and peered out through a single pair of eyes: for our lids opened and closed as theirs did, but revealed intermittently different sets of eyes. We could stand at once in a desolate cityscape surrounded by tanks and headstones, and on a school playground filled with the din of laughter and bouncing balls, skipping children. I remember seeing my sisters across that schoolyard and seeing them apart, unnatural among the other children. And when in passing we were close enough to catch each other's eyes, the cognition was both sweet and painful. We had come from a place no one knew existed, from a reality we could not explain to anyone, and we had seen and known things we dared not utter to those around us.

They reshape and redefine you, the dead. They cast their pall over you, draw the pink from your cheek, or color it and your lips a too-deep crimson, and they hold your hand while you skip, climb, and jump rope.

They are loved ones and there are others I don't recognize. The man who carries a book, half-torn, he comes and goes silently. But I do not know who he is, what it is he wishes to communicate, if anything. He isn't in a hurry and seems content to be dispossessed, unbound to land or time. He simply comes and goes over the days of my life—as do the other war dead—carrying the half of a book, a book he never opens, but which seems an extension of himself and the hand that clutches it, as if it is his blood that circulates up and down the spine of the book, and his thoughts that make its pages flutter.

The dead are many and pass through and reside in books comfortably. Perhaps it is in books they find solace and home. They move through this one. And some may stop a moment to gaze up at you. Do not avert your eyes.

moored

And if Mother is the sun, is Father not the moon? See him silently revolve around his daughters, even as they six revolve around Mother. He, the family's steady Timekeeper, paces his own rotation so that he is always in step with his daughters and his wife, always facing them, whether in the shadow of his holy book or brightly illumined by Mother's warm glow at the dinner table.

one

And the sisters, knowing they were one, refused to be separated into fractions of a whole. They held on to their single identity and were like a braid that would not be undone. They were like the woven red rug that covered their entire living room floor, and which knew every footstep, every grazing knee, every spill, and recorded all. Much like this great rug, the five sisters never missed an incident, and recorded every bruise or cut, each exchange, every harsh or loving word, all burdened silences in the home, all telling glances, no matter which body, pair of eyes, or set of ears registered the information initially. If Mother was angry, they all suffered; if Father was silent, they all retreated; and when laughter broke the silence, all sighed and were relieved as one. And who is to say that five is greater than one? If the sisters were not 1, how did five hands, in early summer, simultaneously reach for the first ripe fruit on the apricot tree in Father's garden?

family

In the beginning: blood: a vast network of aunts, uncles, grandparents, cousins, nephews, nieces, and grandchildren spread across
the valley, the hills, the city's bustling streets, the open farmlands,
the foothills of the mountains. And how knowledge, history, and
tenderness traveled these streets and byways! Hear the traffic
course in the middle hours of the night: it hums, it pulses. It is
a full sound! As junctions within this network, the sisters were
never alone in the first life. Their shared knowledge, old and forever coursing, dispensing, collecting, did not begin or end with
them, their time and place, their spirits or their bodies in the first
land. Living in the city, they inhaled the fresh village air, tasted
the quince on their uncle's farm, and listened to the gurgling of a
brook in a distant valley. They donned their father's pride, having
journeyed that long road that changed him from wild farm boy to
steady engineer; were wistful alongside their ailing grandmother,
aware that the old woman's pain did not inhabit her bones alone;
and were not afraid to challenge the crooked grocer's gaze, knowing as well as he the price of walnuts in late autumn. The sisters
were born with the knowledge and expertise of thread, needles,
and scissors already established in their wrists and fingers. They
cut, stitched, knit, and shaped with precision and grace. They were
born with an understanding of hair, knowing how to braid, pin,
and sculpt it on one another's heads. As babies, their need for milk
was far surpassed by their desire for sweet tea, for meat dumplings,
for lamb stew, and baked rice; and their appraisal of these things
was only slightly less critical than that of their great-uncle. Each
was linked by appearance, voice, or manner to this aunt, or to that
distant cousin. In her own way, each echoed the past, reinterpret-
ing and renewing old habits, sorrows, and devotions. Life within

this great and evolved vascular system was familiar, intuitive, and intimate. If a loved one, near or a long distance away, was hurt or ailing, its members knew where, why, and how to help; if there were transgressions, the family forgave or shunned as one, and sent forth its decision through the elaborate network; if a secret was kept it was only as a formality, as secrets too made themselves known to all almost simultaneously. The network was both ancient and sophisticated. It worked using methods sweeping and precise. It carried gossip, blood, and memory with equal force and to all members equally. It connected and collected its members, those living, those buried, and those yet to come, in a great embrace, bound them to one another in ways subtle and intricate. And when the war, that mighty and hungry machine, arrived in the land, it severed more than fingers and limbs. The invasion shut down more than the country's electric grid.

Now, in the sunny land, the sisters are closed, have learned to be so. But the currents start up and sputter still, wake them in the night, or divert their attention at their school desks. The information comes still, in small spurts and flares, and the sisters know whence it comes, but do not know where to send it. It collects within their small frames, eddies in places, and settles in others. It seeps and escapes through the eyes and the nose, or sometimes as laughter, unsolicited, shocking to the girls' own ears. Occasionally, the sisters are conductors still; they exchange the knowing look, rise, unasked, to help Mother when she needs it, speak the words that mend when one or another is unwell. Mostly, the old knowledge shelters within each girl. In the land of the many closed doors, it finds correspondence in other hidden sources: between the pages of old books on library shelves rarely visited; at night, behind drawn lids; at night, outdoors, beneath the stars.

many

The sisters were five. The family, seven. The dead, who immigrated and lived with them, walked with them, sat down to meals and lay down to sleep beside them, were innumerable.

guests

A great deal of pushing and shoving went on inside the house. The sisters, all elbows and knees, like a twenty-legged spider, scuttled over furniture and up walls and raised dust behind them as they went. They howled and hooted, stamped their feet and jabbed their nearest neighbor with a finger or a fist, out of fun or anger. It was not uncommon to have five sets of teeth flash in the same instant out of a wild tangle of hair. Occasionally, the cat was caught up in the scuffle and spit back out, landing on the couch, the dining table, or in the ficus plant that stood in the corner of the living room. Neither was it rare for doors to slam, curtains to flutter, and lamps to fall over without any apparent cause or disturbance as the sisters, a mostly invisible force, raced and scrambled about the house. But if Mother was sitting in her chair, three balls of yarn in her lap and a pair of needles between her fingers, she might catch, in the corner of her eye, a glimpse of pattern—floral, plaid, or striped—the sheen of a silver hair clip, or a fuscia-painted toenail in midair. Or she might hear, beyond the clicking of her needles, the rustle of a skirt, or a soft giggle by her ear, though she alone occupied the room. The sisters were everywhere at once, always shoving, scrambling, whooping. But when the phone rang

to announce the imminent arrival of a guest, knees and elbows
disappeared and pant legs and shirtsleeves relaxed back into place.
Dark locks settled into neat braids and ponytails or were tucked
behind clean-scrubbed ears. The girls were once again models of
demureness and respectability. And in no time, fifty nimble fingers
had restored the house to its humble yet elegant glory.

Guests were treated like royalty. The upper cabinets in the kitchen,
which stored the best sweets, were opened during these visits.
The finest china was brought out for the tea service and the most
delicate platters were filled to overflowing with fine chocolates,
individually wrapped, with an assortment of many-flavored cookies, and with dates, raisins, almonds, and walnuts imported from
the East. When they arrived, the guests received three kisses each
from Mother and the sisters, who lined up by the front door, in
the early years by age and height, which corresponded, and later
by nature—gregarious to timid—to receive their guests. While the
sisters hung the visitors' coats and purses in the closet and neatly
lined up their shoes behind the front door, Mother led her guests
to the highest position in the house and seated them on the nicest
sofa and chairs. Then immediately, the service of tea and sweets
began with one sister after another bringing in trays of the best the
family had to offer.

It was on these occasions that Mother also shared her best stories.
The stories their mother told her guests were nothing like the ones
the sisters heard otherwise. All agreed that their mother was an
accomplished storyteller. But the tales that passed her lips during
the day-to-day motions of their lives were lessons disguised as stories and came with a wagging finger that spoke more of admonishment than of adventure. When guests filled the house, whether

two or twenty, young or old, the sisters watched Mother transform
before their eyes. Not long after the visitors had emptied their
third or fourth cup of tea, shared and further exaggerated community gossip, and settled comfortably into the cushions of the
sofa, their mother opened up like a rose, fuller and more vibrant
than any their father proudly grew in his garden, its color a deep
red, like the ancient ruby that Mother wore on her finger. They
watched their mother's eyes grow larger each second as she took
in the scope of her own story. And they listened to the quickened
pace of her breath, which reminded the older sisters of their asth-
matic grandmother, a woman who still lived in that far-off country,
and was already a legend herself.

"Is she a flower or is she a fruit tree?" the sisters would later argue.
And one decidedly would answer, "Our mother is a fruit tree! See
how she keeps the best stories, the sweetest, juiciest, and the most
colorful, in her upper branches where we cannot reach them?"
And angry that the guests had finished all the best chocolates, the
youngest would add, "And the guests are the ladders that we use to
climb to get to the sweet fruit!"

And the sisters were right. Their mother was a fruit tree who bore
five girls with cheeks like red apples and a thousand tales that
hung heavy and hung light from her many strong limbs. And the
tales, like the girls, were not all-innocent and all-sweet. Mother
told of death with as much relish as she did of angels. She told of
ghosts and of thieves and murderers. She told of displaced kings
and their buried treasure, of whispering elephants that passed
the secrets of princes, and of scorpions that crossed mountains
and rivers hanging from the tails of unwitting horses with the
lone motive of revenge. She picked her apples with care, ripened

for the individual guest. With the old women who came to visit,
Mother shared stories of her own parents and her parents' parents, each generation born in another time and in a different
country. To the young women, she told tales of handsome young
men, of lavish weddings, of love victorious over cultural and geographic obstacles. And to those who had seen and been through
what she had, she spoke eloquently of unspeakable loss.

But who among her guests had not suffered loss? The war they
had escaped was still young, an open and a deepening wound. On
these occasions, when the room filled with silence and women and
men, young and old, blinked dry their tears, one sister or another
would attend to the soft knock at the door and courteously usher
in the other invited guests, those swallowed up by time or by war:
the newly and the long dead, the missing, the lost who'd traveled
not by car over gray concrete freeways, but through the red inner
channels of pulsing arteries and veins, to arrive at their front door.
Like the first guests, they too pulled off their sandals or their shoes
and lined them up behind the door; the shoeless did not forget to
wipe their dusty feet on the doormat. And some of the silent-
invited, hand over navel, bent deeply at the waist before entering
the living room, while others, reluctant to make eye contact, hurried past, awkward and nervous. Each found a place to sit on the
floor or on the sofas' arms or to stand leaning against a wall or a
cabinet. They were mostly men and mostly young. Some came
dressed in turbans and white trousers; others, usually young boys,
came in t-shirts and jeans and took a place next to the sisters on
the floor. There were the aged who arrived bent over a stick or
leaning on the arms of the young. And there were women, some
in white scarves with clinking beads in their hands and others
in colorful blouses, brightly lipsticked and rouged, modeling tall

and perfectly sculpted perms that made the sisters smile into their hands. Some of the dead were regular guests and came often; others passed through the single time. And a few, like the half-book man, never missed a call, though he was always one of the last to arrive and took a seat closest to the door. The sisters knew him by the gray suit jacket he wore over his white trousers and tunic and by the tattered book he always carried close in his hand, a book missing half of its spine and one of its covers. The circle would widen, the mood deepen. The sisters would prepare and serve more tea, pile on more sweets, and look to their mother to conclude or to begin a new story. And as she spoke, the living guests sipped their tea while the silents unwound their turbans or shook the dust from their long skirts, and, settling in, joined the living in the nodding or moving from side to side of heads, with eyes closed and ears bent in Mother's direction.

son

The boy runs into the house. He has seen them coming. A group of five or six soldiers is in the next street, moving house to house, asking the questions: how many men in the household? occupations? affiliations? ages? height? weight? The boy has in recent weeks returned from his uncle's house in the country. The countryside is also filling with soldiers and tanks and is coming to resemble the city. His mother has called him home again to the city, where he now spends his mornings studying with a tutor alongside his nieces at his sister's house, and his afternoons running errands for his mother or cooking alongside her. He finds his mother in the

house and tells her they are coming. They will take him. He is not
a fighter, he will not fight. They took and did not return his father.
They took and changed his cousin into something he does not
recognize. He is young, a boy, but old enough. His mother knows
this. He and she are terrified. They have seen this many times
before. She will not let it be his turn. She tells him to lie down on
the living room floor. She tells him, play dead, they cannot enlist a
corpse. She brings out the white sheets, she cuts them to the customary dimensions. She ties shut his jaw and stops his teeth chat-
tering. She wraps his trembling body in the white cloth and ties the
shroud at his feet, his knees, at his elbows, and his head.

She hears the soldiers down the street. *Shhhh* she whispers to her
son. Lie still, lie still. She hears their boots coming up the path,
through the front door, up the stairs, down the hall, into the room.
She kneels beside her son, cries, moans, rocks to and fro over his
shrouded body. "Ohhh, my boy, my boy . . . Ohh, my boy." She
moans, and cries, and trembles and collapses on her son's unmoving body. The soldiers nudge the body with their boots. They lift
the woman off her son. They untie the shroud and unwrap the
boy. They find a pair of open eyes transfixed skybound, teeth
clamped around a pale tongue, and a small trickle of blood traveling from his nostril to the corner of his mouth. They find his

torso slack and his fists clenched over his unmoving chest. They find a heart not beating in a still warm body. They see a schoolboy recently dead, fourteen or fifteen years of age, between five and a half and six feet in height, equal in weight to the smallest in uniform among them.

seed

Mother says that if a girl swallows a seed whole, the seed will find a warm, dark place within her and, after many meals, many sips of tea, and many nights of dreaming, the seed will sprout, sending roots one way, and branches and leaves another. The little seed will germinate, feed on what the sister eats, grow in height and girth within her over the many years, branch and flower in the internal spaces, then finally grow out of the ears, the nostrils, the mouth, the eyes, the elbows and the knees, the fingertips and the toes. And the fourth girl remembers the cherry pits she swallowed last summer at the beach picnic. She wonders if the seeds have found a bed within her, wonders if any have yet sent up a shoot. She feels and taps her belly and her chest, she checks her ears, her nose, her throat, and her eyes in the mirror.

Father says that an innocent killed, no matter age or sex—infant, girl, youth, or old woman—whether in a time of peace or in wartime, the innocent will become like a seed again, to sprout elsewhere. And the third child checks her ears, her nose, her eyes, and her mouth in the mirror. Who has she swallowed and who grows inside her? She wakes in the night to review her dreams, unfamiliar. She reads aloud the words from her favorite book in order to scrutinize the timbre of her voice, changed. Is she herself or is she another? She finds herself praying next to Father, swaying, reciting the sacred syllables, grieving for the old places. She finds herself crying when Mother hums the old songs.

in winter, the sun

And the sun, as if acquiescing to human needs—not the tree-dwelling human but the recent human with greater sheltering needs: roof, walls, windows, and rug—the sun in winter lay low in the sky. In winter, the softened orb sent in great leaning rays of light through the windows, rays that stretched from windowsill to opposite wall, rays to warm the sisters' backs and legs and feet while they sat or lay on the floor to play checkers, or to crack sunflower seeds between still-neat teeth, or pick a scab from a bent knee, or converse with that near star, photon to cell, beam to muscle, dream to dream. And so the sun, on a winter's afternoon, nods in the westerly direction as the dreaming sister's head sinks into the red patterned rug.

the widow-bride

The municipality has been given its own delivery truck. It is not a large truck, but it is a well-built truck, foreign-made, with an

engine that hums, and wheels that glide. There is room enough in
the bed of the truck for numerous parcels if they are stacked and
arranged neatly. Its cab is comfortable and adequately spacious for
two strong men, men with arms like elephant trunks, able to lift
the hefty packages they deliver. The deliverymen, whom the residents of the municipality have never seen with their own eyes, are
hardworking men who must have day jobs that keep them from
delivering while the sun is still up. Or perhaps the local government, anxious to keep the traffic in the streets of the town running
smoothly by day, has obliged its residents by making its official
deliveries only in the middle hours of the night.

The residents know the delivery truck, not by sight, but by sound,
though it barely purrs as it moves down the narrow streets of their
neighborhoods in the darkest hours of the night. They hear the
truck's firm tires rolling over gravel or paved road long before it
has turned a corner onto their street, and hear it still, long after it
has gone. Since the start of the war, many of the residents swear
that their hearing has grown keener; some would even admit their
ears have grown slightly larger and somewhat more curved-for-
ward to better collect and decipher the sounds from the new world
that has sprung up around them.

The two deliverymen are not talkative men. They are respectful
of the residents and would not dream of disturbing their sleep.
Or perhaps they are tired and have little left to say after a long
day at their first jobs, and after a long evening in the company of
their wives and children. Regardless, they do not talk and barely
do they breathe while they work, though occasionally a grunt or a
sigh escapes their throats as they lift a parcel from the bed of the
truck or bend to drop one off on the front steps of a house. The

deliverymen work hard, seven nights a week, from midnight until five o'clock in the morning. But they enjoy a holiday each month when the moon sits swollen in the sky.

It is on a quiet, moonless night that the truck makes its first delivery to the bride's house. It is the night before her wedding and she wears her hair up in curlers. The bride has not slept for many hours; she has tossed and turned so often, the spines of her curlers have pricked her scalp; blood dots her white pillowcase. The bride has listened for the truck for many nights; she has studied the various sounds of the night and has learned by heart the subtle shades of silence; she has slept with her window open despite her parents' pleas, listening, listening for the wheels, the hum, of the delivery truck. And tonight she does not mistake its approach, though she knows it is yet a mile away. She lies on her back, rests her arms at her sides, and waits.

On the day of her wedding, the bride bathes and dresses, not in the wedding gown that she and her mother have spent one hundred nights adorning with beads and mirrors, but in her washing dress with her curled hair tucked beneath a faded scarf. She does not paint her face and does not send her guests away, though they arrive dressed in the dark colors of mourning. Behind the house, in the open courtyard, streamers made of white paper flowers stretch from tree limb to tree limb to rooftop, and rustle in the mid-morning breeze. China cups and saucers, plates and bowls, piled one hundred high, tower above the red geraniums growing along the stone walls. Cherries and loquats, peaches and melons fill borrowed silver bowls and platters. Large copper pots filled with dry rice and soaked beans sit atop the unlit stone oven in the corner of the yard; she empties the largest of these. The unopened parcel rests beneath the old walnut tree where her father, with the help of her youngest and only remaining brother, dragged and set it, grunting and panting, in the early morning hours. The bride stands beside the unmarked box in the center of the wedding party, a swarming, vibrating, many-armed spiral made up of her: mother, father, little brother, two grandmothers, aunts and uncles, cousins and classmates, friends and neighbors, hairdresser and baker, meowing cats and buzzing insects. She pulls the lid off the wooden box and opens the mouth of the coarse hemp sack that sits within. The wedding guests groan, some swoon, but most cannot pull their eyes away: here is the groom, his teeth and his hair, his fingernails, his toes, his ears and his nose, his kidneys and his heart. The bride is silent and those around her cry and moan, they pray and they curse, but none too loudly; the courtyard contains the sounds and motions of their peculiar celebration.

Some in the wedding party swallow an herb that turns them both dumb and invisible, and which commonly grows in the dry soil of this forgotten land; they exit by the back gate on a silent errand. The bride immediately sets to work. She tallies and measures the pieces, accounting for all of her groom's handsome features, and wonders at the whiteness of the flesh, its bloodlessness. She fills the copper pot with water from the Well of Death and rinses the pieces carefully, lovingly, one at a time before setting them out on a white sheet that has been spread over the hardened earth by her elders. She works her way upward from the toes, mistaking, occasionally, a part of his arm for his calf, a shoulder joint for a kneecap. She calls the children to her; they work together to piece her betrothed back into a man, tall and slender, awkward and modest even in death. He lies supine and naked in the dappled shade, his lids drawn down over eyes recently replaced in their sockets. When all of the pieces are in their proper order, the bride wipes the sweat from her brow. She sits on her heels, her arms wrapped around her knees, and waits in the shade of the old tree. After three hours, her brother returns from the River of Life and reports that it still runs dry; the unhappy party bemoans its lot. The unseen guests who left by the back gate silently enter the yard again and from their invisible pockets draw forth the blue feathers of the whistling thrush. Bride and mother stitch one feather to one piece of flesh. The elders find patches of sun or shade on mats and rugs, seat themselves along walls and against tree trunks and begin to pray. And the children, taking a feather-bound piece of the groom in each hand, make a circle around the bride and sing a song that is not a wedding song. Through the song's old words, they teach the dead man how to change his shape, and at the song's wailing end they throw up their hands, emptying them of man and releasing a whistling thrush, which rises and spirals and sings, circles over the rooftops, and comes back to perch in the walnut tree.

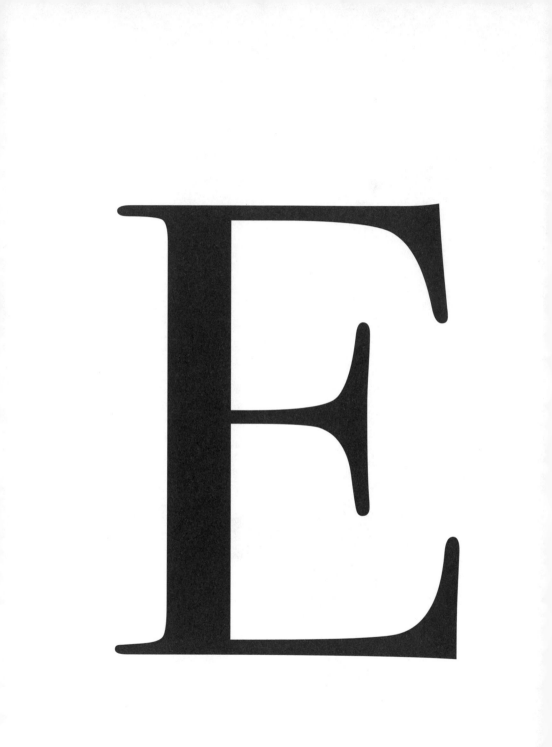

And every so often, the great eye, the eye of that ancient whale slumbering in the depths of the sea, it opens. And in the pitch dark of the sea's depths, it casts its gaze and faint light upon what has brewed inmost and just now is born, sees the thing for what it is and, clearly seeing it, acknowledges it, and so releases the thing, unnamed and unknowable, to the surface, to the outside, where it may be dressed by the letters of the alphabet, soldiers ever ready to advance on Chaos and the Dark. The   eye,   it   seldom   opens. In that instant that the dense lid rises, it is known to the dreamer, whether she lies asleep in her bed or moves and fusses about through her day, for she sees the opening eye in her mind, and it is more than a light coming on in the dark; it is enough to wake her. She knows its gaze, still and keen; she has seen it before and forgotten it each time. She sees the eye even as the eye sees before it the thing newly born and ready to rise up. The   recognition   is   immediate.

division

The sisters had a knack for division. If they could be five, then why not twenty-five? Like cells, each divided, first into two, then four, then eight, and so on, with the occasional mutation that engendered three cells from one, or the unforeseen death that left one cell where there should have been two, or the eager cannibalization of one cell by another. It seemed that each time Mother or Father looked up from a telephone call or from prayer, there were more daughters to count and more to distinguish one from another. Where one day there was one girl, the following there were seven, and the next, twenty-four more. When Father complained about the water or the electric bill, or the great tangle of hair in the shower drain, he did not consider the girls' spontaneous regenerative powers. In the time it took Mother to call a girl idle, three others, identically dressed, finished the chore. The cat had one tail but the sister who would pull it had many dozens of hands. If you say the sisters were five, you are mistaken. You have not paid attention. Look again.

the drifter

And what is written in the pages of the half-book man's tattered tome? Is it his own story, set down there in his own words, by his own hand? In his own blood? Are there lines in the book telling sweet tales of his children, his wife, his village? Does the book tell of his own fate, a fate already delivered and executed? Does it contain the lines of his favorite poet? Does it collect the tattered dreams of his people, people dying, falling daily in that distant land? Does it foretell the future of those still living? Are there more wars to come? The sisters see clearly that the half-book man has walked through more than one, more than a few wars. If he is an oracle, he does not speak. But in the way he holds his head, tilted and still, as though listening, in the way his eyes look into a space far distant from the one he occupies, by the way he grips and caresses his book, and by the way his book seems to speak back to him, the sisters guess it is a past he holds on to. The book holds something beloved and spent, a story of a life lived elsewhere, of life before the knowledge of war. And yet the manner in which the half-book man occupies the present—not aimlessly, but deliberately, walking the halls of the sisters' house, the streets of their neighborhood, the alleyways of their city—tells the sisters that though he is homeless, unbound, he is not superfluous to the spaces he now drifts through. And that the book in his hand is something like a towline, which, binding the past, tugs and heaves it into the present, moment by moment.

Enter and Exit

as you like, dear reader.

rice

So the family continued to practice the old life in the new land—scouring the rice for stones, plucking the feathers from dead chickens, draining the curd to form cheese, growing the grains to make porridge, stirring the porridge for twenty-four hours while praying to the dead saints.

the first river

The first river ran through the house and had its source somewhere unknowable and only guessed at by the sisters. Perhaps the source of the first river was the kitchen faucet, which sometimes in the late evening or the early morning hours ran of its own accord. Perhaps the river had its beginnings in one of antique teapots that lined Mother's china cabinet shelves and bubbled out from that pot's chipped spout. No, looking back, the source of the first river was Father's bosom. It was, after all, where his sensibilities resided. His heart, like a spring, filled, spilled over, and murmured even as he slept; he was a silent man otherwise and kept his emotions hidden by day. He moved wordlessly around and between the six females in his life. He ate their many hand-prepared dishes with childlike relish, listened to their conversations, adding a nod here, a smile here, tended their garden of fruits, herbs, and flowers (his roses were their pride and they, his roses), and with his handyman tools built the sisters their first swing set, their first tree house, a grape arbor to give them shade from the unyielding late summer sun, and an office for himself in the garage, a room within a room,

and not anywhere in their way, a private space that told of man
alone.

With their father at work by day, it was the same river that carried the girls to the shores of this quiet room in the garage. And
this room was sacred to the girls, who left the sun and the grass to
sneak into the dark space in search of treasure. Once inside, they
shut the door behind them, keeping out the river that had delivered them there, for they didn't want Father to know they were
rummaging through his things. At the right time of day, the tiny
window that looked out onto the garden brought in sufficient light
for their explorations. But more often, the girls worked beneath
the buzz of the single fluorescent tube that ran over Father's desk.
On this man's island, there was, among the many dead timepieces,
an old wristwatch that gained sheen over time from the girls' curious fingers, which never tired of pulling the old timekeeper from
Father's top drawer, rubbing it, wrapping it around their skinny
wrists, once, twice, winding it, and replacing it in the cold drawer.
The old wristwatch had a history, but it was not theirs; Mother
had bought it secondhand. There were, also in this room, boxes of
chewing gum and mints, an olive-green typewriter, which Father
kept covered with two handkerchiefs, several dozen news magazines lined up against the wall, and an old tape player, stapler,
and broken key chains awaiting repair. Here in this space that
was Father's alone, the sisters pulled out compasses and rulers
and drew their own bridges and skyscrapers, cars, moons, con-
stellations, and coastlines. The sisters hummed along to the river's
song as it ran outside the office door. They took in the smell and
the character of everything that was not girl or woman: Father's
sweater hanging on the back of his chair; his forever near-empty
bottle of cologne; his green glass paperweight, which they picked

up with both hands to hold against the light; his nail clippers, too large for their small fingers to handle; his filing cabinets filled with carefully tallied and marked bills, letters, and documents. Before leaving Father's treasure island, the sisters closed and locked all the drawers again, pushed in the desk chair, lined up the pens and the pencils by color in their trays, and listened once more for the ticking heart of the old timepiece through the closed desk drawer before shutting the office door and stepping back into the river.

The first river traveled through the house, around the bases of lamps, beneath the sofa, and over the tight weave of Eastern rugs. It flowed beneath the dining chairs, ran in, then out of closets over the girls' shoes, into and out of his wife's coat pockets. The playful river chased the cat, soaked its tail, then gurgled before it continued out the back door and into the garden to water the beds of herbs and the fruit trees. If the girls were not paying attention, running too fast in the house or fighting too roughly with a sister, they might slip and fall into the water. The river shifted its course daily, though over time it was evident to the sisters that it had its favorite paths too. It formed channels at the base of the kitchen sink and the stove, where it ran regularly to cool the feet of Mother and the sisters, who daily cooked and washed the dishes. Though Father was not home in the afternoons, the river that had its source in his chest ran alongside his daughters as they lay on their stomachs on a rug or in the garden, calculating numbers, drawing flowers, reading tales. Its sounds, as it ran past them on lazy afternoons, reminded some of the sisters of the brook that ran through their uncle's farm in that other distant country, the little brook that meandered through the fields, past strawberries and reeds, through peach and quince orchards, and at the feet of ancient goats and sheep.

And was this river running through their small and neat house in the sunny land that same little gurgling farm brook?

Yes, the first river had its source in Father. By day the house vibrated with the many voices of the girls, of family, of living. Only two occasions silenced the boisterous house: Father's regular prayers and deep night, the hours of sleep. Father always chose the quietest corner of the house to set down his prayer rug and the moment he had, the entire house fell silent. The sisters, playing a hand of cards or scratching their names into the heels of their tennis shoes or hanging upside down from the limbs of the tree in the yard, all fell under the spell that was their father's solemn prayer and blessing. And the reverent words that fell from his lips traveled downriver through all the corners of the house, lulling the sisters, Mother, and the cat into meditation. But no sooner was the prayer rug lifted from the floor than a yell or a roar of laughter lifted the veil of silence and drowned out the river again. At night, when the family lay in bed dreaming, the sister not sleeping would listen to the gurglings and whisperings of the river as it tumbled beneath telephone and chair, meandered over rug and around table legs, slipped over cushions and beneath beds until it carried the sister into dreams of endless fields of watermelon and clucking hens perched in the limbs of quince trees.

the second river

The second river that ran, ran hidden and deep. This subterranean river traveled through the cavernous earth a mile below the house, whichever house the family lived in that year. The sisters had little knowledge of the existence, let alone the source, of this river, though somehow they sensed it and were not entirely surprised when occasionally it traveled vertically, found a gap between the red rugs, rose into the air, and silently writhed like an angry serpent in the middle of their living room. At other times, one sister or another, digging deeply enough on a hunch, discovered the flowing water and drank thirstily from the well. But the ancient water had dissolved strange minerals on its journey, and no sooner had the sister satisfied her thirst than the memory of the river was all but erased from her mind and her tongue dry again. This great and terrible river ran from sources secret and took courses deep and meandering. Yet still it reflected the Milky Way on the surface of its waters roiling and its waters silent as it journeyed from unknown to unknown.

If the sisters had stopped to marvel, they would have wondered: how old was this river and where had its travels taken it? What pressures forced it down which pathways? The sisters knew that earth was heavy in all places, but more burdensome in some: did the river flow freely here and back up there? Was the river born of two parents or one? Did the earth not hoard its treasures? Had the river, on its journeys through the cavities and vaults of the earth, not seen its stores of rubies, emeralds, and jade? If the sisters had consciously known of the river's existence, they would have asked it these questions and more. But endless and great as the second river was, it ran mostly silently, and the sisters remained ignorant.

It seems that both fortune and misfortune had joined hands to wed this river to this family. The family did not speak of the second river. Though they each sensed it, they knew not what to call it. It was nameless. Each thought it was her or his own alone. So each kept it secret, hidden beneath skin, muscle, and bone; his or her subcutaneous secret: unnamable, unnatural, cursed. They felt gravity drawing them down but felt more than just the ground pushing back against their own earthly weight. The river too pushed and sometimes pushed hard. Each felt it uniquely: as a pressure below the diaphragm or at the base of the skull; as a terrible itch on the soles of the feet that peaked in the middle hours of the night; as a burning sensation in the corners of the eyes; as a rough and permanent stone in the back of the throat. And each hid the sensations in her, in his own way: Mother swallowed and swallowed again the saliva that ran endlessly over her tongue; Father kept silent by day and kept his feet uncovered by night, summer and winter, autumn and spring; one sister pushed back, into walls and cupboards and sisters; another sister, not knowing that the source of her tears was this same great river that pushed on all the others, let its mineral-rich waters run freely from her eyes behind closed doors in the few momentarily empty spaces in the busy house.

In the backyard, the girls mined for earthworms and gemstones. At the base of the rosebushes, they dug shallow wells, which they lined with shells collected the previous weekend at the beach. They attached a miniature plastic bucket to a string and let it down into the well. But the greedy roots of the many-colored rosebushes absorbed the cupfuls of tap water the sisters poured into the hole before they were able to draw any back out in their doll-sized bucket. The little engineers took the well apart again and used the wet earth to fashion cups and beads and bird whistles, which they baked in the noonday sun. And they came back the following morning to collect their cracked earthenware, to begin anew the digging and construction of a shallow well.

Had the sisters guessed, they would have dug deeper. Had they spoken to each other of the pressure on the soles of their feet and on their kneecaps as they knelt beside the rosebushes, and had they discovered that the moist earth pushed hard and mercilessly on all of them, they would have brought out Father's picks and shovels from the garage. They would have dug a mile down and questioned the river themselves: *what is your message and why do you trouble us? Do you have no shame, at your age? Are you not the same river that supplied the well on our uncle's farm? Did you not reflect grandmother's shrinking image over the many years she bent over the edge of the well to let down to you her chipped pail? Did our widow-aunt not flavor her morning bread with your salt?* The eldest sister distinctly remembered the hiss of steam that came off the shaped dough after it was slapped against the side of the hot clay oven in the farm's courtyard. She knew that hiss and would have matched it to the river's had the sisters known to dig for the source of the pressure on their small bodies. But each kept her secret to herself. And each used a shell, a rock, or her fingers alone to dig the shallow well that refused to hold the many cupfuls of tap water the sisters brought to it from the kitchen.

winter harvest

The people of the small, mountainous kingdom lived quiet, industrious lives that peaked at dusk and dawn with the first and the last stars. By the faint light of the stars, they celebrated births and weddings, vegetable harvests and animal sacrifices, and the visions and words of their dead saints. The people of the land loved their

mountains as they loved their saints. On holidays, they traveled
over desert and down river to picnic or play at the foothills of the
many-mountains: tying rope to the limbs of strong trees, their
youth swung over seas of blue poppies or red tulips; old men lay
in the shade of wild orchards, taking in the delicate scent and
color of apple blossoms; in summer, lovers walked off to fill their
skirts or caps with mountain strawberries and shared them as they
shared kisses; in winter, the adventurous sledded joyfully down the
mountains' many faces.

To their towns, the people welcomed commerce, which traveled
over roads direct and roads winding to deliver pomegranates,
pine nuts, and ice from the mountains, and rhubarb, quince,
and carrots from the village farms. Milk, meat, fruits, and grains
were ample. The people blessed the mountains and thanked the
farmers. And what they could not presently use, they shared, or
preserved for the long winter. Neighbors passed loaves of bread or
baskets of ripe peaches over their walls in every direction. They
gathered in this or that yard to preserve this or that bounty. Entire
days and many strong arms were spent driving the cranks of small
grinders to turn whole tomatoes into pulp, which filled the air with
the fruit's sharp-sweet scent, and jars to the brim. Miles of wash
line were volunteered, cleared of laundry, and draped with herbs
or salted meats left to dry in the crisp air. At the end of such days,
the neighborhood women returned to their own homes and husbands smelling of tomatoes, spearmint, goat's cheese, or slaughtered lamb.

The people of the land honored their king. When their beloved
king took to the sick bed or left to visit neighboring lands, they
prayed for his recovery and blessed his travels. And when their

benefactor opened his arms to his helpful neighbors who, traveling the long roads over mountains and across deserts, arrived to build the highways and the many-tiered spires in their cities, the people blessed their king for his grace. When the visiting neighbors gazed too long upon their arid landscape and saw that it glimmered, the people of the small kingdom shivered but looked to their ruler for comfort and guidance. And when he disappeared, as if into thin desert air, the people knit their brows and pondered. Though soon, others came to take his place and dressed in his clothes and waved their arms with great fervor and bowed their heads in deep piety. But not all of the people were deceived. And those not deceived vanished. And those who went asking after the dis-appeared did not return. The people saw that the new leader was hungry and not satisfied with the tulip or the apple. They watched in awe as he himself vanished before their eyes and was followed by a succession of new leaders, who appeared and disappeared equally abruptly. Each arrived hungrier, with even more ardor for the land, more zeal in his fist. And all this disappearing, so abrupt and sweeping, vexed the people who were accustomed to account-ing for all that came out of the earth and returned to it. So they took to hiding their loved ones. And still the new leaders were not to be put off, needed to be sated—for the taking of a land requires the letting of blood to be authentic. The newcomers looked beneath beds, stairs, and skirts, in attics, cellars, and chicken coups. They dragged out daughters and sons, expectant mothers and bridegrooms, old men and goats, and slaughtered all.

The people of the land looked to their beloved mountains and, contemplating the ways of the mountains, remembered that in their depths the great giants stored the kingdom's many treasures. Thus, the people who were accustomed to burying their own dead resolved to bury their precious living instead. And within their own depths. So the cutting, grinding, and eating of the young and the bright, the learned and the prized, looked from above not unlike the great harvests of peaches and watermelons in late summer. The migrating bird, countryless, flying over the kingdom that winter, and seeing that arid land brighten with the colors of sweet summer fruit, was for a moment disoriented.

F   l   o   w   e   r   s   .
The sisters were like five flowers, bloomed precociously. Nurtured by knowledge untimely, each developed into a curious blossom.

Follow.   Come   now,   do   not   be   hesitant.
You   do   not   need   a   yarn   to   draw   you.

Forward? Did I say the only way forward is through the alphabet? In jest only. You see, here, all of the pieces are movable. And all of the days are one, the same. So please, enter, commence, reside, depart freely, anywhere, anytime, as you like.

holiday

Mother is happy. It is only her third year celebrating the old
holiday in the new land and she has brought together enough
friends from the first land, introduced them one to another over
the months and the short years, made uncles, aunts, and cousins
of them for her daughters, and bound them all enough to one
another so that the old holiday this year will be something of what
it once was. They have secured a place at a city park, beneath
a large wooden canopy and adjacent to a small lake and a playground. Because the holiday falls midweek, the many families will
hold off and gather at the park on the weekend to enjoy the festivi-
ties, to grill the marinated meats, to feast on the vibrant sumptuous
fare laid out across the picnic tables by the many families, to share
the tea and gossip over hands of cards, to toss the balls, slip down
the slides, and feed the geese and the fish at the water's edge.

In time for the holiday, Mother has sown, sprouted, harvested,
and ground the ancient grain. She has acquired an enormous
enamel pot for the cooking of the sweet porridge and has washed
and scrubbed the walnuts in their shells to add to the pot. And
now has spent a full day, sunrise to sunrise, cooking the sacred
porridge over coals on the grill in the backyard. The five sisters
advance and recede in twos and threes or singly to stand by her
side, to take the paddle, to stir the immense pot, to make their
secret beloved wishes, to sway with the old tree's branches, to
utter the syllables that honor the prophets and remember the
dead, to listen to Mother's tales or Father's prayers over the bubbling pot, and to swat at the flies that attend the ritual like many
murmuring pilgrims.

When it is dawn in the new land and dusk in the old, when the porridge is cooked and sanctified through and through and the old grain is sweetened by the stirring and the bubbling, by the tales and the prayers, by the dead and the pilgrims, Mother enters the house to call her family in the first land. It is only her third year in the new land, but already she is able to make a phone call across the distances without bringing harm to her family there. The girls know with what enthusiasm their mother enters the house to call her own mother and sisters. They know she is brimming to wish them a joyous holiday, to hear their voices and, for a moment, to be transported into their midst to share the felicity of their celebration, truer than any she can construct in the sunny land. When she returns from her phone call, only minutes later, she is subdued and walks directly into the garage to tell Father news she will not share with her daughters. She had found, on the other end of the telephone line, mourners, not celebrators. Her niece, across the past five days, was wed and widowed. On day one, the young woman was married to her childhood love. On day two, she lost him to the new forces, who picked him up from his home, carried him off and into one of the newly constructed buildings on the outskirts of the city, and tortured him there for three days before releasing him. On day five, her family could not drag her away from his gravesite.

After the phone call, Mother is somber, she is silent, and she fills the dishes with the blessed porridge and lets them cool on the kitchen counter. She will deliver a dish to each family at the holiday picnic. She fills her daughters' bowls and sets them before the delighted and eager girls at the breakfast table. The bowls are filled with a flavor and give off an aroma that have been distilled by

ritual and through stirring by many hands over the many generations, a flavor and an aroma that still cling to the girls' memories,
and take them back to the beginning days. Mother does not put
any porridge to her own lips, and neither does she color them with
lipstick this morning. She dresses, then leaves for work. It is not
until the day has ended and Mother has found her way into bed
that the newest death accosts her. She knew the boy, had watched
him grow up alongside her nieces and nephews; he was a neighbor of theirs, always present, another child playing, studying, and
helping out among her older sister's large brood. Mother is unable
to sleep and rises often to get air at the window. Father is awoken
by the sound of her body slumping to the floor. Her cries are muffled, held back, but he knows she is in intense pain. In the middle
of the night, he dresses her and walks her past their daughters'
bedrooms. He puts her in the car and drives her to the hospital,
where Mother's body, unable to house any more grief, more death,
or life, unburdens itself of a son, her only one. She does not know
when she wakes in the hospital bed that she has lost a child. She
did not know that she was carrying one. But once she learns of
her loss, she decides she will not have any more and returns to the
same hospital a few months later to assure she does not.

In the hospital, after yet another surgery, Mother is asleep, she is
herself a child again. She murmurs, *there will be no more children falling from the sky. There will be no more airplanes dropping babies into the sky
and onto the land. The land is barren, the sky is filled with planes. The babies
fall and land and they are not babies, flesh and blood; they are dolls . . .* The
words follow her out of the dream. It is a dream, but it is not her
own dream that Mother remembers as she comes to in the hospital. It is an old dream: her younger sister's. Her sister told Mother
the dream of the falling babies on waking one night, many, many

years before, when the two were still girls sleeping next to each other on the family room floor and among the others still unmarried, still at home.

And Mother's dreaming sister *finds and collects the babies and fills her arms with many blue-eyed dolls who move and shift—though she holds them close—and speak and sing in a language she cannot decipher. But the sister loves the dolls still, though she understands them not, loves them all, and is made happy. And are they not precious filing out of the door of the airplane, diving into the sky, their skirts ballooning like parachutes, their hard plastic arms held over their oversized heads? Are they not precious collected in her arms, all radiant, smiling?* She wakes happy. She wakes Mother-the-girl sleeping next to her. She tells her the dolls were plastic, not cloth; their eyes blinked, their lids revealed blue, not brown, eyes; their arms and legs turned in their sockets. She is ecstatic, she beams. It is night and Mother's little sister whispers, yet her eyes beam. She says in her dream, the dolls spoke and she clung to them; they sighed and she felt their breath on her neck, her arms, her cheek as she tried to collect them all. They had fallen from the sky for her; the airplane had dropped them for her, but she would share with her sisters, and would keep the prettiest for herself. Though the dream dolls are not there when she wakes, she cradles her empty arms and hums to them.

Mother in her hospital bed remembers the old dream that was not her dream. And she recalls that it was this same sister who loved the stillborn child that arrived late one autumn to momentarily add to their great number. And while Mother-the-girl and her older sisters had run back and forth between the family room— where their mother writhed and wailed in agony on a cot—the kitchen, and the courtyard, bringing in buckets of heated water, taking out blood-soaked sheets and clothing and washing them in buckets of cold water drawn up from the well, her younger sister, ardent lover of all things small and lifelike, had stayed near their mother, who, after the birth, held the six-month-old fetus cupped between her breasts. She stayed near and begged and begged their now-silent mother to let her play with the tiny, unmoving, red baby boy, perfectly formed in every way, and for a long while still warm.

And this small lover of small things, later, in her teenage years, liked to pinch the arms and sides of all the little children in the family and in the neighborhood, loved to bite their plump red cheeks, and squeeze them until they laughed, cried, or turned blue. She did not marry young as her sisters before her had. She finished school, and finished college, and became a high school teacher, one beloved by the young women she taught for her beauty and her dress, and feared for her strange and, often, cruel humor. She looked as young as many of her students, and was walked home after school, as some of them were, by doting young men. She had many admirers, and cultivated their devotion, wore their many gifts on her fingers, in her hair, across her shoulders. There were those who came to the house, to meet her parents, and brought their womenfolk, their arms laden with presents, and with dried fruit and sugared almonds to begin the long process of asking for her hand in marriage. These devotees she demurely turned away from the house, and laughed at when next she passed them in the city streets. There were others whom she met at the clubs or restaurants or private parties held at the home's of the city's artists and musicians. Was it not rumored that after teaching school in the daytime, she spent evenings in the company of the King of Music? She enjoyed her youth and her liberties, liberties that none of her sisters before her had sought or even envisioned. She was fierce and took for herself what her brothers were freely given.

Mother in her hospital bed thinks about this sister, now a grown woman, recently married to a government official who has helped secure the release of their oldest brother. Married to the official in exchange for the release of a brother who spent months in prison, months being questioned and tortured. Not long after his release, when Mother called the first land and heard her younger sister's voice, she heard in it something missing, something forfeited. It was the loss of her sister's freedom, the loss of a life lived wildly, fiercely. And this sister, always jesting, had said to Mother on the phone, "Of course I am happy! I have exchanged an innocent torturee for a true torturer! What they did to him in there! And you think our brother could have stood it any longer? There was no one happier than he at my wedding! How our brother smiled his now crooked-permanent smile. How his one good eye shifted from bridegroom to bride while the broken eye stared ahead at the merry dancers!" And Mother in her hospital bed wonders now about this sister, about her husband, feared both within and without the family for his politics and his methods, a man trained in the finer arts of official interrogation and torture. Mother wonders will this sister now have her own children? And how many? How many more births will Mother miss living in the new land? How many more weddings? Funerals? Holidays?

differentiation

The sisters needed one another to discover themselves. Each sister was a many-sided cell and had her heart and her outlook shaped by the pressures of being up against the others, within the boundaries of one small house, and beneath the awning of their parents. Each saw her parents in herself or in the others and was proud, envious, or hateful for those resemblances small and great. And what they saw and did not see in one another told them who they were and were not. Without the others, each would have remained too-many-sided, therefore nothing at all, or a soft and yielding sphere. Like cells specializing, they differentiated into themselves among the others. The gum-smacking sister was not the sleep-deprived sister was not the melodic sister was not the daydreaming sister was not Mother's pet. But all of the sisters gave with both hands, pulled up with both hands, shared easily. And the two sisters who would skate around the neighborhood together did not mind sharing the cool shade, after a morning spent conversing and laughing over the hum of wheels, with the book-reading sister who'd never left her place on the porch. And the sister who would hide did not mind being discovered by the sister who would set off on adventures with the cat at her side. Each looked to the others for reference and tried on the others' ways: their timbre of voice, their gait, and their ardor. But seeing themselves reflected in the others, they saw what was false and what was true. They each recognized who they were and were not. They knew their place in the family and in the world. They found their vocation and set to it. And like many specialized cells pressed together, into one being, they were greater and grander than the sum of their sister-parts. Together they were an immense and glorious thing, with many busy hands and many skipping feet and one massive blazing heart.

birth

And Mother remembers the birth of her first daughter in the first land in the newly constructed city hospital Father had her admitted into. Father would not have his young bride deliver at home as her own mother had, as her sisters before her did. He took her to the hospital early, before the pain. He walked her as far as the maternity ward and was guided back to the lobby by the nurse. The room was already occupied by five other women. Mother, a child herself, was the youngest among the women, the only one carrying her firstborn. Timidly, she undressed and put on the nightgown she herself had sewn and embroidered for the occasion. The nurse hurried her into her gown, rushed her into her hospital bed, under the covers, and commanded her to lie still while she tucked the sheets and blanket under the mattress. Mother's form, like the forms of the other five women, bulged beneath the neatly and tightly tucked bedsheets. When Mother shifted to adjust her nightgown or to scratch her shoulder, the nurse yelled at her and returned to her bedside to remove the wrinkles that had appeared in the sheets. If one of the other women moaned in pain, the nurse shushed the woman and threatened to release her before she gave birth. The window that looked onto the room from the corridor brought past it visitors who looked in at the bulging, silent women, and nodded their approval. When the wife of the leader of the country, who had helped to fund and design the ward, came by to look in, Mother was pinched on her arm beneath the sheets to induce her to keep still and to wear a smile. She spent two days in this state in bed as the other women, each in her turn, were wheeled away to the delivery room, until she was no longer able to suppress her cries, and it was her turn to deliver. And Father, all this time, patiently paced the corridors of the hospital, wilting flowers in hand.

type

So, the movable type, ears pricked, eyes dotted, shoulders rounded, legs set, travels backward, travels forward. In time, it will work out what is missing, what has been lost.

unbirth

Mother meets others like herself in the new land. Others recently arrived from distant, once-peaceful befores. Others recently arrived in the land of the sun with little more than their scared fixed eyes, their tired heavy ears, their broken tongues. They speak with voices colored by disparate landscapes, histories, and horrors. They come from lands east and south. It is an age of disruption, of governments toppled, of covetousness and invasion from with-out, of ideology, blind and ravenous, unleashed from within. She meets these new arrivals at one job or another; she meets them at her night course, where they all learn to speak a common language; she meets them in the aisles of the grocery market, where they coach one another on how to cook an unfamiliar vegetable or together make out what a box or a bottle holds inside it. And she brings these displaced newcomers home to meet Father and the girls, who recognize themselves in their new guests. So the girls open the door. And the immigrants file in. They enter the home, some bowing, some holding out their hands, some offering their cheek. Some left their lands in a boat, others on foot, others in the beds of trucks, or hidden beneath their seats. They have all left much behind and they find comfort in what they find common among each other. In the land of the sun, they are invisible. In the land of the sun, they are welcome. Mother too welcomes them. The girls open the door, and the guests file in, bringing flowers or a loaf of bread, a cake or a stew.

There is a young woman new at work: small, quiet, solitary, frightened. But Mother, her adopted language limited, knows how to speak to her, knows how to host even in the bare lunchroom the women gather in at their workplace. Mother brings the food and shares the stories, and soon knows this woman too. The young woman is a more recent arrival, unsure of herself, moving through the new world with the old world still on her skin, in her nostrils, in her throat, and much in her thoughts. In her own country, she was a teacher of small children and lost two of her boys to the militias that efficiently made soldiers of them. Soon her girls stopped coming to class. Then the school closed down. Her father did not return from his walk down the hill to the fruit stand. Her brother collected his small family and, with two strange men, left for the border in the night; but she would stay with her mother and younger sister. Her neighbors began to shut their doors and board up their windows. The dry season set in. Hunger set in. She tells Mother she lost much and many but stayed despite the regular disappearances; the daily state-ordered beatings and shootings in the street; the roving ideologues with guns strung across their backs, who shouted their righteous slogans at closed windows and doors; the nodding heads on TV, who mouthed words but said nothing; the regular funeral processions; the hushed children; the strange new order/disorder. She stayed and adjusted each time. She stayed until the day her uncle came to their door to silently lead her by her sleeve to her sister's body lying in the weeds along the side of the road. She did not recognize her at first. The corpse wore her sister's dress, her sister's ring, her sister's shoes. But her sister was a virgin and this headless girl was pregnant. It was their mother who understood first. Who fell onto the body and, wailing, choking, claimed it as her own. It was their mother who stroked the raised belly and shed her tears, delivered her kisses there, onto that taut, unnatural mound. It was her mother who forced the young woman to leave her home the same night, with the same men, by the same road her brother had taken months before. She did not stay to see her sister's head removed from her abdomen, though her uncle promised her the dead girl would go into the earth as she was delivered to it: whole. Mother's new friend understood that her sister left the world through the same channel that she had entered it. It was an image and an understanding she brought with her to the new land. It was an image and an understanding that was seared into the surface of her desiccated eyes. And Mother's grasp of such visions and of eyes wrung dry by unnatural events was great. She had five small girls to raise and a meandering line of multitudinous dead behind her.

the grandfather tree

The sisters agree that he is a tree; he does not move as they move; he has no legs, no feet. He has only his trunk and numerous arms, two sets of many-arms: those that always reach skyward and love the radiant sun and collect nourishment from it and splay their many broad leaves like a thousand open hands giving thanks to that distant orb, and those that forever reach earthward with their many fine filaments-like-fingers that love the cold dark places, the wet mineral-rich places, the secret-giving places. The sisters see that without legs and with two sets of vigorous forever-reaching arms, persuaded by divergent needs, pulling in opposite directions, the tree is incapable of lateral movement, immobile, bound and locked in place, in a small yard, in an ordinary neighborhood, in a valley near the sea. He is their grandfather yet he is unable to understand their own tired legacy of feet, of forever-movement over an earth that spins, though not steadily enough. And they know that the soughing in the old tree's leaves or the occasional rattling of its limbs is nothing more than the wind moving westward from the mountains toward the lapping sea.

But the sisters also know that movement alone does not generate dreams. So they listen to the old tree's stories and through them know him and find that he is more kin than blood-kin. He too holds memory in his cells, opening their gates to unlock the secrets of his history when the mood suits him or the day is ripe. He too makes use of the inner channels and senses without knowing that they transport more than life-sustaining nutrients and fluids. And his memory, like theirs, reaches back to the beginning days.

Because of the nature of the sun and its seductive relationship to the leaves and upward-reaching branches of the tree and because of the nature of the earth and its intimate and secretive bond with the downward-yearning roots of the tree, the indolent sister, resting in the grass in the shade of the grandfather tree's mighty canopy, will not hear the same story that the intrepid sister, climbing the tree's heights and placing her ear against the tree's uppermost appendages and its whispering leaves, will know. And the mechanism that generates the earth-dreams is the same one that orchestrates the transport of minerals on the backs of water molecules. And it is the sun and his sibling stars who rejuvenate the ancient tales in their churning centers, drawing them out and sending them on their way as sky-dreams across the limitless cold spaces.

On a certain day of the week, at a given hour, in the early morning or at the sun's setting, the sister who wishes to hear the tree's
first story will be obliged. She will sit in the grass with her back
against the tree's forever shedding trunk, her shoulder blades
curved around one of its rough burls—forms that the girls call
knees or shins, though they know well that the tree has no feet,
does not move. Holding a leaf of grass or a segment of tangerine
in her mouth, with her eyes closed or looking out over the boundless yard, she will listen with ears and spine to the tree's tale. It is
an old story, a common story ubiquitously written: in the zigzag
trail left by the slow-moving snail across the garden wall; in the
morning dew dotting the spider's web; in Mother's eyes as she
irons on any Sunday afternoon while she listens to the old film
songs. But the sister prefers to hear it from the tree.

The grandfather tree's first story is also the earth's first dream and it
is the dream of water. The great tree will tell again the tale of water,
of its pooling, its trickling and meandering through the labyrinthine
channels within the rocky earth. It will next tell of water's murmur
and caress, its push and fall, its great roar across the open terrain of
that same earth, giving shape to its many surfaces. And, finally, it will
tell of water's absolute need to travel also in the ascendant direction,
against the force of gravity, in order to find its destiny in the sky. The
listening girl will learn of how water, in it's upward drive, brought
the tree up along with it from its former prostrate position, cell by
cell over the millennia, until the tree too stood upright, looked skyward and found there over its head a floating lake in the form of a
cloud, and understood that the same lake once pooled deep within
the cavernous earth, far below its roots.

The sister who listens to the tree's earth-dreams understands this
story and feels it within her own body, a body governed by the

same forces, the same desire to travel in the skyward direction, to
find its own portrait drawn with lines and points across the dome
of night. The sister knows well the upward movement of water,
knows keenly the gathering force of saliva in her mouth and of
tears in her eyes. But the sister also knows the circuitous movement
of a second force within her of which she cannot tell the tree. She
knows of blood, of its diurnal and nocturnal meanderings through
her own channels. She feels its iron-rich drive, no less powerful than water's roar across the earth. She has watched it pulse
beneath her skin, up and down the tender inside of her arm, and
has seen it break that same soft surface to pool in place like a ruby
unearthed, or to trickle down her arm and burst onto her skirt
like nectar from a pressed pomegranate seed. She has licked this
liquid from a knee or a knuckle after a fall or a fight and knows its
elemental flavor, understands that blood has a color, a density all
its own. She cannot tell the tree of this second force, though she
has read in books that others have tried. She knows of sacrifices,
of pacts made by humans with the green world: those ancient
exchanges of blood for sustenance. But she guesses that the tree
would not ask such a price. The tree knows of life and of death, it
knows of water but not of blood. It has no feet.

The grandfather tree dreams of stars. He studies numbers and
measures distances not in inches or yards but in the age of stars
whose long light has traveled far and carries with it rumors and tales
that tell of distant places and earlier eons. And the grandfather tree
mourns the death of the ancient stars whose last light falls on his
leaves and he divines and celebrates the births of new ones. His own
ancient age is minuscule next to the youthful stars' and this makes
him mourn also the death of the girls who spend their days swinging from his many limbs. He knows that there are many beginnings
and many endings but does not know which comes first: the nascent

bud or the burst star. Years spent in the service of the sky, counting stars and measuring time, has taught the grandfather tree that light courses through the cosmos as water courses through his many limbs. The grandfather tree knows that light too travels a circuitous route and that: what turns will unwind; what enters will out; and what travels will return home again.

mirror sisters

The house was small, the sisters many, and the mirror one. The five sisters shared one bathroom and readied themselves each morning before its small mirror. The rectangular glass hung over the bathroom sink, onto which the youngest had to climb in order to see her image. To this mirror, the sisters were drawn to: brush, braid, and feather hair, rouge cheeks, make faces, admire lashes and tonsils, and practice the many smiles, those polite and polished, and those bare and wild. But their time before the mirror was brief, for the sisters were many and were always coming and going: to school or to bed, to a party or to the store with Mother, to their chores, their homework, or to their guests. And while the house was always humming with their moving bodies and various activities, the many rhythms in the house rose and fell at different rates so that unexpectedly, after a great peak of bustle and push, a deep trough of silence and stillness emerged in that part of the house. In that space, a sister might linger before the small bathroom mirror without interruption.

And the sister who stands idle before her own image and whose gaze long remains on the line of her chin suddenly sees this line blur. For a moment she loses her face, familiar, as her image softens and blurs, then finds it again, clear and close, but ever so slightly changed. Not in form but in gaze returned. And she recognizes that gaze and welcomes it as an old friend. Then seeing her own enthusiasm and warmth returned, she smiles, jumps. It is not long before she finds that she is two in the looking glass—the girl she is here, the girl who runs and climbs trees and walks to school over flat concrete walkways, looking twice before crossing the many streets, and the girl she is in the beforelife, the girl who runs and climbs trees and walks downhill past pine tree and fruit vendor to get to school, routinely stopping along the way to pick the red poppy or its musical dry seed head. The sister finds over time that she may come to the mirror to brush teeth and hair, or come to the mirror to visit the self she is in the first life and with whom she will onc day merge again, for the war will not last long.

So all of the sisters, by accident or through searching—for each knows she exists in the duplicate and lives two lives simultaneously on two continents—all of the sisters early on see the first self in the mirror. And each finds time and space to steal away from the family to come to the mirror-self to converse, to exchange notes, to find out what has changed and what remains the same in each life. And the sister in front of the mirror sees that in the first life her hair still glistens, her brow still knots when pondering a question. The one shows the other a purse she has recently sewn, or shares a new song, or whispers gossip about the older sisters. And the sister asking her mirror-likeness how her day went, hearing of another rocket attack or a school closing, and finding her image in tears, tries to soothe her. And the girl behind the mirror asks the girl in the land of the sun, does Mother still make the barley soup? Does Father still recite the many and melodic names of god? They compare the heights of the mountains to the depths of the sea. The sister and her mirror-self talk of homework, boys, and the color of the sky at dusk. And the two discover that winter makes the one but not the other shiver. But the moon in both lands follows the sister when she is moving, on foot or by car, on Father's shoulders or in Mother's lap on the city bus. And when the immigrant sister praises the airplane, she sees instead of enthusiasm a forced stillness upon the other's face who remembers that fateful day of separation on the tarmac.

Time moves in each land, for each girl, but at different rates. The sisters looking into the bathroom mirror see their images mature, their hair grow in length or get cut or become hidden behind a scarf. They celebrate the piercing of ears, giggle at the donning of eyeglasses. They ask one another what she'd like to do and be and are surprised to know that though their wishes change seasonally, the two are the same and remain alike beneath the surfaces. Both

love and dream alike. Both celebrate and suffer alike. And when
Father is taken and not returned in the first land, all ten sisters
mourn as one, and Mother in the land of the sun wonders why at
the evening meal the dishes she has prepared go uneaten. News of
the war enters the house only in this way, for the television is silent
on the subject. And the resilient sisters living through the unend-
ing war have to console the immigrant sisters, whose hearts have
become timid and tender even as their lives have blossomed in the
sunny land. And the tenderness by and by draws them away from
the bathroom mirror. And over time, they say that the mirror-self
has shifted significantly: she dresses strangely, speaks with an accent,
is bound by rules and rituals of a nature deeper than the sisters in
the new land can fathom. By and by, the mirror-selves come only
to share news of a marriage or a birth, or come dressed in the dark
colors of grief, mourning a death or a disappearance, or they come
not at all, and the sister in the new land wonders and knits her brow
and returns to the brushing of teeth or the trimming of bangs or
the dabbing on of lotion. The war runs on. And the sun shines year-
round in the golden land. The sisters forget the first self or let her
be as they try to dispel the first land and let it be. And over time, the
mirror begins to reflect only the surfaces again so that the contours
of a sister's face hold no matter how long she stares at her reflection
or how much she crosses her eyes. But very occasionally, a sister
thinks she sees a smile when she's felt none or, frowning, finds that
the mirror does not follow suit.

Grandparents: those beings of long ago, mysteries to us. A series of curtains, one after another and with each subsequent generation, had dropped behind us as a result of too much movement over the face of the earth. Our parents and the five of us were all born, but just barely, in the same country. My father was born in the same year his family, escaping invasion and war, crossed a border to seed a small farm in a new land. My youngest sister was not yet one when we left that land. Three of our four grandparents were born elsewhere. Our great-grandparents were shadows, nameless, their bones and their stories buried in other places. Our entire history was unknown, a great and an unyielding mystery. But we picked at it and drew bits enough to tell our story by, bits enough to sustain us, so that we did not feel entirely cheated of a history. We had no records of births or deaths, no facts or dates written on paper, no family trees embroidered on linen. Days before my eleventh birthday, I found out we had been celebrating the wrong birthday for years; with different calendars, the conversion of dates was easily miscalculated. On my thirty-ninth birthday, we worked out that we had left our country, had taken that fateful flight, on the day I turned seven. We arrived in the new land the day my younger sister turned six; against the din of war, birthdays were peripheral, forgotten, and, besides, what have numbers to do with age in wartime?

Of my mother's father, I remember only the single formidable photograph that hung in my grandmother's room. I can easily recollect my grandmother; she was with us when I came into the world. She held the great clan together with an unfathomable strength from her sickbed. Her power, along with her illness, made her as inaccessible to me in my earliest years as were the other three grandparents who had already passed before I arrived. And then we left, and were further removed from her and from the others. We gathered our history from my mother, who was its only source

after we left our birth country. She alone knew of the generation that came before hers. She had her childhood with her own
family by which to recall that more distant past, which she did with
a nostalgia that regularly broke my small, young heart. And she
had for a short time known my father's mother, who had handed
down to her my father's history, what little there was to pass on.

From my mother's stories, whole or fragmented, we put together a slim
history and fashioned a larger one using our own imaginations. Our
mother took up and left off at any point in a story, depending on which
guest listened, or which fragment suited her when she disciplined us,
or when her powerful nostalgia pulled her back into herself. She introduced her people to our guests as living and present beings and found
ways to connect our story to theirs. She knew who had lived where,
on which street, in what year, and how any two people may have run

into each other in the market or at a wedding celebration. She called on our history when she corrected us, drawing ancestors out of the air to aid her in her examples and admonishments; she was mother and village at once. And these people, our grandparents, great-aunts and great-uncles, however they arrived, they were large, heroic. Their stories were not common; they had all come from elsewhere, forced from their homes by war and treachery. They had traveled by foot across mountains, floated on the inflated skins of goats down churning rivers, accompanying deposed kings and their many consorts, or carrying their own children on their backs or in their bellies, as my grandmother had carried my father. They had seen and lost much on their journeys, and started again, then again in the new land.

Her grandfather's people on her mother's side, who had been exiled for decades and then recalled by a fickle king, brought back with them new members: wives and children with cheeks like red apples. Her father, the son of a vizier, had lost his entire family to invading armies and run away with the king of that ancient land. My mother often told us of how, then a youth, her orphaned father had buried his family's treasures—while he could not bury his slaughtered parents—in the soil of his birthland before fleeing it, never able to return and reclaim his property. And I always imagined the colorful gems, the gold fashioned into beautiful and intricate forms, still glimmering though hidden beneath a barren and torched landscape in our distant past. But the ancestors glimmered more brightly. I was separated from them at once by the ages and by a mere series of misty veils. Their stories were somehow my own, or rather, mine was theirs repeated. I knew the roads they had traveled; I had traveled them too.

Of my father's parents, I know only that they were forced out by the same armies that came to occupy much of that part of the world. His parents arrived in the new land in time to deliver my father to it, and took up spade and sickle to live by, though my mother, reaching back, remembered that perhaps theirs had originally been a line of merchants. At another time, she recalled that perhaps my father's father had been a simple village holy man.

As children, we did not have grandparents who came regularly to spoil or to squeeze us. We were separated from our grandparents, first by death and second by enormous distances over uncharted memory, and were separated even further from our great-grandparents, who were nameless, wispy things. The distance was not a mere generation or two, but many centuries in time. They lived in another age altogether; they were farmers or merchants, holy men or viziers to kings. They plowed the earth without machinery. They wore gold in their hair and rare gems on their fingers. They traveled by horse and wagon, and sat cross-legged on rugs woven by their own or their servants' hands. Somehow this moving over land across three generations had moved us centuries, perhaps millennia, through time. And the distance is immeasurable. It is not one that can be reconciled, except in the imagination, and through my own memories, which still reflect the landscape of my early childhood in another country, a landscape that is vivid, one I know well and often traverse to reach those I have not met in life.

gravity

And, of course, it was not blood alone that coursed through
their veins and bound these seven to each other. It was, first and
foremost, gravity, that undeniable and elemental force, which
pulled them into each other, so that all were as one. It was gravity that towed them here, shuttled them there across the wide
empty spaces, and drew them endlessly toward that great internal
cauldron.

the cat

The cat always found the family, a wandering family that left one
house for another because it was easier to take the path unwritten
than it was to settle down and tally how many: cups of tea sipped,
pounds of rice soaked, coats of paint brushed, roses clipped, light
bulbs changed, prayers recited, funerals attended, days, weeks,
months, and years elapsed, since the war began. It was easier to
fill and unpack boxes than it was to admit that the red rug looked
rather at home in the living room. And it was wiser to *choose* the
day and time of departure and arrival. The family came to the
new neighborhood, put down rugs, positioned furniture, unpacked
clothes and dishes, cut open and devoured a watermelon, adjusted
the TV antennas, watered lawn and tree, planted flowers and
herbs, hid treasures, set clocks and polished mirrors, cooked a meal,
hung curtains and a swing, and soon after the cat appeared in the
yard, or by the back door, or sometimes inside the house, curled on
a shirt or a skirt, in a closet or beneath one of the girls' beds.

The girls loved the cat, and each with a child's ardor, one that
suffered love on an enormous scale, in magnitudes at odds with
their own small statures or the size of the thing beloved. They
loved with an ardor that utilized all parts and faculties: hands, eyes,
scent, teeth, heart, dreams, appetite, memory, and breath. The
girls recognized the cat as their own upon its initial appearance,
saw it first as fur and ears and lit eyes, then perceived an outline
drawn around its small form, a neat contour that distinguished the
cat from all that surrounded it, all that was new and strange and
limitless, and belonged to others. And although they had never
had or held one before, the cat was theirs upon arrival, and introduced itself as such, though it did not speak, had no words. And
each time the cat arrived, in a black or a striped or a spotted coat,
with blue or green or golden eyes, it made itself at home among
the family, in the house, beneath the car, in the tree, and in the
neighborhood, which was new to the family but not to the cat who
knew its conduits and its hiding places.

With the sisters, the cat played and purred alternately. It hid
silently behind doors or beneath tables, then pounced suddenly
on their shuffling feet or tapping fingers. It lay across their books
or their backs as they read for school or studied ants. From its
higher perches, atop the refrigerator or in the limbs of the tree,
it leapt noiselessly to land in and swing from their long hair. The
cat woke them in the night to stare deeply into their eyes and hum
soothingly into their chest cavities. By day, thin red lines appeared
across their skin, running the length of the girls' forearms or across
the backs of their hands, though the playful cat was not to be seen.
The cat, which enjoyed play as much and as often as the girls did,
kept its nails sharpened, its whiskers groomed, and all lids over its
bright eyes ajar.

And the sisters did not fight over the cat because the cat belonged to each girl and was devoted to her alone. It was in five places at once and attuned itself accordingly, becoming humble, silly, or ferocious, light in weight or upright in posture. It fell in line with each sister, knew who moved with ease and who moved sharply, understood who was and was not speaking to whom else, sensed who was and was not dreaming when the lights went out. And each sister held the cat close, shared with it her best secrets, and kept for it her tastiest morsels at dinner.

But where the cat went or what it did when the sisters were not looking, not petting, or pulling, or chasing, no sister knew. In regard to its nocturnal practices and wanderings, the only certainty was that the cat always returned. Whether gone for hours or for days, it faithfully came home, always their cat, yet each time altered. And attempts by the two small brave sisters to follow it out into the night disclosed none of the cat's secrets. Instead, the sisters' ventures revealed a neighborhood changed by moonlight and silhouette, a place unfamiliar, filled with shadows deep and shadows tall into which the cat leapt and disappeared. The neighborhood at night was a place shifting. Houses shrank as the sisters neared them, and cars and street lamps receded so that a block that was now fifteen houses in length was in the next moment fifty. Trees doubled in size to tower over telephone poles, and shrubs ballooned to block interior lights streaming forth from windows, while porch lights flickered and grew faint. And lawns, still twinkling with the sprinkler's dew, like many small lakes, swallowed toys left out by children now in bed, to grow denser, darker.

The sisters, who would not disturb the night, peeled off shoes to walk with bare feet, and took in soft, measured breaths, not eager to steal oxygen from the respiring trees, which swayed deeply though no breeze lifted the sisters' hair. With limber necks, they peeked beneath cars, over neighbors' walls, and under the lids of trash bins, but the cat remained elusive. They turned two corners and found themselves again on the same street, in front of the same house. When they stopped to wonder, they saw that: puddles reflected more than starlight; flowers, which had closed at dusk, now bloomed again in colors richer and emanated scents sweeter; large sycamore leaves, in twos, stepped, not aimlessly, down sidewalks and up walkways; stones stirred, disappeared, then rematerialized ten steps away; and street lamps pulsed blue then red as if the stars themselves had alighted in the sleeping neighborhood. As their eyes adjusted, the sisters came to see that within shadows resided deeper shadows still, and from the depths of the darkest corners, eyes languid and eyes alert appeared and watched them in return. Where initially they'd strained to hear distant horns in the night, they now heeded each crackle, whir, slosh, and sigh by their sides or at their heels. The sisters were not afraid. The trees spoke, and the flowers spoke, and the stars whispered. And all that they said was wonderful. The sisters looked about them and laughed. They grabbed each other's hands and skipped back home, jumping puddles, kicking stones, and left the cat to its own amusements.

anger

When Mother was angry, she was like a dragon: her fiery breath blew hot words through the halls and doorways of the house, singed the sisters' brows or the fine hairs on their long arms and legs, and melted the cubes of ice in their cups. Mother's breath created hotspots in the corners of rooms, and eddies over the sisters' heads, forcing their hair upright, to sway and swirl like small tornadoes, which made their heads nod yes or shake no in answer to her questions: "Did I not ask you three times this morning to take down and wash and iron the curtains?" or "Did we leave everything and everyone behind to bring you here to speak and dress and behave like this?" or "Was it you who hid your sister's book in the rice bin?" And the offending sister who liked to wear her hair in braids had them undone by the turning, hot currents of Mother's words. And the sister-in-trouble whose hair was loose was left with it knotted in a great mass and standing askew on her head when Mother was done with her. Before her anger erupted, Mother swelled, measuring her intake of air, first shallow, then deep, first rapid, then deliberate. And the girls sensed this recalibration of Mother's great instrument long before Mother spoke, long before she entered the rooms they occupied: one sister felt it on her face, on the side not covered with the telephone receiver, another felt it brush across her fingers, which held a pencil raised above a sheet of paper. And each sister froze in space and time and took the opportunity before the storm to assess her day and her actions, those taken and those not accomplished, those categorized and those forgotten across the stretch of day. And each sister wondered, is it me? And if me, *how shall I brace myself, let me first put aside my homework lest it get scorched, let me hang up the telephone and move gently across the linoleum to the kitchen sink to finish rinsing the pile of dishes, so as to counter Mother's impending words with the chiming of glasses and the tinkling of spoons and forks.* But much like the dragon's scorching breath, just as suddenly as it appeared, her anger dissipated, and the girls were left with a glow on their cheeks.

When Father was angry, the house filled with a white fluff, like
the cotton he'd picked and cleaned as a boy for his mother to spin
on her wheel, and which he now seemed to unspin back to the
natural fiber—rarely, a sister listening might make out the whir of
their grandmother's spinning wheel and guess Father had somehow brought that machine with him, managed to sneak it past the
guards and out of the first country, in one of his many pockets,
perhaps. The white stuff that was Father's anger was born in the
remotest parts of the house: the inner corners of closets where
Father kept his old shoes, his umbrella, and his holy book, and the
spaces around the appliances he maintained for the family—the
nooks behind and beneath the refrigerator, the washer, and the
dryer. The cotton stuff silently filled these spaces first, generally
unknown to the sisters, who went about their day, ignorant and
noisy. But once started, Father's anger did not retreat, as Mother's
did when she found herself rushing in judgment or felt herself
unfair (Mother's memory kept her always in two worlds—that of
motherhood and that of her own girlhood, so it was not difficult
for her to feel with and for her daughters). No, Father's disapproval had a mission and would fulfill it. His anger grew silently
and after filling the quiet spaces of the house, it softly tumbled out
of the closets, the doors of which gave to the growing pressure
from within, and pushed out from the sides and tops of the large
appliances. Father's anger-like-cotton fell forth in silent clumps and
grew into small hills. It moved down the hall, along baseboards
and over rugs. It climbed up the corners of each room while the
girls played or read or cooked, each busy and unknowing until
the last moment when, looking up, they saw the avalanche and
panicked at its imminent cascade upon their heads. Or they felt
it from below: tipping their chairs this way and that; lifting their
arms so that they dropped and immediately lost markers and

crayons, nail polish or forks, in the white clouds; causing them to spill water or tea on the Eastern rugs, which were now no longer visible, covered as they were with Father's unspoken disapproval. The billowing mountains muffled the girls' voices, covered their ears and their eyes, left them floating in a white fluff. The movable sisters feared Mother's tempest but were more affected by Father's silent disapproval, which was rare and potent with its enveloping, noiseless pressure. His anger did not make them take action as Mother's did. Instead it made them consider, forced them to turn inward, to knit their brows and become humble.

scene

The girls jump. The planet spins. And when their feet find earth again, they find themselves in a new yard, in a different neighborhood, welcomed by the grandfather tree—who does/does not travel—and peered at from beneath the rosebushes by a new cat with the old familiar eyes.

brother, sister

The two are small boys, aged five and six. They chase each other about their neighborhood, down alleys and over mounds of refuse and rubble. They throw stones and make faces at one another, call each other the cruelest, dirtiest names they can muster or imagine with their small-boy minds. They hide behind the trunks and in the canopies of trees, climb them to reach ripe fruit, to rob nests of colorful eggs, or to spy over walls into yards and through windows. They have recently met and are friends already. The five-year-old is new to the neighborhood. He goads the older boy and lets him hold the lizard he has captured. He shows him the large scab on his elbow and drops pears into the waiting boy's outstretched shirt. He whistles and snaps his fingers and the older boy, with diligence and aspiration, learns to do the same. They line up marbles and squint their eyes. They squat as the adult men squat; they spit, and click their tongues. The foreign soldier passing the boys in the alleyway pays them no heed. He stops beside a house, looks over its garden wall, enters its yard through its back gate to use its outhouse. He has leaned his rifle against the outer wall of the house, beside the gate. The younger boy does not hesitate. He runs over and picks up the heavy automatic rifle. He has seen it used more than a few times. He knows how to hold it, how to engage and release it, and he uses his whole body to brace the machine. He yells to the other boy, "Look up, look up to the sky!" The older boy looks up, squints, makes out a hawk circling high up in the air. The boy with the machine gun empties it of its rounds into the squinting boy's body, in a straight line from the ground to the sky. The older boy is split in two cleanly, vertically. His two halves fall backward and away from each other onto the dusty earth. The soldier, hearing the shots, runs from the outhouse, the yard, climbs and jumps the front gate of the house into the busy street, races down the hillside, down into the city below, leaves his helmet, his gun behind. The younger boy too falls backward, under the weight of the gun. He scrambles out from beneath it, runs to his house, to his grandmother and his sisters, in the wrong direction, bewildered. The boy split in two lies staring with dust-coated eyes at two separate skies. The hawk returns to circle in one of them. One by one the people of the neighborhood venture out. They scream, they heave air, and else; they run from and return to the body; they pull at their hair and chew on their knuckles and on their sleeves.

The cleaved boy's mother is brought to him. She sees her son in two, two small halves, neat, mirror images separated by a pool of red, she falls to her knees, silent, unable to take in what is before her, she is herself split, never the same again. The break is instantaneous. In her mind, she returns to the days of her own childhood, becomes sister to her small daughter, becomes a muttering and obedient servant to her husband, who soon takes on a new wife, younger, keener, not unhappy to take the position of first wife. The mother/child/sister/servant ages even as she lapses back into her childhood. Her dark, flowing, silken hair transforms into a white woolly heap on her shoulder. Her morning-dew skin grows leathery. Her teeth twist and turn, crack and brown in her mouth. Her eyes lose their acuity and turn inward. Sleeping under quilts next to a fire one winter night, she dreams of a long-ago school outing to the city's flour mill and stretches her feet into the nucleus of the coals, which take her toes gladly. Her young daughter/sister dreams of a roast goat on a spit, and waking, smells it roasting still. She finds her mother asleep next to her, unconscious, unperturbed, unaware of her toes burning among the coals, toes melted, then fused again. The cleaved woman can nevermore walk on her feet. She further ages, is bent farther forward in body, further back in mind. She is a child, a not-yet-wife, a not-yet-mother standing over a small boy who is split down the middle and lies in two in the dust with his sundered eyes bound skyward. The transmuted woman's daughter/sister, now mother/

servant to her, metamorphoses into a beautiful young woman herself. She betrays her legacy and exhibits the silken black hair, the soft milky skin, the steady, knowing eyes. And though many come to win her hand, she does not marry. She is her mother/ sister/daughter's keeper. She bathes the leathered skin and combs the rough woolly hair on the aged woman. She brings the tea and sweets and lays the cushions and quilts nightly. She empties the bedpan and dances while her mother plays the tambourine and jubilantly sings the early songs. She ushers the guests away from her mother's hidden quarter of the house, keeps her mother engaged while her siblings, her step-mother, and her father attend the parties, the parades, and the festivals.

coil

And all that winds will unwind.

the sisters did not fight

The sisters did not fight. They simmered, dug into memories of yesterday or yesteryear, and excavated old hatreds for one another. They revisited old hurts caused by this or that sister to add to their personal brew of present anger and new grief; each sister kept a bubbling cauldron into which she regularly dropped her hurts. They picked old scabs, nearly healed, and added these too. They

stirred in Mother's look of admonishment from the breakfast
table, that silent but potent drop of "never-you-mind" or "shhh,
not in front of the guests" or "sinful, insolent girl." Each sister
tended her own cauldron, though sometimes two or three gathered
around a single large pot to whisper and bemoan shared injustices,
to stir and stew, to add their own heat for fuel and gripes for flavor.
They sprinkled in grievances over promises not kept, rights denied
by, or injustices suffered at the hands of, the offending sister. And
the sister unloved was always a different one, though each had
her preferred target/offender. Into the dark and cloudy brew, they
dropped in and pushed under those possessions especially prized
by the hated sister   pages from her beloved book, a single earring,
a section of her dark hair clipped in the night, her best music cassette, a doll's shoe, a blue jay's tail feather.

And as she stirred, the wounded sister swore and, beneath her
breath, recited rhyming hexes using both of her two tongues.
The pot sputtered and popped, it spewed its caustic solution into
the air, onto the girl's hair or clothing or bare feet, which scalded
and blistered and formed new scabs. This cooking and stirring
and this regular adding of fuel and seasoning soothed
the sisters to a small and necessary degree. But it was not a
release in any true sense. No, the sisters did not fight. They held
in and held back anger, spite, and hurt. Each nursed her own
cauldron of unexpressed emotions and when she felt she could
no longer keep it in, when she felt that her pot might crack from
the heat of all that was unsaid, she simply dipped her cup into
the murky, hot liquid, filled it to the brim, and drank from it
swiftly but deeply with tightly shuttered eyes and plugged nose.
Then she went on with her day as if all were right with the world
and in the house.

The five sisters suffered to keep peace within the walls of their home while conflict festered within their small bodies and in the distant and war-sealed country that was their birthland. They deceived nearly all who saw them with: their large, sweet eyes; their timid, smiling lips; their deference and modesty, worn well; their eagerness to help and serve; their quiet tones—unmusical, unpretentious; their spare frames and spindly limbs; their color- ful and peculiar, thrift-store and hand-me-down garb. They were slight but cavernous, unassuming but knowing. Early on they had been entrusted with the darkest secrets of the human heart and mind. They understood the power of words spoken and understood that words kept in held equal power. The utterance of a few words in jest had put their young uncle into an early grave, a mass grave, with others still breathing. The utterance of their father's name on national television, broadcast belatedly, a week after their silent departure from that first country, had fallen on the relieved ears of the few family members who'd been burdened with and kept the fleeing family's secret. But the list had contained the names of many others who did not have the means or the forethought to escape, and each name spoken was a sentence passed.

The sisters knew the uses of secrecy for good and for ill. They understood the consequences of each—the consequences were life and death. They had been initiated into that murky world and learned to navigate their way through it with little help from the adults. But these were not the only codes they lived by. Mother and the first culture had instilled in them the innumerable direc- tives governing the proper behavior of proper girls. These were principles of decorum and etiquette, which the sisters could not shake or shed, though, at one point or another, each tried to

unburden herself of the old customs. They knew, every one of
them, how to keep and exhibit a proper-girl surface. The sisters
knew they were judged by: They who ruled from above and
Those who had passed (the many, the countless); Mother and
Father; aunts and uncles (though they lived many thousands of
miles away, could rarely be reached by telephone, wrote letters in
a different script); their parents' friends and *their* families and *their*
friends; neighbors; teachers; dentists; policemen; school bus drivers; grocery clerks; televised politicians. The sisters were reminded
often that the adult world watched them with a keen eye. They
knew the price of too much wisdom shown, of secrets revealed,
and of loose lips. And so they kept these things to themselves and
hid them even from one another.

But the keeping had a price as well. The cooking and simmering
of solutions and the drinking and reabsorbing of these noxious liq-
uids had a price. These practices and rituals were corrosive; they
ate away at the delicate sprouts of the various flora of wisdom,
emotion, and vision within each girl, which endlessly produced
beautiful buds that never reached full blossom to leave their lips.
Feelings and thoughts were turned in and under and created teeming gardens vividly real, beautiful, and harmful within each sister.
Mother had said that a seed swallowed would one day sprout and
find an exit to the external world, but the sisters knew that what
went in only festered, then bloomed silently within. Emotion was
looked down upon; expression became a solitary and internal
endeavor. In this environment, secrets proliferated, the sisters
created imaginary sisters who spoke in loving, sisterly tones, and
held one another's hands. They envisioned sisters who played and
moved lightly through the world, as did the happy children on television or in their neighborhood. In this way, the sisters multiplied

again. They were five, then they were twenty-five. They were ten, and then they were one thousand.

It is true. The sisters did not fight. They did not express or share emotion. They kept hurt and anger and grievances to themselves. They kept dreams and stories hidden. They knew the cost of war and knew it was greater than the price they paid in silence and self-absorption. This is true and it is the way it was in the house and in the yard. It was the same in the car on long drives through infinite loops of freeway or on the walk to school over the uneven concrete sidewalks of their neighborhood or on a solitary bench in the schoolyard in the shade of a large sycamore tree.

like cats, like cats

It is all fiction. In truth, the sisters fought like cats. They were like many angry cats with piercing eyes that cut through laughter and conversation at dinner; like cats with ireful hisses in pitches Mother and Father could not hear; like cats with razor-sharp claws that flashed for an instant and left neat crimson lines across naked skin. When infuriated, they called each other *dog*, that vilest of curses in the first tongue. When hurt, they buried, burned, or tore-up the other's beloved possessions. It was not necessary to tiptoe into the hated sister's bedroom in the middle hours of the night, scissors in hand, to steal a lock of hair. No, the aggrieved sister, in broad daylight, simply grabbed and pulled a fistful from the other's head. Yes, the sisters fought: they pushed and tugged; scratched and spat at each other; sprang out of nowhere onto another's back, bringing her to the floor where the two writhed, bit, and screeched.

It was when Mother and Father were away at work or visiting friends that the sisters' claws and teeth were bared. Once the adults had left and the house was theirs entirely, it did not take much, or long, for a fight to break out between any two or three of the girls. But there were always another two or three who sat it out to watch with trepidation, or amusement, or who were simply too engrossed in their own activities or daydreams to take part. Sometimes the fights were purely vocal, angry shouts or empty threats launched back and forth across the house or screamed through walls and doors. Occasionally, quarrels escalated, turning into a war of words *and* claws. But the most treacherous battles were those that were purely physical and that took place as if within a void, outside of time, in sheer soundlessness. Then the two sisters fixed their gaze on something beyond each other, on something recessed further back in time or abiding in a different place altogether. In silence, their bodies coiled and uncoiled. In silence, they lurched and fell back. Their teeth, their fingernails blindly sought a patch of exposed skin on the other's thigh, or neck, or belly. Their elbows and knees, their chins or heels, sought the vulnerable recesses where nerves collect and breath resides: the dips just above and just below the sternum. And the sisters who stood apart witnessed the background of television and window recede and imagined space swell around the two who were fighting. They recognized their sisters in the brawl; saw the flying braids or the familiar cuff of a sleeve. But they also glimpsed: a grown man's unkempt beard and brow, a torn and blood-soiled trouser leg, the dull flash of a helmet, the burnished handle of a knife, yellowing teeth in a gaping mouth—and the hot breath that hung to it—life-weary eyes filled with loathing and animal terror.

When it was over, after the feuding sisters had exhausted their limbs and their spirits, each returned to her chores or her home-work and carried on not-speaking. With minds turned inward, roiling stomachs, and busy fingers, they went about their daily tasks, awaiting the adults' return. And in that strange calm of the fight's aftermath, each sister created half-truths and untruths about the other. In her mind, she worked and unworked scenes and plots and dressed the sister-villain in suitable garb. Each was a master of her art and crafted a tale worthy of her rage or her injury. When Mother and Father returned, all of the sisters went on as usual, in the usual tones, employing the usual proper-girl gestures, asking polite questions of their parents: "The drive was not too long, no traffic, I hope?" or "How many were invited on the bride's side?" or "Did the old woman die here or in the first country?" or "What dishes did they serve?" But all the while, each battle-worn girl endured the many minutes and the encumbrance of too much family. She bided her time until she found Mother alone, winding her hair around plastic rollers in front of the bath-room mirror or turning down the blankets on her bed. And in that abridged and rare moment of confidence, the sister looking for sympathy, with raspy voice and tear-filled eyes, recited her well-practiced tale to Mother:

"Look, Mother-Dear, at this fistful of hair, which she has pulled from my head and that I found hidden beneath her pillow. And look at the tears in my drawing; she clawed at it with her long, dirty fingernails. Had you not arrived when you did, I'm not sure I would have any hair left on my head—and the others, they did

nothing to rescue me; they aren't true sisters. But she, she is a wild
animal! She cannot be of this family; she doesn't resemble us in
the least. Maybe it's true what the others say. Maybe you did find
her in the desert, roaming the hills, barefoot, shirtless. Well, she's
little better now."

"Ma-Dear, see how she parades around the yard, doing cart-
wheels no less, and in my beautiful new skirt! And when I
threatened to tell you, she said she doesn't care because she is
the youngest and you like her best and she has the prettiest eyes
and she can wear anything she likes, whether or not it belongs to
her, whether or not it fits her. And how poorly my skirt fits her,
Ma-Dear."

"Do not tell Father, but I found her looking through his desk
again, taking his pencils and his mints once more. And, this time,
scratching her name with a razor into the back of the antique
watch he keeps in the second drawer. What will others think?
They'll say we are not raising her properly, not teaching her our
ways. I think she may turn into a thief; I felt I should warn you.
She doesn't listen to me, doesn't appreciate my guidance or my
kind, sisterly words. You know how others talk. It's your reputation
I worry about, Mother-Dear."

Mother did not know all that passed between her many daughters
when she and Father were out. But often she guessed correctly
what did not. She herself had grown up with no less than a dozen
siblings and knew the tale-telling ways of sisters and brothers.
Mother knew how to sift truth from falsehoods and exaggerations.
She knew that the watches in her husband's desk drawer were
broken and awaiting repair—a testament to her husband's thrift

and industrious ways—and that the skirt her youngest wore was
neither new nor beautiful. Like most of the items in their home,
it had been purchased secondhand, with her thrift-store employee
discount. She saw clearly that the hair her third daughter presented as evidence was her very own, wavy and fine, and that the
clean tears in her drawing had been cut with scissors, not made by
little hands. But still, she listened to her many daughters' tales with
an easy ear and hidden smile as she clipped the ends of peas or
stacked cans of tomato sauce in the kitchen cabinet. It was Mother
who kept the peace. She knew whom to reprimand and how
severely, which girl needed a gentle word and whom she needed to
send to Father for a quieter and briefer, but more potent, scolding,
and how to coax the feuding sisters into forgiving one another. Her
own father, full of laughter and a strong distaste for conflict, inside
or outside their home, had taught her and her siblings a simple
yet powerful gesture of reconciliation: the hooking together of the
feuding parties' pinky fingers. She had passed this on to her children, whose proud and stubborn feelings never failed to give way
to the power of a pinky-finger truce.

After a quarrel, Mother would bring the two sisters together to
face each other. And the seething sisters, silent and defiant, with
eyes averted, would inch their clenched fists toward each other,
deeply sickened by the prospect of making the slightest contact
with the hated sibling. But Mother was patient and, looking on
from above, spoke the words that the sisters could not or defiantly
refused to say to one another: "But you know she didn't mean it;
she is sorry and did not escape unscathed either; look at her shin,
it's blue beneath the scratch already." or "She didn't steal your
magazine, she only borrowed it to do her homework; there it is
now, in her hand behind her back, neatly rolled and ready to be

returned to you." And while she spoke in pacifying tones, the sisters' fists relaxed and inched closer, until each girl's pinky finger opened, trembling, to meet the other. The effect was immediate; the slight but intimate touch of bird-like bones hooked about each other smothered the storm within each girl and set things aright in the house once again.

eyelid

The sisters slept nightly and woke each morning, but it took the moon many nights to close its heavy lid and many nights to lift it open again. And how genial and diverting was the moon when wide awake, cheering up the gloomy sky with its radiance, dressing itself alternately in clouds swollen and clouds trailing, outlining the rooftops, the telephone lines, the apricots, and the swing with its soft spray, bobbing, as the night went on, from hilltop to hilltop, to chase the cat out of its hiding place, and finally, at its peak, filling the valley with its liquid blue light so that the basin became one large pool for the sisters to swim in. And how sluggish and reluctant a playmate the moon was when, in daytime, a sister met the faded friend lolling over the school playground with lid half-drawn, with little to say.

brothers

They are brothers. The more clever of the two—the one who runs his father's business, knows his customers, listens to what is exchanged and whispered in the city's clubs and back alleys—he reads the signs early and joins the party of the new government. His younger brother, a youth still in school, is taught the new dogma, learns to dress conventionally, speak softly, and avoid eye contact with those in authority, those carrying rifles, riding tanks. But his heart is with the cause of the rebels in the mountains. At home, the two brothers, once inseparable, grow suspicious and watchful of each other. Their mother says, "You are like dogs, sniffing, circling. What will come of this?"

One day, the student yells across the courtyard of their sprawling house, "I will tear you to shreds in your sleep!" His brother yells back, "In bed or at your school desk, sipping your tea or squatting on the toilet, look up and find me ready to skin you from navel to toes." The young merchant leaves the market early one day and comes home with forms, with pamphlets. The student, looking out over his schoolbooks, yells to him, "You are official now. Okay, come here." And he strides across the courtyard, past the rooster, past their mother peeling carrots and, though smaller, lifts his brother into the air and slams him to the earth.

Their father, on hearing the official news, says to his older boy, "You are a merchant's son, you will amount to nothing under them. Those that rise in the party are the poor—the farmer's son, the delivery boy, the fruit vendor—not the likes of you." Still, the young merchant and his three penniless friends enlist in the military and pledge their allegiance to the party in power. He comes home one final time to show his family his uniform and his gun, and departing, tells them, "My uniform is weighty, but I leave you lighter, unburdened of family and God." His young brother shortly leaves school and exchanges his school uniform for a religious cap, his schoolbooks for the holy book. He listens to the radio and to the neighborhood murmurings in order to keep up on the advances and the losses made and suffered by the rebels in the mountains and in the countryside. He studies his book diligently and begins to preach to his mother and father, and to the children of the neighborhood. He grows his hair long and spends his days walking about the courtyard, clinking beads and hissing prayers, peeking over the garden wall to watch for government vehicles or neighborhood children, so that he may hide from one and scold the other.

The merchant-turned-soldier serves four years emptying homes of those disloyal to the party, tracking well-armed rebels over mountains, and driving officials from the city to the villages, to the borders, and back again. The three friends he enlisted with have each advanced to become a general in the military, a consul to a neighboring country, and a minister of construction, positions that keep them occupied and unable to see visitors or respond to letters from former friends. At the end of his fourth year, while clearing mines, the soldier steps on one, and loses a leg and half of his face. He returns home bandaged and penitent. His mother says, "This. In shreds." The devout brother brings his holy book to his ailing, disfigured brother, who kisses it and rocks it against his chest and, drooling, begs for god's mercy and forgiveness.

gem

Mother wears a ruby ring on her left hand. And when she braids
the sisters' hair or rinses the rice in the sink or readies herself for
work, the girls hear it clink and clink again against the handle of
hair brush or the dish in the sink or her car keys. And the small
and rhythmic sound of her ring against other objects, and its brilliant color against her skin, their hair, the teacup in her hand, this
sound and color are as much a part of Mother as is her voice. The
ring is old, they can see. And Mother tells one of her daughters
that when she was a teenager, she and her best sister had identical
rings made from a single stone to honor their sisterly bond. And
she tells another daughter that the ring has been passed down
from mother to daughter for many generations in their family.
And each of the girls believes one day it will be hers. Though they
are five and the ring one, each sister knows it belongs to her, and
momentarily borrowing it, the girl admires its color and form on
her still-small finger.

pride

The sisters are proud. They do not share their fears, their loves,
their secrets, their visions, their wishes. In the land of the many
closed doors, they too have become closed.

tenderness

But beneath the pride lay tenderness, a soft and unspoken devotion practiced between the sisters. The five girls, full of dignity, loved deeply. The girls who held in hurt and disappointment, who suffered loneliness and misunderstanding, were adept at loving one another tenderly, without cause or obligation. They showed their love in small and dear ways. Proud and unable to express love openly, they often worked surreptitiously. When a sister fell asleep on the rug, over a book or in front of the television, another lifted the sleeper's head to place there a pillow, and draped a sweater over her bare legs. In the car at night, the sister falling asleep on the long drive home from a party draped herself over another's shoulder to enjoy the closeness she would not by day. (And the sister leaned-on did not shrug the sleeper off.) A sister-not-in-trouble took another's blame, and Mother's admonishments with it. A sister-not-involved stood up for another, during fights great and small, in spite of consequences, in disregard of current peril or future strife. And their love for each other flowered through the smallest of openings, mimicking the poppies that emerged in summer through the cracks in the concrete sidewalks of their neighborhood. And it showed with all of the beauty and the grandeur of that papery blossom against and despite such a backdrop.

The sisters gave joyfully and often. So giving was an art form with them. One gathered flowers and grasses from near and far, wove and bound them, dried them in the cool space beneath her bed, and placed the finished bouquet in the intrepid sister's favorite hiding place. Another woke early on a Saturday morning to bake the sick sister, listless and dull-eyed, her favorite dessert for breakfast. The gregarious sister stopped mid-play with her friends to

smile at the timid sister across the schoolyard. The fashionable
sister neatly folded and placed her best top in the awkward sister's
dresser drawer. And the two sisters who shared adjacent birthdays
made, wrapped, and delivered each other's gifts three months in
advance. All graciously shared clothes, toys, pencils, books, time,
talents, sweets, and friends. They were patient and forgiving, sin-
cere and sympathetic. They were, after all, movable. Kindness
came easily to them. All were sensitive and had lived with hearts
and eyes open. Mother taught them to not shun, look-down-upon,
or think-better-of-yourself-than. They observed Father and saw
that he did not judge, gossip, or resent. So they practiced with one
another the kindnesses they'd witnessed bestowed on others. The
movable sisters suffered for and through each other, understanding
the why's and how's and even-so's of a life lived in two. They lived
closely, suffered one another's proximity, and loved and admired
each other gingerly, joyfully, deeply.

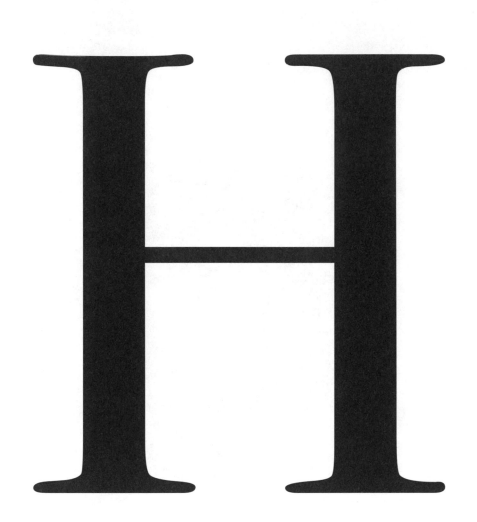

Home. What we carried with us no matter how often we moved, who and what we left behind. And while we were separated from our larger family, from what was familiar, the seven of us had one another in that space. Home was a world unto itself. A boundless, pulsing universe. And there were enough of us to make it so. There was the outside world, which called and to which we each went dutifully, to school or to work. And the outside world was open and wide and full of wonder, and yet small and precious, ever creating moments like scenes inside a snow globe. We each, awkwardly and tentatively, found our way in the outer world of school and job and market and highway. And over time found ourselves through the books and films, the friends and play, and the curious objects and experiences that world offered. It was the outside world and it was large and luminous, but somehow, home, however cramped and modest in size, home was always grander and more expansive. During those first years, home is where we knew ourselves for who we were. It was where we could be what we were: a many-limbed, vivid, young thing. Yes, even Mother and Father were new and young. They were young parents separated from their families, their land and language, taking care of a brood of small girls in an unfurling, unfamiliar world.

We carried pain and horror always with us. Deep within us when we were out in the world. And this burden is what turned things inside out, what made the outside world innocent and precious next to what we knew, had brought with us, and carried internally. We were not innocent but we were young, and youth gave us the courage to play, to be still-curious, to grow and take form as a family. We had one another, and it was all we needed in those first years. But we came with more than knowledge of death and war; we, five girls between the tender ages of one and twelve, arrived knowing already how to cook, wash, sew, knit, saw, hammer, harvest, cut, glue, paint, dream, and invent. We were creators, each of us. Next to our love for one another, it was this, the making of things, that made home so vast, and so formative. We were never without something to shape. Inside the house were needles and fabric and yarn, scissors and pencils and paper, onions and flour and eggs. Outside, were dirt and water and seeds, tree branches and flowers, bricks and stones, and any tool we wanted in Father's garage of wonders and supplies. We were forever making alongside Mother or Father, with one another, or off in one or another corner on our own. We made dolls and dollhouses, tree houses and tree swings, guitars and flutes, skirts and scarves, books and pictures, bowls and vases, soups and cakes, masks and swords. And with each creation, the world grew larger, more pos-sible. If things could cease to exist, other things could be brought into existence, to fill our vision and our hearts. With little hands and small weights thrown into fleshing things out, the world was trans-formed again and again, endlessly to our great joy and fulfillment. Home was Mother and Father and sisters. And home was a workshop.

the begetter

Mother says, there is an old man, an ancient man, who sits by a river. *You know the river, you have been there, have played at its edges.* In his hand, the old man holds a pen, and in his lap are long strips of paper, unmarked. When a child is born, the old man takes up a strip of paper and, down its length, he writes the name of the newborn, the moment and date of its birth, the moment and date of its death. This is all he writes: name, time of birth, time of death. He then throws the paper into the river, which takes it, swallows it, and, churning, racing, carries it away. Mother says, *we are all born, we will each die, and the number of our days here was set down in the beginning. The old man has written all of it down.*

And the sister listening sees the river in her mind, remembers it as the one the family stopped to picnic by on drives between the city and the village years before in the first land. Mother would roast potatoes and a chicken the night before. Father would rise early to pack the car. The girls would pile in, conscious/still-dreaming, in the pink early dawn. On the drive, Father sang the folk songs that made the sisters laugh, and wrapped his hand around Mother's knee or her neck, as Mother, always nostalgic, reminisced about their last trip to the farm, or about grandmother's first trip to the city to meet Mother years before. The road was long and, at its peak, the mountain pass was year-round under snow, winter and summer, spring and fall. The road was long and Father and Mother had a spot along the river, among the trees and boulders, they liked to stop at to enjoy the mountain air and the packed cold lunch. Down along the banks of the river that wound its way through the mountain gorge, the air was raw and crisp and did not filter what the equable mountain, the effervescent river, and the

trembling aspens murmured to the girls, who sighed or giggled or
whistled in response. They climbed the boulders and hung from
the limbs of the trees. They shaped boats with bark and sticks and
leaves and filled the boats with berries or pebbles and sent the
boats sailing down the white river. They hid and called out and
teased each other and teased the mountain sparrow. They roared
and chased one another and stumbled back to where Mother sat
handing out red clusters of grapes and chicken wrapped in springy
leaves of bread.

The sister now listening and imagining sees the old man sitting
on a boulder worn smooth by time. He sits along the river's edge,
lean, wrinkled, and bent over the roiling waters. She sees his bony
hand resting on his stiff knee, pen ready between quivering fingers,

a lap full of long curves of paper, listening for something more subtle than the call of the mountains, the river, and the trees. The sister remembering the picnic and the cold, salty potatoes, Father's intrepid rock-hopping, Mother's dark, shiny locks and overlarge sunglasses, her sisters' laughter, and the warm sun overhead, this sister wonders, was the old man there, just around the bend in the river, behind the peeling white trunks of the whispering close trees; was he there all the time we played and climbed and threw pebbles in after the quick glimmering fish?

record

And the letters of the alphabet stand tall, stand keen, look left, look right, and spring, dive, splash into the river after the stories.

Father, the boy

The girls can see, vividly, and not without a tickle, Father, as a little boy of five riding the wild village dog, his small body shirtless and mud-speckled, in muddy cotton trousers, drawstrings hanging, single earring in his left ear, hair long, dusty, and unkempt, feet bare, eyes intent, mouth like a lantern. It is Mother who tells them these tales; Father does not remember or refuses to see the impor-tance of remembering. *It is a time long gone, why not feed the cat now, take out the trash, sweep the porch, water the roses, do your homework, check on your sister, hand me the pliers, look at the time, it is nearly 7, your mother needs your help.* It is Mother who recorded the stories as a young bride on visits to the farm Father had left years before. It was the new bride who listened raptly to the many tales her mother-in-law told her about her youngest child. Mother: the young city girl in short skirt and lifted hair, lipsticked and eye-lined, solicitous and spirited. Grandmother: timid and tender, weathered and small, with long white braids, in white shrouds, and mirror image of the girls' city-dwelling, maternal grandmother. The two women sat together for hours in the dappled shade of the old fruit trees, in the packed-dirt courtyard of the life-churning, food-churning farm in the ancient village. And the sisters who remember for themselves know that courtyard for the place: where the morning bread was daily baked in the early dark; where the harvest, planted, tended, collected, borne, and stacked by the elbow—the farmer's humble fulcrum—was stewed, baked, boiled, roasted, fried, and set out by hands coarse and hands agile; where the members of the family gathered, alone or with visitors from near and far, to partake of food, shade, rest, story, and company.

The remembering sisters know the trees of the courtyard and the various fruit of those trees, know which limbs are good for climbing and which limbs bear the tastiest specimens. And they know too that those are the trees Father is forever trying to raise again from the new soil of the new land in each new house the family occupies. The past they hope to unlock is Father's, but it is Mother who pulls out the fragments of story like sweets from her pockets. Mother who hands them out to the girls between chores, after meals, in moments of collective reverie that all of the sisters delight in. *Your Father wore an earring, rode a dog, stole melons from neighboring farms, chipped his teeth cracking the shells of almonds and walnuts, begged to go to school and snuck in in his brother's place, lost his own father at nine, ran away at fourteen in search of more learning, nightly climbed up and crouched in the uppermost limbs of a tree to study by moonlight, found his own way to the city, to the schools, to me, found me amid my many sisters and brothers, behind two gates and three walls in a house on a hill in the city four hundred miles, a mountain range, and many rivers' distance from the farm where his brother tilled the earth and his mother and sister kept their eyes on the dirt road, awaiting his return.*

And the girls study Father in search of the little boy. In search of story and evidence, they check his ears for the piercing. He pulls out his dentures to show them yet again, *this is what happens when you break walnuts with your teeth, chew on your pencil, chomp on hard candies.* He pulls off his glasses to teach them, *this is why you must*

halt your reading to switch on the light at dusk. And some of the girls
know he is not all human, he whose people came from an earlier
and an enchanted land, a place of elves and jinn. Father does
not deny the girls' claims that his origins are magical and neither
does he offer an alternative explanation for his singular ways.
Father does not talk as other men talk, does not boast or brood,
yell or curse. He speaks little but smiles often with his mischievous grin and impish eyes. And Father prays for many hours a
day, and when he prays, the girls' limbs feel the weightlessness of
time expanding, their stomachs become restless, grumble more as
lunch, dinner, or tea await the lifting of the hush and the prayer
rug, as even the cat, overly lulled, head nodding, awaits Father's
return from the netherworld.

And while Mother draws the girls, the family, in and holds them
near with her warmth, her will, and her stories, Father, the
Timekeeper, lets them see that there are doorways through which
they can exit and return regularly and with ease. He departs for
work at a precise hour in the morning and each afternoon returns
at a precise hour, keeping time by the company clock. Keeping
time with the sun, he recedes several times a day, as a tide recedes,
into prayer, and returns as if from deep waters, unhurried yet
revived, to take part again in the family's activities, to listen to their
stories, their gripes and gossip, to play a hand or two of cards, and
even to sit still for a few minutes in front of the television, which
transports his wife and his daughters but leaves him disengaged
of purpose, restless, and too aware of time desecrated. Each
afternoon after work and early morning into late evening on the
weekends, Father toils in the garage, on the rooftop, in the yard,
or beneath the hood of the car in the driveway in the service of
Time, and, depending on the job, calls out one or two or three,

the second or the middle, of his daughters to hold a lamp or a ladder in place, to pass a tool or hammer in nails, to dig a hole to remove or to plant a bush, to coax the cat out of the crawl space beneath the house, or to untangle and reconnect wires in a broken appliance. And whether he works alone or with the girls, leaves for minutes or for hours, he returns to the family, like clockwork, and returns bearing herbs or pears or flowers from his garden, and returns wearing his half-drawn mischievous smile that precedes or caps a joke or a short tale of his own, quietly fashioned during his time of focused work or prayer.

And the way he orchestrates the growing of things in the yard, and accomplishes the making of things in and around the house, shows the girls that Father does have powers unusual, that perhaps what he does not say is tilled under and transformed into the doing of things. Father who climbs the ladder to the roof to patch leaks, and walks with ease from eaves to apex, just as easily climbs the heights of the tree, unharnessed, to cut and clear dead branches. With his tools, Father: builds shelves to hold the many objects he makes or collects, and all of which have purpose and place in his mind, for *what in this world is purposeless?*; takes down walls to put up new ones better aligned with those in his mind's eye; digs earth to find the source of a leak in the old house's plumbing; builds a tree house in each yard the family occupies so that his girls too will know that time spent in trees is more elevated, more evolved. In his doing upon doing interpolated with momentary rest, Father, the eternal farmer, regulates time and pushes time's usefulness to its extreme, so that toil eases the heart, and rest and food fully, but not overly, sate the spirit and the stomach. All this in order that remembering, which is cluttered with the dead and the usurpers of life, is given the smallest sliver of the clock.

When the girls ask him when he was born, Father says at the blossoming of the peach trees. And when they ask how and when their grandfather died, he tells them that they found him lying, lean and spent, in the fields, atop the tender spinach. Mother tells tales of his boyhood, youth, and courtship and the girls listen raptly. But eager to understand the enigma that is their father, wanting more information yet, the sisters question the juvenile fruit trees, the roses, and even the herbs that rise year after year in one or another corner of the yard and which originated from a small handful of seeds transported by Father from the old country. They marvel at Father's love for his plants, seeing how much care he puts into the soil at their roots, into the pruning of their leaves and limbs, into the fighting-off of their pests. They see what pride he takes in each ripening plum or apricot, each sprouting leek seed. And the knowledge he has in his skin, eyes, and nose, given him by the sun and the seasons, the air and the clouds, impresses the girls. And they guess that the many watches and small clocks in Father's desk drawer do not await repair but rather unwinding: the unlearning of regulated time. Perhaps Father's aim is to coax them to keep time with the plants. And if the broken timepieces are not swayed, the sisters who come to the garden to learn about their quiet Father, slowly and incrementally, come to understand the moon and its steady math, the sun and its oscillating ways.

Father, who, indoors, silences the house in order to send out his blessings, like many doves, over their heads, Father, outdoors, draws out lightness in the girls who play and run about him as he clips dead roses and rakes the earth. He hums, smiles, and laughs to himself or with the girls, inviting them over to show them a grafted branch, newly budding, or how much to cut back an overly eager mint plant. And in his loving, devoted care of the garden, the sisters see that Father is still the farmer, though he left the farm early to pursue the learning, and that he shows the care, caution, and pride of the farmer, distilled. But when the light changes and along with it a breeze arrives to pass through the grandfather tree's branches, they find that Father is up in the tree, sitting with the small animals of the canopy and speaking to them as the sisters have heard him speak to the cat on occasions he has thought himself alone. And coming across the creatures, he is for a moment again the boy, the strange, impish boy who wants to show the girls his find of grasshopper or caterpillar or bird. And the sister who loves the various-legged creatures shares in his delight. And the sister who hates spiders and insects, desperately screaming and many-armed herself, runs from him as from a pesky little brother. And all the remaining sisters listen to his nonsensical clicks and trills, and wonder at their effect on the hushed creature in his hand. They add this to that growing pile of evidence that supports Father's mystical origins.

ubiquitous

The sister remembering knows that time does not stand still, but neither does it travel in a single direction. It is many-legged. It rushes past, it scuttles back, it spins in circles. It finds the openings and passes through them. It is there, it is *there*, and it is here. At once, simultaneously.

the idolater

The sun does not ache for the stars. Blinded by its own churning brilliance, it knows nothing of the night and nothing of its siblings in the sky. But it knows of the grass that grows over pastures and in valleys, that covers lawns in a regular patchwork and forces cracks in concrete sidewalks. The sun is drawn to the infinitesimal grass even as it draws the spinning earth to itself and keeps it there in deliberate and perpetual orbit. And with its far-reaching fingers, the sun travels across great distances of space at a fervent speed to hear the song of the grass for which it wistfully yearns, to find an answer to the grass's apparent and uninterrupted state of ease, to probe into the soil of the living planet for this logic.

The grass, which seeks nothing but water from below and light from above, works diligently in both directions to achieve its modest stature, laterally making up for that stature by sending out roots, just centimeters below the earth's surface, over distances short and distances long, roots forever evading the sun's soft fingers, which cannot penetrate earth. And the grass's own tough, green fingers, having broken through earth, humbly receive the daily offering of light. Knowing nothing of the sun's need, it cannot give away its underground secret to the aching star. And the sun, knowing no night, untiringly and without satisfaction, brushes the surfaces of the earth with its incorporeal fingers, petting the grass as a child, standing still, attempts to pet a dog running past her. The grass's secret: an intertwining, forever-advancing network of persistent roots, nodes, rhizomes, and intrepid blades that toil to colonize the many faces and planes of the spinning earth in a silent attempt to find and keep family. But the sun, blind, is alone in the heavens, its radiance obscuring its relation to billions of others like itself. Unaware that it possesses its own living network over spaces vast and mysterious, it pines after a nearer idol.

the mourners

The sisters forged an alliance one still and sunny day. It happened during a time of peace; recent battles had been resolved, lingering wounds healed, and old animosities forgotten for the day. It happened on its own, for there was no planning involved and no intention on the part of any of the sisters to act on such a thing. On that day, the mediator, taking respite from her usual work, the work of undoing rivalries and bringing sides together, was preoccupied with a different task. Using a rusty nail, her finger, and her saliva, she etched then filled in, etched then smoothed out, then scratched again, a tentative note of condolence into the hardened earth beneath the wilting leaves of the tomato plants in Father's garden. *It is difficult, I know, it is hard for you . . . It cannot be easy producing fruit under these conditions . . . In your condition, it is difficult, I know . . . It is hard, yes, in this weather, the condition of the soil . . . It is the soil, it refuses, I know . . .* In another part of the yard, the giver, that other sister full-of-good-intentions, was lying on her back watching the small mechanical movements of a robin's head in the branches above her. Under normal circumstances, the giver would have been the first to take advantage of the uncommon silence and peace among the sisters to call for a picnic on the lawn, or start a spontaneous game of hide-and-go-seek, or offer the services of her nimble fingers in the braiding of the younger sisters' hair. But she, like the other four, and like the still air and the dry earth, was under the spell of the sun.

The treaty that was formed on this day had not been foreseen in a dream or foretold by the garden oracle. There was no specific event that led up to it. On the contrary, what united the sisters on this day was a lack of circumstances. They had made no plans, and set no agendas. The day's sweetness lay in the absence of responsibilities—of housework, yard work, schoolwork. On this common-uncommon Saturday: all chores had been accomplished in the morning without the slightest nudge from Mother; the sisters more fastidious had bathed early; the sister who preferred bare feet to a bright smile, on this Saturday, joyfully chose to forgo all rituals involving the grooming of hair, teeth, and skin; and all, even the studious sisters, pushed the responsibility of homework aside, onto Sunday, or erased it from memory altogether. It was the absence of duties—whether through completion, denial, or rebellion—and the much-felt absence of adults that brought the sisters together. On this Saturday, neighbors slept in or drove off early in their long cars loaded with children, sandwiches, beach-balls, and towels. And Mother and Father, who usually took the day to put back to order the house and the garden and the girls, left them all shortly after breakfast to visit an old and distant friend of the family, a woman newly arrived from the first country.

Mother and Father traveled over concrete highways, through many adjacent and indistinguishable cities, and to the side of a woman newly arrived from the before-country. This elderly woman arrived from that landlocked and war-isolated land with recent and unsul-lied news. She was received by her hosts in the land of the sun as a monarch bringing lavish gifts from distant realms, though she arrived without a suitcase and wearing a man's coat over a hand-sewn, unembellished long tunic, loose cotton trousers, and worn plastic sandals. She'd traveled with only a large wool purse that contained her passport, unchanged money, a few photographs, a large bag of golden raisins and withered almonds—*from the home-land*—a handkerchief, a prayer rug, and her prayer beads, which she now held in her hand and which softly clicked and slipped under her thumb continuously, seemingly of their own accord. The news she brought was not the kind published in papers or prompted from the mouths of broadcasters. She had her own personal accounts, tediously recorded over the months and years and now held pain-fully, but preciously, within her person. And some of these records were like small, tightly coiled scrolls, which she kept tucked in the oily canals of her ears or under her red wrinkled eyelids. Some of her articles of news were like gossamer webs—thinner than the aged scarf that covered her head—folded into quarters, and placed beneath her breast, over her heart, or wrapped around her kidneys. And some were like impervious raw jewels stuffed into the soft cor-ners of her mouth, a mouth which had learned to hold its secrets tightly, even as a running murmur of prayer passed from her lips from morning to night. The old woman, once her family's story-teller, had chronicled their quick demise, and the destruction of the wider world about them over the previous half dozen years. Much had shattered and she had done her best to gather the fragments. Illiterate, she set them down within herself, hoping that someday she could relay them, deliver them to rational minds that might make sense of the horror.

The woman sat on the couch, not hungry, not thirsty, not touching the many small mountains of sweets that her host, her niece, had set before her on the coffee table next to a dish of the almonds and raisins she herself had transported. Gathered around her on chairs and cushions and bare floor were men and women who'd traveled from the many adjacent and indistinguishable cities to receive her news. They sat with eager eyes and humble folded hands. The only news they received during these years was delivered in person by newcomers fortunate enough to have escaped the brutal war. The new arrival pulled out her chronicles and organized her facts. She adjusted her headscarf and smoothed out her skirt. And the news-like-gossamer the old woman brought out from the hidden places. She looked at the many faces about her and began with a story about the beginning days of the war. In the beginning, war was only a trickle, a new spring born on a distant hillside: far off, unsteady. But the trickle grew into a running stream, which the people still did not heed or hear for they were preoccupied contemplating the sudden proliferation of wildflowers in midwinter. And when the meadow flowers turned into giant trees overnight, the people, too busy looking up, did not notice that their feet were wet and the bottoms of their trousers and skirts soaked. It was only after their children, their in-laws, and their grocers disappeared that they perceived the red river at their knees. Only then that the outer mind grasped what the inner mind and the heart had known for many months: the lives they'd had, nurtured, and claimed for themselves were no longer their own; the landscape they'd inhabited had fractured and shifted. Though many of the listeners knew this story intimately, had lived it for themselves, heard and recited it many times in disparate company, still they listened as a child listens to a fairy tale: hopeful and bound. But by and by, those in her audience who had left the first country during the beginning days, or shortly after, filled in the gaps in her story, for they had left with that tale intact while she had put hers away in order to record the onslaught of each advancing year, each unfolding barbarity.

She continued with a tally of the dead, recorded not as integers but as names. Looking to the small group to her left, *Do you remember*

B——— who lived five houses from your aunt's, and raised doves on his rooftop and took them to the Saturday Market, not to sell, of course, but to show to the young female passersby, hoping the birds would do for him what his people could not accomplish for twenty-five years. Yes, that fortunate-unfortunate man found a wife, a pretty villager, a widow, and not long after disappeared, then reappeared in a gutter, leaving her his cooing doves and his three-story house, which was blown up by rockets even as his stepchildren were preparing it for his funeral. And turning to another, *Z——— who was a good friend of your eldest brother, he was one of the first to go over to their side; you did not know this? Well, my son, his disloyalty to his family was not enough, and when they were finished with him, his mother alone might recognize him . . . though the poor woman was not so lucky to have him back . . .* and turning to another, *He was useful to them for something. After all, it was through Z——— that they acquired your uncle's name, learned of his illegal newspaper, located his distributors, then his readers.* She told of hillsides flattened and charred; of daughters hidden from the occupiers for days beneath mounds of sawdust or sacks of potatoes in cellars, or inside clay ovens in courtyards under snow; of sons lost to that bitter cause in the cities' outskirts, pulled from their mothers' arms in the night, lured by the call of the barren mountains, whither it was said sanity and valor had retreated; and of animals unhinged—goats from their craggy perches sprouting wings and adopting flight, chickens mating with apples, and dogs returning to the desert in search of the jackals they'd once deceived and replaced.

And when her throat was dry, the newcomer stopped to sip tea, to look about her at the people who had gathered there, at the photographs hanging on the walls in her niece's apartment, at the too-bright sunlight on the balcony outside. After many cups of warm tea, the news-like-jewels dislodged, were brought forth, and shone with such glitter that many in her audience shut their eyes.

The old woman now shared her own private tales. She told of her youngest daughter's inability to hold a single child in her womb for the duration of a pregnancy through two marriages, two widowhoods, and three rapes. She told of her niece, the bright one, fond of letters and numbers, who climbed into, but never again out of, a neighbor's stove, though, in turn, the occupiers, the preaching men of god and guns, her family, and her neighbors called and called for her. She told of the rocket that fell in broad daylight onto the small shop across from her house. Of whole melons, peach pits, gum wrappers, marbles, mud, flesh, teeth, and hair caught in the limbs and needles of her pine tree.

Her now thin, now low voice shuddered and quaked as it recalled the myriad events, stages, and transmutations of the war that would not end. And other news tightly coiled for years, months, and weeks, oily and warm, now uncoiled to run like a film. The images played over the curtain of many-faces before her, cinema for her eyes alone. She put together the disparate stories and put words to the images that shuttled through her mind and simultaneously transposed themselves over the silent visages of the company gathered about her. Tired as she was from her travels, she kept pace with the moving images, translating all she witnessed into a language her audience understood well. The voice that struggled to hide anguish soothed her listeners, who found much knowledge in its peaks and valleys. And happily/unhappily, the visitor unloaded her burden of gifts into the arms of the veterans of life in the new country, a people whose relatively softened skin now puckered again, its sensitive hairs standing upright against the assault of wanted/unwanted information.

This woman, like those who came before and would come after her, held court (as Mother and Father had on their arrival) and sat like an aged queen, alone on her throne, meting out what was left of her dying empire—her many and painstakingly gathered memories—to her subjects. And those who were lucky to have known her or of her in the first country were seated in the first circle, having the most to gain or lose, waiting for the name of a loved one or a description of a beloved place to fall from her lips. And each name she spoke reverberated through the crowded living room of the fifth-floor apartment, traveled through all who sat there as each tried to put a face to the spoken syllables. Many names found a home within the lucky/unlucky person who recognized and claimed it as one of her or his own. And in that moment, the receiver performed all rites, shedding tears, reciting prayers, and burying the loved one in a fleshy grave within themselves. But other names roamed about the room, entering and exiting ears, trying to find a foothold in the memories of those gathered. Then, unrequited and homeless, these unclaimed letters of the alphabet slowed and settled into a single mass grave in the middle of a small living room in an unfamiliar land.

With great reverence and patience, the audience waited for the woman to finish her telling and showing before asking her their own burning questions. And the concentric circles took turns, those on the inside taking the longest to question and reminisce with the old friend, to ask about sisters and mothers and neighbors and relations of neighbors, and parts of town, and customs, and pined-for foods, while those in outer circles waited with tear-stinging eyes or sat simply nodding, taking part in what all there shared: their collective and great loss of home, kin, history.

It was the absence of responsibilities and the presence of five sated bellies, drifting minds, tapping fingers, the hot sun at midday, and the dry grass beneath their feet that allowed the sisters to be girls, just girls, and to form their unforeseen alliance. It was the lazy swing of the screen door that led from kitchen to yard, and the perspiring glasses of water or fruit juice, which traveled in the same direction. It was the open but unread book, the dreaming cat's arcing tail, the beetle's dainty march across a shin and over a kneecap. It was all of these things—the clearing away of responsibilities and the lingering of the sun at the noon hour—that opened up a door never before seen or imagined by the girls, one that led from a child's backyard to a castle's courtyard.

The sisters did not expect this sudden change of scene: the many tall towers of a pristine and enormous castle, with walls of stone running three hundred feet into the sky and dotted with small dark windows; an expansive courtyard, open and empty, save for a single fruit tree near one of its walls, and sunlight that filled the desolate courtyard as hot tea fills a cup; and above it all, a still, brilliant blue sky. The silence mimicked the stillness in the yard they'd left a moment earlier. The sun hovered high above the spires of this castle as it had done above the telephone poles in their neighborhood. The sisters did not expect this sudden change of scene but neither were they startled by it; they were movable. Each of the five took a separate course to discover the place in her own leisurely and indolent manner. The first sister wondered to herself why the

courtyard had no doors leading to or from it to the rest of the castle grounds, forgetting that she and her sisters had arrived through
a door only moments before. She marveled at the vastness of the
castle, the towers of which seemed to stretch for miles toward an
unseen horizon. And though she could not see the many winding
pathways and stairways, the heavy wooden doors, the tables set for
forty, the long, lamplit halls, the four-poster beds, the wardrobes
filled with silks and laces, the jewel-laden tables, the first sister knew
these things existed within. The fifth sister played a game she often
played at home. Starting near one of the walls of the courtyard,
she walked deliberately, with her hands clasped earnestly behind
her back, and followed a spiral pattern that started wide and very
slowly narrowed. The fourth sister, squinting, tried to see into the
many dark windows above her head, and imagined not only their
interiors but also what might be visible of the surrounding country
from their apertures. She did not wonder about the castle's inhabitants. In fact, none of the sisters ventured in this direction, for they
all knew that the castle was deserted, as their neighborhood had
been deserted on this Saturday. The second sister measured the
perimeter of the courtyard using her small outstretched hands, one
over the other. And as she counted, she felt the texture of the wall
and wondered at the close fit of the heterogeneous stones, which sat
one atop and one adjacent to another without the slightest gap; she
studied them and hoped to take what knowledge she gained back
to Father, who had been working on mending the garden wall. The
middle sister, attracted by the only color in the place, visited the
fruit tree, which bore a single ripe pomegranate on one of its lower
branches. She helped Father tend the garden at home and knew this
tree was thirsty, could tell from a distance, but confirmed it by putting her fingers in its soil. Eventually, all but the youngest gathered
around the tree and spoke for the first time, their small high voices

bouncing off the walls of the enclosed space, and traveling skyward. They forgot about the castle and took council over their concerns for the tree. Behind them, in another part of the courtyard, the fifth sister walked ever more deliberately, in ever tighter circles until it seemed that she was spinning in place. But soon she came to a stop, her small feet positioned atop a single stone. And just as deliberately as she had walked, she came down to her knees, then to her elbows and shuffled back in order to put her ear to that single stone. Beneath the stone: the murmur of running water.

Without tools and without knowledge of a way back home to retrieve them, the sisters wondered how they would bring water to the parched tree. They sensed the water ran deeply and saw the roots of the tree lie in a single plane, confined in a shallow bed by stones on all five sides. They guessed that tree and water were not aware of their proximity—a few dozen feet—to one another. The stones covering the ground were heavy and their joints but thin lines; the sisters' hands were small, their fingernails short. They were aware that they had arrived with nothing and would leave with nothing. Without Father's tools or Mother's knives or hairpins, without a telephone or pencil and paper, without books or the cat, the sisters had nothing but their words. And their voices were clear and the unblinking sun was stark and the stones would not budge. The water ran and the sister who held her ear to the ground gave testimony that it did not falter. The fruit tree, its leaves wilted, its roots wrinkled, stood upright and held on to its single pomegranate. And the sisters came together. And an alliance was forged. And it was agreed by all that time would stand still, though the sisters might age, until a solution was found. Without picks or spades, ropes or pulleys, the sisters would find a way to bring the water to the tree's roots.

And time has stood still. And the sisters have remained in the courtyard even as they have returned home. And even after Mother and Father have returned home, and the neighbors have put tired heads to soft pillows, the sisters still muse, purse their lips, twist their brows in both lands, and hold hard to their resolution. Though the earth spins and the days fold one into another, though the girls, like spires, rise in height, leave the house, the yard, to study or roam or marry, the pact to rescue the pomegranate tree stands. Through time, the sisters curl and open in bed and at twilight, they bend and tug, they release and gather, they gesture and sing to charm the sun to shift the stones to open a path through which the water might course to the tree.

old woman

The old woman walks to the market. She is following their proscriptions: she is covered head to toe; when she speaks, she speaks softly, briefly; she walks with someone of the male gender—her small grandson. He carries her empty shopping bags for her over his shoulder. He kicks the stones that come before his feet. She keeps hold of his small hand, tries to steady his speed, and steady her gait beneath the enveloping garment; her tattered shoes peep out from underneath its hem as she walks. At the intersection of two narrow streets, she meets with the roving men of god who see her white shoes and are alarmed by her impudence, by her flagrant disregard for their rules, and the desecration of their flag. They grab the small boy from behind her and push the old woman to the ground. They pull off her shoes and beat her with them;

they whack and kick her ankles, her shins, her back, and her arms. She is a small heap beneath the garment; they lift it and see she is an old woman. "Granny, you should know better!" The oldest of the men steps over her unmoving form. The two younger kick her again in her ribs, her spine. "Take the old mother home!" they yell. "Teach her modesty." The beaten woman lies in the street as the men move on to continue their rounds and others cautiously pass and regard her from a distance. A young woman, walking alongside her brother, leaves him to run over and draw the voluminous garment over the woman's legs and feet to cover her, then catches up with her brother again. Unmoving, the old woman lies there until her grandson returns with a neighbor, who lifts her, sets her down in his cart and tows her home.

celerity

So our earth reels. So our galaxy hurtles through the vast deep. So.

ghosts

The sisters are not unfamiliar with ghosts. They were taught and learned early that the world they inhabit is not theirs alone. Mother, who was raised in a land where the living fill all the indoor spaces, the courtyard and the garden spaces, the street and the market spaces, and who now raises her own brood of five in a small house that is rarely silent or empty, Mother has met several ghosts in the few solitary moments of her bustling life, and heard tales of many, many others from the living who were raised and walked alongside her. Mother, who might write a natural history of spirits were she inclined, recalls them by name, type, and origin. Her native taxonomy includes not only the specter but the spectator as well; she lists sightings and encounters by: year, *your grandmother was pregnant with your aunt R*——; time of day, *on her way home from the bread maker's*; specter, *Sheeshak, who sits in the tree, long hair, long nails, red eyes, envy*; location, *in the wood behind the house*; and effect upon the spectator, *she gave birth two months too early to a fragile and birthmarked son.* If Father does not speak of ghosts, it is not for lack of belief; he simply is not one for stories. But the sole time he has mentioned his own father, it was not the man he described, but his spirit, who continued to walk and work the fields, to converse with the goats, the sheep, the roosters of his farm long after his natural death.

The sisters love to read tales of terror by candlelight or flashlight, and to watch horror films alongside Mother into the early hours of a Saturday morning. But they know that true ghosts are not the wispy, pale things or the lurking, shadowy things that haunt the hallways and attics of old houses in the books and films they relish. The sisters know that ghosts are what the living carry within themselves their whole lives through. Ghosts do not hide in closets or beneath beds, though the sisters have checked and checked again. Ghosts are housed within the living, in the cavities of the skull and chest. The halls they walk are the passageways of breath; the doors they rattle are the tongues of the living. Their voices echo within the head, their torment bursts within the heart. And the dead glimmer within the living, as do jewels in the cavities of the earth; though no light reaches them there, they glimmer.

Did the sisters themselves not let the dead in? Did they not collect them even as they gathered memories and visions, as other
children collect flowers into a basket? Did the girls not utter, with
open arms and bowed heads: *come, I will give you a place though this
world may not; I will lend you a warm bed and shelter from the elements; you
may use my own eyes as windows through which you might, if you please, look
out on the world that has relinquished you.* And did the dead not take
up this offer? Homeless, they had nowhere to go. They accepted
politely, wiping their feet before entering, with hearts heavy and
eyes dazed. And once inside, did they not tint the windows of the
girls' eyes with a myriad of hues: with their crimson blood, which,
continuing to spill, saturated the cells, painted the cheeks, and
filled the small frames of the welcoming girls; with the hazy or
the crisp blues of their unfulfilled dreams; with the green of their
unharvested fields. Did the dead not shift the sisters' gaze and
focus it on yet more suffering outside? And when the sisters shivered, was it they or the dead that yearned for the sun? When they
bit into a mulberry, who savored the familiar sweetness? Whose
hands stroked the warm grass? Whose dreams moved the sisters'
eyes behind their curtains at night?

The dead litter the faces of the earth. The sisters have collected
and house many, mostly men and boys, mostly the casualties of the
war they themselves just escaped. And their tenants, having sharpened the girls' ears, attune them now to the voices of the women
they've left behind: wives, brides, mothers and sisters and daughters. Though they live half an earth's distance away, the women
speak and the sisters listen. Those left behind whisper, pray, moan,
and anguish day and night through. The wives, mothers, and
daughters speak the names of the dead and call out to them. And
the sisters who've grown accustomed to these voices respond in

tones and with words not their own. The sisters nod and smile. They feel their hearts within their chests flutter or fix, and their breath catch or release in great sighs. Their bodies stiffen. The palms of their hands moisten. And they cry. Though no wound originates in them, the sisters cry. And the wounds not their own pain them still and perhaps with greater acuity, for their sources are unfathomable, lie elsewhere, in a ditch or in a tree, or left to the birds on a mountainside.

It seems that war was written into the pages of the family's history long ago. Did the garden oracle in the new land not foretell of the war years before the family arrived in the country to water that thorny plant's roots and take in the scent of its dark flowers? Was it not war, another, earlier war, that lifted the girls' grandparents from their beloved lands and placed them in strange cities and on unfamiliar soil? And the sister who looks back, wonders: *Why was I preserved while others were felled like the fields of corn on our uncle's farm in late autumn? But who then lives and who is dead if the ghosts that haunt the world reside within us who walk the earth and breathe its air? Did I strike a bargain with the dead? If so, when, why, and what for? How will I fulfill my end, and when I have, will it come as a release or a death repeated? Will I recognize the sound of my own voice in an empty house once they have departed?*

And the sister who accepts the dead within her and knows their presence, as she knows and accepts the birthmark on her forearm, says: *It is me, it is of me, it is a simple fact of my life. And those I carry around are as much a part of me as is this birthmark, and they move and shift within me even as this birthmark, apparently motionless, moves up my arm, ever so slightly, across the unfolding days of my life. And the unfolding, is it not also only apparent? In reality,* is it not a folding in, a forever turning inward into the very center of existence? Is life not like the many-armed galaxy, which spirals in even as it spirals out?

And those who fell, who were mowed down by that monster-machine that is war, those whose natural lives did not unfurl as the fern's green fiddlehead unfurls, did their spirits at the moment of death not snap inward, spiral back toward center as do the dry arms of the geranium's seedpod at the moment of dispersal? And the sister who tends the garden alongside Father asks: *From the beginning, did I not collect the dead as one collects seeds that have fallen to the earth? And later, did I not swallow them and give them a place to root and sprout within me, into my own flesh and, further, did I not irrigate the fields in which they grew with my own blood?*

And the sister who feels with the dead, wonders: *When I curl up, breathless, from pain or horror, when I can no longer bear to keep the windows that are my eyes open, am I mimicking the same automatic action/reaction as did they whose lives were violently, suddenly extinguished? Will I forever cave inward, chasing the death that should have been mine too?*

And the sister who blesses the dead, wants to know: *Are we not all forever fleeing, forever chasing the gaping mouth, the bottomless well, the black hole at whose edge our feet are permanently strapped, as we furl and unfurl, live and die, receive the dead and honor the dead, collect the flowers and scatter the flowers?*

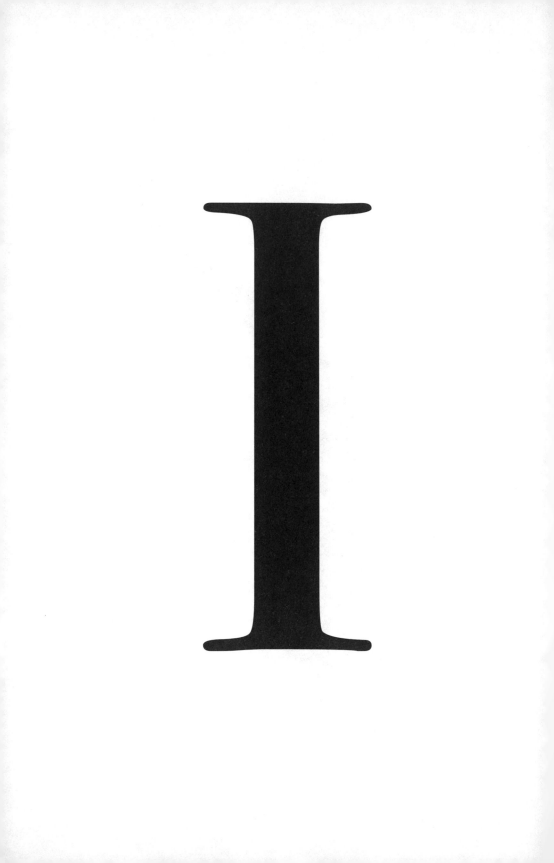

The interior. It is in the internal that this story was born and there that it took on its form. It follows the laws of that place, where everything happens simultaneously, and an entire childhood spans a single day. The logic of the interior is not the logic of the temporal. The vast interior takes all that happens externally into itself over many of our days, our years. It folds our hours, our gesticulations, our utterances in on themselves, again, then over and again, to draw out another tale entirely. What I tell you is not the story of my childhood as it occurred neatly, chronologically, but of my childhood as I experienced it internally. It is in the silence and dark of the interior that story is able to ferment, to burn off excesses, to distill down to its essence. In the great internal sea where story seethes and writhes in perfect darkness, new tales are born, unknown to the one dreaming them, until they are ready to be drawn up, as if from a well. That is in fact how this book was written, its tales pulled up by rope and pulley, bucket after bucket over the many days and recent years of my life. And I see them now before me, the tales that do and do not tell of my childhood. I have dreamed them often. And I know that it is in dreaming nightly, in drawing up and remembering regularly, that I have learned to fall in line with the laws of the interior.

It is repetition that aligns us: the cycling of days, of deeds and gestures, of a single dress passed down f r o m   s i s t e r t o   s i s t e r t o   s i s t e r , of one home left for another, of one tree welcoming the ghost of a former, of the heart's measure that clenches and releases, of the breath's rhythm that fills then falls. S e e   t h e   r i s i n g   a n d   f a l l i n g   o f   b r e a t h , and of the head as it looks up to the sky then down at the earth, and of the body in the morning and into bed at night, and of water into the air then onto the land. See the turning of the seasons, one into and out of another, of summer into fall, and spring out of winter, of man into woman, and child out of mother, again and again repeated over the many generations. It is repetition, do you not see, which aligns us with the internal. It is incantation, which stirs the cauldron and burns off the excesses to make what is nebulous formful.

My story was born and brewed in the internal; it will not follow the form or the logic of one shaped in the external. I cannot give you the arc you desire; if you seek biography, look elsewhere. It is a dream I offer you.

the pond

There was a small pond on Father's family farm. Though the farm was boundless and teeming with delights for eyes, hands, ears, nose, and mouth, it was the pond which often drew one or another sister to its edges. The small pool occupied a peculiar space on the farm. Here, nothing grew but a slender small tree that made a graceless arc over the pond in which it barely forged a reflection. It was a spindly tree, a tree perhaps long dead (for it never bore a leaf), a tree perhaps not a tree but a root misguided, a tree little taller than the sisters who carefully walked around and squatted at the pond's edge in an attempt to fathom its depths or find their own images in its cloudy surface. The pond was in a barren dusty space: past the courtyard where Father's sister baked bread every dawn in her clay oven; between the two fruit orchards, which took turns bearing their bounty through the seasons; many yards' distance from where the beet and cotton fields began; far from the little brook that ran the length of the farm. It was a murky and still pond. Its diameter, which the chickens could easily flutter over when given chase, was no greater than two cow lengths. Its depths were unknown and unknowable—for the girls had driven in reeds and branches of varying lengths and never sensed a bottom. One might fall into this pond and never come up again. It was narrow and deep and quietly swallowed up whatever slipped or was plopped into it. One might fall in and come up somewhere entirely different, somewhere different and a long distance away. If not careful, a sister might slip along its muddy edge, fall into the pond and rise up elsewhere, might rise up a fish or a frog in another land under a different sky. In this other land, a sister might sprout wings to take flight, or a powerful tail to hang by. The new skin, the new visage, the new sky might be green or speckled. A

vigorous and many-limbed old tree bent over the pond where the
sister comes up in another land might house a witch. Or a pea-
cock. Or a house of glass and mirrors might sit near the edge of
the pond in the alternate land. A blue boy, many times reflected,
might glide through and disappear in the rooms of this glass house
and might finally open the front door and signal an invitation to
the traveling sister. All was possible beneath the murky surface that
barely yielded a reflection of the sisters' images. And it was this,
this delightful and frightful unknowing, that brought the sisters to
the pond's edge again and again on their visits to the farm. This
that called them out from the blooming quince orchard, that lured
them away from the friendly donkey, that made them forget the
ripening strawberries on the brook's banks.

the letters of the alphabet

From a distance, we appear not unlike the well-ordered rings
around the girth of a giant planet. Come nearer, and you will recognize us as the remnants of dead stars caught in the gravitational
pull of a persuasive and beautiful dirge, swooning.

alchemists

And the girls were master transformers, making the world over
again for themselves and for one another. They shaped and

converted the materials about them into objects of function and
wonder. They sewed handbags or headbands, molded clay into
miniature trees or teapots, shaped dough into rings or braids, fixed
flowers to skirts or hair, altered the color of their eyes to match
those of the sea or the schoolbus. They knit scarves many hundreds
of feet in length with bits of yarn of various diameters, colors,
and textures collected over the months and the years to keep all
the cats in the neighborhood warm in winter. They constructed
worlds within worlds within shoeboxes that were then placed on
cabinets or desks or in the branches of the grandfather tree just so,
to catch the sun just so, to lengthen the day by minutes or hours
or to push the clock forward by entire seasons inside the shoebox.
On random sheets of paper, they painted rivers against mountains
against clouds against a keen azure sky, and placed a giant ant on
the mountainside and a girl on a bicycle crossing a bridge over the
roiling river to reach her beloved cat on the other side.

Birthdays were holidays observed by all and the making of gifts for
the one growing a year older was a ritual that most in the family
performed, and with deep devotion, with set avid intention. This
ritual commenced days or weeks or sometimes months in advance
of a birthday. The gift-making-sister would find the rare unoccu-
pied space in a bedroom or the garage or the treehouse and put
up a sign to keep the others out. She brought to her workshop
the materials she had collected and hoarded behind dressers or
between the pages of her schoolbooks. She'd fidget and fold her
limbs and find her place on the floor, always the floor, and sometimes necessarily against the door to keep out spying intruders.
Sitting among her materials, she'd set to. She'd gather her focus
and work with her small, articulate hands to bring to life the gift
she had for eons envisaged in the depths of her mind for the

birthday-sister. And the making and the transforming, as all other things in the home, was done in earnest, with the brow twisted and the teeth clamped about the bottom lip. The making was in earnest but the giving on the special day was done with modesty or nonchalance. The sister who had toiled over the gift did not boast or push but waited, nonetheless, expectantly for her present to be opened, to be cooed and delighted over, and to finally release its spell, the charm she had worked into it with her imagination and her fingers. And when thanked, she would respond, "It is nothing. It is nothing, of course."

It was first and foremost from Mother that the girls had inherited this desire to please with gifts made by hand and with tenderness. Mother looked on with the same quiet smile as her birthday-daughter opened Mother's gift, and the one "from Father," wrapped in the same paper. Mother was a fount of giving, and never tired of it, was rather made larger, pulsed brighter by it. On Sundays, she prepared her meals with this same intention. And the aromas that wafted beneath doors and out to the farthest edges of the garden, down to the ends of the block, whichever block they lived on that year, called in each girl, Father, and the cat long before it was time to gather to eat. Mother cooked a food that fed their noses, their eyes, their tongues, their stomachs, their dreams. The meals she imbued with her love fed them to the bottoms of their feet, and its effects traveled further still through those feet and deep into the ground to come up elsewhere, the girls were sure, as flowers and herbs, as clear mountain springs or brilliant rainbows, as agates and opals.

The family were always bringing forth something new into the world. Father planted trees that bore peaches and apricots, sometimes on the same tree, bushes that churned out rose upon rose, onions and potatoes that multiplied, as the girls did, unseen and furtively. He constructed tables and ladders, and under his quick and steady hand, brick walls went up. In the garden, the sisters stretched a bed sheet this way and that way, hung a lamp, gathered the neighborhood cats, dogs, rabbits, and birds, painted their faces, and a circus was announced. Mother set out an old nightgown and a sister made a new top and a purse with it. Pictures were cut out from old schoolbooks to make masks or to people a cardboard train. Socks became dolls, and twigs were lumber for the doll's house. When a thing expired, another was born of it.

The materials were all around them; their lives were unsteady. Their imaginations were fertile and restive; the distant goings-on made them so. Their own strange, unfolding history in a bright and sheltered land made them so. When a sister felt unmoored, she cast out her yarn and took out her knitting needles, or she painted the solar system and its imaginary ellipses and marked her place along one of them. When Mother remembered her lost loved ones, she rolled out dough and cut it into neat long strips, hung them to dry, and the next day cooked her dead sister's favorite noodle dish for her daughters. In the house, the transfiguration of the used into the new, the overlooked into the wondrous, the pain into delight, this was common, was necessary, and was, in nature, devotional.

tireless

And though the sky had no feet, it seemed to the sisters that it walked and walked tirelessly around them, dawn to dusk to dawn again, year after year, neighborhood after neighborhood.

But they also sensed in their slender bodies that it was they who whirled and whirled endlessly. It was they who careened through the blinking heavens.

conveyance

The sister-always-flitting-skipping-sprinting caught a glimpse of the cat in the corner of her eye as she bounded diagonally across the yard, from the scorching patio, over the hissing sprinklers, to the back gate, up which she routinely liked to climb barefoot, and over which she liked to keep an eye on the goings-on in the alleyway the gate bordered. Having spotted the cat, she stopped before the gate and, rather than climbing it, leapt again over the sprinklers in a direction perpendicular to the fence to slide into the cool, dry, shade under Father's grape arbor. The cat, unperturbed, lay in a corner stretched out along the arbor's trellis; the sister sat cross-legged in front of it, so that the two met eye to eye. She looked over her shoulder and about her, across the expanse of lawn and toward the house: she and the cat were alone. The midday sun kept the others indoors; Mother's cooking on a Sunday drew them to her circle. The animated sister settled down and began to match her breath to the cat's idle, resonant purr, and tried to elongate her pupils to match the cat's vertical slits. The cat stared. The sister stared. The two respired in synchrony.

The sun pushed its rays through the grape leaves onto the cat and the sister's fur and hair, warming them in patches. The sister and the cat gazed at one another. The sprinklers pattered softly across lawn, rosebush, and patio in the distance. And then the girl fell, head-first, into a slumber that was not a slumber, into a world that was mirror-image to her own world in all but one way: here the cat spoke in the sister's first tongue. Yes, the cat, in this world, very plainly spoke in the sister's birth tongue. And the cat asked the sister, *do you truly enjoy running through and leaping over the odious wet sprinklers?* To the cat, the sister looked happy enough, her wild hair swinging across her shoulders, her flushed face revealing teeth and tongue, which released the intermittent whoop and roar as she bounded here and there. *Or have your Mother or sisters doled out the terrible punishment because you have misbehaved again? Have they discovered your collections of dead flies and beetles?* The cat stared and waited for an answer. It was familiar with the family's ways but didn't always comprehend them. The cat waited. The sister purred.

boy

He was not a soldier: not a rebel soldier, not a soldier by training
or by force, not any kind of ————. He had picked up a rock.
And then a second, and a third, and a fourth, and so on, until
his fists were like two large, knobby —————, his mother
said. He held fast to the rocks-smooth and rocks-jagged, clenched
tightly his fingers around them until blood ran over his knuckles
and up his forearms. He was not innocent; they said his eyes were
like coals, his lips like barbed wire. His fists were two large, ripe
pomegranates, she said.

look out!

Look in,
says the book.

the library

And the sister who reads, who has just learned to fathom the new
alphabet, on any day of the week, after school, or before a trip to
the sea on a Saturday morning, is called to the library by a force
not dissimilar in strength to the one that draws her to the ocean's
edge. She enters the great public institution, and makes her way
to the shelves that hold the tales. The fairy tales, the ghost stories,

the adventures, and the mysteries have drawn her across the valley, down the streets, up the avenues, past the convenience stores, the mechanic shop, and the basketball courts. Once inside the quiet sanctuary, she finds her way to the tales and reaches for the books, stoops for the books, fits her small frame through the narrowest spaces to angle for those that have called her. These books have made promises and will keep their promises of adventure, fright, kinship, wisdom, and wonder. On the shelves she finds the faded-thumbed volumes. Between their pages the sister discovers the beautiful forms, the ancient forms, and the novel forms. And it is all an enchantment to her. She is spellbound. The fairy tale, perfectly and concisely, illuminates the marvels of the world and categorizes its atrocities. How brilliant! The dead haunt the passages of the ghost stories and, through their wailing, rattling, and floating, defy the grave and impart sweet terror! Sublime. The romance brings the sister and her true kin, the fearless harpooneers, together on the roiling seas. At last! The library has a limit of 11 books and the sister walks home each week testing her strength and her balance with three adventures, five ghosts, myriad friends and foes, and immeasurable wonder in her arms.

wind/unwind

Everyday, the girls feel the wind/unwind of the coiled universe. They are one moment child, one moment aged: a result of too much growth while tender. The sisters, unnatural, share in common: a much quickened metabolism, a ravenous appetite for things living and dead; nails and hair that pay no heed to clippers or scissors; a history that holds fast to their small bodies to pillage the present of peace and security, great and small. The sisters were not born old but age was fast at their heels and with it wisdom unnatural to children, a wisdom that marked them, shaped them, aged them. When the sisters are simply girls, the other self is forgotten, and literally behind them. They are human chimera, split in half, a child on one side, an aged woman on the other. Each faces her own direction, but somewhere within, at the meeting place of the two, perhaps at the heart, the gut, where time is irrelevant, each is aware of the other. When the child is tired, the old woman bends further forward to carry her on her back, to put her to bed, and lay her down to a child's dream. When the old woman is disheartened, the girl makes her a cup of tea, sits her down on the softest chair in the house, tells her a child's story about the earthworm or the helicopter, and plays her a song in the second tongue, which the old woman's mind cannot decipher, but which nonetheless tickles her ear and makes her smile. The one climbs trees and skips rope; the other waits and watches, counts the days and the dead, and prays to the heedless male god. This wind/ unwind between innocence and burden pierces the surface of the earth where it is soft, leaving many holes in the neat and manicured grass in the yard. And Father treats the lawn with gopher poison, unaware of his daughters' drilling, thinking the past is his alone, shouldered by his thin frame alone, thinking he has sheltered his girls sufficiently. This turning of faces, girl-to-hag-to-girl, exhausts the old woman and electrifies the small child. The withered hag, she is ready for the grave, her feet drill in, kick dirt up. The child darts up the tree's trunk to drape her limbs around those of the tree, singing nonsense with her child's mouth, a mouth still new and discovering. She whistles and chirps. She attempts the finch's song. She dangles her limbs, releases her hair. She suctions her cheeks to suspend a long string of saliva out into space. In these moments, her disregard for gravity, blatant and wild, slows time, rebalancing the ratio between the two rulers. She alone exists, she, her saliva, and the grass below, all suspended.

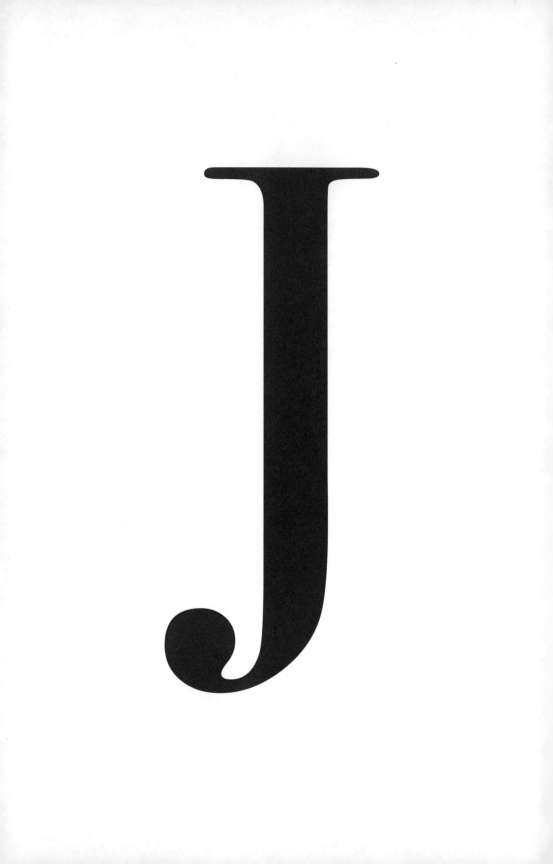

J   o   y   .

And we had it in abundance! It made the brightest scenes more vivid, and bloomed even in the darkest corners. It was something to cultivate while we turned our eyes away from what besieged us. We were never without the war; its long tendrils traveled smartly, using shortcuts to find us at work or school, singing over a birthday cake, or delivering a new plant into the garden soil. Joy, a precious thing, a thing to procure at every turn, to draw from the most modest of sources, to raise with gentle caresses and soft encouragements. We were adept at finding and cultivating joy. And well aware of its worth and its power.

confetti

The girls spent hours and took turns making confetti out of old homework, colorful drawings, or mail catalogues using the hole puncher. For occasions special or nonexistent, they spent entire afternoons after school cooking great feasts, plastering the walls of the living room with garlands and bows, and setting up a restaurant using the sofa cushions, cardboard boxes, Mother's linens and china, and roses picked from Father's garden. They wrote up menus and dressed as waiters, cooks, and musicians, covering their faces with black ink to fashion mustaches and beards, or applying Mother's lipstick to color cheeks and lips. They drew the curtains and blinds and lit candles to transform day into night. And when they heard the key in the front door, they all ran to it to toss confetti over Mother and Father, to take their bags, jackets, and shoes from them, to lead them to their table in the middle of the living room floor. And Father enjoyed ordering items not on the menu. And Mother said of everything, "delicious!" And the two youngest sisters stepped out in the traditional dress of the first country, in costumes over or undersized and loosely authentic, made up of items gathered from every family member's closet. While the older sisters, the tired and perspiring cooks and waiters, looked on from the kitchen, the youngest took the stage to sing, dance, and play the two traditional instruments the family owned, but which none could play with the least skill. And Father clapped to the music and Mother showered the girls with confetti and praise.

Mother, Father

The girls admired Mother in the bathroom mirror as she unwrapped rollers from her hair, or ran mascara over her lashes, or plucked her eyebrows, or applied color to her lips, and did these things without fuss, expertly, and often without looking. They marveled at how, leaning into the sink, in high heels, she zipped up her skirt with one hand and simultaneously put on an earring with the other. Or how with hairpins between her teeth and a hair dryer held over her head, she gossiped with the older girls about the previous weekend's party and mused about the coming evening's attendees. While they were girls, Mother was a woman and something else entirely. Mother wore a slip and stockings. She fastened and unfastened jewelry and her bra with long, shaped fingernails, elegantly painted. When she left the bathroom, she left it smelling of perfume and hair spray. And the sensitive sister coughed and gagged and returned to the living room. And the sister accompanying her parents to the party stayed behind to absorb Mother's scent and to study her own lips in the mirror.

Father, in front of the mirror, as elsewhere, was unhurried and meticulous. He drew out his razor, shaving cream, brush, and cup—articles pristine though used a thousand times and transported from the first land—and neatly laid them in order on a hand towel beside the sink. The sisters lingering in the door watched him lather cream with tepid water in the tin cup and spread it over his face, from one to the other ear, over his lip, and under his chin, using the soft round brush. And the helpful sister learned to lather the shaving cream for him, and the curious sister was allowed to brush it over her own cheeks and used her fingers to clear paths and make patterns across her face in the white foam.

The girls watching squinted and braced themselves as he drew
the shiny razor over his tautly held chin and along the corners
of his mouth. The sister who thought she might grow up to be
like Father recorded his gestures as he made the knot in his tie or
combed his hair close to his head.

the valley

In summer, by day, the valley is scorched and the girls run from
freezer to sprinkler to fan. The doing of homework, packing of
lunches, wrapping-about of sweaters and scarves, raking of leaves,
cooking of stews, tucking of blankets all cease and are replaced
by the refilling of ice cube trays, donning of shorts, lifting higher
of t-shirts and hair, fanning of necks, chasing of musical trucks,
unwrapping of sticky-sweet treats, licking of pink or blue dye off
wrists and kneecaps.

In summer, at night, the greedy valley clutches its heat and the
girls leave their bedrooms to lie five across on the living room floor.
And the industrious sister pulls the sheets off their beds, moistens
and wrings them in the tub, and spreads them over the hot bellies
and legs of the not-sleeping sisters. And the fidgety sister rises to
open all windows and doors and tramples on shins and knuckles as
she steps over the sprawled, sweltering bodies in the dark. And the
thirsty sister alternately sucks and rubs ice cubes over her face, her
shoulders, her arms, and finally lets them melt in the pool that is
her bellybutton. And the sisters curse the sun, long set, and though
they beseech, the wind sends not a breeze.

two

The sisters were five and divided down the middle into two groups of three. The first group consisted of: the first-born, the second-born, and the middle child. Mother and Father called them the Girls. Girls, because they were not yet women, though they carried laundry and the younger sisters on their narrow hips with ease. Girls, because their strength and their wisdom had earned them the title. The second group—made up of the baby, the fourth-born, and again the middle child—were called the Children by the parents and by the Girls. Though the youngest three, in their few short years on earth, had seen and heard nearly as much as the oldest three, they were still children and allowances were made them for childish things.

This classification was not arbitrary: it was born in the minds of, and placed upon the sisters by, Mother and Father, who believed that while offspring are all born equal, they should not be treated so in a large family. To their eldest three daughters, they gave the many and various responsibilities of housekeeping and childrearing. When Mother and Father left home for work, to attend a funeral, to purchase an electronic appliance for the kitchen, or to look for another house with a larger yard in a different neighborhood for the family, they left with their minds at ease, confident that the Girls would take care of all. When they returned home, they came bearing gifts, offerings of sweets or modest playthings for the Children, with the singular hope of extending the dream of childhood in the ever-widening eyes of their youngest three. The Girls were often treated as adults, but the Children could get away with: running wild and barefooted in the yard; wearing a short skirt or a sleeveless top; feigning a sore throat and a runny

nose after a meal to avoid sweeping the kitchen floor; furtively
feeding the cat or reading a book beneath the dinner table. And
the Girls, in turn: went on long, meandering walks through the
neighborhood with girlfriends; sat and conversed with guests as
adults, balancing teacup and saucer on knee; were taken into the
confidences and conspiracies of Mother, who shared with them
secrets kept from Father or gossip ripened on the boughs of the
community tree.

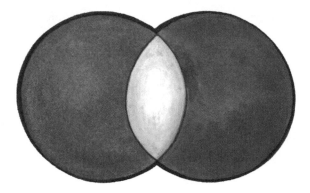

And because the middle child fit into the two groups simultaneously, she was cut off from both. Because she held the designation
of both Child and Girl, she was neither. A line ran down the
middle of the family, who had chosen odd numbers over even.
This line ran through her as well. A clean rip, a tear traveled from
the pit of her neck down to her navel. She was one and the same
sister: the middle child. But filling two posts simultaneously, she
became two and spoke in the playful and nonsensical tongue of
the child and in the authoritative voice of the adult, alternately.
She benefited from the two roles, giving orders to her younger sisters when Mother and Father were away, receiving gifts alongside

them when the adults returned home. This double nature allowed
her to be in two places at once: up in the tree's canopy and at her
school desk; at a wedding reception and crossing a mountain pass
on the back of a mule; rummaging in her sister's closet and lay-
ing her head across Mother's lap. The line that ran through her
occasionally pulled her completely in two and left a void in her
place. She was forgotten and: left out of conversations and unseen
around the house, though she sat next to and laughed along with
the others; left behind when the car pulled out of the driveway;
uncounted when Father paid for tickets at the amusement park.
She enjoyed her invisibility and suffered by it. The middle child
was not a whole number; she was one divided into two = 0.5. This
left her searching for: ten missing digits, her other ear. She was five
divided by six = 0.8333333333333333. She sensed that she ran
on, was one of those numbers that futilely resists infinity: a number that is but is not because it fails all attempts at wholeness.

And so she spent her days hungering after wholeness, gathering
all she could draw to herself: rose petals and snail shells; beetles'
wings and cats' fur; paper—white or colored, blank or covered
in the letters of the alphabet and bound between two covers;
Mother's broken jewelry; Father's precise gesture of adjusting
the watch on his wrist; the shame and agony of the family when
yet again they were forced out of an overheated car and onto the
side of the freeway; the school bus's diesel fumes; the schoolboy's
smile; her sisters' meaningful looks, looks piercing and looks tender. She gathered from far and near and, through the slit in her
chest, she dropped her many treasures into the slender cavity that
would not be filled. But her two small arms, lifting and dropping
buses and houses whole, became powerful and out-proportioned
her middle-child frame. She swung from tree limb to arbor beam

and remembered the beginning days, the earth's young days, and picked grapes as she went, filling her mouth but not the void that had produced two of her. Invisible to the others, and mindful of what feeds the grass and the trees, she went out daily to draw the sun into her. But unimpressed with its minuscule size in the infinite spaces within her chest, and never quite warmed by its generative powers, she searched farther out and farther on in the sky for more and ever greater stars. And there, she glimpsed the edge of things: the falling away of stars, the disappearance of galaxies entire. Shivering, she returned again, then again to be and to play with her sisters, to welcome the small space offered in their midst, the one simultaneously warm, buttressed on each side by two sisters, and suffocating, for it left little room for two of her.

and Mother

It makes the sisters glad when Mother speaks freely about her own childhood. Glad when Mother admits that she too fought with sisters and brothers, over friends or clothes or sweets, and went to bed not-speaking, woke in the morning to not-speak to the brother who sat on her right at breakfast or the sister who avoided her soapy and agile elbows over the laundry tub. But when Mother sees her daughters exchanging lifted brows or staring at her with mouths incredulous, jaws hinged open, she adjusts her story. And Mother tells them that in her time, she and her sisters: stayed up for endless hours, whispering and sharing dreams and secrets while the others slept on in the room the siblings shared at night; fell into deep sleep in the early morning hours with arms wrapped around each other's necks; held hands all the way to and from school, to and from the market, to and from the kitchen; mended one another's clothes; combed each other's hair; rouged each other's cheeks.

Mother says that unlike her own five daughters, in her time, she obeyed her elder sisters and brothers, no matter the request: in all seasons, washing and hanging their clothes to dry; before breakfast, lunch, tea, and dinner, pouring a neat stream of water from a jug over their hands and collecting the rinse in a basin; on bended knee waiting for the return of the hand towel before moving on to the next brother, while other sisters, directly behind her, set the large platters of rice, vegetables, and meat before the men and boys. We never complained, she says. *There were many of us. We cooked daily for 15 or 50—there were always guests—and every meal we prepared by hand, from scratch. There was always work to be completed: bread kneaded, rice and lentils scoured for pebbles and pests, eggs collected, floors scrubbed, fire tended, water drawn up from the well, carried in. Red knuckles, bothered hens.* And they know she is still being truthful. Mouths closed, the sisters hang their heads.

But they want to know the other truth as well. Want to know that Mother too was a girl, and suffered as a girl, not as a martyr. So they ask about grandmother's reprimands and whether or not she spoke them with the same asthma-labored voice some of them recall. They wonder how their stooped and bedridden grandmother managed to chase her many children around her many-roomed house: did she shuffle in her leather sandals, leaning on her cane, or was she lifted and bolstered under each arm by the older siblings, her white skirts and scarves trailing behind her as she floated down stone hallways and over crimson rugs, her eyes and teeth set and stern, the fingers on her right hand counting

prayer beads, while those on her left pointed and scolded? The
sisters who remember their grandmother remember an old
woman small and gathered—folded pale limbs, plaited gray hair,
white skirts in layers around a small body seated on white linens
atop a thin, cotton mattress on a low wicker bed; bed and linens
and old woman gathered in the corner of her otherwise bare room.
Notwithstanding the meager furnishings, Grandmother's room
was not a quiet, peaceful space. Those who entered it brought with
them the noise and life from elsewhere in the house and from the
neighborhood and the city beyond its walls. Like envoys, the passers-
through retrieved and delivered news during their comings and
goings to the room that functioned as a nerve center in the great
house and in the great family. Grandmother's was a room between
rooms, with two doors leading to disparate parts of the sprawling,
single-story house, and as such, was a sort of thoroughfare for the
family—the children, the grandchildren, and occasionally a stray
hen from the garden. The sisters remember: the ancient woman's chest working up and down, suffering for breath; her moist
mouth, sputtering words of judgment or reprimand or praise; her
large, warm, heavy hands caressing their heads or cupping their
chins or lifting their wrists and ankles to make sure they weren't
adorned with the bangles or anklets she detested. They sensed and
witnessed that a great love emanated from this breathing, pulsing
nerve center as they crossed her bedroom from living room to
kitchen. But they knew also to not unduly disturb the white-
gathered corner, sensing that at all times, whether she spoke
or listened to her visitors and passers-through, grandmother
simultaneously held another conversation. The girls knew their
grandfather only from a single and imposing photograph, which
hung on a wall in grandmother's room; for them, he existed in
periphery. He was grand, but separate and distant, a family legend

framed in wood. For grandmother, he was near, his presence
beside her as material a thing as the photograph on the bare wall
directly across from her simple woven bed. But for the family it
was she, small and concentrated, who ruled the home and from
her corner gave orders and passed judgment on the many children
and grandchildren always at her house, by her bedside, running
her errands, passing through her room. She was their great leader,
and her grown daughters and sons, heads of their own broods,
were like her viziers, never questioning, always attentive, arriving daily from across the city to bow their heads, kiss her hands,
deliver to her the day's news, and mete out her decrees. Had she
always been so severe, the girls ask Mother. No, Mother tells them.
She was a kind and warm mother. *She was a whole woman, strong
for raising ten children, losing three, spoiled and daily softened by my father's
adoration of her. He was shameless and in front of all embraced her, held her
hand, kissed her face, and sang her praises. He traveled often and brought her
gifts from near and far, sitting at her feet as she opened them, watching her face
like a child, devoted and giddy with expectation. It was this she was given and
this she had taken away when your grandfather died. It was not common, his
love for her. And we were many, arriving early in her marriage, having our own
early and often. And there were ones who did not survive, ones who died young.
With each new birth and each death she was splintered and the folds in her
skirts and in her skin multiplied, while she shrank, became more concentrated,
more severe beneath the garments, mind sharpened, body more poorly each passing year, unable to leave the corner of her room. This is what you remember.*

And the fickle sisters move on to ask about the broken nose given
Mother by an angry and spoiled older brother, the evidence of
which still sits on her face now, though barely visible to their accustomed daughter-eyes. *He was angry, yes. He woke me in the middle of the
night to wash his police uniform—in those days, he arrived late each night and*

left early each morning, always tired and made more proud by the rising-early, the coming-home-late, the spotless and tidy uniform. I fell asleep over the wash tub. It was two o'clock in the morning, a school night. He was young and proud. He was angry and brutal. He didn't speak to me for weeks after. The sisters study her face, see their mother in her perfection, and know that she has lived many days and many lives.

It makes the sisters glad when Mother lets down her guard, sheds her mother-role to reminisce about evenings spent in the company of sisters, listening to an adored singer on the radio. *So Mother too swooned.* She tells them about their grandfather's intolerance for rules and tradition. It was their grandfather, an immigrant from a neighboring land, who encouraged his daughters to be playful, to be girls, to dress as they liked in modern clothes, to wear their hair out and up, unveiled and beehived. He who, notwithstanding his disdain for the cinema, gave them the bus and the film fare, and sent them off to the city's central marketplace to shop and watch foreign films in the new theater.

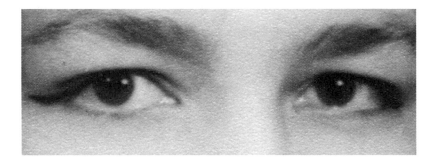

And the girls delight to discover that Mother's initiation into the dreamworld of the cinema, her first love, followed the natural pattern of girlhood ardor. They see the marquee, the bright colorful posters; they wonder at the soft rise of the velvet curtain, the white letters over the silver scene; they hear the bells on the dancers' feet, and perceive a shift in Mother's quickening speech as she describes the dancers' mirrored, sequenced dresses, their arms adorned with lustrous jewels, their eyes cast upon their beloved. Mother recites the titles of films, the names of stars. She tells them how she grasped the meaning of lovers' scenes and songs with her heart first, and through her love for the form, learned to speak foreign languages. With her eyes alone, she gave color to the black and white screen, painting flowers red, fields green, and silks golden. The five sisters elbow each other and nod significantly. One thing Mother cannot hide from her daughters is her complete devotion to romance. Around the house and over her daughters' heads, she preaches innocence, chastity, and duty, but when the sisters push a button for her to play a favorite film song or a beloved scene while Mother irons or files her nails, they watch her recede and return to her girlhood. The lights dim, the red curtains rise, and Mother remembers her allegiances. And these are not religious or familial or civic; her loyalty is to the lovers and their cause, no matter the barriers—ethnic or geographic—between them. And though she's watched the same films countless times since girlhood and knows their tragic outcome, still she urges the lovers across the desert or out of their homes, urges them to break their fetters, deny their parents and their customs, and sacrifice all for love. And if Mother could read well in the new tongue, the sisters guess that her shelves might be lined with books instead of silver and china—and they know which books would dominate those shelves. If Mother could write, the sisters imagine that her stories and her girlhood might be hidden from them.

madness

She is a neighbor girl. A single child. The sisters befriend and
invite her in. Mother welcomes her as she welcomes all her
guests: she brews the tea, sets out the sweets, asks the girl about
her family. And the girl, not younger than the oldest sisters, but
bigger, softer, and more innocent, finds comfort in the strange
home. It is a comfort she cannot find in the schoolyard or in the
kid-filled streets of their neighborhood or inside the shuttered
house her mother occupies day-through dressed in a nightgown,
day-through filling an ashtray at the kitchen table, in front of the
television. The girl comes regularly and over time finds her place
with the youngest sisters, who play as she does, but are many
inches shorter and several years younger. The neighbor girl is
joyful and innocent, forever ready for an afternoon of dress-up
and make-believe, a walk to the corner store, a game of tetherball. She is all-child and, as an only child, she is all-sharing, bringing over her dolls and her board games, inviting the sisters over
to her house for hotdogs or to record songs on her tape player or
to wonder at her pet rabbit—its ever-twitching nose, its menac-
ing pink eyes, its snow-soft fur. The neighbor girl is all child, all
innocence, all joy: she celebrates the call of the ice cream truck;
she swings and slides with glee and abandon; she puppy-barks at
the cat in the tree. Slowly and before their eyes, over the months
she transforms from girl to madwoman. And the sisters, always
obliging, invite her in, play along, and watch, helpless. But
Mother's heart grows larger, sadder, more welcoming. Madness
finds an innocent vessel in the golden land. It rises through the
neighbor child, enters and distorts her pliant, biddable face,
and leaves her twisted mouth as curses vile and precocious. She
hisses and spits at unseen demons; she glares at houseplants, at

bicycle wheels; she tries with her strong, soft hands to choke the evil spirits out of the neighborhood children. She screams and thrashes, curses as grown men curse, and is dragged home by her mother, her father—called home from work again—and returns to the sisters' house the next day a child afresh. But over time, the neighbor girl comes less and less often to school, to the sisters' house, out to the curb to meet the ice cream truck. On their way home from school, the sisters pass her house and meet her eyes through a slit in her bedroom window curtain, which drops, then quickly rises to reveal her hand, waving. When the gone-mad girl comes again to visit, she comes with her head tilted, her eyes questioning and unsure, and her lips curled in a permanent smile that releases a girly titter when she drools or knocks something over in the house. And daily, her large drooped frame swells so that she comes to tower even over the older sisters. They bring out their toys, their drawing materials; she smiles and she nods. She picks up the cookies Mother places before her, then sets them down again, uneaten. All the while, her mind regresses until it is the toddler, the youngest sister, whom she comes over to play with. Then one day, she leaves the neighborhood entirely. And the vanished neighbor girl's house takes on a new appearance: its lawn is regularly mowed, its exterior painted, its shutters opened. Her mother purchases a car, takes a job, cuts and curls her hair, dresses in a suit, and joins the other wage earners.

signpost

The only way forward is through the alphabet.

the stalker

And violence in the sunny land takes a strange form. It adopts the guise of a willowy young man who visits houses at night, exploits the giving nature of suburban windowpanes and screen doors, and enters into the bedrooms and kitchens of the sleeping valley-dwellers to shoot, rape, hammer, mutilate, and murder them. And the family sleeps fitfully through one winter and two summers; they sleep with all doors, windows, and the cat securely barricaded.

heritage

The girls know very little about their grandparents, and have even less knowledge of who came before these filmy legends from long ago. But the sisters know that as a lineage they have never stayed any one place too long. Movement is their legacy. It is a heritage that courses through their liquid channels and marks their features. This movement has contoured and colored their biology over the centuries. Chased by war and called by the unknown, their ancestors moved from land to land, over sea and mountain, across the faces of the earth. As an itinerant beggar collects alms on his travels, the sisters, over the many generations, collected their traits from this or that ancestor in this or that land. The girls' languid eyelids are an artifact of earlier lives lived in the frigid northern peninsulas, where plump lids keep dreaming eyes warm through the long, dark winter nights. Their spindly fingers, assuredly, were given them by a mathematician of the westernmost East, who, because he had the night sky wide open to him above the still desert and the roiling sea, learned to count and to measure distances with his digits, and passed down to the girls his passion for numbers and rulers and, through it, his ardent love for the night sky. The girls' red-apple cheeks, and the smiles that produce them, they picked up in the very heart of the old continent, the native home of the fruit that has traveled farther and wider than the sisters. The various colors of their eyes were distilled by the rug weaving women of the mountains who knew the secrets of drawing color from roots, nuts, beetles, and stones. And the color of their hair, which they all share, was sanctified by the priest who slept by day in the hot climes and stood chanting at dusk and dawn in the smoke of the funeral pyres. When a sister lies napping facedown with arms spread wide on a rug in the house, it is because she and the rug have traveled great distances and find comfort in their shared odyssey. When a sister finds herself spontaneously chanting while washing dishes or raking leaves, she guesses, correctly, that another family member, somewhere, has passed. When a sister tastes a supermarket apple that Mother has reluctantly brought home, she wrinkles her nose and, at the same time, mourns the imminent loss of her own piquancy. When a sister stares out at the sea, is she remembering the great merchant ship that brought her ancestors across the frozen waters? And when a sister looks out into the night sky, she knows already the distance to the nearest star, and, knowing it is not great, she playfully closes that distance by pinching closed her forefinger and her thumb.

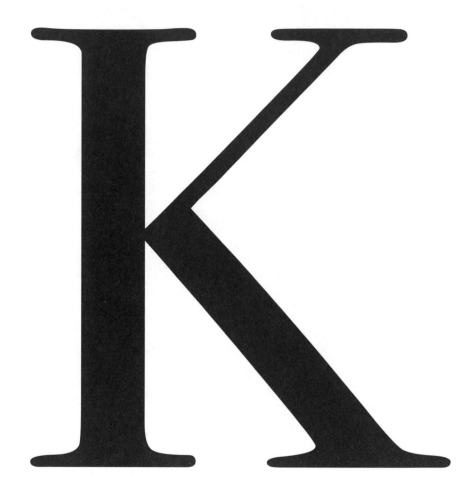

K a l e i d o s c o p e .
And this book is one. See the little movable pieces, watch the bright
colors arrange and rearrange to tell ever new, ever different tales.
Did I not say that you can enter, turn, and return as you like?

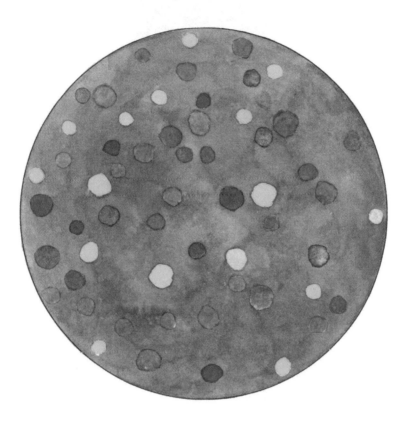

Key. Are letters not keys? See *them* arrange and
rearrange. Lock and unlock. Turn. And click.

ardor—birds

The bird-loving sister follows the winged creatures she admires with her eyes, and with her arms and legs, which help her eyes climb trees, fences, and even the rooftop to catch a better view of a robin hatchling, or the distant perch of a red-tailed hawk. She loves the creatures and knows them each by their size, form, color, sound, and movement. She knows their individual calls and the turbulent or dull flutter of their wings through the air when they fly near or high overhead. She knows the different birds by their proud or cowering postures as they perch on the

topmost frond of a palm tree or walk to and fro along a rain
gutter or scuttle across the sand before an incoming wave at the
beach. She is enthralled by their mechanical gestures when they
nod or turn their heads, peck at the earth or into the weathered
trunk of a utility pole with their pointed beaks. She knows the
many birds by their shadows, cast across the lawn or against the
side of the house when they soar overhead or dive deeply after a
smaller creature nearer the ground.

She dreams of birds, though in her dreams they arrive with longer tails, taller crests, and brighter plumage than any bird in her
neighborhood or her schoolbooks. In her dreams, birds of myriad
shapes and colors congregate in the grandfather tree or in the
sycamore on the front lawn. They meet at dawn or in the middle
hours of the night, when the neighborhood and the family sleep
and the sister alone stands outside to receive the visiting birds.
They arrive from all corners of the dream realm for occasions
she clearly senses are important, epochal even, but the purpose of
which she cannot fathom. The dream birds collect, some hovering,
others perching on or moving through the limbs of the tree she
stands beneath, their long tails hanging down to the ground, their
crests and bright plumage filling the tree with shimmering color
and movement. Though the birds arrive from great distances to
meet in *her* dream, in a tree in *her* garden, it is she, the sister, who
feels the interloper at these conclaves. It is she, the wingless and
earthbound ambassador, who steps awkwardly, stands deferen-
tially, and waits patiently below them as they hold their raucous
assembly. She counts the birds, classifies them by size, color, and
plumage and sees that they organize themselves by something else,
by a social order that has little to do with their appearances. She
is patient and waits and notes when the meeting becomes heated

or distressing or somber, and when it lightens in mood again. And as these assemblies come to a close, she eagerly stands on tiptoe to raptly listen to a small bird—their envoy—who descends to speak their message to her. It is a message that is neither song nor speech and fills her mind as warm tea fills a cup. Yes, I know it now, I understand, she whispers, then wakes suddenly. On waking, try as she may, the sister cannot grasp the message given her. It is one moment there, whole and of the greatest import, and the next moment gone from her, like a breath exhaled. And shortly, she cannot recall the number of birds attending, their colors, or their activity. The only thing that abides is a small thrill in her chest, a tingling sensation, as from a flutter of wings, within her ribcage. The featherless sister watches birds, dreams of birds, draws and colors many pictures of birds.

ardor—the sea

The sea-loving sister sits at her school desk and draws and colors
a scene she knows well—it is a picture of the ocean. She is drawn
to the ocean by a force she cannot deny or explain. It is an old
attraction. She felt the pull and dreamed of it long before leaving
her landlocked birth country. It was there in her dreams from
the beginning: the water that ran in all directions but up. In the
dreams, she was often in the very middle of this great expanse.
Though she did not know then the sensation of swimming in a
body of water, in her dreams it was not unlike flying, which she
had also done many times over in the dream realm. After arriving
in the new country, the family did not wait long to visit the beach.

When first she saw the great vast blue in the land of the sun, the sister stood before it frightened and with an awe her small body could not withstand. Though a hundred paces separated her from the water's edge, she stepped back, and stepped back again at each wave's lapping. Comfortable in the limbs of trees, she climbed a small one near the picnic tables where the adults sat gossiping, drinking tea, and playing cards. From a distance, she watched the waves advance and recede, advance and recede, and felt the old, familiar tug in her chest. She watched and listened and heard the call and she held on more tightly to the branch that supported her. And she went home that night to sleep with her head beneath her pillow, trying to keep out the enchanting thrum of the ocean's call. When next she visited the beach, she watched the waves from her perch in the same small tree, listened to the froth of the surf as it disappeared into the sand and, feeling a sudden joy she had not known before, she climbed down and stepped on the sand. And the loose, coarse grains warmed her always-chilled feet. And her parents, the tree, the picnic table diminished behind her. And she stood in awe of the great ocean before her. That awe, though it expanded to great proportions within her, did not threaten to break her skin this time. With each subsequent visit to the beach, she moved closer, and closer, until her feet, having traveled far and tentatively over the increasingly hot sand, felt the cool relief of the water. It was not long before the small tree by the picnic tables was forgotten. Not long before she began to chase the waves she'd once feared. Not long before she disappeared giddily under those same waves, and rose beyond them with a length of kelp worn around her neck and a seashell or a stone held triumphantly over her head. Long ago, the sea cast a spell on her. It is a spell that called her to its edge, then called her into itself, then drew her deeper and deeper in, for longer and longer. And now, Mother and Father grow tired and grow hoarse calling her out again at the end of a long Saturday. She is drawn to the ocean by a force she cannot deny. After each visit to the beach, sun-tired, she comes home feeling more sated, more sure of her place in the world: her place is in the water. And she wonders, what is this force that emanates from this most vital and persuasive element, that calls me to it in dreams, in daydreams, on the weekend, and midweek at school? And at her school desk, she paints regularly the picture she drew years before in the first land—the blue ocean, a thin strip of green land in the far distance, a boat shaped like a slice of watermelon, a single bird flying overhead.

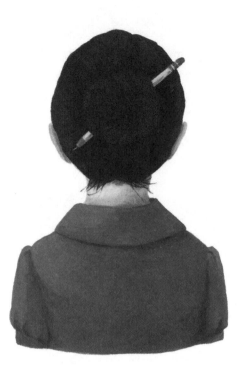

ardor—pictures

The renderer draws and colors all that she sees around her and all
that she sees within her. And what is within is no less compelling
than what is without. She knows because she is able to turn her
eyes quite around so that she can, when not busy with something
that requires her entire attention without, look into the body of
her. So, after she is done drawing cherries, cats, trees, hills, her sisters, their toys, Mother's sunglasses, Father's roses, the neighbor's
cars, her teacher's shoes, the ice cream truck, robins, and sailboats,
she rolls her eyes under and back to look into and throughout
her body; she is keen to accurately draw the nerves, organs, and
bones that make it up. She draws landscapes of violet blood vessels

snaking through pink muscles set against white bones. She out-
lines the quadrants of her brain and tints each a different bright
hue. She draws her heart, large and pink, and can't help placing
her cat, fast asleep, atop it. She draws her skeleton and observes
that she has an extra bone in each of her feet and that her broken
arm has healed well. Inside her rib cage, she draws the bird that
has made a home there. Then, anxious that the cat near her heart
might be too much attracted by the flittering bird in her ribcage,
she erases the cat and replaces it with her new crush, a boy with
hair no less wild than the cat's fur. The picture-making sister is
fascinated by her circulatory system and draws it in its entirety on
a large piece of paper. She comes to understand that in structure
it is not unlike the roots of the grandfather tree. Peeking closely,
she sees her blood cells coursing through this system, tripping
over one another as they race from organ to organ. Looking deep
within the cells themselves, she finds atoms quivering and sliding
past other atoms, equally spry. More closely still, she locates last
night's dream, even now playing, but faded in places like a tattered blanket. In the dream, she climbs a ladder, up and up until
she arrives at the gate of an enormous overgrown garden. The
doors open and she is welcomed in by a guard in a suit of armor
who hands her a blue rose and points to a group of sheep on a
hillside. The dream looks as it did the previous night, but is now
missing bits of scenery—the sky in places, the guard's arm, the
trunks of trees—and is moving much too slowly, as if the machinery required for motion in a dream is in use elsewhere, or is being
serviced. Watching and drawing, drawing and observing, she sees
that the dream shifts and a new one begins to take shape in its
place. Seven large stones, each larger than the previous one, rise
out of the hillside. The sheep move up into the sky to form clouds
and fill in the empty patches. The guard dissolves and spreads as a

small pond at her feet. As she draws and observes, the construction of this dream falters; the stones tip and are swallowed again by the hillside, which has turned into an elephant's back. Perhaps this is the coming night's dream that she is viewing too early; it is not quite ready yet, the players have not all arrived, the machinery is still gearing up.

ardor—the dead

The daydreaming sister lives too near the dead, and catches
them passing in the corner of her eye as she reads from a book
or clips her nails or stares at the passing clouds overhead. She
is/is not afraid of the dead. She does/does not question them.
She follows their tracks. She understands their restive tendencies.
They are a moment here, in the next gone, and return again
to the same spot regularly. The veiled woman, she wears bare,
down its center, the narrow red rug that lines the hallway and
connects the sisters' bedroom to Mother and Father's. Nightly,
the stooped woman walks across this rug down the short hallway from bedroom to bedroom, never entering the rooms but

appearing at one end of the rug and disappearing at the other
end, continuously. And the sister watches her through the opening in her bedroom door and lets the old woman's step and the
soft rustle of her long trailing veils lull her to sleep. When the
sister sleeps lightly, she is woken early by the soldier's footfall. On
these mornings, she sits up in bed and looks out her window at
the young man on early morning duty in the peaceful suburban
neighborhood. The soldier turns the same corner of the house
over and again until the roses too are roused from their slumber
and turn their faces to look after him, and the soldier himself
adopts the scent of the large sleepy blooms, a sweet-bright perfume that wafts through the neighborhood in the predawn hours.
The half-book man returns regularly to monitor the traffic on the
suburban street. Hours pass. The sister watches/does not watch
him from her perch in the tree, or through the curtains in the
kitchen window. When he grows tired of the activity, the poet
stands up, and walks into the trunk of the tall sycamore. The
dead are more restless than the living. And they are more patient
too. They return to the same station—in the same city, the same
neighborhood, the same house—as the ocean tide returns to
mark the same spot on the intertidal rock. And the dead are
helpless in their comings and goings, as the tide is helpless, and,
like the ocean tide, are animated by a source outside themselves.
The dead are driven by loss, though many do not seem to know
what it is they are missing, what it is they have mislaid. But they
search, regularly, rhythmically. The dead are patient, they are
steady. The months pass, the years pass. The sisters grow taller.
The days are all one to the dead. And the living to the dead are
like shadows, like whispers. The daydreaming sister to the half-
book man is like the fleeting shadow cast across a garden wall by
a bird passing before the morning sun.

ardor—numbers

The sisters are five. They are one. They are ten if you count
their shadows, who are ostensibly attached to their feet, and live
sometimes above ground, and sometimes below. It is the counting
sister who has figured this out. She has tallied each sister *and* her
shadow. She has watched their shadows do as the sisters do: jump
rope; swing high into the canopy of the tree; scramble up the tree
or over the large arms and curved back of the couch like a lizard
or a spider; pick Father's flowers and the petals off of those flowers one by one in the alleyway behind the house; take large, then
small steps to sneak up behind the cat; write, with a mud-soaked
finger, on the garden wall, the name of the new beloved. She

has watched as shadow and substance have danced, leaped, and twirled together.

Yes, the dark counterparts do as the sisters do. But sometimes they do more, when they are inclined. See the shadow continue to swing even after the sister has tired of the repetitive motion and gone indoors for a snack. See the shadow leave the sister and follow the cat. And sometimes the analogs do less than the active sisters. A shadow who no longer wants to run around the school track will find the shade of a tree to meld into. A shadow who does not feel well on long car drives—who does not do well keeping up with the car's occupants as she moves at great speeds over highway and pinned to the sides of passing cars—will remain behind at home. The sisters' shadows are loyal, but sometimes it is the dark silhouette that gives a hiding sister away, as it can be seen before the sister can. The lovelorn, petal-plucking sister stands hidden in the alleyway outside the garden gate, but her shadow remains within the yard for all to see, point to, and giggle at. The camouflaged, leg-swinging sister up in the tree forgets her silhouette on the grass below.

The number-loving sister tallies ten, and subtracts down to five as one after another shadow disappears into the ground at the noon hour or when the sun sets, and counts back up to ten as the after-noon wears on or the lights come on in the rooms of the house in the evening. But not all of the sisters' shadows appear or disappear at the appointed times or places. The sisters and their shadows are not one. The loyal/disloyal silhouettes share/do not share a common life with their more substantial counterparts. Sometimes the shadows lag behind; sometimes they refuse to show at all. And a sister missing her shadow for the day feels suspended and unmoored. Without the dark partner to mark her way, to signal the angles and turns in the world about her, she bumps into walls, or trips and falls more than usual as she walks and plays. The counting sister wonders where it is the slippery contours go when they go away, and wonders why sometimes they do not show up at the agreed-upon time or location. She has a sense that her shadow returns to the world beneath the surface since her dusky companion attaches to her where her feet meet the earth. Further, it must be true that this shape, which remains un-illuminated even on the brightest of days, must originate from the sunless countries below. Perhaps the shadows disappear early or arrive tardily because their world beneath ground is more fascinating than her world above. After all, the underground wonders—the mineral caverns of many colors, the close and meandering byways connecting them, the milky pools of emerald and topaz waters, the creatures that scurry, burrow, and swim there—must keep them better occupied and entertained below. And how the counting sister wants to follow her shadow there! She knows that her shadow drives her aboveground; why else would she, shy and turned in, suddenly twirl and twirl and leap across the school playground, or shoot her hand up to answer a difficult math question when all other hands and heads are weighted down? So she closes her eyes tightly at night in bed, and uses her will to drive her shadow this way and that way through the earth to discover this and that unfamiliar route or creature or sound. And oh, the wonders she discovers!

the sister

And it seemed that all of the sisters folded one into another so that there was but the single one.

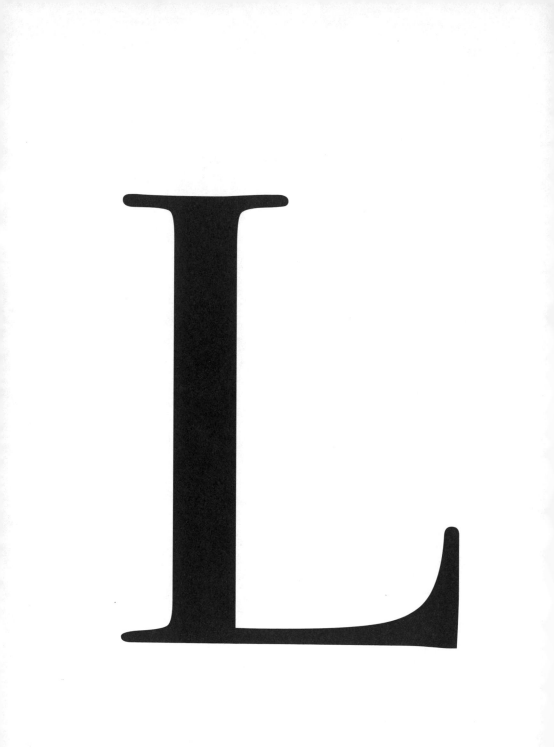

L   o   v   e   .

And is there anything else to write of?

This is not a book you read. This is a love letter.
A letter of love to the sky and the stars that dot it.

the days were one

And it seemed that all of the days folded one into another so that the sisters lived but the single day.

And the daily repetition—the stirring, the rising, the holding up and holding in, the pushing out and pulling up, the turning under, the dreaming and not-dreaming—the repetition functioned to score a notch into the fabric of the illimitable universe, to cause a small disturbance or a deviation in its calculated rhythms, to wear a shallow groove into the face of that mostly invisible system, so that a record, however dim, however slight, a record of the sisters might persist in the realm of the windy stars.

And the repetition—the stirring of heads and of shoulders in the morning; the morning rising of bodies, of hunger; the regular holding up of unyielding custom, of decorum, of delicate chins; the awkward holding in of ardor and loss, which combined to produce that singular ache that some of the sisters called *longing* and which all of them felt keenly, held closely; the pushing out of stars and of laughter from eyes bright and bodies slender; the pulling up of roots and tubers out of a yielding earth, the pulling up of more chairs for more guests at the table; the turning under of memories beautiful and horrific, the turning under of kittens born naked, born dead, into the eager soil beneath the rosebushes; the dreaming of things and of people passed, the dreaming of a day spent under the sun, the same one, the same day repeated now in sleep even while the body lay still, untwitching, and the eyes flitted in their sockets, as if reading, not dreaming—the repetition produced a record, small but not mislaid, slight but not fleeting.

And all of the days were one. Folded into the single one. And were recorded as one.

Above   us   the   Milky   Way,
so   resplendent   that
I   can   write   this
by   its   light.

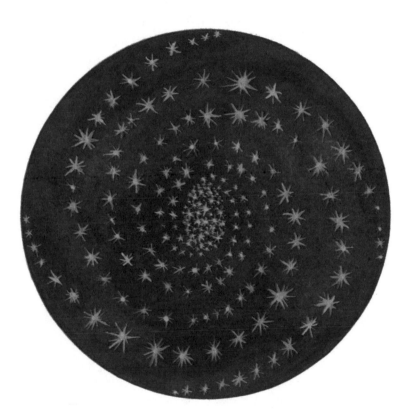

unsleep—the insomniac

The sister who could not sleep often shared a bedroom with the
dreamer. She wondered, as she tossed and turned, how it was that
her sister, who searched all day between the covers of books and
beneath insect wings, among blades of grass or within Mother's
jewelry box, did not tire of seeking at night and slipped directly
into her dreams, as if slipping into the next room, to begin her
search anew, to follow a new hunch, to pick up yet another silvery
thread. Each night, the insomniac kept her eyes on the ceiling
while her mind walked up and down the same thousand steps—
up to the locked door that was her future and back down to the
locked door that was her past. Though it was her mind that made
this nightly journey, the balls of her feet and the knuckles of her
right hand ached in the morning and calloused over time. And
who were these doorkeepers, she wondered? Did they not hear her
desperate knock? Did her pleas not move their cold blood?

It was when she thought she had made her last descent and taken
her final step, when the knees of her walking mind were ready
to give, that the ancient knob on the door to her past would turn
and the door open. Behind the door: the scent of lilac or of mint;
the creaky voice of an aged aunt or the call of a beloved teacher
across a familiar schoolyard. Also behind this door, the sister's
best friend, who wore her hair in a single braid down her back
and nearly to her knees, who took the sister's hand and whispered
schoolgirl tales in her ear. All about her, an ocean of blue and
white matching uniforms, the din of many dozen feet running, of
balls bouncing, of laughter booming and breathless. Behind this
door to her past, the light, whether gray or warm, dim or bright,
the light was different and somehow more natural than it was in

her current life. Behind the door, the air was filled with the scents of a less sterilized life: of rising dough, of the street vendor's ripe melons, of onions frying in animal fat, of mint leaves drying on Mother's clothesline, of snow and ice covering every surface and every article left outside in winter. Did the cold snow not have its own fragrance there? Behind this door: the laughter was of a different pitch; the milk was sweeter and the chicken more tender; the hills were nearer; her mother, taller and thinner; her family, much, much larger. How many sisters and cousins she had carried on her own child hips up and down the steep hills of their neighborhood. How well she knew the gender or the age of a child by its weight or its movement on the edge of her pelvis. So many hands—large and small, graceful or strong, calloused or withered, sticky with sweets or with the steam of baking rice—she had held in her own. So many cheeks she had kissed. So many elders she had bowed down before who had kissed her own cheek or the top of her head with their soft, crinkled lips. So many eyes she had met straight on or with her own averted. Behind this door there were customs and rules that were familiar to her. Behind this door: the questions ceased; she simply was and simply lived the single life; she knew and had her place and cherished it.

The sister who could not sleep did not choose to haunt the world on the other side of the lower door. The war that shut this door behind her had also closed paths of communication, cutting down telephone lines, shutting off borders, searching then discarding letters at these borders. This was the only way she knew to get back to who and what she missed and once was, and often the only way she knew toward sleep. And once asleep, she did not dream but continued her ascent/descent in the stairwell, wondering: where were the eyes, the cheeks, the hands she once knew? What did those eyes now see, if anything? How many dropped bombs, how many dead bodies, how many missing relatives had they silently counted? What color was the night sky during an air raid—she herself remembered then unremembered red. When the loved ones in the first land gossiped with neighbors, did they look over—as they once had—or through the walls that perhaps no longer stood? How tired now were those hands and how sunken the cheeks she had once held and kissed? Was it these worries that kept her from dreaming?

It seemed to her that in her current life, her family was an abridged version of the greater family she had known before and left behind. And within this new family in the new land, she, no less than Mother and Father and the younger sisters, played more than one role to all the others, comprising aunt and uncle, cousin and hairdresser, schoolmate and neighborhood gossip within a single skin. Was she not her sisters' ancient great aunt with the stooped shoulders and spirited laugh? Was she not also the spinster schoolteacher with ruler forever in hand? The cook? Did her ankles not ache from standing before the kitchen stove all afternoon, a schoolbook on the counter beside her? Or was the cause of this ache in her legs those same thousand steps, the ceaseless march that kept her up and kept her from dreaming at night?

The keeper of the door at the top of the staircase, the door to her future, did not bleed as the other did, refused to open the locked door despite the sister's tired pleas, despite the ever-growing pile of gifts—of thick, sweet honey from the corner shop, of blood-red roasted beets purchased from the street peddler's basket, of lace from her grandmother's cabinet, of cured meats from her second aunt's cellar—gifts pilfered from her previous life each night and offered to the keeper of the door at the top. In exchange, a single request: a return of her original, unopened future. A future once promised her as the eldest daughter. Among the gifts she left were pictures she drew and colored with care, images of a grand and multitiered family, of big gatherings and celebrations, of bounteous tables laden with an array of ancestral dishes. But the keeper of the top door, standing behind it, peered out of the peephole with an unblinking eye. He kept his hand on the lock and denied the sister a look into her future, refused her a single night to dream her first fate.

No, the eldest sister did not choose to make this nightly trek, to wear thin the soles of her sneakers and slowly over time wear out her welcome in that world that was her past, with the friends and family who slowly grew to not recognize her, to suspect her and occasionally mistake her for one of *them*: those who walked with too straight a back and too stiff a gait: the pilfering invaders. This endless ascent to nothing and descent to less and less was not of her own making or of her choosing. It was her vocation, just as it was the dreamer's vocation to search over rainbow and beneath mossy bridge for the thing *she* had possessed in her early life but lost in the chaos and wished only to bring back to the family who had lost alongside her.

outside, the rain

Outside, the first drops of a light rain begin to fall on parched concrete walkways and well-watered lawns. The swing raps against the tree that is the sisters' grandfather. The tree's broad leaves, covered in dust, resist the feeble rain. Up and down the block, color television sets flicker blue images and information into living rooms. The street is quiet. All the streets in the neighborhood are deserted and quiet; the people have gone home, turned in. Above, it is only a partial lunar eclipse that makes the moon blush: an act of love performed against a twinkling backdrop on the firmamental stage. The rain clouds, like a curtain, close over the scene, and the sisters' cat does not return home tonight.

rocket

The two are brothers, farmers, young fathers each. It is a close summer evening and they remain outdoors with their uncle. The sun has set but the sky in the west remains lit, flecked with herds of soft golden clouds. The sky shifts and, liesurely, one by one, reveals the stars. The spent dusty men stand among quince trees that have only recently been unburdened of their crop. Night advances slowly and the day's heat lingers in the orchard. The brothers say tomorrow will bring more heat; there is no moon to draw the clouds over the mountain peaks. They say, a break by week's end. They say, God willing. One brother leans against their cow, the other squats on the ground, his arms slack over his knees. Their uncle smokes his pipe, tells the brothers about his day, his journey that started in the early morning hours and took him to and brought him back from their nearest neighbor-village to the north. Their uncle is a driver, has two horses that pull his wagon; he makes deliveries and transports people and goods about the

village and occasionally farther. He is tired. The journey was long,
hot. He has not washed yet, and has yet to fulfill the day's missed
prayers. But he has put his horses, hungry as he, in the stable, put
out their feed. He looks over his shoulder, through the orchard
toward the light that is his own house, a short distance up the
road. His wife will step out soon, calling him in to wash, calling
him to dinner. He laughs, tells his nephews about the beet sugar
factory owner's plans to marry his second daughter to an eye doctor in the capital. They will have two weddings, he says, one here,
another in the city. What feasting, what a pageant it will be! Three
nights and three days of celebration! How ugly she is, he says.
The young men smile, nod. Their father's first wife and her grown
children raised the brothers, who are close in age and together
cannot remember their father and share only the few memories of
their birth mother. She died young and her brother stayed near to
look after the boys. But they do not look to their uncle for fatherly
advice or direction; he is a friend, comes daily as a friend to share
news, gossip, the small goods—leather, string, buttons, glue, dried
fruit, candy, tea—goods he has picked up on his drives, from his
fare. One brother holds the rope, holds the cow near, though the
animal strikes the earth with its hoof, pulls in the direction of
the barn. The other picks up pebbles and flicks them against the
trunks of the quince trees; the chickens roosting in the boughs stir.
A window shuts; a door opens; the older man clears his throat.
Together the three men leave the orchard, lead the cow toward
the barn. The night is still, clear, dark now. Several miles away,
the men who fight for the country's freedom load and send out
half a dozen rockets, each in a different direction, not particular.
Their work is brief; it is important; the countryside belongs to the
people. A single missile, shot from a shoulder miles away, hits the
three men and the cow. The hens flap their wings, kick out their

legs, and settle again. A measured breeze, like a long exhale, moves over the orchard. Indoors, their women and children tremble, they wait. In their pots and on their plates, their dinner cools, stiffens. At the first light of day they venture out. It is easy to see where the rocket hit: it has left a great dark bruise in the ground near the rows of newly sown beets. But the flesh is in tatters and strewn broadly, and it is difficult to make out what was man and what was cow. This news does not leave the country for many years: who will tell their older brother in the golden land that his family contracts further still? Who has the will? It is enough to tend to the turning of the earth.

loss

And the weeping old woman finished her story, looked at the five
sisters, still small, still tender, and said,
And the grandfather tree balanced the five small bodies on his
many limbs and said to girls,
And the red rugs felt the girls' anxious steps across their sensitive
pile, and said to them,
And Mother hung up the phone, stared at her trembling hands
and, once again, said to her daughters,
This is how the world is, one dies, one remains.

eyes

The sisters had eyes, five pairs of eyes that took in all they saw—
and there was much to see—in the ever-expanding universe
around them. And while their ten eyes were like the dark, feeding
mouths of fish—gaping, keen—they were also like small mirrors.
It was with regular frequency that one sister looking into the eyes
of another would see reflected there her very own thoughts and
visions. In this way, images multiplied as in a hall of mirrors and
filled the house with multitudes of others. But the ten eyes were
also like living marbles of different sizes and hues. The daily
visions rebounded off the firm, wet, convex surfaces of the girls'
eyes without entering the girls' minds. They reverberated off walls
and chairs and dishes. They filled the rooms and increased the
heat, the energy, inside the thirty-five-year old, single-story house,
little different from others on the block. Occasionally, one vision or

another that one sister or another had captured and released left
the house through a window or an open door and made its way
into the street, so that a neighbor climbing out of her car at the
end of a long workday, or another trimming the hydrangea bush
in front of his house might stop a moment and look in the direction of the sisters' house with its verdant and neatly mown lawn,
its many-colored rosebushes forever in bloom, and imagine for an
instant that she or he had seen in place of the sycamore on the
front lawn a peach tree in full bloom or had seen a man, barefoot,
with tattered book in hand, sitting on the curb looking expectantly
in the direction of an advancing car or had seen the polished
rifle butt and muddy boot of a soldier rounding the corner of the
house.

News. And how little we had of it! How little we knew of what happened, continued to happen in the first land. For many months at a time there was no news. Nothing at all. Not from family—who dared not send word for fear of reprisal in the first land, or fear of wounding us in the new land with unwelcome information—and nothing on the television. Yet our father watched the news nightly, first thing after returning home from work, and last thing before bed. And he called us with great urgency when he thought there might be a news piece about the East. We all gathered around the set, seven faces, homework or toothbrush or teacup in hand, and waited. More than not, we went back unsatisfied, disturbed, but perhaps relieved, when the news story turned out to be about another conflict, elsewhere. On those very rare occasions when there was something reported about us, we drank it in with great thirst, however brief or uninformative the piece. How little anyone seemed to know or care.

The other news, equally rare, which arrived by post and was written in a script only a few of us could read, this news was always potent, filled with too much information. We wanted and did not want to know. Each letter, each audio recording, added to the tally we all kept within us: bodies, limbs, homes, livelihoods. On these occasions, Father was reluctant to gather us around. If he did, we knew that he censored as he read. He passed along the love from the uncle or the aunt who included all of us in their letters, with terms of endearment specific to each girl. And the love was always palpable, visible, even in that other script that was indecipherable to my eyes. As the years went on, I wondered how it was they remembered us at all. And as the years went on, it became more and more difficult for me to remember them. I did not want to know about them, about their lives. Did not want to hold their lives up against my own. A n d   y e t   I   w o u l d .

A g a i n   a n d   a g a i n .
It's a strange connection, blood. It delivers the news using its own
channels and it demands a gentle regard. And so I tallied and noted.

sleep—the forgetter

By day, the giver bestowed on the other sisters all that she earned for herself. After she dusted shelves and vacuumed rugs in the living room, she called in the others to play again, to make a mess again of the space she had put in order. She made a game of all she did with and for the younger girls. With cardboard, crayons, and a single nail, she fashioned a wheel, her own wheel of small fortunes, which she held in midair and which the girls spun with delight, landing on: one dollar or five, a bag of potato chips, a one week's holiday-from-dishwashing, a bottle of nail polish. In a separate game, called *prisoner*, she locked the younger girls, joyful, in the garage to let them play *magician* or *mother*, while she ran back into the house to finish for them the chores they'd put off, scrubbing sink, tub, and toilet in the bathroom, washing plates, cups, and pots in the kitchen, raking leaves into small mountains on the front lawn. Between chores, she stopped to fix them an afternoon snack of french fries and soda or cake and tea, which she slid through the tall gap beneath the garage door. And the younger sisters who stood on the other side of the locked door could not see the giving sister's smile but knew it was there despite the sternness in the prison guard's voice.

The giving sister gave daily and nobly. She gave of things great and small, never complained, nor cried, nor demanded anything in return. Tirelessly: she pushed the others on the swing; amused them with jokes, with the latest music; shared with them her clothes, too large, her friends, much older. She saved money only to spend it again on them; she put off her own homework to bring them soup or extra pillows when they were ill. When she had nothing else left to share, she presented her smile: the too-large two front teeth, the single dimple in her left cheek, the squinting watery eyes. And in exchange for her daily giving, she slept each night the sleep-of-forgetting, undoing by night what had been done by day, unknowing each morning what had been learned the evening prior.

This was no accident or grievous twist of fate. The sister who would give was not by coincidence the same who would forget. It was the war that had orchestrated it. In the first land, the war had unraveled her childhood, taking from her what she wouldn't have given freely, and turning the native act of gathering memory into something unnatural, perverse. The war entered suddenly her child's eye and, while others looked away, she took in: the too-perfect lining up of clear-eyed soldiers in brown uniforms along the sidewalks of her then-neighborhood; the winding of enormous, unseeing tanks through its too-narrow streets, and later the blood that ran down those streets; the falling of stars not from the cosmos; the felling of trees and cornfields; the folding of women's hands to hide missing fingernails; the folding of men's heads to shelter shattered pride; the biting of tongues lest too much be said; the perking of ears lest anything be missed; the going gray of heads; the turning putrid of mouths; the taking off of limbs; the magical vanishing of grocers and taxi drivers. Her eyes ached. The parched earth, the arid climate, the dusty streets, the ruthless doings of strangers and friends alike, took their toll on the gaping eyes that would not shut, leaving them desiccated. And so one day in that former life, the sister who would not look away lingered behind the others after school to walk home at leisure, to take a side street, to stop before the washerwoman's gate and offer that old woman her cheek in exchange for the gift of daily forgetting. And the laundress who had once used all of her charms, so often in vain, to coax children to her gate with sweets and toys, to enchant them with her honeyed voice in order to steal their dreams, now labored beneath the weight of her two jobs—that of neighborhood laundress and that of capturer of children's visions—as day after day the children came, now of their own accord, faded and unblinking to offer her their nightmares. With one waterlogged hand, the old woman balanced the basket of wash on her hip, and with the other, raised the girl's chin, to stare into the dry pools that were her eyes, to steal from the child her nightly and her daily visions, and then in exchange, to plant on her cheek the kiss of forgetting. So thenceforth, the sister who would give away her memories and her visions would also give freely, selflessly of all else, forgetting not only the first land's dust and the old violence, but also herself, her own needs, her own wishes. Daily in the new land, she gave of her time, her patience and care, her abilities and humor, and her few found and earned possessions to those around her. And whether engaged in the act of giving or the act of sleeping, the sister wore a smile. Her eyes, which had once owned then lost luster, now held pools of water forever on the verge of overflowing.

While the dreamer, that other great basin of brine, sleeping in the first bedroom, cut down bramble and vine with her glass axe to find a way into the heart of the forest where the jewelmouth giant lived, the sister who would forget slept a breathless sleep. In the second bedroom, the second sister lay immobile, unknowing, in the bed that was not a bunk bed. Above her, the window that would not shut let in the night air: a constant and soft sigh, a cool pressure across the girl's cheek. Carried in on this current: a cat's cry or the screech of tires or the scent of geraniums. Carried away: her burdens and memories, her dreams and her nightmares.

the twin stars

And so fortune-misfortune, circling about one another across the cosmos, smiled upon this family.

Father, ill

Father is healthy, always moving, making, doing: productive. In body, he is at once the farmer, sinewy and strong, and the engineer, precise and mechanical. The two reside in his small frame, which never pauses, is never idle, always efficient. And Father is sick but the single time. He falls ill after receiving the rare and precious communication from the first country. This time, it is not a telephone ring in the late hours of the night, stark and demanding, but a package, quiet and humble, left in the mailbox by the mailman in the bright middle of the day. It is a small parcel containing an audio cassette, a recording made by Father's sister, who does not read or write, who tends a farm, looks after chickens, goats, and sheep, plants seeds and harvests vegetables and fruits, bakes bread and cures meat, and lives in a small village many hours from an official post office. She speaks to him through the cassette player he keeps on his desk in his office in the garage. Speaks in the familiar sister voice, loving and soft, but still audible through the crackle of machine and distance. Her words unwind slowly with the spools of narrow tape. She blesses him, sends her love and blessings to his wife, to his five girls, and she tells him of the poor state of their crops, of unsold cotton and mildewed beets. Then faltering, crying, Father's sister tells him about her most recent loss, her third child, and her last child of five dead in a handful of years, this son cut in two, cleanly. This is not her first recording, and she does not want to deliver more such news, yet she must; she does not know when and if she will see her brother again: the war rumbles on. Her soft familiar voice, the telling, and the listening make Father ill. He remains in his garage-office through dinner, through tea, then makes his way directly to his bedroom. He calls his girls to him, calls them away from the television, from the women modeling evening gowns in the beauty pageant. He asks Mother to bring them to his bedside where he lies beneath the covers, shrunken, desperate. And Father, who does not cry, who speaks few words, tells them each he loves them, chokes and whimpers as he blesses them, speaks to his daughters as if for the final time, then turns and disappears beneath the blankets. Mother sends the girls back to the television, to their books, and does not question Father the next morning when he rises at the usual hour to dress, and to leave for work on time.

suit

He is young. He wears a suit. Is proud to do so. He walks the village roads proudly to the main street where he is employed at the repair shop to fix radios, clocks, and watches. He is a farmer's son but keeps his forearms level, his elbows against his ribs, and his shoulders drawn back and down, even when he is bent over his work. His wrists are agile and steady. His fingers are adept at turning screws, uncoiling springs, connecting wires, and adjusting gears, tubes, circuits, wheels, and weights. His eyes are sharp,

and made sharper by the loupe he keeps in his pocket. His ears
pick up sounds faint and sounds amiss in the broken instruments
before him. He understands gravity and temperature and works
his materials accordingly to achieve precision. He loves accuracy
and dresses smartly. But what is fashionable in the city is not
appropriate in the village. Moreover, in wartime, propriety resides
more with power than with custom. The men who have appeared
recently to oversee village affairs tell him it is indecent to wear a
suit, to emulate the ways of the godless enemy who occupy the
cities and infect the people. The dress suit he wears is not new, was
purchased from a friend in a neighboring town, and fits tightly
across his shoulders. His neckties were cut and sewn by his mother,
who used the spare scraps of fabric to finish a quilt for her grand-
daughter. And the village leaders, the new men of god who have
recently appeared, warn him a second time about his dress. But
he is young and cheerful and proudly walks the same village roads
to and from work that they sternly walk to keep order and keep
an eye on the prideful. Coming home in the evening, the repairman is stopped by two men and knocked to the ground onto his
hands and knees to be made an example of. The first man turns
and cinches the fallen man's tie around his neck and uses it and his
own knee braced between the repairman's shoulder blades to keep
his clean-shaven head steady. The one wielding the sword lifts his
arms high above his head and relies on the strength and heft of
those arms to bring the blade down swiftly, to cut the young man's
head off cleanly with a single blow. They know where he lives and
know his family; they drag his body over the dusty earth and drop
it in middle of the road in front of his house. They toss his head
over the wall, into the courtyard where his mother, rising early, will
feed the chickens and bake the morning bread.

loss

And Mother says, It is not that they have passed, but that their
simple innocent lives were *taken*, senselessly. The legacy they leave
is one of futility, of nothing where there should have been *something*, of a small void where a modest life might have been lived
fully. A small void left by an insensate war that suctioned each life
up as a vacuum suctions up dust. If you hold up to the sky the
fabric that was once our land, Mother says, you will see these apertures and you will know that our dead dot our land as the stars dot
the sky: endlessly, mutely.

O.   The   character   that   is   and   is   not.

O.   The   form   that   is   both   letter   and   number,
and must be, for the duty it performs is one in the two
lands, and is vital to both language and mathematics.

O. The only form. The single One. The one that encompasses all others.
It   harbors   nothing   and   all,   simultaneously.
It   calls   and   it   hears.
It   is   blind   and   observes   perfectly.

O. It is the wail. The eardrum. The lens. The bullet hole.
It   is   the   opening.   The   first   and   the   ultimate   one.

O. The great Open. Ocean. See it. It goes on and on and on.
And   its   depths!   What   dazzling   creatures   reside   there.
Hear   it.   It   calls.   O,   Oh!,   oh...
And   the   stories   therein...

Once   upon   a   time,
there was a family: a mother, a father, five girls, a cat, a tree.
Nearby were neighbors and grocers and friends, guests and ghosts,
soldiers with rifles and peddlers of melons, drivers of school
buses, of taxis, of tanks and bound bodies, teachers and butchers
of cows, of women and children, launderers of dreams, of uniforms, of news, hairdressers and deliverymen, fixers and farmers.

No,   there   are   not   so   many   characters.   I   have
strayed   again.   There   is   the   single   ONE.
Do not all books contain the single character and use their many
pages like mirrors to reflect and divide her so that she is at once

whole *and* all of her many parts, so that you see her simultaneously from all sides, front and back, afore and after, from above
and below, within and without? And is a book itself not a mirror?
My dearest reader, be still a moment. Focus. Look intently.
W h o   l o o k s   b a c k   a t   y o u ?

unsleep—the somnambulist

The house, always a different house in a new neighborhood, never had more than three bedrooms. The five sisters shared two between them. The first room, with two twin beds, lodged two sisters, while the second room, with a twin and a bunk, took in three but not always the same three so that the legs that climbed the ladder to the top bunk were not always the same pair that climbed down in the morning. In some seasons, in the second bedroom, in the upper bunk, beneath a hand-colored picture of a seascape, lay the somnambulist. She, like the dreamer, searched, but only at night and not in the dream realm. To prepare for bed, she followed all of the customary rituals of face-washing, hair-combing, teeth-brushing. In fact, she was more fastidious than the other sisters, picking up all of her toys and organizing her books and pens before settling in for the night. She always changed out of her day clothes and into her nightgown and never forgot to kiss Mother and Father goodnight as the others too often did. When she climbed up the ladder to her top bunk and slid beneath her neatly tucked linens, she did so with ceremony, as if climbing into a carriage, as if displeased with the state of the disordered room beneath her, as if only too eager to escape that unenlightened province.

Unlike the insomniac lying awake in the first bedroom, the sleep-walker did in fact fall asleep once she crossed her arms over her chest and dropped her heavy lids over her tired, day-filled eyes. After two or three hours, these same lids, now weightless and unburdened, lifted again, and the eyes that stared out reflected lights that did not originate in the dark room. The sister who'd climbed up to the top bunk climbed down again, with as much ceremony, using the same diminutive, tight, and pretty movements as before. And now, she smiled and bowed; she raised the hem of her sleeping gown with the tips of her fingers; she glided across the bedroom and through the door, mostly in silence, but sometimes with a giggle or a verve of step that softly filled the quiet house in the midmost hours of the night. And the sister who could not sleep, taking these sounds for ones in her own mind, incorporated them into her own schoolyard reveries, unaware that another moved and shifted within the house.

The somnambulist searched nightly. She had left her birth country too young to remember faces, names, or places, or to tell stories of that former life to her now-friends by day; her memories were half-formed and unfamiliar, not her own. Unsure, she let them go and lived in the now-world, unconvinced that there ever had been another country, a former life, a host of relatives, endless mountains, a time when she ran freely and giddily like a child. And what was she now, small limbs and teeth forever coming in, bangs forever in her eyes? But at night, the need to fashion whole memories out of fragments half-woke her. What made her unsure and awkward by day gave her poise and purpose at night. The house, which was her home by day, became her empire at night and she walked through it as one sure of her mission in life. She walked about the house opening and shutting doors, lids, drawers, or envelopes in search of the missing halves of things. She was and was not dreaming. She fell into the space between the two states and, half awake, she moved through a silent house and a lonely world, part queen, part child.

In the kitchen, she opened the door to the refrigerator and delicately pulled out a weighty plastic bag. Taking the bag to the living room, she sat on the edge of Mother's flowerpot, crossing one leg

over the other, prettily undoing the mouth of the bag to take and
eat from it slices of cold wheat bread: the bread limp in her hand,
her pinky finger poised in midair. She knew bread and knew its
dense, chewy texture, its sweet, earthy flavor, its warmth, feel, and
color, but could not find it in the bag she held, though she chewed
through half a dozen slices. Unsatisfied but full, she placed the
near-empty bag inside the washing machine. This sister searched
for scents as she did for flavors, removing the cap from a tube of
toothpaste to sniff and sniff and not find the scent of the spring
flowers that refused to bloom in her night-world. She searched for
the owners of voices lodged in the broom closet. She opened and
shut her mouth to form the same words or names that fell from
Mother's lips so easily, but no sound left her own. She held the
partial memories in her arms like the many limbs of broken dolls,
but unable to find their missing pieces, she dropped them one by
one even as she searched for memories: for the sunny afternoon
in the green hills in that photograph that held her likeness but
not her memory; for the voices and faces of the many relatives
she heard tales of from Mother and the older sisters; for the dress
which they told her had been her favorite for far too long and
which, in the hurry to leave the country, had been left behind.

She searched and came up with nothing but continued night after
night to open and close, and open again the drawers, the bottles,
the boxes that promised her their secrets and pledged to help her
solve her many mysteries. She opened cupboards and brought out
Mother's china, one plate, one cup at a time to set a table in the
dining room for twelve. And she sat at the head of the table and
ate warm food from empty plates with half-formed guests, who,
missing lips, tongues and teeth, could not partake of the meal she
set before them, nor laugh at the jokes she told with so much spirit.

On one occasion, the somnambulist donned a coat and boots and marched over to the hallway closet as though marching through a snowstorm to the outhouse and, once inside the closet, pulled down her underwear to pee in Father's work shoes. On another night, she mistook the toilet for the trunk of a car and, opening its lid, dropped in a ball and a tennis racket, in preparation for a picnic with cousins and friends who never arrived or came nameless and faceless or with missing appendages, unable to catch the balls she threw or to smile for the camera that refused to take pictures of her play. Then sometimes in her search and in her play, the sleepwalker, opening a window, let in a music that was not hers and which she couldn't even half-place because it traveled from so long ago. Yet somehow she knew the lyrics to the song, though it was sung in the first tongue and in the language of the poets, poets long gone, tilled under and asleep. And sitting by the window in the middle hours of the night, with wistful eyes, which reflected a distant blue sky and another sun, she sang out with her child-voice the lyrics to songs long forgotten by everyone but Mother. On these nights, Mother woke but did not rise or wake Father. She listened, with heart and lungs stilled, to her daughter's unfaltering voice and felt the same sunlight on her skin, watched the same clouds cross the same blue sky and remembered her own childhood, its very scents, textures, and colors replete and palpable.

outside, the wind

Outside, a wind, moving from sea to mountain through the slumbering valley, rustles the leaves of the grandfather tree and he, as

if aware, awake, respiring, releases his most restless leaves into
the neighbor's yard, where they spiral into a small mound against
the sleeping dog's side. The recently watered lawn now passes
its moisture to the driving, parched air. The sky above, cloudless
and moonless, casts shadows of trees, telephone poles, and power
lines across lawn and roof with the light of the stars alone, and
summer's unripe grapes, hanging beneath the shadowy arbor,
like many dull eyes, watch the living scene. Across the street, the
wind/unwind of a tetherball around its pole attracts a dozen of
the neighborhood's cats, who, sitting around the base of the pole,
follow the swinging yellow orb with the untired, unblinking eyes of
the nocturnal.

policeman

The land is arid. Though many rivers lace through it, and the
peaks of its mountains are winterlong covered in snow, it is an
arid land. The young policeman is not on duty but he is called
into service. He leaves home at dawn and travels for two days
in the bed of a truck with the military men and the engineers.
Their caravan is long and winds through the mountains and
rumbles through the desert. They travel away from the city and
travel morning to night with the sun. At dusk on the second day,
the caravan stops, and the military men, the policemen, and the
engineers step down from the beds of the uncovered trucks. The
young policeman is handed a shovel and follows the military men,
who follow the three engineers, who follow the two senior officers.
They work by the beam of the trucks' headlights; the policeman

lowers his cap to cover his eyes. He wraps a handkerchief over his nose, his mouth; the trucks' lights are strong and thick with the earth's rising dust. The sky above is thick with a band of stars that the working men cannot see. They use shovels and picks to dig the great pit and are relieved to see the headlights and hear the engines of the construction vehicles start up across from them. It is a large pit: it takes the three hundred men and the twelve excavating vehicles seven hours to dig it to the depths and dimensions dictated by the engineers and the officials who've tallied all but make adjustments still by the trucks' bright beams. In the middle hours of the night, the policemen and the military men are given orders to unload the cargo trucks and to line up the prisoners who, bound at the wrists and ankles and blinded by the light in the desert, need the aid of the working men to walk to the pit's edge. And the cavity fills quickly along its four sides. And the policeman is ordered to jump in, to drag, roll, pile, and evenly distribute the bound men's bodies, which writhe and coil in the dark, dusty cavity. He and the other contractors work until the sun's rising. He rests with them against the truck's tires, drinks from the thermos that is passed down, and, in the pale light of the early morning, watches the working vehicles spread and flatten the desert earth again. And the vehicles' engines do not dampen the voices of the buried men. And the policeman imagines he hears his own name called and called again through the earth. And he tells himself it is not so, *the desert does not speak, its earth is level, has always been so, and the sun has risen to prove it, this is what I believe.* He sits silent, immobile against the truck's tire. But later, at home, in his dream, he does move, breathe, blink, put down the thermos, get on all fours, and crawl to the place where the earth speaks in a thousand voices. His wife wakes him, yet he returns to the dream. He rises for work, and at the end of the day returns to the dream. His hair grays, his shoulders stoop, his children grow and wed, and he heeds the voices and crawls to the pit in his dream.

immovable

And the letters of the alphabet, the movable type—immovable in their mission—combine and recombine, turn and click, circle and search untiringly after meaning, after sense.

before, so

And Father, squatting, swaying, harvesting leek and basil in the garden at dusk for Mother's dinner, says:
Before the war, life was simple.
The earth was giving, it was bountiful.
The farm produced beets and melons, corn and cotton.
We carried the beets in two hands, they were as large as our heads.
Watermelons ballooned before our eyes, until the earth cratered under their weight, until they split.
Before the curse, life was sweet. It was simple.
Before the curse, life was simple and blessed.
The sky was blessed; it poured rain.
The earth was blessed; it produced bounties.
Our lives were blessed, simple, before the war.

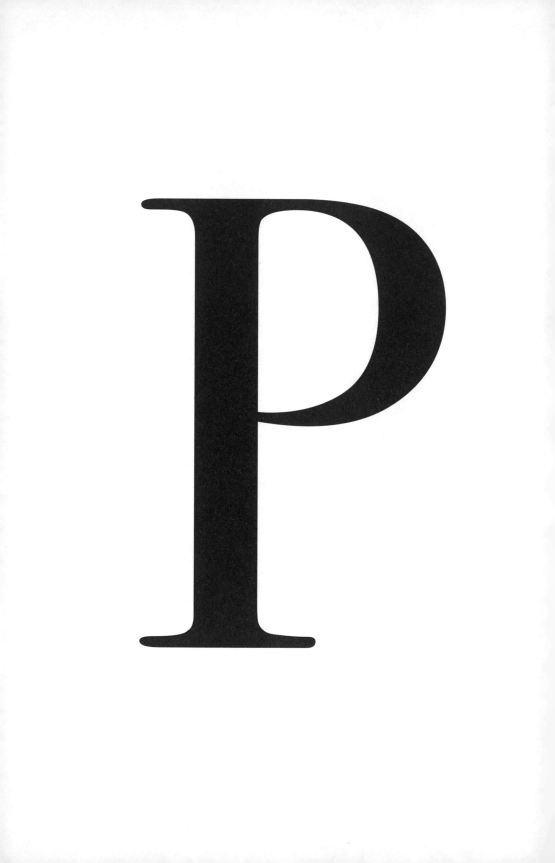

Plants, the great chroniclers of human history. They gather our annals diligently with root and leaf, store them in rings, blades, flower, and fruit, and pass them on, without review or censure, neatly packaged in seed and pollen. The voiceless, immobile plants see without eyes, listen without ears, speak without tongues, and travel far and wide without feet. The upright tulip, the papery poppy, and the tart crisp apple, like silent ambassadors of their native land, spread the history of that deep ancient land across the globe. And who is not transported in their presence? Whosoever reads the chronicles of the planet's flora, backward from the present, will discover the old places, witness the early events, and glimpse answers to the many questions. The farmer's practicality and good sense, the king's ardent desire for riches and novelties, the investigations of the meddling scientist with his thin blade, the blunders of the explorer on his great ship, and the lover's fondness for expression are all collected in the earth's vegetable libraries. Read the flora, and you will know the history of the roads and the trades, the wars and the famines. Hold the firm ripe fruit in your fist and sense the voyager's lust, the conqueror's appetite. Gaze long into the center of a flower and you may come to know the suffering and the ecstacy, and spontaneously recite the poetry, of lovers and saints. And all this the photosynthetic historians accomplish without aim or intention; they simply occupy the same space in the same time with the human species. But every so often, the garden rose, having listened much to, and lived long with, the one who tends it, picks up the ways of its caretaker, and having come to understand her needs, it desires to return the tenderness the little gardener has always shown it. Knowing that history alone will not sate her, the blossom speaks back to its caretaker in her own tongue. Listen, the rose says, I remember your people. Let me tell you a story.

sleep—the image-maker

She was not shy, not proud. If she wished it, she could have asked openly and outright: "and what happened next," or "who was she to us" or "but where was Father that day?" Instead, she, who was the youngest, listened and took in all of their words, watched her many sisters and mimicked their many faces and guises, their dress and their walk. She had questions, she yearned to know and to grasp, but she held back, afraid to give herself away, afraid that in their eyes and in her own she would become superfluous, an unnecessary cog in the story-making machine that was her family. It was common for them to say to her: "but you were only a baby" or "it was before your time" or "how you used to cry in Mother's arms." She knew she was of them and had touched, if not with the soles of her feet, then with the palms of her hands and her soft knees, that other land; had taken in the perfume and smoke of that previous life with nostrils that were her own; had tasted the honey and dust with her moving, though still inarticulate, tongue. By day, she watched and gathered, absorbed all that was theirs because, by birthright, it was hers too. She did this not with greed or envy but with care, cutting out one image at a time, one phrase, one sound, placing it in this pile or that, to tell this or that story, in a style befitting each, and marking them with labels: in-the-be-ginning, good, fearsome, brave, happy, the-end. She was watchful for their memories muted and memories vivid, their tales true and imaginary, their many emotions hidden or volatile, and nightly stitched every emotion, memory, and word into a moving-picture reel that was all her own.

The family-machine that roared by day reached a pitch before the evening meal as Mother and the older girls set to, to prepare the night's dishes. And she, the youngest: was not trusted with a knife; did not know the difference between a pitcher and a bottle; could not help it if her hands were too small to carry a platter of hot baked rice from the kitchen to the table; could not help it if the plates, the cups were stored in cabinets beyond her reach. But she chased the cat out of the kitchen, swatted away the flies that landed then landed again on the same fork, and when all was ready, she ran out to call Father in from the garage. The whir that moved above her head and within her chest settled after the sun did, after the evening meal was eaten, dishes were washed, and books shut for the night. It was the brewing of tea, the pouring of tea, the intermittent nibbling of sweets, and the mesmeric sip-ping of bottomless cups of tea that settled all and invited the cat back into the house. Then the four older sisters, tired and undone, withdrew into one bedroom or the other. But she, the youngest, remained and turned her face to Mother, that warm sun, who at night, after a long day's toil, after Father and the older girls had gone to bed, emitted a warm glow, cast her light, now soft, on all that surrounded her, on coffee table and couch cushions, on lamp-shade and wall. In this light and by the blue light of the television set, the sister who would go to bed late stayed up to watch old films with Mother. Spellbound, she took in the songs, the dance, the dramatic sighs and glances, the swordplay and the airplane crashes. She did not look away when arms were severed or blood ran down a flight of stairs or vampires bared pointed teeth. She took this in as she did all else; she was no younger than any of the others. It was here she daily came into her own, in Mother's company, sharing Mother's love for the form that would open and close worlds entire in the space of two hours.

Later, long after the mechanical sounds of her family's doings and undoings had quieted, and even Mother's light had diminished, she made her small way to her bunk bed, content that she had not missed a thing and had recorded all, but not ready yet to leave the world of the movies. Though she slept warm, she drew the covers over her head and drew down her eyelids. Onto that soft, dark curtain she projected the day's various articles of interest and fell asleep to the soft whir of her own movie-machine: here was a face, still and nameless, yet vivid and familiar, cut out from a hand-tinted photograph found in the family's photo album; and here Old Man Thunder, who plucked reckless red-garbed children from the city's streets and carried them away into storm clouds—her older sisters had witnessed many an abduction and disappearance of children into the dark, rumbling, slow-moving thunderclouds in the first country; on their heels, Father, with long hair and a single earring in his right ear, riding on the back of a giant and ferocious bear through furrowed fields of rubies on golden stalks; next on the screen, a mountain pass forever covered in snow and in danger of avalanche—this she'd collected from Mother's own lips, from the oft-repeated story of their red car stopped at the snow-blocked mouth of the forty-mile-long tunnel; and at the other end of the tunnel: a tall green glass filled with a wintertime treat of snow, milk, and sugar from the first life, which the eldest sister had tried and tried again to recreate, with little success, in the land of the sun, using refrigerator ice and a dull pick.

In her sleep, the sister who would cast shadows brought together image and sound in order to give new life to an inaccessible past, in order to give gesture to the static limbs, and expression to the fixed gazes, she'd memorized in the family's photographs. She switched out the hero of one tale for another, added flowers where before there was only a wasteland, gathering tulips from here, pushing them down there, no matter the dryness of the earth, no matter the sun hidden behind a dark smoke. She recalled stories of their uncle's farm: if cotton grew there, why not here, along the fence; if cows and roosters roamed freely there, why not here alongside the cat, up and down the sidewalk? In this way, she built a world of mismatched faces and voices, memories and facts. In her world, the war too needed a face, a voice, and a reason. War was a red, scaly, many-horned, sixty-foot-tall creature. In search of home, abandoned and hungry, it walked and shook the earth with its angry roar and step, knocking over power lines, flattening cars and playgrounds, devouring people and trees as it went, unaware of its size or its power. In her cinema world, it was not the vampire alone who hid by day and roamed by night in search of fresh blood; she'd heard of others in the tales Mother whispered to guests or the older sisters, and she placed those villains here now, where she knew they belonged. Here, her sisters were the heroines who quenched War's thirst with snowy milkshakes or pierced the vampire's heart with hammer and nails from Father's toolbox. In this world of cast shadows, the warm, smiling woman standing next to Mother in the old photograph, with headscarf and flowing, rose-covered skirts became the school lunch lady who filled her plate with sweets alone. In her world of shadow play, cities went up and went down, heroes appeared and disappeared, goats took flight on immense diaphanous wings, stars circled around Mother's head as she gathered her children around her, holding them to her trunk with her many leafy limbs while Father, now a small bird, sang to them the old folk songs as he flew overhead, and her sisters changed form continuously, shifting from rocking horse to swordsman, from airplane pilot to whale. And she herself sat back in the audience, directing even as she winced or laughed, answering for herself the questions she would not ask the others by day: "and what happened next," or "who was she to us" or "but where was Father that day?"

revolution

Outside, the air is still and the sky clear. The sister who swings by night lets her head loll back and with her bare feet touches alternately the dewy grass and the tree's tender leaves. The sturdy limb of the great tree bobs but does not creak. The neighbors turn in their beds. The sister who has wiped the kitchen counters, swept the floor, washed and dried the last dish, steps outside and leans against the laundry room door to take in the cool air. And though it is still below, the stars above are turbulent. There are two sisters and two cats in the garden tonight. The cat, the one newly arrived, is introducing itself; it rubs itself against the tired sister's calves, turns, steps over her feet, then pushes into her ankles, her calves again. The other, the one departing, leaves its hiding place beneath the rosebushes and, with something small and still-stirring clamped between its jaws, the cat lifts into the sky. Drawing crumbs of soil and a stream of crushed rose petals in its wake, it rises above rooftops and telephone wires, glides over trees broad and trees slender. High above the sisters' heads, the cat sails gracefully through the windy stars.

Mother, ill

And Mother, strong like a mountain, is underneath ill. The sisters have heard her tell of her five pregnancies. Of how she carried on, while she carried, until the last moment: uncomplaining, preparing throughout, and at every moment primed. And in those last moments in the house, after she had swept the floors, ironed Father's suit, curled her own hair, packed a suitcase, cooked a feast, fed the guests, and set out their tea, she snuck out with Father to the hospital to deliver a daughter. She labored, silently and cooly, for minutes or hours or days, and each time returned home with her hair pinned smooth and high, her eyes outlined and her cheeks rouged, holding in her arms a glowing baby neatly wrapped, not crying.

So in the new land, Mother continues to bear her pain unde-
tected until the last moment, and the girls come home from school
in the afternoon to find her absent and Father fussing over the
small things—the running of the house, the cooking of dinner,
the how-to's and how-so's, which the girls understand better than
he, who knows garage and garden but not house or kitchen. But
they let him run on in place of Mother, see him try to exhaust his
frantic worry through his lists and his instructions, and see him to
the door, then to the car to return to the hospital to speak to the
nurses, the doctors.

And Mother's internal mechanics falter, one after another each
year. She is young, tall, and strong, but within, she falters. And the
doctors chase the illnesses from one anatomical system to another,
removing, adjusting, and adding as they go, prescribing the many

medications and suggesting the rest that she cannot and will not take. Mother herself does not guess that what ails her is the loss of life elsewhere. Her internal landscape of bones, organs, blood, and tissue is connected still to her birthplace. And war rages and pillages in both lands. Mother loses a nephew and simultaneously loses her gallbladder. When her cousin, raised from birth alongside her—suckled alongside her on her mother's other breast, on long winter nights enchanted alongside her by the same fairy tales and family legends, nightly set down to sleep and dream alongside her beneath the same quilt—is gunned down in front of her young children, Mother clutches at her heart, which clenches and sputters inside her. Her niece's young husband is taken alive and shortly after returned dead, so Mother miscarries. Her first brother is taken and tortured and she tries to shelter and keep him, as a mountain shelters its gemstones, painfully, within her kidneys. Her stifled moans wake and collect the girls about her bed in the middle hours of the night. They become accustomed to seeing their mother stand tall by day and bent over with pain on the edge of her bed at night. Her glands and her feet swell and shrink; her blood rages like fire or it courses like honey; her heart pauses and starts again; her bones splinter; her nerves pinch; her lungs spasm. And she does not allow anyone to see this, not by day, and not by choice in the single-lamp-lit hours of the night. She is strong and denies the war, its heat, its hunger. She has five small girls to care for, a husband whose life she has barely escaped with, and siblings trapped in the first land who look to her as to morning's first light, as a singular hope in a distant sky. Mother is not ill, will not say she is ill; her surfaces are still, they are solid.

Perhaps the doctors do not know what they look for when they chase the pains and diseases inside Mother. Perhaps the true cause of Mother's ailments is the piece of lead she accidentally swallowed when she was a little girl. Mother scolds her daughters when she finds them lost in thought, over their books, chewing on their pencils. It was the same daydreaming rumination at her own school desk that caused Mother-the-girl to snap the point of her pencil with her busy teeth and inadvertently swallow the sharp lead. She had felt its tip, like a minuscule scalpel, score the back of her throat as she swallowed. Perhaps it is this piece of pencil lead that has traveled through her, nicking veins and arteries, slicing organs, severing nerves, and, over the years, writing a tale of terror within her steady frame.

loss

Father says,
This is life.
This coming, this going.
We are born, we die.

the lodger

The neighborhood, empty for three years, has filled again in recent weeks, house by house, with its former residents. But the families returning find they are not the sole inhabitants of the streets and the homes that were pillaged, occupied, then deserted as the war rolled on. There are others who dwell here now, who have nowhere to go, who cannot be turned out. And this house, near the base of the hill, is no different from the ones farther up; it hosts its own lodger. He visits nightly. Though this is not his birth-house or the land of his forebears, he comes through nightly.

They found his body in the next-door neighbor's well. They pulled him out, still fresh, only a few weeks dead, a young man of eighteen or twenty, dressed in cotton shirt and trousers, wool vest, leather sandals on his swollen feet. He comes through nightly, enters and leaves the same room at the back end of the house. Through an interior wall, he enters the room where the young woman sleeps, exits through the large window overlooking the yard, the grape arbor.

No one recognized him; he was not one of theirs. They buried him on a hillside nearby, with others, one body to one grave, graves marked with small green flags on poles of various heights. And across the city, strips of green fabric dot the hillsides, fluttering, prayers written across them, marking the graves of the numerous, nameless dead. He was not one of theirs; they'd only just returned. He enters and exits nightly. Leaves through the glass, stops to look back at the house, its living, dreaming inhabitants, then continues on into the arbor, where the ripening grapes hang, swollen. He has no voice, he speaks through her, the young woman who has returned to her childhood bedroom. And nightly her people wake her to tell her *it's okay, no one hurts you, no one holds you down or under, the guests will wonder at your vile cursing, your kicking, you are a young woman, what will your future husband say?*

outside, the moon

Outside, the moon, like an egg's yolk, full and golden, threatens to break its diaphanous membrane and run down over the hills, flow into the hushed valley.

Questions. And there were many in the sisters' minds. They flitted about, burrowed and rummaged, rang and knocked, and were mainly left unanswered. But the questioning itself was not unfruitful, for it bred new worlds. And what strange, what terrible, what marvelous worlds!

Questions. Yours? How many you have! How little help I am.

sleep—the dreamer

The dreamer's work was never done. She dreamed a hundred dreams each night. She woke up full, unable to ingest anything superfluous—food or drink or words spoken—for she had already feasted and held lengthy conversations, attended conclaves and funerals, chased monsters and saved children. Yet she woke up alert and ready for the long day's work. While the others filled the kitchen with their busy bodies, vying for the toaster or a favorite teacup, preparing this or that for breakfast, discussing the coming of things, the dreamer prepared herself for yet another solitary adventure. She tied her shoes with expert and fastidious precision using two knots instead of one per shoe; she rolled up the hems of her pant legs, twice each; tucked in her shirt and rolled up its sleeves to her elbows; turned the watch face so that it might be guided by the sun; and depending on the day of the week, she either plaited her long hair into two braids, one over each shoulder, or tied it into a single ponytail on the right side of her head. Because she was always in two places—in the dream realm and in the day-world—she was simultaneously here and not-here and, therefore, was unable to commit to a full smile. She half-smiled in school pictures, at her sisters across the playground, at the schoolboy over the library book.

At school or on the walk, then the bus ride, to school or back, she took mental notes of all she witnessed or heard: a bee caught in a flower's sticky trap; a silver car moving too fast in a direction perpendicular to her own; her sister's mismatched socks hiding and peeking out alternately, blue, green, blue, green, as the younger girl walked ahead of her; a toothy-grinned boy panting and nodding while he crossed the monkey bars; her teacher staring with eyes crossed out of the classroom window; a dead silvery balloon caught in a small tree's branches, a fly envious of her sandwich. She looked for clues everywhere, collected them and, one after another, registered them in the catalogs, and placed them upon the shelves, of that place in her mind that was her memory library. She could not help but tinker with the articles she collected before recording and placing them, turning the popped balloon into a mechanical bird, lost and trapped in a world that was not its own, or seeing, through toy binoculars, a fire-breathing dragon miles up in the sky where there was a glimmering dragonfly in the air a few feet over her head. She gathered clues as one gathers seashells: methodically (turning them over in her hand or in her eye alone), deliberately (she was aware of her duty), and yet unmindfully (she daydreamed even as she collected). She searched for and gathered by day the clues that might make sense of the world around her even as she copied the blackboard or rinsed the dishes or banged on the bathroom door. She collected her articles—those pure and those tinkered-with, those precious and those dull, those clear and those ambiguous in her child's far-reaching mind—and found a place for them, one and all, in her limitless and private memory chamber, knowing that each had worth and would one day contribute to solving the riddle: why are the flower beds colored here, devastated there?

The sister who would dream knew of secret doors and hidden passageways in the backs of closets or at the base of old trees. She was aware of underground tunnels and of the creatures who resided in or traveled through them. She knew that if she climbed high enough into the canopy of the grandfather tree she could converse openly with the tree, the insects who made their home among it leaves, or the small clouds that descended to halfway meet her

there. She worked alone and worked in secret because she had
taken an oath to do so long ago in a dream. She knew that dreams
were neither tidy nor considerate; she knew that often they spilled
out of sleep and over into the day-world just as that world crept
or pushed its way into the space of dreams. It was her job to rec-
oncile the land of dreams and the land of the sun. Where the two
collided, she found additional clues or doorways that furthered her
endless hunt. And because the two continually collided, in darkness and in broad daylight, her work was endless, and she tireless,
or seemingly so, as she stepped from dream into daydream.

She discovered that beneath the vast memory chamber in her
mind lay a vast briny sea (a trapdoor and a narrow spiral staircase
took her from one to the other efficiently) and on the reflecting
surfaces of this sea she saw not only her own face but those of
others, many she knew and recognized, and multitudes she did
not. And because this ocean was immense and had many tributar-
ies feeding its brackish edges, she guessed that the tears that made
up its waters were not her allotment alone. And yet she saw no one
else cry as she did, shamefully and needlessly, at all hours of the
day, evening, and night. Had she made an oath to all the others
who kept their grief in this ocean, to cry on their behalf as well?
While the pain she felt was familiar (when had she not carried it?),
she felt it could not be hers alone. Who else contributed and why
did they not come to take back their share? She could not contain the waters that pushed with unrelenting pressure against the
cavity of her chest, gurgled up the pipes in her throat, and filled
the narrow passages in her skull. She leaked. Huge amounts of
saltwater poured from her eyes and filled her mouth (how well she
knew the taste of brine) with little warning (she was forever ill-pre-
pared) in the cafeteria lunch line, or in the middle of a game of

hide-and-seek with friends or sisters, or over the pages of a book, or deep inside of a dream. Was she a prisoner of this subterranean sea? Did it not seem that her feet were forever soaking at its edges, forever wrinkled and sodden? She needed ten thousand eyes to release the waters of this sea. She hid her tears as best she could: she hid behind doors and sofa cushions, beneath blankets, and in the limbs of trees. On the bus to school, she opened the window, let down her hair, and let it fly freely in the wind, across her face, to hide and to soak up the tears streaming down her cheeks. In the schoolyard, she found a bench beneath a tree or against a wall and settled behind her embroidery hoop or her knitting needles. How familiar she became with the corners of things: of walls, of books, of her hands brought together over her face. And not knowing that the cool spaces of her mind were buoyed, in fact, fed, by the warm waters of her heart, she cursed these waters and the constant leaking that clouded her vision, hindered her work.

The sister who would cry understood only too well the value of, and the danger involved in, dreaming. Though she looked forward to the end of the day, to the coming of night and the world of dreams where she no longer had to work clandestinely or don the guise of a little girl, she could not enter sleep unarmed: she knew what perils lay there. Over time, she had learned that the language of dreams was not the language of the day-world. So the dreamer collected the many and myriad names of her sisters by day to form a new alphabet. By night, she set to tirelessly arranging and rearranging the letters of this alphabet in order to speak in the language of sleep, in order to write her sisters' stories anew in this coded language, in order to fight the demons and marauders of her dreams with these stories. When she drew her eyes closed, the girl who cried at all hours saw that her sisters had yet more names, dressed in yet stranger garb in the other worlds. One night, she saw clearly that the sisters were five and whole and complete as such, like the five fingers of a hand. On a separate night, she witnessed the sisters double, then multiply so that they were now ten, then a hundred, then five thousand, and she knew that still they remained whole and complete, as an oak tree bearing two hundred thousand leaves is whole and complete.

Because movement was in her blood, she found that even in sleep she could not keep still. Though her body lay immobile in bed, she traveled far and wide and met with those familiar and those she did not recognize from dreams or from her day-life. She visited the before-life and saw it as it was and saw it as it was not. She spoke and laughed and ate and sated herself in sleep with loved ones and strangers alike. She ran and was chased by bearded demons with skin red or skin blue, with horns curved or horns hidden, with eyes hungry and eyes clouded. She hid atop buildings, beneath cars, inside dryers, or behind sacks of rice. From her hiding places, she saw others who were not so fortunate as she, and she became used to witnessing the letting of blood, the splattering of blood, the running slow and the running fast of blood, the shallow and the deep pooling of blood. And the dreamer collected what she saw as evidence. And the dreamer used what she collected to save herself time and again. She learned to fly through air as a bird or a kite, or to swim in the skin of a snake through water, or to cast light, brilliant and particulate, as one casts seeds over the earth: by the handfuls; and to raise more light.

Through time and across a thousand and one dreams, the sister who would sleep sensed, and then eventually witnessed, an undercurrent that told a story subtler than her own, and which made her own story small. She saw the living world, as it was at its birth: green, unspoiled, unknown, and unknowing. She witnessed the various manifestations of its inspired youth, let run before her eyes the long, shifting, branching courses that produced its many lineages. She heard its laughter and laughed along. In the acquired dream tongue, she conversed with the many faces of the earth's diverse outcroppings and loved each with a child's easy devotion. Over time, she saw a new face, one open and forward-gazing, and looked on it as into a mirror. She studied the creature's form: upright and bilateral, full of vigor and ability. And in this new offspring's eyes, she recognized joy, awe, and resolve. And in its long, dark shadow she made out the fallen buildings, the deserted streets, the rivers not running, the endless and empty horizon. And here at this place, always here, she woke up with a start, facing the dark corner of her bedroom wall, ashamed again for having soaked her pillow with a brine that could not be hers alone. She cursed the depth of that ocean that kept her tethered night and day. But the dreamscape called her back, promising that down in the depths of the well or within the heart of the shadowy forest or past the sleeping giant lay the key, the answer for all that was irreconcilable by day.

taxicab driver

The taxicab driver brings home a chicken, washed and plucked—this is the city, not the village; he has purchased the chicken from the butcher at the central market. He asks his wife to make a soup, start it early; he will be home before the evening prayer. They

were children together; their families farmed adjacent plots. They
married in the village, came to the city where his uncle lives. He is
independent now, lives with his pregnant wife and baby daughter
in an apartment above a garage. He has worked the many odd
jobs and driven his cab the many hours, early and late, and paid
his uncle back the full value of the taxicab. He keeps it clean, daily
wipes the dust and moisture from its seats, its hood and mirrors,
and pays to park it in the repair shop below his apartment. His
wife makes the soup but the taxicab driver does not return for the
evening prayer or the warm meal.

On the morning of the third day after his disappearance, they
find his cab in front of a government office building. The minister
tells the cab driver's wife and his aunt: he was found out, we know
he was a spy, a criminal, a traitor, do not worry about him, he is
done. The taxi driver's wife listens, unable to say a thing. The man
behind the desk is a minister, a senior government official, he has
found other traitors—musicians, shop owners, professors, bank
clerks—announced their names and crimes on state television; he
has saved the nation many times. The family nod, they rise and
they leave, they are not persuaded.

They search about the city, follow the rumors whispered and the
trails warm, and wait outside the jails with others, hopeful. They
drive out to newly constructed buildings-like-fortresses at the far
edges of the city and morning to night await the release of prisoners, with hundreds of others like themselves, hopeful. The few
prisoners who are released, who tell or do not tell tales of the
goings-on within the walls of the utilitarian buildings, do less to
elucidate the taxi driver's fate to his family than the passing of
days marked on their calendar. And questioning, searching, the

family gather some information, enough. And there is one who is released who tells them: yes, I have seen him, your husband, heard him, *his voice, his feet, shuffling,* he was earnest, *not silent,* pleading, he was marched along, *shuffling, there are places, great pits,* bound, *his feet, they do not bother with bullets or hammers or blades, shoveling, at that stage they do not trouble themselves, I have seen, they fall, I have heard them, falling, the living, they breathe, still, they have fingernails, still, many of them, and voices, still, without tongues some, still, they call, through the earth, they move, they have feet, I know the urge, the urge is great, from the beginning, it is great, the urge to walk, we are human, and underneath, and against the others, too close, the others, neighbors, the urge must travel from the feet, bound, upward, through the torso, to the wrists, bound, to the tips of the fingers, to the nails themselves, claws, the urge to walk releases there, at the end, it is basic, the earth in the gullet, it is basic, it is backward, the earth within, it is too soon, I know, I was with them though I stood without, still, I was there, and I heard him, your son, he was mine too, and I have others, too many and I am young, still, I have a mother, I am her child in two now, below and above, I have feet and fingernails and swallow, cannot stop, do not stop me, I swallow, I was there, below and above, they have not saved me, will my mother know they have not, they employ me, I have feet, fingers, claws, tongue dry, bound to the earth, I cannot return to the sky, I have seen within, the earth is thick, a heavy blanket, the earth, dust, it covers the stars, I heard them, they said they are not dead if the sky is covered so, they said, death comes to those above, who breathe air, see light, in the end, it is the order of things, the earth cannot fashion it, death, as it fashions life in the beginning, it gives, but cannot take, in the end, in the wet gullet, it is not its place, the taking is backward, and some fell so, and others forward and I with them, and still, though I walk, innocent, I am, falling forward, I am, not living and I will not meet my end, it was taken with theirs, with his, he was there, I heard him, your husband, your son, he was there I was with him, he said, in earnest, he said, I am, he said I.* The cab driver's wife returns home to her village to have her second child, a boy. There are no television sets in the village; she does not hear the names of traitors nightly broadcast. She learns, a month later, in a letter from her husband's people in the city, that the name of the same government minister they visited was listed, was read and broadcast, and he taken in. He too was a spy, a conspirator against the new and the beloved state.

speechless

And while the tongue grows thick, lies immobile in the mouth, while the heart pounds impotently against the chest cavity, though the lids drop to switch on the dreamless sleep, the pen labors, it scratches and claws to tell the story that is not the writer's story.

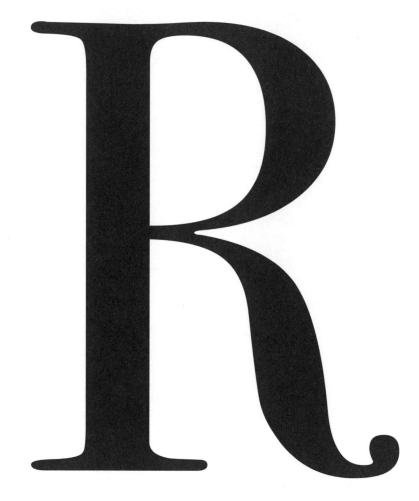

Does the river not return to its source? If you follow it long enough, with a steady gaze, you will see it returns there again. Runs, then returns again. Then runs again. And I find I return to the beginning. Again. Then again. Perhaps the river has misplaced something, as I have, and scours its route over and again in search of what it is missing. It scours and wears a winding and an ever deepening groove into the earth, though it stays nowhere long.

Faithful reader, perchance this is how you now read this book: you return again and again to the beginning for answers, scouring the text, turning the pages, staying no one place long, but ever deepening the furrow in your brow. If you think me unsympathetic, you are mistaken.

released

Father receives the rare bright missive. His close friend and former colleague has been released from prison after suffering years
of torture, hunger, and isolation in the buildings-like-fortresses
constructed by the occupiers in the first land. His name was read
along with Father's by their colleague-under-duress on public television in the beginning days. But Father had just fled the country
and was just out of their reach, long and capable as their reach
was. At the time, his young friend had been married a month
and, despite the war and despite the threats all about, he looked
forward to a joyful and new future in his homeland. He was not
difficult to find; he was at home, with his new wife and his mother
when they came for him. They came for him in the middle of the
day and kept him for eight years. In the beginning, they came for
him daily. Daily, they collected him from his cell, took him to the
windowless interiors of the building to pry him with instruments
and with questions. He had nothing to tell. Few prisoners had
anything truthful to divulge. As the years went on, and as the most
avid of the torturers and prison guards grew tired of their voca-
tions, and themselves chose to leave the country for the brighter
lands, there was a reduction in the physical torment he suffered.
But his spirit diminished continuously and was kept alive only
by a single thought: his wife was waiting for him. And now he is
released and has hastily written Father two lines to share the good
news. Father suppresses a cry as he smoothes out the letter that has
traveled the distances to reach him in the land of the sun.

Though Father writes several letters in response to this one, he
hears nothing back from his friend for another year. When he
does, it is not from the first land, but a neighboring one. He braces

himself for more good news. Here it is, Father's name and address written in the hand he remembers well. And the envelope is dated only two weeks prior. Surely, his friend has removed himself and his wife from danger and left the first, the relentless, land for good. But still, Father turns over and pats the unopened letter, finding it difficult to face its contents, guessing somehow that it contains unwelcome news: the mind-splintering, heartrending news he has become accustomed to receiving and logging and hiding from his daughters. He has learned that good news does not have the endurance to travel such distances so quickly. It is bad news that flies like an arrow.

His friend writes that he has finally left the smoldering land, the well-fed furnace, as he should have many years ago. He writes that he was released into his wife's arms and, though his mother had passed and several family members had left the country while he was in prison, his return to his remaining family was more blissful than anything he had dreamed while locked away. He slept enfolded in the warm, sheltering arms of his still-new bride for two nights and followed her about the house like a devoted dove for two days. On the third day, his sister and brother-in-law invited the couple to their house for a meal. His brother-in-law prepared a lamb to celebrate and bless his release and had set up a grill on the veranda for the occasion. While the released man and his sister cut and dressed the vegetables in the kitchen, his wife carried the marinated lamb to the veranda. She was not gone a moment before the house trembled. Then wheezed. Then sighed. It was the neighbor's house that was hit by the rocket. But something of the rocket, or of the neighbor's house, or of the tree outside, or of the dusty cosmos above, landed on their veranda, on his wife and brother-in-law, killing both of them instantaneously, and soon burying them under inches of soot and debris. Her ears, her eyes, her nostrils, her mouth were filled with the stuff, he writes. I was eight years in prison, and 31 days with my bride.

Father folds the letter, folds it again, runs his fingers over the creases, and stands up to walk to his office in the garage to file the letter away with the others.

the immigrants

And war in one place is like a wound in all. What are walls and borders, disparate tongues and dress, to the free flow of blood? When the throat releases the singular wail in each place wasted by the scourge, do not all ears, everywhere, perk up? Do not all bodies shiver at once?

nocturnal

The sleeping girl, lying on her back in bed, breathes deeply, rhythmically. The purring cat, crouching on the sleeper's chest, careful
not to tickle the sister with its whiskers, holds its nose to the sister's
nose and breathes deeply, eagerly. Every time the sleeper exhales,
the cat draws into its own lungs the scent of the small bird that
lives inside the girl's lungs. Every time she inhales, the bird senses
the crouching cat's sulfurous purr. Its wings flutter against the sister's ribcage and cause the girl to shift to her side in her sleep, and
to dethrone the cat.

the uninvited

The innocent and the persecuted were not the only ones who
crossed the borders on foot, in the beds of trucks, by car, by plane,
through snow, through mud, in the dark, across desert, around
mountain, over limitless expanses of sea to reach safety. So too did
the persecutors, the torturers, and the butchers who infested the government, methodically shot the prisoners lined up, indiscriminately
launched the rockets that killed multitudes of innocents, avidly cut,
bled, and dismembered their own people, buried the dead and the
living in single or mass graves, or left them to the animals and the
elements out of laziness or hubris. These people also emigrated in
search of the quiet life, in search of anonymity in the new land.
They quickly found their countrymen and unabashedly slipped into
their midst as members of the displaced people, attending their
weddings and their funerals, arriving, uninvited or accompanied

by acquaintances and relations, at the homes of the immigrant community's members. And Mother in the new land, knowing well who her guests were, having heard the many stories, old and recent, would have to serve them tea, fill their plates, nod and smile as they praised her dishes and her daughters. And the former torturer would squeeze Mother's shoulder or pat the back of her hand and call her "sister." And the girls, unknowing, thinking, here is an old friend of Mother's newly arrived, would force a smile or a laugh at his poorly delivered jokes, and would pour him another cup of tea or press on him another pastry. And it was so with the former rocket launcher/arms procurer/god's devoted servant. And it was so with the former government official responsible for collecting, imprisoning, and sending to death thousands of innocent city dwellers.

ears, eyes

Yes, I was there. I heard, I saw,
says the book.

engraving

Reader, look about you, at the trees, the grass, the flowers, the bright star overhead, the markers humble and ornate, the limitless sown horizon. Here rest the dead. Here the letters of the alphabet remember them.

once upon a time

Bood, nabood, a taxi driver.

stillness

The sisters did not know stillness. But day in and out it was what they longed for and worked to achieve. When a sister opened a gift, it was this that she looked for inside the box, though a doll or a wristwatch put a smile on her face. When another vacuumed the ancient red rugs on a Saturday morning, it was stillness she tried to gather as she sang in the first tongue. And when an older sister snatched her dress from one younger, it was time she was reprimanding, not her sister. But how were these tender and core years of their childhood not steady? Were not their fixed, gazing pupils backdrop to that ever-burgeoning dusty universe? Did the sisters not enjoy a periodic repose within the walls of their childhood, having fashioned their own timepiece, one separate from and, by design, at variance with the cosmic one, that churning light-con-suming-dark-begetting-life apparatus? While four sisters slept, the one on duty slipped out of bed to unwind the great clock, to hold it to the hour of two—or three, should she have overslept—so that the others might lie motionless a few hours longer. Did they not escape, in those early years, the cosmic eye of the unruly universe through buttressing the four corners of their house with rope and stakes, and with furniture and their own slight bodies, doing all they could to hold down the house that shook and flapped like a tent in a tempest in the wilderness? The careening universe slowed neither for war nor the garden snail, but against it, with it as constant contrast to their lives of play, school, and slumber, did their childhood not take on at least a semblance of stillness?

These, the central years of their childhood, when all sisters lived under one roof, were not steady because their blood roiled at all moments, in sleep and at school, within and without the walls of their home. These were not motionless years because their minds lurched forward one moment and suctioned backward the next, into adulthood and all of its mysteries, its callings, then backward into the womb, that country that had birthed them all and continued to birth others, now joylessly, hidden from the eyes of an incognizant world. They did not know stillness because the warmth of that womb, even the now-war-torn womb, continued to call. They did not know stillness because it called Father and Mother with yet greater insistence and the girls saw it in the adults' faces, read it in their tea leaves. How many cups they emptied each night! What stories written there!

If the universe was unruly, then so was the blood that pulsed in the chambers of their small hearts. And each girl was a universe unto herself, a churning loss-consuming-life-begetting-tenderness system. And did she not fold/unfold like the great spiral galaxy itself? If stillness could be achieved, the sweet-toothed sister might enjoy her daydream even as the popsicle melted down her fore-arm. If stillness could be achieved, two sisters walking side by side to school might hold hands for a long moment before pride broke in to part them. If time lingered, then perhaps some of the photo-graphs in the family's albums might look plausible.

The sisters knew honeysuckle and jasmine, but the scents of these flowers never belonged to them, were always of a different and a distant past, which belonged to Mother's stories, or were locked away in Father's far-off gaze. And these scents, though they wafted in through the living room windows, did not belong to the present because the memory of things weighed more than their experience. The girls knew that the weight of a single memory is greater than the weight of all objects within view in any present moment, yet still they wished for time to linger, for a scent to pass through the nostrils and not through the longing heart alone. Wished for the great dial's mechanism to lock the sun at a definite hour, or to keep the moon's face open. What was stranger still was that these things not belonging to the present somehow but with certainty seemed to await them, as if all the turning away from their past only led to that same distant past in the far-off future. And always the distance! The great and the growing gulf between what had been and what might have been. There was no now because the war might end in the next moment and the family return to what had been steady and knowable in the before. There was no future because that steady and knowable before had long since been consumed by the war. There was no stillness in the present, only a lurching forward and a suctioning back, as if the first life, though a handful of years in length and long vanished, was the only reality for the sisters, and everything else and since was but a long night's dream.

sleep

Shhh . . . close your eyes,
says the book.

laundry

And the girl dreamed that she and her sisters stepped outside and,
in the pale light of the late moon, together hung the corpses of
the dead on a clothesline that traveled from tree to telephone pole,
from one to the other end of the yard. And the dead filled baskets;
and the girls worked steadily. And when they were pinned to the
line, the corpses resembled well-worn garments, in places thread-
bare, in places discolored, and were flat and stiff like laundry
frozen on the line in winter. And the quandary of clothes hanging
on a line outdoors in the dead of winter is something that some
but not all of the girls can remember from their former life. And
the sister dreaming remembers, even in the dream, sucking on the
sleeve or the hem of a frozen garment: she knows well the texture of frosty linen, the flavor of soapy ice melting in her mouth.
And in the dream, the sister wonders and asks, why do we hang
the dead outdoors in winter when they and all around them must
surely freeze? Should we not bring them inside and lay them about
the stove where they and we can keep Mother company while she
cooks the soup that will warm us?

shadow play

Some of the girls remember where Father was raised. In the first
land, the family lived in the city and had to travel through the city,
over the hills, across the desert, up, up, up the side of the colossal
mountain till they reached the clouds—where they stopped to
pack, throw, shape, and eat snow—through the endless dark tunnel, and back down, down, down the colossal mountain, across the
colorful fields, and through the small, whispering forest to get to
their uncle's farm. And they made this trip regularly, and looked
forward to it always. In Father's birthplace, the nights were long
because they were lit by candles, lanterns, the moon, and the stars.
With electricity a full day's travel away, nights came alive, entered
their aunt's small mud home through its door and single window
and called the sisters outdoors.

Indoors and out on the farm, nighttime teemed with shadows
that abducted the girls' imaginations. And the sisters loved the
shadows and the mysteries they promised. The darkness held and
hid the dead ancestors, whom the girls expected any moment
to materialize, dressed in the garb of the old land, speaking in
strange tongues, bearing fantastic sweets and opulent jewels.
The shadows loomed, then sprang suddenly. They swallowed the
farm animals whole—though the goats' eyes always remained, to
hover and float across the courtyard or over the pond—and then
released the animals, changed. The cow transformed into an elephant and stomped into the quince orchard, knocking fruit off of
trembling trees. The hens morphed into kites that floated up and
away into the inky sky. Little demons peaked out of the pond, as
curious about the sisters as the sisters were about the fiendish, shy
creatures who followed the girls with their large eyes, blinked and

blinked, blew the occasional bubble through the soupy water, but refused to answer the sisters' questions and taunts. The intrepid sister entered the peach orchard by herself to spot the elusive sparkling cap of Sheeshak, the tree-witch, whose feet and dark locks dangled beneath the canopy as she hummed and ran her long, curling fingernails through her long, oily hair. The witch, whose glance they were instructed to avoid at all costs, promised those brave enough to speak to her a look into their futures. Darkness on the farm made other promises to the sisters. It promised ripeness, an early and untimely harvest of sweet fruits and crisp vegetables, always more tasty when picked directly from the source plant, and picked at night. Listen to the corn stretch, rasp, and quiver. The sugarful melon's skin cracks in the field. By the moonlight, the sisters plainly observed the strawberries on the brook's edge lift their leafy skirts and walk into the water to rinse and cool themselves.

On the farm, the days began early and were long, colored by the sun and by their adventures. But the sisters rediscovered the farm after the evening meal. Once out of doors, they stepped tentatively or boldly here and there. They carried candles or lanterns or used wattage from the sky to gather ripe/unripe fruit; to visit and converse with the tired farm animals now bedding down in their own mud dwelling; to climb the aged, bent, barren fruit trees at the far edge of the farm; to seek out the flower oracle that opens between dusk and dawn; to watch the glistening earthworms that dive in and rise out of the soil as whales dive in and rise out of the sea. When they tired of their explorations and wanderings and grew hungry again, they, each in her turn, returned to the enveloping mud house where the adults were already on their third or fourth pot of tea. Each girl found her place between the adults and the cousins and the visiting neighbors and poured herself a cup of

tea and helped herself to sweet milk-rice, fresh almonds, dried
peaches and plums, and fried bread. And they sat back to listen to
Mother, Queen of Stories, who even here, and perhaps especially
here in the humble lantern-lit room, was in her element. And the
girls, sated and shadow-tired after their rovings, teacups in hand,
settled back into the giving pillows. They and all others listened to
Mother and saw the miles and miles of tales that lay in Mother's
swaying shadow as she sat cross-legged on a floor cushion, lit by a
single lantern that hissed in rhythm to her telling.

in summer, the sun

And in summer, in the new land, the sun beckoned the sisters out of doors. From where it stationed itself, directly above and near, it sent down pulsing rays to heat their heads, covered in dark hanging tresses, to guide their hands into cool earth, and to call forth minerals and moisture from the girls' glands. The sun instructed them on all that blushed and blistered across the face of the earth: the ripening peach, the naked hatchling, their own hearts. The great orb bleached out rooftops, illuminated the timid spider's silk, and divulged the pattern of the fickle bee's flight. Because it knew the girls' thirst for color was great, the giving sun by turns separated, then stacked its light to color the many flowers, fruits, leaves, birds, and insects before their eyes. It made the girls intimate with and sympathetic to all that was not human yet still breathed, writhed, and quivered. And that which was inert—the pane of glass, the wide expanse of uncracked concrete, the unearthed marble, the smooth stone shaped like a small whale—it offered as a point of respite for the sisters whose roving, reeling, busy legs, hands, eyes, and shoulders sought these places and objects even as the girls flitted from activity to activity and place to place in the garden. And in summer, the unblinking sun saw all that the girls were and were not, in the world, among each other, and unto themselves. It witnessed their ways, what they hid and what they bore proudly, and showered them with silent praises and condolences. It applauded their exploits, those heroic, and those sensible. The sun, in summer, measured the depths of their calluses and the arcs of their smiles. It reddened their cheeks, and browned their skin. It warmed their hearts and soothed their brows. And it was the sun who named the sisters. And knowing the girls, the sun kept their names hidden.

the sea

The sisters, who were born landlocked, live now in a valley near
the sea in the land of the sun. It is the sun that charms them out
of doors the year round and it is the sun that calls them to the
seaside in summer. And the ocean receives them gladly as it does
all the other valley dwellers who travel to it by car, bicycle, and bus
over the concrete highways and byways, and the hills great and
small, to rinse off the heat and the dust from their oily skin, to play
and toss, to lounge and feast, to tease and chase the bold seagulls
and the lapping waves. And the sisters see that they were called
to this continent's edge, were towed, as in a skiff, on currents of
warm air, from the beginning, over desert, mountain, and valley
by this sea. They know that the call comes from its depths and that
the ocean draws with an undeniable power its devotees from the
interiors of continents.—Yet they cannot guess that this immense
force tows from farther out still, has its origins in a center more
dark and fathomless than the ocean's mysterious depths. And perhaps more beautiful, more wondrous.—It is a call they would not
deny. They are invited and they come regularly to: drift with the
sand from dune to wave; wonder at the anemone's dance at the
tide's edge; sort the shells, broken and whole, by hue and texture;
mock the pelican's comical form and envy his intimate flight over
the ocean's still surfaces; laugh, tumble, splash, and float in the
turbulent surf; and be lullabied into a soft dream by the sea's pacifying tongue and the sun's tender fingers. It is in the bright middle
of day, at the water's edge, that the sisters sleep the joyful sleep.

open

And Mother's heart was big. It was deep. It was soft, warm, pulsing, bright. Open. Like her front door, her heart was always open
to woman, child, man, friend, neighbor, guest, ghost, god, infi-
del, immigrant, vagrant, stray, invalid, sufferer, dreamer: being,
living or dead; being, real or imagined. Mother's heart was big,
its interiors vast and limitless. And the girls were at once within
and without it. Her great heart was the universe they inhabited.
Everywhere they turned, there was Mother's heart, encapsulat-
ing their turnings. Everywhere they turned, there was Mother's
heart, stretched far and wide across the dome of the sky, smiling
down on them, illuminating their tender emotions. And when
she held them for even the briefest of moments, the girls felt the

red living thing pulse and press through Mother's ribs, through her breast, through her bra and her shirt, pulse and press to reach them, to touch their beating young pink hearts within their small narrow chests.

13

Mother, on a Saturday, drives the many miles over the concrete highways, past the contiguous cities great and small, towering and highway-flush, to reach the doctor, the distant acquaintance, for whose efforts she collects money and clothing regularly. The immigrant doctor, long established in the new land, brings the injured and the maimed from the first land for intensive and immediate surgery and therapy. The war, now sufficiently rooted, and the visiting forces, now satisfactorily assured of their hold on that country and its enervated population, allow the occasional opening of its border for the temporary release of the handpicked woman or youth, orphan or widower. Those whom Mother visits are the few, the lucky/unlucky, able to take respite from the never-ending war for a few weeks of treatment in the sunny land. They arrive to see the interiors of airports and hospital surgery and recovery rooms and, if capable, ride in the back of a comfortable and air conditioned van to the seaside, the city center, and the amusement park, before being flown back to the war-land. And when they arrive in the golden land, Mother takes her Saturday off of work to deliver what she has collected from friends to the temporary patients, and to spend a few hours with them to salve her own ailments, her longing and her guilt.

The patient sitting up in the hospital bed sways to and fro, beats her thighs with her fists, only occasionally stops to adjust her head scarf, and all the while screams, "Thirteen, thirteen!" She is unaware of Mother and the doctor who have stepped in to visit with her. Mother next stops with the two young men in the adjacent room. The one in the first bed, the older of the two, is unable to communicate, having lost his sight and speech, and his right arm, picking up a mine in an empty lot behind his father's vegetable stand. But he is happy to hear Mother's cheerful and warm voice speaking to him in the familiar tongue and tones and holds her hand in his hand as he might his own mother's. His friend in the next bed, bright and talkative, speaks for both of them. He is all in one piece and tells Mother that his injury, and the weapon that injured him, are inside, trapped within his skull just above his left ear. He pulls back his hair to show her a small scar and asks Mother to come back the following week to celebrate with him post-surgery. He will show her the piece of metal the doctors remove. He plans to make a necklace of it and Mother promises to bring him a leather cord for the purpose.

Mother visits with the other seven or eight patients, kisses their faces and hands, sets out pastries, pours tea from the thermoses she's brought with her, and shares stories and gossip as she might with her own siblings and aunts, though she has only just met these patients and will likely never see them again. She returns to the wailing woman in the first room, the woman oblivious of Mother and the culture that binds them, and yet only too aware of where she is and what has transported her here. And Mother, whose charm and warmth open a line to everyone she meets, is unable to reach this woman who sways and pummels and moans, "thirteen, thirteen . . ." Mother sits and waits. The tea she has poured cools on the table. The woman rocks and moans. She falls

back into the headboard and the wall, pushing buttons and setting off beeps and alarms, unintentionally calling in nurses, who
repeatedly come and go as Mother waits, as the sky outside shifts
from midday to afternoon. And the woman falls back into the
pillows and the wall, lies staring at her lap or the end of the bed,
then sits up to begin the cycle again, the rocking, the beating, and
the wailing. She rises. She falls.

The doctor has told Mother what has brought the patient here.
And it is this that keeps Mother in her chair at the woman's bedside. Only months prior, the woman was at home with her family.
They had gathered, as they regularly did—her sons, young and
grown, her daughters-in-law, her grandchildren—to share a meal.
They began to set out dinner, and she went up to the rooftop to
collect the laundry. As she pulled clothes off the line on one corner of the roof, two rockets sent over the city hit her house, nearly
simultaneously. The house crumbled and gave way beneath her,
killing everyone inside. She was left standing on the one corner
still erect. Though it is growing late and Mother has a long drive
home over endless miles of freeway, she remains beside the moan-
ing woman. She rises to pour out the cold tea and replaces it with
a fresh cup. She uncovers the meal the nurse has brought in and
pushes the table nearer the swaying woman. She straightens up the
hospital room, leaves momentarily to retrieve more pillows from
the nurse's station, and returns to place them behind the patient.
Mother pulls her chair nearer to, and attempts conversation again
with, the now humming woman. Finally, the woman looks/does
not look at Mother. She speaks/does not speak to her.

And what is left? Tell me. This? What is this and what am I and
what for? I know where I am. *Why* am I? This? Here, I sit. In this

bed, under these cold chirping lights. I ask them to shut them off.
But the sun outside! Here, the sun again. And I, plucked from the
debris, from the waste. Pulled down, carted over, driven there to
here, here to there, lifted from there into the glaring sky, dropped
here, hospital to hospital, desert to desert. Here. A cold hospital
bed. I asked for none of this. Why am I still here? That blazing
sun looks in. Gapes. Am I fated to suffer this? This? I had thirteen
boys. I am their mother. I did not send them to fight. I kept them
here. Under my skirts, within my arms. Protected. Then I stood
above, as they were buried beneath my feet. I have no feet. Look,
the two are gone. This! This is why they have brought me here.
Footless. What need have I for feet? I had thirteen sons, torn from
me like limbs, like flesh ripped from my body. My womb inverted,
sucked out by something, what? A cloud? Count. Thirteen. Before
you reach it, they will have all vanished. Count! Thirteen, all
smothered. Extinguished. Thirteen. What use this tongue? It flaps.
Thirteen! They said I was blessed. They said, thirteen! All boys!
All healthy. All strong. All safe. All whole, limb and livelihood. I
went to gather the laundry, their things, trousers and shirts, underwear and socks. Bricks like cards. Like biscuits. The dust. The
cloud. They told me it was immediate. But the cloud rising out of
the gaping hole below me spoke, it whimpered, it gurgled. Beneath
my seared feet, it moaned. And I stood, teetering. Listening. Past
my own choking, hearing. Below. In my girlhood dreams, the
cloud descended from above. A soft feathery cloud, descending
softly from a clear blue sky. It spoke, softly. It said to me, you are
blessed. Tenderly. This? This sun you have here! I have nothing
to tell it. Do you have no shame? An old woman. My breasts are
dry. My hands dish rags. It swallowed my feet, yet I stood. Two
pegs. I stood, tottering. Welded to the rooftop. The dusty dull
cloud moved up my pegs, between them, inside me, and suctioned

out my womb, turned it inside out, and tore it clear away. It knew
where I kept them. You'll see no scars there now. They said it was
immediate. They say these things. I know what I heard. Here,
in this hospital bed, clean, dry desert, through that window, the
shameless sun. The same one. Has it not seen enough? It was
there. And there are others, plenty. Places, plenty. Smothered,
plenty. Sons. Mine. Sun, away! Ramble on your course. Turn.
Totter, I. What need have I for feet? I teeter. Ramble. This flap-
ping tongue! I have no rest. So. This searing brain. They say eat.
This? They say rest now. I ask, this? So.

leaves

I have led you astray again. The dead do not reside in or pass
through books. The dead author the books. It is the living who
arrive from disparate stations at various hours of the day to enter
the books. It is the living who come to rest within a while, who
stop to fan their flushed cheeks, or to amble in the shade of the
many leaves.

the Straw Road

Take this path through the alphabet, steady reader.

Will you think it strange if I confess that I have a deep sense of myself as something like an astronaut, floating weightlessly out in space, high above our tender earth, there to do naught but marvel at the absolute beauty of the stars. Sometimes, I feel that it is the thing I was born to do: love the sky with all of my being. And if my eyes, naked and unblinking, fixed themselves upon the stars for a thousand years, it would not be long enough to quench their thirst. How beautiful they are. How absolutely and fundamentally beautiful.

one

The sisters are one. It is their fascination with numbers that sees them multiply and contract, tally and deduct.

subtraction

When they brought her first one home, her knees buckled and she collapsed onto the floor before anyone could catch her. She didn't try to regain the breath that had been clapped out of her and, somewhere far back and deep within her, she worked to will it away, as she worked to will away the image she'd glimpsed of her boy carried in through the door in his uncle's arms. But her breath returned of its own accord, and then the wailing began. The following year, her eldest was driven home by strangers, fellow soldiers of her son who'd taken care to cleanse his wounds and wrap his body though they knew it was not their place and his family would see to the ritual and see what was left of him when they did. She heard the army vehicle's motor, listened for the truck to slow as it advanced up her street and, hearing the squeal of brakes and the grinding of gravel, began to sway and reach out with her hand for the nearest wall to brace herself, while her other hand went to her scalp to grab her hair at its roots. A scream gathered itself within her belly, thrashed within her ribcage, rattled up her throat, and released before the front gate was opened. It silenced the entire neighborhood. In the fall of the same year, her third boy came home; his body was followed in by a procession of neighbors with bowed nodding heads who were now adept at the routine and were prepared to take over her household duties. This time, the void that opened before her allowed her entrance. It closed about her for several days, let her sleep the sleep of oblivion, and released her changed to a changed world. She missed this third funeral and her family and neighbors were not sorry for it. The dimmed world she returned to operated by rote, like a mindless machine. The dull sun rose and the dull sun set. The moon ballooned and dissolved and looked in her window six nights a month. The new world was occupied by people, some familiar, who spoke words that blistered and popped like water in a kettle and evaporated before she could grab hold of their structure or arrangement. Her neighbors and her cousins, her brother and her own aged mother were the gears and cogs that operated the breathless, mechanical world. In bed, she was shifted and turned over, undressed and dressed again, fed and wiped clean. In the bath, her arms were lifted and set down, her legs stretched out, kneaded, and folded again, her upper and undersides scrubbed and rinsed, her hair shampooed and combed, her nails clipped. And in time, she too was a gear, and her turnings produced steaming meals and neat piles of laundry and spotless windows. When they brought news of her fourth and last son, a young man forcibly conscripted, whose body the military was still negotiating to have released, she dropped the needle and the handkerchief from her hands. She stood up and stumbled out into the courtyard, into the daylight, tore open her shirt, pulled down her bra, and, near the feet of the neighbors duly arrived, she threw herself to the ground and grated her breasts across the dry, pebbly dirt, crying, "I'm burning! I'm burning!" She ground her flesh into the earth and cried, "I'm on fire! Let me in!" But the earth did not extinguish the inferno in her chest. And the earth did not open up to take her in, though it sopped up her blood and her milk.

riveted

And what have they not been witness to—the sun, the stars, the moon, the planets, pinned to our firmament like many captive eyes, blinking and unblinking?

in the first land, childhood

In the first life, all was sound, and color. The street peddlers' calls—*lab-lab-ooooh* and *puqhana-puqhana-puqhana*—reached the sisters' house long before the itinerant traders themselves did. But it wasn't the peddlers' melodic proclamations, describing the names, qualities, quantity, or value of their various wares, that excited and entranced the sisters; it was the bobbing of their boiled red beets, or their innumerable and colorful, buoyant balloons, or their hand-painted, jingling tambourines over and along the garden wall. With the peddlers hidden by the towering walls that enclosed the garden and the five small girls, the wares seemed to have lives and personalities of their own as they bounced and danced first above and along one wall, then around the corner and above and along the other wall. And the sisters themselves jumped up and down and they beamed ear to ear. The older sisters loved the sweet boiled beets, while the younger ones gagged at the sight of them. The younger sisters each had their favorite color of balloon, which changed with the seasons or the day. All expertly examined the fit of this or that tambourine in her hand, the jingle of these or those bells in her ear. And Mother could only occasionally deny them, only sometimes stop

her girls from opening the garden gate and chasing down the
peddler, who never looked as he sounded, who always looked
shabby next to the riches he peddled.

Depending on the aunt or uncle they visited, depending on the
day of the week or season of year, the girls were often treated
to music and dance. The young aunt who adored the new films
always had cassettes of the new film songs and they were songs
to be danced to. Danced to just so with one's hair tied up just so
with red and gold bangles clinking on the wrists just so. The young
aunt with the glimmering dark hair taught the precise but fluid
moves to the older sisters while the younger ones watched longingly or timidly. And the beautiful aunt danced with her eyes set
on something far-off, elsewhere. And the sisters all set their eyes
on her. Their uncle, who adored food and loved to cook above all
else, loved music second-best. On the rare occasion that he hosted
a funeral or a man of god, he forwent the musicians. But at all
other times, at the many and regular gatherings at his house, the
musicians always arrived first and were seated on the best cushions, and not far from the bounteous array of drink and food. And
the singing and playing commenced before the last guests arrived,
and the dancing not much later. So all ate and imbibed and sated
themselves even as they danced and applauded the musicians and

shouted out song requests. And the sisters bounced, swayed, and clapped to the singular rhythms and melodies even as they chased, teased, or gossiped with cousins among and through the warm swarming crowds.

Mother rocked the sleeping baby sister on her outstretched legs, in and out of the soft sunlight, and the older girls sitting beside her on the floor cushions begged to have a turn, squirmed with anticipation to play mother. At the park, Father lifted the two little sisters into the air, one hanging from each arm, and swung them back and forth while he whistled the old folk tunes. He tossed the intrepid sister and caught her in midair before placing her on his shoulder so that, walking through the avenue of trees, he might show her what lived among their leaves and scurried over their branches. The sister happier with her feet on the ground and her eyes, nose, and hands nearer the velvety radiant flowers and the scurrying shy bugs skipped and tried to keep up with him, and was in awe when she calculated that three of her steps equaled every one of Father's.

orbit

Did I not say I would return again to the beginning? Write, then whirl again. Then write again, in search of what has been mislaid.

in the beginning: innocence

Innocence lost on a grand scale, an epic scale. The innocence of:
a girl,
of five girls,
of a young family,
of an ancient city,
of a land entire,
lost in a twinkling.

shelter

During the years of steady bombardment, when more rockets than
rain fall on the city of hills, the inhabitants of this city under siege
learn from their neighbors the secrets to remaining alive another
day. And the family of seventeen—made up of brothers and sisters, their husbands and wives, children, and two grandmothers—
who've come to live under the sole remaining roof among them,
set out to apply the latest scheme. They collect rubber tires off of
abandoned vehicles in abandoned neighborhoods too far shelled
for even the rocket launchers to use as a hub. Or they purchase the
tires in the back alleyways of the squatted neighborhoods where
orphaned children, making a living among the chaos, barter tires,
doors, chairs, picture frames, frying pans, bedsheets, grenades,
marbles, eyeglasses, and soap. The family load their car or roll the
old tires home, up and down hills, and into their buttressed yard
over days and weeks. Soon, they have a myriad and sufficient collection. And they place the tires two layers thick over boards that

cover a cramped but ample bomb shelter they have dug seven feet into the rocky earth. The rubber tires, they have recently heard, will protect them from the rockets and the artillery that regularly shell the neighborhoods on the hillside. The day arrives when the last tire is in place. The family celebrate in their regular gathering spot, the porch beneath the grape arbor and adjacent to the new shelter. They bring out the bowls and the fresh bread, they ladle the soup, and sprinkle the garden herbs over it. The rocket that hits the group on their porch is the first of hundreds sent out over the city that afternoon. The family is one moment here, the next gone. Two of their children, who have been shooting marbles with friends in the alley, dazed, dusty, and bleeding, stagger away from the rubble and down the street.

the return

What eclipsed the sky? What great catastrophe? Which omen, what deeds? All labored under the darkness. Civilizations and forests fell beneath its weight. And villages whole huddled together to die. The earth gods, weary of floods, quakes, and other play, returned to the bowels of the earth, whence they'd come, to slumber, and were replaced by the gods of the sky, who after eons, turned their gaze once again toward our milky arm.

mirror

And blood ran under doorjambs, along gutters, down hills. It filled basins, wells, and valleys. It colored rivers and lakes. And soon the clouds reflected red.

twilit

So, the exiled jackal learns to feed on the bodies of the dead, the dead who have suffered their own exile and are no longer welcome in the world of the living. The dead who call back to the living, *let me in. Were we not lovers, not schoolmates from our earliest days, not brothers, not mother and child, not neighbors on the same hillside sharing the same wall?* The loyal jackal, still pining after its human companions, longing for its lost home, for warmth at the human hearth, comes to occupy the ruins of their felled cities. The disgraced jackal lurks at dawn and dusk among the rubble, uses its keen senses to locate the decaying flesh, the rotting food left behind in the upturned stove, the singsong springs of the old mattress. The warm tones of its human keeper's voice from long ago still haunts its ear. The exile futilely attempts to call to its old keeper from the borderlands, howling in the human's voice, begging the old companion to let it return home. But who hears the jackal or the dead without shivering? Who would let them in?

antidote

I am unwell.
Read me the alphabet,
says the book.

There was,   there   was   not,
B o o d ,   *n a b o o d* ,
once   upon   a   time,   a   family.

straw and silver

How are the fates written? Or are they spoken? The sisters have heard of the many oracles: the mountain spring, the regenerating garden flower, the opening in the rock, the bird in the dream. There are many destinies for the many people, and the girls were dealt theirs early, and had it written long before. They inquire of the oracles, wait and listen attentively, but receive no response, for while the destinies spoken repeat and resonate through time, those written are read but once.

Was it not the mule and the horse, traveling side by side over the dusty mountain pass—that long winding pass connecting the Northern to the Southern lands in the heart of the great and ancient continent—who read the family's fate in that much traversed mountain path beneath their hooves? Did these two animals not come to know over the many trips, burdened beneath burlap, straw, and silver, that all paths are laid for future travelers? All paths are packed down, tempered over the many years by hoof, foot, and wheel, so that one day they might be conduits, not just for the trader, but for the adventurer fleeing the life he was born into in order to shape the one he has dreamed for himself, or the refugee fleeing the invading armies, or the pilgrim returning home after a long absence. It is the mule and horse who see the markings. The companions spend their days in the service of merchants; they know the mountain pass better than any open field or covered shed; they have made the journey a thousand times, carried the goods and tempered the path. The two animals that practice the steady gait have learned to read the marks and come to see that besides the travelers who go by choice—seeking adventure, wealth, or safety—there are others who are bound to the path. There are those whose footprints are etched in its hard earth long before they are born into the world, those who are not drawn or pushed but simply are a part of the fabric of the path—that very one wending its way over that very mountain. They are those who are bound to approach the mountain, climb and traverse it, and, putting one foot before the other, reach their destination with eyes half-closed, as in a dream state. And these people find themselves one day in a new and strange land and set down tote, put out stale bread and dried meat, gather about them the earth's materials—stone, wood, brush, and clay—and lie supine, with legs and mouths open, crying out with the howl of the mountain pass, driving in and pushing out the new generation in the new land, paying the valley the mountain's tariff. The mule, looking down, sees the footprints of such a person now, knows that the very boy the marks write of will one day cross this pass, carrying his germ with him. The horse reads also the footprints of his unborn children and his children's seed, and knows that fate has cursed them even as it has blessed them each, and will move them from valley to valley, over river and mountain, across the seas and the many faces of the globe, for generations to come.

red tulip

In the first land, near the edge of the yard, beneath a lofty aged pine tree, each year, a single red tulip appeared. And though the sisters were young and their memories cast shadows shorter in length than the tulip's, they knew in late winter to await its appearance. The sisters went daily to the patch of dirt between the old tree's exposed roots to celebrate the red flower's arrival, to witness the chilled earth tremble and finally give at that tender point. They went daily to that place and watched the plant start in early spring, watched it rise and rise and rise, then settle and fix. They went daily to adore the single flower unfolding and to wonder at its glow in the shade of the towering tree.

the begotten

There was, there was not, once upon a time, an almond grower who put his crops before his happiness. In his fiftieth year, the almond grower marries, and in his fifty-second, he fathers a single child. The child grows up to marry a sailor who takes her far from her own land to a distant and strange one where she conceives three daughters and a son. The boy, her youngest, leaves home while still a child in pursuit of adventure and glory. He sows his own seed into the cavity of a woman he acquires in exchange for a she-goat in the desert. In her eighteenth hour of labor, his wife gives birth to a kicking and silent baby boy, its mouth still full, its tongue not yet released, uncrying. The child, born of blood, dressed in the residue of blood, rides that fluid's single surge into the withered, deft hands of the recently arrived laundress with skirts covered in village-road dust, with eyes red from the same dust and the flaming midday sun, a sun now feebly denied entrance by two boards nailed across an opening in the mud wall. The laundress delivers the baby unseeing—sees nothing in the dark and dust of the house-shed—but feels the small body, a thing new, a thing simultaneously solid and liquid, come free, slip

up her bare forearms with a force all its own, and she, the laundress, momentarily totters in her squatting position, forgets in that
moment the shed, the pail of well-water, the broken mattress and
the flies, senses instead the red river fish that has eluded her her
life long, and imagines for that instant that she sits at the river's
edge, a pile of wet twisted laundry beside her, her sleeves pulled
up past her elbows, her skirts wrapped tautly around her thighs,
balancing on stones run smooth and round by water over the millennia. In the silence of the unbreathing shed, its single window
shuttered against the unrelenting sun, the newborn takes his first
breath and hears his mother choke on the same blood that now
pulses through his tiny beating heart and across his thin, red lids,
which cover eyes yet unseeing. His legacy is binding. He carries in
him the almond, the desert, the fish, and the she-goat, and will pay
the price in blood and exile.

the emigrants

And where the dead in other graveyards have tombs worthy of being plundered and desecrated to feed the appetites of the living—those native and foreign—the dead here, in the war-torn land, lie under small mounds on hillsides with the single tattered green flag to mark their resting place, or wedged between two stones in a riverbed, or packed like many clammy worms in an unmarked common grave beneath the desert earth and sun. Many of the war dead—the disappeared and the missing—are entombed in the weary minds that in the early years had capacity enough to inter them: for the heads of the war-living are now like graveyards filled from one to the other edge, and have long since lost the ability to take in more bodies and limbs. But the war rolls on and the living join the dead. And these new unburied dead, homeless, restless, travel in ever-widening concentric circles, farther and farther out over the landscape, crossing the mountains, the borders, the oceans, following the still-crackling lines that connect them to loved ones who've immigrated and who may yet have space enough in their weighty heads to entomb them.

shhh . . . listen

Sit here quietly a moment, dear reader. These whispering leaves have tales to tell, fates to read.

the sisters will marry

When the time comes, the sisters will marry: a bird or a prince, a
magician, a lion, or a weaver. And this, after twenty or one hundred moons or fifteen of the earth's revolutions or the infinitesimal
shift of the sun, like a birthmark, across the growing arm of our
galaxy. With their husbands, they will live in the palace of the sun
or in a garden beneath the sea or atop a snowy and perilous peak
or beside a prattling river on a grassy bank or among the ancient
small inhabitants of a dense forest. And their daughters and their
daughters' female brood in a long line will carry their ruby blood
in the sacrificial vessel till the end days. And always on this delicate
journey across the spinning globe, their blood will course, it will
roil, it will spill, though the maidens hold firmly the vessel and
walk with eyes steady, eyes bright.

nebulae

And are the sisters' eyes not like nebulae, churning the cosmic soil,
pushing out stars, consuming and reflecting light?

scene

See Mother. She is a wizard with her machine. Her hands fly here, they settle there; her fingers turn that knob, press this lever. Her eyes are quick and keen. They follow her nimble fingers or guide them to where they are forthwith needed. Together, eyes and fingers thread the needle, measure lengths and circumferences, tuck and pin. Mother snips thread with her teeth, tears cloth precisely with her hands alone. She drives her machine forward, backs it up, guides the cloth beneath the humming foot, commands its speed with her own foot on a pedal beneath the table or with her hand on the wheel. She curls over her machine, hums with it, feeds it yards of colorful fabric, which disappears between her elbows and reappears, transformed, on the other side of her machine. Here is a dress, all color and form: red flounces, white collar, curved pockets, three golden buttons, and white-laced hem. And here a curtain, endless and stiff, forming a small and ever-growing mountain range on the table before the incredulous sisters. Mother effortlessly produces a shirt and tie for Father; tops, shorts, skirts, and headbands for the girls; dolls to replace those they've mislaid; dresses for their dolls; and finishes with a blouse and jacket for herself. And though each piece is unique, and fits its individual wearer perfectly, all are in the same colors. So, the family on their rambles and travels across the first, the easy and the innocent, land are like a spring bouquet of daffodils and narcissus, or like autumn's turning leaves.

not-home

And like the displaced jackal who inhabits the borderlands, the sisters will never return home. If the doors to their birth country should open and the sisters file again onto a plane, lift and land, lift and land to reach and enter that country, they will not have reached home, because the doors once closed, the curtains once drawn, never open upon the same scene again.

balloons

The sleeping, turning, sighing sister dreams of the house on the hill
in the first land. She is in the garden; she runs to the base of the tall,
ancient pine to find her old friend, the red tulip, who rises year after
year, during springs dry or rainful, in times of peace and in wartime,
in the waking world and in the dreaming world. It has been several
years since the family left the first land, and the sleeping sister knows
that though she now lives a great distance away, and she is no longer
there to tend it, the tulip still rises dutifully each year. Family after
family have come to live briefly in the house that Father added two
stories to. They have looked out through windows Mother once
dressed with colorful curtains sewn on her machine. Other mothers
and fathers and children have strolled through and played in the
garden in which the sisters once chased, climbed, sang, and swung.
The sister knows of these others because she continues to return
yearly to meet the old vibrant friend in her dreams. And through
the dream window, she has watched these other families come and
go, live and push on despite and because of the war that voraciously
and relentlessly plunders the first land.

It is spring again, but for the first time, the dreaming sister cannot
find the tulip. She kneels at its yearly birthplace and lightly runs
her fingers over that little patch of earth to see if she might sense
the flower beneath. Perhaps spring this year is late in arriving in
the first land. She digs, carefully at first, then more despairingly. A
hole forms and grows as she scratches and scrapes. The sister stares
into the empty cavity then sits back on her heels and looks over her
shoulder at the house. Its exterior paint, a pale blue she does not
recognize, is chipped and peeling away, exposing layers of colors
beneath. The door to the kitchen is attached only at its bottom

hinge and rests at an awkward angle against its frame. The concrete
Father once poured for the patio, and which must still hold the sisters' many palm prints, is broken, altogether missing in places. And
that ancient pine above her, its needles gray and listless, has aged
another hundred years.

The sister looks up at the tree and down at the earth; she sets her
forehead against the trunk of the pine: so this is what has happened
in the first land: all has fractured, withered, and aged, and the tulip
has immigrated to a new home. She feels the old familiar stir in
her belly. Then the surge and rise. She tastes the salt in her mouth
before the tears have risen to her eyes. A distant song, a faint but
familiar sound suddenly wakes her in the dream; she listens. A call
she knows well grows closer, louder, more urgent. Or rather, her
physical response to it becomes more acute. She jumps to her feet,
stands on her tiptoes, and listens to the approaching call with ears
perked and hands clenched. *Puqhana-puqhana-puqhana . . .*
And just over the wall she can make out the tops of the swaying,
bobbing balloons coming up the hillside. *The balloon peddler is coming!
Here comes the balloon man!* And his globes grow bigger as they come
nearer and she strains with eyes and toes to see them. *Puqhana-
puqhana-puqhana . . .* But wait! They are all the same color, these
advancing balloons. All red. They bob and bounce along the top of
the wall as they should, but they hardly resemble the old balloons;
these are like many oversized cartoon tulips. Now here they are
rising, moving closer, rising higher. The sister attempts to call to the
peddler: I am coming, Mother has given me money for five! But
no sound leaves her mouth in the dream and the huge bouquet of
balloons-like-red-tulips rises up and rises up and draws the ragged
peddler into the sky. And the peddler, kicking, holding fast to the
tulip stems, looks at her bewildered, looks to the clouds, then at the

earth, loses a sandal, desperately sings *puqhana-puqhana-puqhana* . . . and disappears into the clouds. The sleeping sister turns in her bed, moans, grabs at the blanket hanging over the edge of her little sister's top bunk, and tugs.

darkness

The sisters were not afraid. They saw darkness. They stared deeply into its hideous face. And they found that it was nothing, that it had neither eyes nor stomach. They found that there would be no chewing on young flesh because darkness had no teeth. Because darkness had no tongue, there would be no howling. Without feet, darkness could not chase them. The sisters laughed.

the dancing dead

And the country, so neatly organized and administered, so well groomed, and efficiently operated, fell into chaos absolute. The country, which for a decade had been cinched and held firmly together, beneath fist firm, fractured into many parts when the powerful fist lifted. Lords took their places right. Equipped with armor sophisticated and elementary, supplied by forces great and minor, distant and neighborly, they carved out their kingdoms. And the bloodletting began in earnest. Heads and limbs fell from torsos as overripe fruit drop from trees. Fissures like mouths opened in the earth to swallow one and all, bodies whole or in parts, charred or swollen, old and young, man, woman, and child. And the great lords had each their particular appetites. And those with a taste for women gathered them as they passed, in the marketplace and in the alleyway, removed their garments and their full breasts whole to fill the many crates. And the crates full of women's breasts were sent between kingdoms and the king receiving the gifts was amused and, according to his own tastes, filled his own crates with whole men. And the windowless metal containers filled with the living men were sent out to the parched deserts where the men might bake and stew in their own steam. Still not sated, the lords sent after the girls and boys still budding. They collected the country's children by the wagonload and wed and plundered them and ate their flesh and were not sated, needed still further amusement and so sent for the dancers. And the dancers arrived with eyes covered and mouths gagged. And the lords who enjoyed the traditional melodies and new entertainments brought in the musicians and the swordsmen. And the swordsmen struck cleanly with keen, heated blades, and sealed quickly the open arteries of the neck with clear, hot oil so that the dead might dance. And the headless corpses jerked and swayed, clapped and stomped. And the lords were amused. They leaned on their cushions and sipped their sweet tea and shouted for more.

witness

The sun does not blink, nor ever avert its gaze. It looks on while the earth giddily spins and totters on its axis.

offering

And Mother looks at her girls and thinks, this is what I have delivered to this world.

These girls.

This world.

A Thousand Tales

The book shivers, its pages flutter.

Count these pages, tally the dead. Before you are finished, they will have doubled. There are others, plenty. Places, plenty. The living are cut down. The dead rise. They circle.

There are words. Not condolences. Not dirges, not blessings. Stories. Plenty. Each their own. Come, read with me, says the book.

The sisters, Mother, and Father were not bound to the earth. They lived also in the upper realms: up in the sky each night, they assembled, bright, twinkling.

See their lids grow heavy at night; watch them close. See the rungs of the ladder glimmer in the moon's light. Watch them climb; they are expert. In their nightclothes, barefoot, softly they ascend, the seven. Listen to the rustle in the grandfather tree's leaves; the same breeze clears the sky of its misty veil. Look up, as I do, at the starry archipelago.

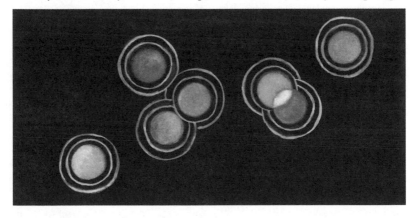

the three astronomers

The early astronomer observed and calculated the distances, orbits, and motions of the planets to create a novel picture of the cosmos. He placed in the center of this system the sun, that brilliant and ever-lit lantern, so that it might illuminate all things at once. About the sun, he stationed the roving planets in concentric rings so that each might have its own smooth path to travel upon. And what order! What logic! How perfect the image of sphere within circle within circle!

Three centuries later and in the land across the river, the reticent poet, after spending a lifetime gazing at his own image, awakened to the beauty of the stars over his head. He, both poet and maker of mirrors and other convex surfaces, was not unaware of his own beauty, equally bright and transcendent. The poet and the polisher of surfaces looked long into the sky and long into the mirror. He reevaluated the early astronomer's calculations, drew his own diagrams, and formulated his own equations to generate a new vision, one more exquisite, more truthful than any previous: he imagined himself in the center of the great system of moving bodies; who else but man could occupy such a seat? But the poet was not long for the earth and his short romance with the stars produced only the single poem, which he recited but once. It was spoken even as it was created, traveling from his bosom to his lips in a continuous stream, beautiful. In that moment, in the dense hours of the night as he paced back and forth in front of the stove in his small apartment, he knew that everything he was, had ever been, and would be was concentrated in this single poem. And while it streamed forth, he was whole and all of life and all in the cosmos was of one piece and complete. The verse said everything that could be said,

contained all that ever was and would be, and expressed it more
perfectly, more beautifully, more elementally, than it ever had been
expressed or would be again. But as he spoke the final verse, the
poem, which had contained him and all else in it, was gone, from
him, from the room, from the town. Though he labored through
the night to bring it back, pacing back and forth, his hands in his
hair, over his clenched, tired eyes, or gripping his ready pen at his
table to set it down on paper, the poem was gone and not a solitary
line was left him. In the early morning hours, the poet fell into a
feverish sleep from which he did not regain consciousness.

The poem was recited the single time and heard only once by
another: by the new astronomer, the steady mathematician,
that lover of integers, the poet's own countryman, two centuries
earlier in a dream. And the poem, the same one, expressed the
harmony among the stars and contained the absolute truth of
all things in the universe in the mathematician's dream just as it
would when the poet later recited it. And the poem, which was
whole and complete and beautifully recited by the pacing poet in
the mathematician's dream, filled the scholar as he listened, and
left him afterward despondent when he awoke without any trace
of its rhyme, and only the echo of its beauty. So the new astronomer returned to his work and fell wholly into it as never before.
But one day, while looking deeply into numbers and geometries
he saw there an image of the poet from his dream. And leaving one idol for another, he revived the poet's cause, making it
his own. He found his way to a distant graveyard, to a plainly
marked plot, and dug out the clean bones of one long dead: the
early astronomer. In his laboratory, he worked the many hours,
early and late, to take precise measurements of all the bones in
the body—their lengths, circumferences, and densities—and he

molded these calculations so that they fit the laws of the poet's cosmic system, which showed man in the center of the universe. The new astronomer/mathematician took down his model of planets in elliptical orbit around the sun, a model over which he had labored for ten years. He hung in its place a new model, which consisted of the 206 bones of the dead astronomer hung by string and balanced perfectly, each bone placed so as to be in supreme harmony with every other. And the mathematician, who knew numbers and geometries and had applied them to the cosmos with great success, no longer gazed skyward but spent his days dusting the early astronomer's bones, and listening for the poet's verse in their sometimes dull, sometimes ringing chime.

tender

Yes, Father's heart whirred like a finely tuned, smooth-running mechanism. Having many small legs and two deft wings of its own, his heart followed the trails of the little things: the ants marching up the trunks of the fruit trees; the snails inching across the cool cement patio in the early morning hours; the spiders spinning their intricate webs beneath the eaves of the house; his girls' tentative dreams and ideas knocking against walls and slip-ping into dresser drawers; the squeak beneath the car's hood; the small fissure forming in the wall behind the washing machine. Father's heart was aware of, and friend to, the small things, the invisible things, the unobtrusive creatures, the whats and whoms others missed and stepped on or over. His was a tender heart and it listened tenderly to the new shoots that came up in his vegetable garden, to the broken wing of the disoriented bird, to the small stirrings that muted the expectant mother cat. And his sympathetic nature sharpened his daughters' senses so they could better see in the dark and better hear, through the din of daily living, the subtle and the quiet energies.

below

Gentle reader, come, come! Place your eye here. Just here. Look, the earthworm wriggles, it glistens, it glides in and out of the crumbly earth. Look here, at the beetle! It has been out all day, now it shambles over the dry teetering leaves and disappears into the inky aperture in the garden wall. It takes its iridescent jewel home with it.

rotation, revolution

There are the fixed stars and there are the whirling stars. It is the transfixed new astronomer who sees that a need in the wandering planets causes them to turn and turn, searching outward, searching inward.

voyage

The stars and the planets went tumbling through the cold dark
spaces, unknowing, unmoored, until caught by this or that force.
What tugged the family—Mother, Father, the sisters each—this
way and that way? What brought them to this destination, drew
them to that port? Here is a job. On the library shelf, a book.
This is your friend. Around the next corner, a wonder awaits you.
What guided each: the nose, the heart, a whim? Did they make
deliberate calculations before making decisions important and
trivial? Each holds a small notebook and sharpened pencil in her
and his hand. But each also keeps a coin, ready, in a pocket. And
each, at least on occasion, makes her or his way to the hall closet,
pulls down from its upper shelf the wooden box, takes out from
it the cloth-wrapped tome, unwraps and kisses the sacred book,
and opens it to read the old script. No, the family practice neither
deliberation nor speculation nor faith. The planets themselves sail
without oars and without charts. The family too sail with the giddy
winds. They close all fourteen lids and lie back to float upon the
fathomless dream.

canopy

The Milky Way, illuminating the darkness above, travels across the
dome of the sky in a continuous stream, beautiful.

the dream

The new astronomer had his eyes drawn to the cosmos by a passing swift comet in his sixth year. His small feet planted on a hilltop, his thin-cold hand wrapped in his mother's, he gazed into the marvelous sky. The child's eyes, still tender, still gaping, took in the mysterious body's radiant flight across the peaceful firmament. Even as his eyes were drawn to the sky, the strange image—the luminous orb with trailing blue tresses—drew itself upon his brain. And so his gaze was thenceforth fixed skyward, and his mind began working on the task of explicating a firmament that was, after all, not fixed.

He attended the schools and found the masters who would teach him numbers and geometries. He studied the figures, shaped the models, observed the sky, and returned to his notebooks to adjust his calculations. Over many years of observation, rumination, and refinement, he came to discover the laws of the cosmos, even while the laws of the lands he crisscrossed, in search of a living and a station, could not be sequenced into any system of order. Fickle kings, men of power hungry for more, and for status, war, revolution, disease, fear and superstition, made disorder of all things across the myriad lands. The sky was not fixed and neither was the astronomer's life. The many years of his life were not steady, not still, because war raged wherever he went. They were not fixed because kings came to power and lost power, honored him and exiled him. They were not steady because his children's lives were cut short after only a handful of revolutions about the sun.

What was steady was his devotion to the sky. And he loved the sky with an ardor unmatched in all of the lands. And what he found there through his diligent observations, his computations, and the expert use of his implements told him that the sky moved and shifted according to the laws of harmony and attraction. But when he pulled away long enough to see to the necessities of his earthly life—to beg for the promised income, to uproot his outcast family yet again, to soothe the kings and the generals with false readings of a false sky, to bury his children, then his wife—he saw that the fundamental laws of the sky did not correspond to those that were in place on the surface of the earth. What he read in the stars he could not translate to those about him. The more he turned away from the sky, the more desperately he turned back to it. And through his many turnings, he came to accept this lack of consonance between that above and that below as a tragic and insuperable predicament. He wrote the papers and sent them far and wide to the great thinkers and tinkerers of his time, but few grasped his meaning. So he lived outside his time. Cast out of land and time, the new astronomer dreamed of an automated mechanism, which, though it would not bridge the great divide between the laws of the earth and the laws of the sky, might at least, through a simple and repetitive gesture, express the comedy that is life: the universe has produced, out of dust, a wet convex lens in order to see itself reflected on that surface, but it is wholly unaware of the pining soul the lens in turn has produced in order to reflect upon the universe.

center

Look at Mother. She is one and she has produced five. And she keeps her girls about her through a force of attraction unnatural to any but the bright star in the center of a planetary system. Mother is all warmth, all gravity, at once radiating outward and drawing in. She is all love. And the girls have no need to acknowledge or articulate this truth, for their minds cannot fathom their hearts beating, their eyes blinking, their breath rising and falling, their fingers wrapped about a pencil, their legs wrapped around a tree limb, without Mother in the center of their world. But they sense it in their bodies, and their elliptical perambulations about her from the moment of their births, and across the years and the landscapes, are record of it.

the astronomer's book

The sleeping sister, lying on her back, hands folded over her narrow ribcage, flits her eyes to and fro beneath her resting-closed lids. The sleeper dreams. The dreamer reads. The reader recognizes the story in the book as her own story. And she asks the librarian in the dream: who is the author of this book?; this is an old book, yet I recognize the story; it is my own. The librarian takes the book from the girl; she tilts her head; she pushes her glasses farther down the bridge of her nose; she turns the book in her hand, back to front to spine; she sets it down on the counter before her, and opens it to its title page. Oh, this book, she says. Yes, this is the new astronomer's. One of two works of fiction he wrote. The other is about a dream of the moon. This one, about an automaton.

five

The sisters are five. Like the five openings in the face, they let in and let out the world. See this sister, she rises on her toes, raises her arms above her head, spreads her fingers, and arches her back; she is all force, a silent gale. The others run from her, giggling, peeking back. And look there at the sister lying prostrate on the lawn; she adores the scent of living soil, of crushed grass, the beat of an ant brigade across her forearm and into the hollow of her closed hand, the beads of moisture that release at the nape of her neck. Is not all life a letting in and a letting out? And if you rest your fingers lightly on your lips, can you not at once sense your heart and your breath, your mind and the verse it is at this moment delivering to your tongue?

And the reader dreams.

moon

The sister dreams that she rises from bed and walks out into the
garden. The others sleep within. Her family, the neighborhood,
the city sleeps and she is drawn out into the night. She steps outside and can do naught but look up. Above her, the moon fills the
sky so that only in her periphery and along the horizon can she see
and sense the muted stars. The white sphere has descended.

It is a hundred miles above the earth and it fills her vision, fills
her mind. She is aware of the space between herself and the
moon; it is not a distance she can travel and it is not an empty

space. It is suffused with something invisible that emanates from the white orb as the air around a rose in full bloom is suffused with the flower's scent. The moon has no scent. It radiates no heat. It accommodates no shadow; it is not borrowing light tonight. It has and issues its own soft particulate light, a luminescence rising from its own skin, a light equally bright everywhere and no brighter than it is when the moon is in its cradle in the sky. But now, close, the light is multiplied, not in intensity but in sum and area. And so the sister can look on it with eyes open, studious. Here is the moon, still subtle, still soft, and obliterating all sound, all thought, all drive with these qualities multiplied. Here is the silent satellite freed from its steady course. The girl sees clearly the moon's face, its pits and peaks, its continuous open fields, its arid shores, the rising crests of its mountains, the sheer walls of its craters. The moon is close; it is white luminescent. Its texture is vivid and its presence keen. It is not unalive. It demands her attention. It is awful and beautiful. She wonders, why has the moon left its path in the sky to come so near? Has it a message? It smiles, it does not smile at her. It speaks/does not speak with her. Why has it woken from its slumberous turning and turning and dreaming and dressing/undressing in the sky to now stand unmoving, demanding, playful? And where are the calendars, the celestial atlases, the paper wheels and dials that predicted *this* phase of the moon? The sister is alone with the white vivid orb while the others sleep. Somewhere in the distance, perhaps the far distance, others are awake and though she can neither see nor hear them, she senses them, their toils, their practiced gesticulations, their rise and fall utterances. The earth will turn and they will look up. They will see this new moon awakened.

And the dreamer reads.

Jewelmouths

The earth has shared a minute but generous fraction of its
existence with humans, who are born of it, slip out from its hot
crevices, and almost immediately leave the horizontal position
to stand on two feet and gaze skyward. The human offspring
inherits but one gesture from its progenitor, a gesture born of a
single impulse: the need to find home. It is the gesture that all
others serve. It is the first and the last gesture. In silhouette, it is a
small motion, one barely discernible otherwise: the head follows
the eyes from the horizon to the stars; the chin draws a short arc
over the backdrop of forest and hill. This small motion, limited
by bone and sinew, by the human body's upright structure,
mimics the earth's own tireless rotation: the earth, like a bodiless
head, bound to an invisible neck, uses its small range of lateral
motion through the seasons to search for home and parent from
morning to morning again, from horizon to horizon, across the
great emptiness. And so too, the human progeny, who shares
a biology with its home, repeats this gesture hourly over the
many faces of the earth, in the form of prayer or in the name of
science, out of love or resolution. It is the earth that has birthed
the child, and it is the earth that, out of love for the unintended
offspring, has worn a myriad of expressions, in places tender
and devoted, in others weary and exasperated, in places proud
and triumphant, in others grimacing. The earth, like a mother
half-devoted, gives with one hand to the human child, takes away

with the other in its negligence or its half-devotion to that other cause, the one that gnaws at its own core: the need to find its place among the stars. In its dizzying spin, it guesses of a distant origin but is bound in place by gravity's sinews. And out of pity for the child who has inherited its need, the earth laughs, and a village is born. It breathes, and golden spires rise out of the dust. Towns bud like small blisters over its features. And the human child burning with the same need builds always skyward, builds structures that draw its gaze from horizon to stars. It is the child's need and destiny to claw out of the womb and to the place of mud, to compel something between its frenzied hands out of dust and water, to lay brick upon brick, to steal height from tree and mountain in order to climb upward in an attempt to but lick the light of dead stars.

And so the earth and the human, each half-oblivious of the other, singe the other's brow or spill the other's blood. Cities, even in their sanitary nascence, arising out of desert sand or ocean mist, have their ruin written across the walls of their towers from the first moment of erection. Like tulips they push out of the soil, ever skyward, their feet ever bound, only to fall under the pressure of their own grandeur into the earth again. Towers, built on silt or on rock, crumble back to earth. From dust rise the cities, to dust they return. It is all that the child's hands, the little engineer's tools, can fabricate: the temporary spire, the pining spire, which hides its skyward obsession beneath the mark of dwelling and tomb. And so the two, parent and child, practice the gesture, lift their gaze from horizon to sky, from land and sea to stars. And the one forgets about the other, does not realize that it shares a common goal with the other. The human child fights against the earth's gravity to build his cities; the earth acquiesces, then erupts. Two forces battle selfishly across the earth's revolutions and over the child's many generations.

But from underneath the same silt or rock of felled cities, something else pushes: a third pressure. This pressure from the buried dead, those who have fallen but have not given up the yearning and who practice still the single gesture, the arcing of the head, searching skyward, clearing earth. They who push upward saturate the earth with their bones and their singular desire. They are many who fell in centuries or millennia past, after the way of the grand towers, and have been there, underground, keenly awaiting the day when the dust storms, the cleansing winds and salts release their forms from their too-early graves: for the arcing chin accomplishes little underground but to clear the space around the skull. And the gemstones they wore heavy once around their necks, they now wear in their mouths. Gemstones lining the jaw like many-colored teeth and filling the sockets of the eye with splendor. But in the mouth, the jewels speak of underground truths that the living child's mind aboveground cannot fathom, truths hidden in the earth's burning heart, cooked there over billions of years by that singular and repeating gesture—the head tilting from horizon to sky, horizon to sky—truths unknown to the spinning sphere itself. And it is that mineral eye that charts a course home: the ruby eye housed in the skull of the human child that once was and ruled the earth and inherited from its mother the need that death would not sate. This gem child now finds his way out again. The ancient child returns in newfound glory, rises to bring with him his daughters and their sons and the many generations that joined them there beneath the earth's surface in death. And it is with an awful lease on life, with the coiled hunger of hundreds of thousands of years, that they come back to take what is theirs and to eat the fruit on the distant boughs of their own tree in order to make the ascent. The jewel-mouthed mother takes from the earth that was her tormentor and her tomb the fruit of her own loins and eats also the earth's fruit, fertilized and harvested by her own living descendants. She and her brood eat the earth out of bread and blood and leave not the rotting flesh of the fallen apple, nor the steady breath of the sleeping child. And the twinkling twice-born with the ripe fruit of the earth reflected in their jeweled eyes and firmly clutched in their jeweled mouths return, blood and brood, to the sky. Having at last charted their course home, the dead return to the dead.

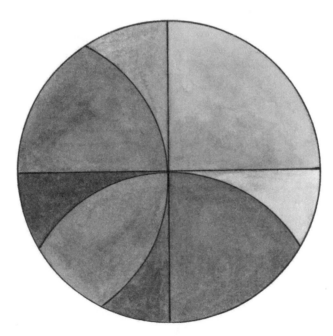

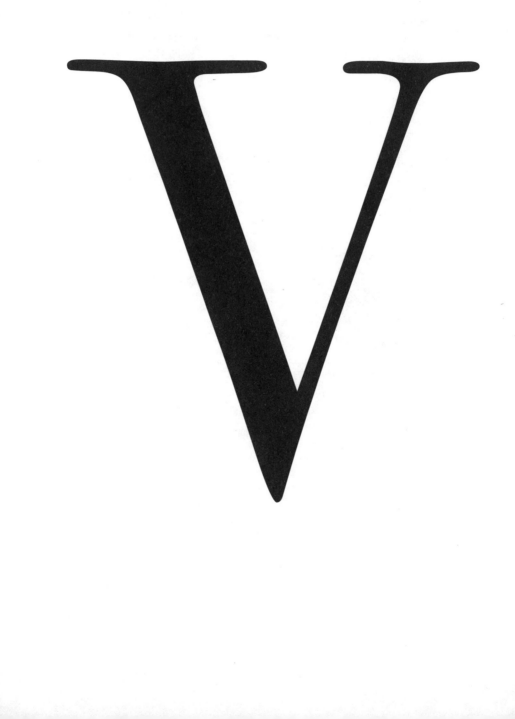

Vowels. Such a small handful of them, and yet they do what no consonant would dare, or could, do. They are openings. To what, you ask? Openings. They are like your eyes, your nostrils, your mouth, the orifices leading into and out of your body, which let in and let out the world. How far have you traveled into the interior? How far do you dare? What are you willing to ingest? Take a vowel. Take two.

automata

The sidereal yearnings of the sisters drew their eyes upward and upward, skyward and skyward. Performing the single gesture, drawing the singular arc with their small chins across the backdrop of schoolteacher and blackboard, or breakfast nook and stove hood, or car interior and indistinct fleeting cityscape, or flowers and fence—wherever a window or other opening presented itself—they were like automata, preset to perform their function: to love the sky and the stars that dot it with the ardor of a child. And did the astronomer/poet/mathematician not dream them, these five sisters, nearly four centuries prior and in a distant land? Was it not he who drew up the plans, envisaged their silhouettes, and calculated the arc of the chin in its motion from horizon to stars? Searching for the perfect geometry, in agony and discontent, he worked at the mysteries, he pored over observations and numbers, he drafted papers and letters, year after year, there in his laboratory. Nightly, he peered into the sky, pen in hand, and traced the courses of bodies, measured their distances, and recorded their peculiar motions. And while war and pestilence raged outside, he remained inside, steadfast. There at his window, the astronomer dreamed the sisters. And dreaming them, he came to see that there is a force in the mind that causes the eye to shift in the ascendant direction. And this nameless force draws curves even as it draws objects directly to itself and holds them there in perpetual orbit. In the archives, among his papers, you may find the drawings: the small nose precisely depicted in silhouette, lips set, lashes curved upward over an open and bright eye, which reflects the stars above and etches their forms onto the mind within. In the drawings, the automaton is sitting at a desk, or on a park bench or, like a giant, with her legs draped over the curvature of the earth, always gazing

skyward. In her hand she holds a pen, or a compass, or a paint-
brush, or some other crude implement with which she is meant to
depict her devotion to the sky.

motion

There is a force in the _____ (fill in with larger being/object in
the center of any system, e.g., sun, earth, mother, mind), which
causes the _____ (fill in with smaller being/object that is in orbit
around aforementioned being/object, e.g., earth, moon, daughter,
eye) to move.

the mysteries

It seemed as if the atmosphere, that thin gaseous blanket
enveloping the globe, was where understanding lived, and the
mysteries of the world lay cavernous beneath and vast above.
Between the forces of the sky and the forces of the earth: the
atmosphere: a thin bright line, like the opening in a door left ajar
at night. This opening just wide enough for measured breath and
measured thought, which might draw meaning from the great
mysteries. And the inquisitive sisters, living in that measured
space, reached into the earth up to their armpits in the day and
stared piercingly into the sky at night to extract knowledge.
But the mysteries retreated. And the earth was cold at shallow

depths. And the eye looking upon the beauty in the sky misted with liquid emotion and with longing that rose from the body's interiors. Yet the unknown called and spoke to the sisters, sometimes in dreams, sometimes through the distorted words that effervesced from their lips when the two languages the girls spoke faltered, blended, and metamorphosed on their tongues. The line where the two languages met on the tongue was not unlike the thin line of clarity in which the girls lived, not unlike the line between the mussel and the barnacle on the intertidal rock, a line that draws stories from the deep-wide ocean about the moon and the clock. And in that bright space, where the two mysteries rushed one upon another, a third was born. And out of the tension between the forces of sky and the forces of earth, a soundness evolved. In this space, the sisters were happy to put on hold their search for an answer to the lack of correspondence between the two forces. In this space, they were happy to play, to laugh, to be children. And there were boundless moments when though the mysteries called, the sisters did not listen, would not heed. Boundless moments when they gathered the bright azure line about their shoulders—as the earth gathers it around its girth—comforted by its clarity and its independence from the two forces that gave it rise. And perhaps the greatest mystery was that life could prosper and proliferate, could shift and evolve on its own in that luminous space, despite the tension. And in spite of the tension, life could use the great fuels from above and the great fuels from below to churn new life in that slight opening, so that the arm that reached into the earth brought it out in handfuls to craft bowls, towers, and telescopes, and so that the eye, when at night, looking out on the vast dark open, instead reflected the great vast internal.

Sunday

Father tinkers in the garage, hums the old folk songs to himself.
Outside, in the shade of the grape arbor, the two youngest build
a wedding cake for their bride-cat and the neighbor's groom-dog
out of mud, vines, tendrils, leaves, flowers, grapes, and shells. The
middle child, unseen, unheard, sits in the treehouse, chewing gum,
reading a book of fairy tales collected in distant lands, in distant
times: she is transported. Inside, the second girl paints her nails
with the five colors she has collected over the past year. She paints
snowfall across the fingernails of her left hand and a bonfire over
those on her right. The eldest has her bedroom to herself and
sits against its closed door gossiping, giggling with her best friend.
She has stretched, and uncoiled, the telephone cord its full length
from kitchen, across living room, down hallway, to just inside her
bedroom door. Mother, in the kitchen, listening to the melodic
film songs, drops the filled dumplings into the boiling water, stirs
the pot of simmering lentils and ground meat, mixes the yogurt,
crushes the dried mint leaves. One by one, the others arrive, wash
their hands, set out the plates, pull out the chairs, fill the teacups,
and fill the air with their chatter.

plenty

Yes, the sisters know that they are stories, points of light bob-
bing-embedded in the ever-undulating, ever-swelling sea that is the
cosmos. Points of light, like myriad others, blinking.

inborn

And does the child who has thus far lived the peaceful-joyful-safe life know what terror is when war arrives? When war emerges, seemingly, as from a void, begotten yet motherless, does the girl recognize it for what it is: a god of Chaos and Bloodletting? Does the thus-far-sheltered child know to feel dread at war's approach and appearance? *A guest is coming! Sweep the rugs, fluff up the cushions, put on the tea, set out the sweets, fix your hair.* The girl senses the excitement in the air. But does she absorb the vibration of the exploding bomb a mile away? Can she decode the adults' cipherous speech? When her eyes meet the cold gazes of the foreign soldiers lining her neighborhood streets, can she read in them the story unfolding? Does terror rise in her small frame when she watches the news alongside Mother and Father, aunt and uncle, neighbor and milkman, as all sit around the television set and listen to the newscaster describe the many and precise methods and instruments at the torturer's fingertips? Or does she look to the adults, study his and her face to read and apprehend fear? Does she wait for Father and Mother to return from the prison yard, from the graveyard, from the countryside, and from the government office building in order to study their dusty shoes, their bent-haggard shoulders, pale faces, red eyes, dry lips, in order to know terror? *Look how Mother's hand twitches, then freezes, then sets the teacup down again, lips trembling, tea unsipped.* Or is terror a thing innate in the child? A thing fecund, ready to rise up, as from a void, to meet war eye to eye when it arrives?

Enter War

So the eyes tender, the eyes bright, the eyes trustful and steady, primed by biology and destiny, the child's eyes look on, agape.

the five

And how far can the small child's mind enter the sterile torture chamber, the gaping pit of the mass grave, the cold and damp well bottom? Once in, how deftly do her eyes see, her fingers feel, her nostrils scent? What odors are there? Which notes resound off steel doors and concrete walls, off flesh and off damp-bunched clothing, off earth-soft and earth-dense, off a small disk of fathomless water? DRIP DRIp DRip Drip drip. And her eardrums are taut, they are new; they are like the goat's skin stretched across the street peddler's tambourines. And her taste buds line up like many eager anemones at the tide's edge. Are there not scents that are more flavor than odor? Does the throat not swallow what the eyes take in? And what visions there, in the torturer's tidy room, in the dank subterranean pit, in the close wet cylinder! How vividly the child's imagination colors the scene! A pencil behind each ear, a rainbow of crayons clamped between all ten fingers, the little illustrator's imagination sings!

What is it the newscaster said? Shhh, listen: they shaved her head, clean. They pulled out her nails, all twenty. They clipped three of her fingers from two of her hands. They sliced off her breasts, both. What else have they taken? The newscaster interviews the

young woman, the torturee newly released, who sits covered
in skirts and scarves—modesty, first and foremost in the newsroom—bald head to fleshy toenail beds. The woman bows her
head and speaks in muffled tones through the veils to deliver the
government's clear message to the population glued to the television screen. They lined them up, she says. My parts. On the table
next to me so I might see them, hear them, count them. They kept
me awake, she says. Though I tried to dream, they woke me. She
hides behind her veils, broken. She hides behind, hideous. But the
little girl watching the tortured woman on the television screen is
able to leave her own seat on the cushion, to glide across the living
room floor past the adults watching, to slide into the newsroom
and past the newsman, to get underneath those garments, pull off
the shoes, finger the ten fleshy beds, climb up the red lashed legs,
over the wasted belly, and put her ear to the concavities that were
once soft mounds. Hear her heart beating? The young woman is
still alive. Hairless, sterile, clawless (and therefore unable to leave
her mark on the grave's edge), she lives; though her life was taken,
she lives. Hear her heart beating? The war has only begun. The
newscaster is doing his job: asking the questions; terrifying the
population. Stay with us. There is more to come.

And the sister travels where the adults dare not; the girl sees with
fertile inspired mind. She holds the torturee's twitching hand in
her own. She swallows the woman's thick coppery saliva. She feels
the pliers clamp down, hears the knife blade hit the table, sees the
blood pool in her lap. The child smells the flesh burned. The child
smells the fresh earth turned. In the crowded grave, she feels over
her belly the weight of an arm that is not her arm, feels beneath
her foot the top of another's head. She feels a hand that is not her
hand cradle her face in the shared loamy bed. She feels her slight

sister-weight stifle breath that is not her breath beneath her; in the space between her shoulder blades, a cyclical warmth, then a rattle. She holds her breath and counts to one hundred. *These are my people. Here I lie with them in the earth, not breathing. Here I drop with them, off of cliffs, off of scaffolds. Here I float with them and with the river's current. Here I sit huddled with them in the well's inky dank bottom.*

Though the war started first in the grown man's imagination, it takes root more readily in the child's. It is she who sees, smells, tastes, hears, feels most keenly. She who cannot turn away when the curtain rises.

a, e, i, o, u

The sisters are five. They are openings.
They are *what*, you ask?
They are vowels, openings. Their fertile inspired minds go where
the adults' dare not.
They are like your eyes, your nostrils, your mouth, the five senses
leading into and out of your body, which let in and let out the war.
See war enter.
See war remake the children into something else.

she

Her husband is not at home. Though it is midafternoon, he has
not yet returned home from prayer. The men do not use the
front door; they kick in the garden gate. She jumps and, despite
herself, lets out a sharp scream, which she quickly muffles by
biting down hard on her lip. She is upstairs and from her bedroom window sees them file into the garden—six or seven men,
rifles on their shoulders or loosely swinging from their lax hands.
She runs downstairs, then room to room, collecting her children,
rushing them upstairs and into her bedroom, into her closet and,
with her eyes alone, daring them to make a sound. They have
rehearsed this; the children know what is expected of them and,
as their mother draws the curtain closed, each child finds her and
his hiding place against the wall or the floor, behind dresses and
coats and underneath bedding.

She inhales and pats down her head covering and her dress and walks downstairs to answer the knocking on her kitchen door. She greets them with her eyes cast down at her hands. "Where's the husband," asks the man standing nearest the door. "He has gone to pray, he will be here shortly, any minute," she answers, now looking at his worn shoes. The other men of god beyond him, standing and milling about the garden, picking at her okra plants, or leaning against the pomegranate tree, or poking into the soil with the tips of their rifles, chuckle and spit. One of them pushes past the leaning man at the door, past the woman, and enters the kitchen. "You can offer your guests a cup of tea, can't you," he says. Her eyes are cast down, but she senses his eyes scanning her, head to toe, and front to back as he passes. The one at the door comes in next, before she is able to step out of his way, and brushes against her with his rifle and his hand. "Come in," she says, "he will be here soon. Seat yourselves in the living room. I will put on the tea." A third man has now entered the house, and the three walk around the living room, peer out the front window, pace the hall, step into the family room, walk to the base of the stairs, picking up photographs, opening and shutting cabinet doors, kicking up the corners of rugs. Two leave and return to the garden, passing her in the kitchen on their way out. "And me, I'm second," says one of them over his shoulder.

The woman sets out teacups and saucers on a tray. She fills a small dish with candy and, hands shaking, removes the towel off of another piled with savory biscuits. She steps into her pantry and steps out again with a rifle held at chest level and already aimed. She walks down the hall, turns into the living room, and shoots at the couch where the man sits, his arm stretched

over the back of the couch, ankle on knee, cigarette midway
to his mouth. She does not stay to see him slump over into the
cushions, then keel over onto the floor. She walks back down the
hall, into the kitchen, and shoots one of the men as he reaches
the open doorway. The woman steps over him and over toppled
shattered teaware into the garden, where she releases another
eighteen or twenty rounds into the other four or five men,
stopping each of them mid-run to or away from her. She walks
out into midst of the crumpled tented bodies, lets the rifle fall
onto the earth and looks up to her bedroom window, where she
thinks she sees the faces of her two youngest. The other armed
men of god, who've been making their routine tours, visiting
other houses in the neighborhood, having heard the gunfire,
rush into the garden and empty their rounds into her back. Her
shoulders and arms jerk and lift, her head tips back, her veil slips
off to reveal her dark curls. She rises in the air. For a moment,
she is suspended, arms lifted, feet pendulous, dress billowing,
eyes rolled back and sky-bound. She is whole. When the firing
concludes, she falls to the ground in a thousand pieces.

laundry

In the first land, the line grows, the children wait, the laundress grows weary beneath the burden of her trade.

system

The automaton, the little fleshy machine, composed of dust, wired by biology, animated by chemistry, she looks up to the sky and looks to the horizon, looks up again, repeating the gesture her small system is programmed to make across time and the solar system. The little automaton's eyes look on, agape. Behind the lens, an intricate, subtle, methodical machine clicks, turns, and whirs unceasingly by day and in sleep to find a resolution to that perennial quandary: the inconsonance between what the lens observes on the horizon and what it beholds in the sky.

the visitation

The sister dreams that she has returned to the first country. Though the distance is great—two continents and an ocean lie between her bunk bed and her first life—and little time has elapsed since she laid down and drew her blanket to her chin, she finds herself in front of her old house in the first land and wonders at the method of conveyance that has deposited her here.

This is how it works in a dream, she remembers. Mother told me
so. Mother said: though your body lies soundly in bed, your spirit
travels where it wishes or is drawn to when you dream. The girl
stands in front of her old house, looks down the hill toward the
city below, which hums under a misty veil, then looks up at her
house, which stands dark and shuttered against a red glowing sky.
She wonders if her family are at her grandmother's. It is Friday
night, after all, and the family may have gathered there for dinner.
She remembers the way to her grandmother's house: it is only
up the hill, past the bread maker's, past the butcher's, around the
next corner, and just opposite the dry fruit vendor's stall. She takes
a step in that direction and is instantly at the door of her grandmother's house. She opens the door, or the door opens of its own
accord, and now she sees it is not family alone who have gathered.
Here are her aunts and uncles, her cousins and the neighbors,
her first schoolteacher, the equally shy friend who shared the first
school desk, the baker, the military men, the nurses and doctors—
all in uniform—the television newscaster, the men who delivered
Mother's china cabinet and carried it up the narrow staircase to
place it in the dining room, Father's coworkers, grandmother's
hens, uncle's sheep from the farm, the cheating grocer from across
the street, and many others she does not recognize.

The sister steps into the house and through the crowd, thinking,
I came here because my dream spirit was bored lying in bed on a
night that is not a school night. I came because I was invited. She
enters the shifting, billowing crowd. Here is the balloon peddler
handing out his colorful orbs, there the cousin showing the small
children how to draw a tiger, here the ice cream maker cranking
his machine, there the musicians sitting cross-legged before their
instruments, awaiting word from their host to begin playing. She

looks for Mother and Father, for her sisters, but cannot locate them. They lie asleep in the new land, too tired or too lazy to make the trip to come to this wondrous gathering. Searching and pushing through the ever-thickening crowd, she comes to the end of the great room. There lies her grandmother on her narrow wicker bed, covered in white from head to foot, eyes closed and jaw bound up with a strip of white cloth. One by one, on bent knee and with heads bowed, her guests pay their respects to the old woman.

The dreaming girl makes it to her grandmother's bedside and stands behind two holy men and a bookseller to await her turn. And the girl sees that it is not the old woman alone who draws the guests to this end of the room; against the wall there is a long table covered with a bountiful array of dishes, from which the guests eagerly fill their plates. She has come to kneel at the old woman's bedside but her attention is arrested by the food on the platters and in the bowls. Here is one filled not with rice and raisins, but with fingernails, whole and pulled clean out. The layers of translucent nails, some yellowing, make a dizzying hatch pattern; peaking out or showing through in places, the bright colors of polish break the pattern. In the center of the table are two large china bowls filled with teeth of many sizes and shapes, smooth or chipped, roots intact, in shades of white, yellow, or gray. And next to them, an oblong dish with eyes of many colors, looking in many directions; round, plump forms that glisten in the half-lit room. Three silver platters at the farther end of the long table are covered with women's breasts of various circumferences and heights, neatly placed next to one another, like many puddings. Nearer the sister, two round trays hold hundreds of fingers arranged as diminishing spirals, some still wearing rings. And she sees it all at once, the entire table, each dish, every wrinkle on each finger, every vein in each eye as her own eyes flit to and fro, as her mind reels and wonders, do the others not see, not heave? Is this what they now eat in the first land?

A soft rhythmic thud and jingle draws the girl's attention away from the table. To her right sits her grandmother on her low bed, playing a tambourine, surrounded by the throng of guests. The old woman slaps her shaking hand against the taut goat skin, and all the while looks directly at the sister, singing words the girl strains to understand in the dream. Her grandmother nods at her; the girl draws nearer through the crowd to stand by her bedside. The old woman plays faster, more forcefully; she closes her eyes, tilts back her head, and opens her mouth to repeat the inaudible lyrics. And the girl sees that in place of a tongue, her grandmother has many rows of neatly arranged teeth, loosely bound to the fleshy bottom of her mouth; she realizes that the rhythmic jingling is not made by the tambourine in her grandmother's hands but by her row upon row of teeth, which strike against each other as she nods and sways. Looking about her at the other guests, the girl sees that now all have their faces bound round with white cloth, their eyes shut, and are moving their torsos in rhythm to the old woman's music.

wake

And is not childhood but a dream? Open your eyes, said the laundress.

childhood

How immense the epoch of their childhood! How timeless those
core years when all five sisters were children. When a walk, measured in steps from one end of the yard to the other, equaled an
entire afternoon! Then, time whispered its ticks, hummed its tocks,
and skipped some altogether. While the greater universe, that mag-
nificent gravity-devouring-death-begetting-light machine, lurched
and tugged, the smaller world of the sisters opened still smaller
worlds, breathed them into being: bees appeared out of thin air
to join the thick summer atmosphere; laughter, while thrilling the
eardrum of a jesting sister, halted long enough to admit a second
joke before resuming; and water revealed its sticky properties to
insect and girl alike.

and water

It is not earth alone that opens up to take and comfort the many
bodies, those dead and those bound for death. And they who push
them, who have been schooled in or come on their own to learn
the subtleties and the physics of the act, they push with equal force
into earthy pits as into rivers, lakes, dams, and wells. A bound
body, a single rope tying it at ankles and wrists, defines the one
arc through the air if the hand pushing hits precisely in the space
between the shoulder blades. Watch the chest lead, the neck snap
back, the jaws snap together the single time, the eyes gaze into
the skull. And they who push, those drivers of small forces, are
surprised at the similarities and come to appreciate the differences

between a fall into the aquatic versus one into the terrestrial grave: air escapes the lungs with a puff upon hitting hard earth, but as a series of gurgles and sprays in the liquid medium; there is equal chance of the neck breaking upon impact with either substrate—it is the angle at which the chin meets the surface that yields such rare deliverance for the body; in the men of this land, who can no more swim as fish than fly as birds, it is a push into water that elicits the coveted scream. And while the great pits are an easier time, a tidier solution, collecting the many bodies at once, neatly concealing them, it is water that holds the attention of the driver of small forces long after that initial arc. The thrashing, bound body fights to stay afloat, turns and turns again in the lake, bends at the neck, hips, knees, and ankles—mimicking the inchworm and not the fish—only to bind itself further, to draw in more water. In the river, the body, like timber, moves with the powerful flow, hits first onc boulder, then the next, at the head, the shoulders, the elbows, or the feet, and releases neat, warm streams of blood, streams that eddy, bead, and sink. Streams that, being of a denser, stickier nature, momentarily oppose the river current's force and freeze the spectator's gaze. And there is also the well, omnipresent in this arid land, which, upon receiving a body, releases the single great exhale. It too is neat, swallows neatly, but it is only for the immediate and small job.

Water takes the many bodies. It enters the bodies, shifts that ratio of liquid to solid further in its own favor, ballooning the dead, coloring their skin a cool hue, and distorting their features, so that the living who go in are not the drowned who come out, should they be pulled out. And water dissolves those who do not find the idle or the brave passer-by in time to be dragged back out onto the dusty earth. The great solvent absorbs and distributes the

molecules evenly through itself and around the globe, in time.
Water returns to water. It receives the dead and comforts the dead.
And what does water learn from the dead about terrestrial life?
What secrets leave the drowned man's flaccid mouth, what stories
are read in his clouded, unblinking eyes? It is the magic element,
water. Watch how the hydrogen bonds snap into place in winter,
collapse in summer. Observe how water changes the landscape,
across the seasons, across the globe, across the ages. See how
water changes form and, in its shifting, rises from the depths to
the heights to fall again, to soar again, then run again, rinsing the
mountaintops, the valleys, and the depths on its circuitous route.
What knowledge does it carry and distribute? To whom does it
deliver its news? Who listens? Is water burdened? Is it joyful? Is it
oblivious? Has it not always carried and constituted life? Known
life more intimately and fundamentally than any other? Does it
not know death equally well? Was it not the first to do so?

In the beginning: water.

I say I am an astronaut. I say I am here to do naught but gaze upon the stars. And even as I fathom the luminous lights above, I sense the wholesome water within. It rises and falls, it fills and buoys me. If my eyes were not firm and not coated with the liquid, what use would they be to the sky? And I think it is they, the ancient glimmering stars, who call water up and bind to it their own salt, so that they might see themselves amplified in my eyes. If I say their beauty makes me cry, will you think me weak? Will you laugh if I add that I know water came to be born in the bowels of rocky bodies, which, blindly hurtling through the empty spaces, grew agitated with an unknown desire, and in their hurtling and spinning and agitation conceived the liquid jewel that would rise and pool on their dusty surfaces so that something might reflect the starry night?

dust

In the beginning: dust: H, C, N, O.

stones

And the dreaming sister observes, as if from a window and across a courtyard, a group of men standing, none too close to another, and staggered over a patch of dry and dusty earth. She does not see the fists that hold the stones or the arms that pitch them—the persecutors are out of view—but the stones come fast from the direction the men face. They hit the standing men on the shoulder, the chest, or across the chin, which makes the head pivot and the body totter momentarily. The men absorb the assault. They falter, bend, sway, and come to stand upright, stand still again, to face forward again. And the sister dreaming watches a stone rush through the air, sees and hears it lodge in the forehead of one of the men, and senses all this closely: the man's face contorted, his eyes crossed and upturned, the lines on his brow deepening, his neat hairline, the moisture collected there, the stone embedded, the blood surfacing. And Mother who is and is not there beside her in the dream describes to her daughter what she is observing. She says, *this is such-and-such*, a phrase in the first tongue, which the girl tries to hear, to decipher in the dream, but cannot. Mother repeats herself, *this is such-and-such. It is when a stone is thrown with a precise aim and with purpose and power enough to lodge itself in the skull, but not so deeply that it causes the man to topple. The stone must lodge and the man must remain upright.* This is the object of their diversion. And the

girl listening, seeing, hears and sees other stones fly, hit, lodge, and
men totter, sway, find their equilibrium again. Beads, not streams,
of blood drip onto their shirts and shirtsleeves, their pant legs and
bare feet, the dusty dry earth. And she cannot turn her gaze. And
Mother who is not there reassures her, *this did not happen in the before.
When I was a child, this did not.*

arc

Against a backdrop of disappearances, drownings, live burials,
hangings, shootings, stonings, electrocutions, beheadings, disem-
bowelments, and dismemberments, the automaton's head makes
the singular arc. And her eyes search the sky for deliverance.

how lonely, how earnest

How lonely we were. We were girls, children. When the gods ventured down from the cosmos, did we not halt our play and climb down from the tree to sit upon the ground from which we had sprung? Did we not bring together the soles of our feet and splay them like the many pages of that ancient book so that the gods might easily read the account of our natural history? Was it not written clearly enough in the lines that perhaps did not score deeply enough into the bottoms of our weary feet? We were born landlocked, surrounded by mountains. Our journey was by land, by air, and over the great swirling sea. All this, and more, was plainly written there. We were wanderers of valleys and hills by day and castaways, adrift upon the bottomless starry sea, by night. Ours was a circuitous route; the gods had traveled directly. Should we have first washed our feet with the garden hose? Should we have bowed, genuflected? We wore our hair long, loose or plaited. They stood about us and looked down at our wide eyes, our moist pink lips and soft full cheeks, our graying hair and wrinkled spotted hands. We were unnatural. Was it this that frightened the silent gods away? Perhaps it was the rustling of leaves in the rosebush at their heels. Did they overhear the garden oracle whisper their fate? Or perhaps the gods noticed the rectangular lawn become more faded at its edges and more vivid, more saturated where we sat in a semicircle before them. Did they, in that moment, learn of our pact with the pigments of the earth? Oh, and how we tried to keep them near with our daily offerings: the sunbaked earthen vessels filled with berries and ladybugs, the bleeding scabs-picked-early, the flowers, the bird feathers, the countless drawings of billowy clouds and snow-peaked mountains. How earnest we were.

forbearance

If you, my constant reader, are sapped by this wearisome method of telling, take pity on me who, at a very great loss of time, had to work through at least a thousand repetitions of it, not to mention the anguish involved in writing with the dead at my side, over my shoulder; nor will you be surprised to know that by now the ninth year is nearly past since I took on the task.

birds

She dreams that she stands beneath a tree and the tree is filled with birds and a din not unlike the one that filled her grandmother's house in the midst of a celebration, just at the setting out of a meal, when all elbows, hands, eyes, mouths, cups, plates, platters, pots, and spatulas were moving, meeting, busy. And the sister dreaming wonders, is this one of the dreams about the birds, the birds that are and yet are not real because their tail and their crest feathers are much too long, too wrought, too luminous in color, and their movements in the air less like flight and more like conversation: at times lively, at others lingering, at times coy, at others insistent. And just then, a bird, a single one, comes out of the clamorous canopy, shows itself to the sister, who sees it is a small tree finch, common in form, size, and plumage. And the sister follows the small bird as it moves from tree to hedge, across a manicured garden, and through the open door of a lamplit house. And she sees that it is day, and yet the lights are on in the house, yet it is the bright middle of day, outside, a thousand birds singing. Entering the house, the sister finds herself in a long dark hall, its two sides regularly opening onto numerous rooms, some grand and others close. And passing the rooms, she sees that each is filled with a variety of lit lamps hanging from the ceilings, sitting atop every piece of furniture, and standing about the floor—filling the rooms floor to ceiling at every level with lit bulbs—each lamp placed so as to be in perfect relation to all the others. She enters one of the rooms at the farther end of the hall and is drawn to a framed image directly ahead of her on one of the walls. She steps through and around the lamps, which glimmer and twinkle, but none too brightly. The sister steps in front of the image, and, mistaking it for a mirror, stares long into it, recognizes the furrow in her brow, the reflective eyes, the earnest set lips. She stares long and wonders at the cropped hair, the pointy mustache, the square beard, the tall, white, stiff ruff. She wonders and scrutinizes, then remembers the picture in her schoolbook, the portrait of the man with eyes like telescopes, the new astronomer who studied the rhythms of the universe, and told tales of order and harmony. The recognition is immediate.

the garden

Enter. There is room here for many. The air is fresh, the sky blue. Find a bench. Set down your blanket. Look out. The garden is in full bloom. Find the chapter, find the page. Look in,
says the book.

. . .

Who writes war? Who tells its story? The soldier? The scholar?
Did the early poets, those great explorers of the underworld,
scratch their knowledge of war into the leaves of dead trees and
bequeath that understanding to posterity or, holding their boon
too near, did they take it back under with them? Does the historian
not have the clearest grasp of events? Perhaps the story belongs
to the traveler who was passing through when war escalated; he
had a camera around his neck and *he* had no stake in the conflict.
Perhaps it belongs to the boy who was tempted by the bright and
idle toy, which ripped his arm from his body and strew his fingers
a hundred feet in each direction. The boy who carried that limb
three miles back to his house, through the wood, across the newly
tilled fields, and into the courtyard to place the shredded appendage before his sisters and his mother. And does the newscaster who
is informed say anything when he moves his lips? *The volume is up,*
Father asked us to turn it up, shhh, this is about us.

Is war a word or a cry? Is it a song, a dirge repeated across time
and space? And who sings this song? Or perhaps, by necessity, war
must be a wail, necessarily howled by invisible lips (for who has
seen such a creature?), carried over hills, through the canopies of

trees, beneath doors, into homes and heads? Is war a man's tale
to tell? Is it his alone, of his mind and calculated there, afterward
incubated in his groin? How carefully he guards that place! Does
woman know the story better, tend to it in her full heart, succor it
at her breast, feel its pain more acutely between her legs, whence
the limbless boy sprouted? The gods, what do they say? Or do
they speak? This one, he watches, his leg twitches, a yawn, the god
surrenders to sleep. Does he dream war? And in his dream, when
he is no longer the great, wise, male god, but a girl, no, five small
girls, does he then speak war? Will war then have a name in the
god's dream? And will the girls, one or all of them, ever speak the
name? The three letters together, they are not what you see, would
like to think they are: they are not tidy, not pure. Inherently, they
lie and can therefore not be trusted on the page or on the tongue.
See how tightly they are bound together, the three letters: consonants, like lips pursed around the single opening where the wail lies,
unwilling to utter the truth, to release the cry within the vowel. But
wait. Separate the letters. Here you have a beginning, or the chance
for one, for the movable type will combine again and with others
and, given a task, will find meaning after much circling, after much
distillation, find meaning at the center, that place of concentration
where the mass of a billion stars is compressed down to a point.

The sisters sit in a circle. And the girl, the middle one, opens her
mouth. She makes a hissing sound, falters, shakes her head, hisses
again. She looks from sister to sister, then at her own hands, which
perspire and tremble, as if crying. She knows she must speak the
word. It is a single word, she knows this, feels it in her own soft,
small belly, sees it in her sisters' unblinking eyes. It is a word, one,
but not the one heard, read, or spoken. It is not war, war is not

what you may think, read, speak . . . think, speak, watch, shudder, read the newspaper, the book, though you might. The sister does not, cannot find the word in the lazy god's dream. Though she dives in and under, she comes up   .

She surrenders and accepts this defeat, breathes in, cleansed of the god's lazy dream. She leaves the search for letters, leaves the letters to their own devices, knowing they will, through movement and rearrangement, through circling and distillation, spell the single utterance that war is not.

She, instead, returns to the first form: the image drawn. Her eyes closed, breath held, against the pile of the crimson rug, with her steady finger, she draws this: ☺ And eyes closed, she knows that her sisters nod in agreement and, with her, exhale.

laughter

What happens when after eons of winding toward center, that light-devouring aperture, our great galaxy unwinds outward? Does it not seem that this unwinding is inevitable, a very necessary release from the draw of the keen orifice, a denial of its relent-less suction? But what is the opposite of the fall toward center? Perhaps a return to childhood? What would be the result of break-ing such a pact, the pact with the grave, the strange cosmic and human pact with gravity? A loosening of things wound perhaps: vocal chords vibrating with the singular sound of laughter.

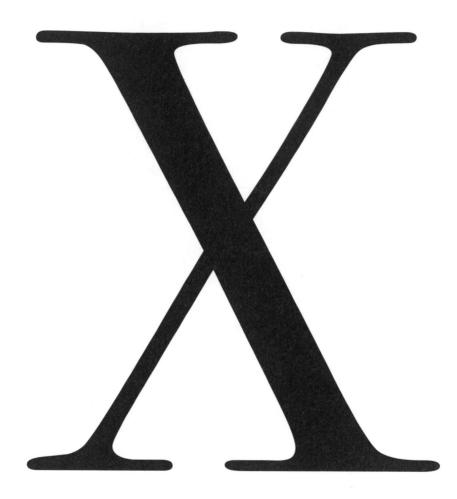

There is no sign to mark where our maternal grandfather buried his family's treasure after the invading armies slaughtered his parents. In a hurry and terrified, just before he fled his homeland, he dug a great pit and in it buried a chest filled with the weight of ten grown men in gold and gemstones. And as one fleeing a new and unfamiliar terror, confident that he would soon return to retrieve his riches, reoccupy his family's land, and repopulate it with his brood, he neglected to mark the location of his fortune or to draw a map leading back to it. And the new life that absorbed the exile in the new land, the wife and the children and the vocation that came to fill his days and his embrace, this new and ever-unfurling life buried the old life with many layers of sediment so that the tales that draw my regard now from the present are the muffled echoes of another time. And how I strain to hear!

X misses the spot where the dead lie, in single or mass graves. Though many feet and the wheels of traveling vehicles cross and cross again over them, nothing signals the locations where the war dead lie. Who and what will honor them? Memory? *It* only lives a generation, a single lifetime. Is it not instead the tale, long and circuitous, which brings the reader to the gravesite? Come, sway with me.

X, that most difficult and evasive of letters. It wants to say so
much, with such authority and purpose, yet it yields so little.
For it is all limbs, pointing to a center, and all limbs, pointing out. I have it, it says, it is here, look! And yet, there is
nothing when we turn. It says there! We look. In the meantime,
it has scurried off, like a spider anxious for shadows and corners.

wanderers

They are a nostalgic people. They stand upright, walk from place
to place, sit, lie down, and stand again, and walk again, and
throughout, the longing, like a plumb line hanging from that soft
pit below the sternum, draws them downward to the earth's dense
core. And against this draw, their eyes gaze upward, as if for relief.

Mother, she listens to the worn tapes that play and play again
the old film songs. The girls need only to press a button and she
is transported, and they with her through the twinkling, wistful
spaces, hanging on her skirts, admiring the whirling planets and
the fixed small lights.

Father, he works the soil with his hands or the edge of a spade.
He pinches the dead flowers and leaves and clips the redundant
branches. He understands and admires the simple forms, the basic
forms, and he works to raise them again from the new soil: the
round apple, the pendulous grape cluster, the vertical leak. And
the girls chase these old icons, running from garden patch to garden patch.

The sisters need not look to Father or to Mother for the source of their longing. They carry the gene; they look back. Though nothing is there, they look.

above us,

The cosmos: where the living and the dead dwell in harmony.

book

Down the centuries, one after another arrives to rule and dictate. They bring their gods and their technologies. And some decree adherence to the gods and some to the machines. The men of boots and rifles arrive from distant lands to annihilate the devout and set up a new godless order. They fill the streets, proclaim their supremacy, and burn down grandfather's bookstore. Grandfather is a pious man who sells holy books to the faithful. His shop incinerated, he knows they will find his home and his family next. In the dark of the night, he and his small family leave with their beliefs, a few articles of clothing, and a single singed book. They arrive in the new land still longing for the old.

Father, born in the new land, falls in love with the land out of which his learned, devout father—exchanging books for sickle and spade—raises cotton, beets, peaches, mulberries, goats, chickens, a home, and a simple living for his family. Father, still a child, runs away to the city to quench a thirst for learning older than himself at his tender age. It is not long before he has amassed the knowledge, gained the experience through the many jobs, found Mother, and sired his own brood. It is not long before the men of boots and rifles and tanks arrive to his beloved land to annihilate the educated, the connected, the wealthy, and the believers. Father and Mother, and their five small girls, leave with a few articles of clothing, a set of porcelain dishes, two red wool rugs, and the old longing for the first land.

Father's brothers, left behind, are killed by the men of god who are next to arrive to cleanse the country of the disbelievers and the educated, the fashionable, and the traveler walking north when he should be walking south down the village road. His brothers leave behind and pass down to their small and yet-unborn children the single book they and Father, growing up on the farm, read as small boys: a holy book with gilded edges, written in a scribe's melodious hand, badly charred along two edges, and smelling of fire.

bright star

The girl dreams that the sun has gone away. She steps outside and sees the night sky, though it is day. It is night, but it should be day. She knows it is true, yet her mind fights it: the sun has left for another sky. In its place it has left behind the billion stars that it once bedimmed with its own brilliance. It has left behind the inky backdrop. And the dreaming girl looks at the stars twinkling against the black curtain. And the dreaming girl falls to her knees in disbelief. She falls to her knees from the absolute shock of this insuperable loss. She falls to her knees and, in falling, bruises and scrapes them. Her knees bleed. In her mind, a thousand small explosions. In her mind, a thousand small   , like many suns bursting. She falls onto the ground, wants to fall into the earth, to disappear into its depths, wants to disappear inside its solid utter darkness. And the earth opens, it takes her in. It is not her mother but it will take her in. She falls forward, her head heavy, her arms limp, her knees bent; falls into the dark cavern that has opened up to take her in. When the earth closes up over her again, she does not draw a last breath of air, she does not look back to take in a final glimpse of the sky. And what are a billion stars twinkling when hers has gone?

the living-on

The living-on after another has passed. The walking-away from a fresh grave filled. As if barefoot, over glass.

longing

So the exiled sisters learn to make their way in the new land: here is a book; here is your school desk; here your friends; here an alphabet to help you communicate with them; if you wear this top just so, comb your hair just so, you will acquire more of them; if you add 2 and 3, you will have 5; if you turn the television dial, you will locate wonders and truths; if you nod when spoken to, you will comprehend the mysteries. The sisters learn to wear the proper articles of clothing, the proper smiles; learn to nod and wave hello; to draw the clouds just so; to fill the notebooks just so with the accurate figures; to speak the proper words in the customary ways to their teachers, neighbors, grocers, school friends: to navigate the new land in accordance with the correct codes and standards of the land.

But the sisters know that 2 and 3 rarely equal 5; that their hair daily sculpts itself according to its own laws and whatever pact it has made with the elements of the natural world; that clouds do not desire to be illustrated, they demand to be followed in the sky by eyes half-open; that the television only displays a two dimensional copy of the external land; and, most naturally, that the mysteries are not explicable.

The sisters remember when and by what means they left their birthland, and when and how they arrived in the land of the sun, but they cannot recall when and why they became exiles of the internal land. And it is *this* exile, and the riddle of it, that produces the keenest longing in their small chests. What the sisters knew within themselves, in the beginning, does not correspond to what they find in the world without. The land about them is a strange and corrupted reproduction of the land within. The two are animated—wind and whir, unfurl and thrum, oscillate and ping—by different machinery. In the first land, the internal land, all makes sense. In the external, the sisters make themselves dizzy chasing the how's and just-so's, the therefore's and must-be's.

Occasionally, they come across someone who seems to share the longing, who returns the candid smile, or gazes into their eyes with a silent affectionate greeting, or are themselves practicing the gesture: the ice cream truck driver who absentmindedly hands them their cones on a late summer's evening, while longingly scanning the red, bird-filled sky in the west; the gleaming toddler in the stroller at the grocery store, present but not yet exiled; the school teacher who says, "yes, this is so and that is correct" but hands the sister a book not on the reading list; the old man at the wedding who folds his napkin into a rotating menagerie of animal figures long after the other guests have risen from the dinner table to dance and mingle.

The sisters live in the new land but long and long to return to the first, to the beginning. How vast, how full, how true was life in the first land, the internal land. In the interior, thought and flight were one and the same; sight and understanding were one; imagination, like a generator, produced both light and heat; ardor simultaneously produced tears and a smile, lifted the body, weight-less, into the air, and compressed it to a breathless point. One imagined, and one was. One did, and one was. One spoke and one was in the internal. All corresponded. In the interior land, the sisters are. In the external, they were but shadows. The external life is a crude counterfeit of the first. No matter how the sisters try to live in consonance with the internal, to allow the logic of the interior a seat in the outer world, the two lands will not meet and, over the years, they shift further and further apart. So the longing grows. So, the sisters, pining after what no longer is, become like dispossessed comets chasing their own trailing locks about the solar system. And it is there, against the black dome of a wintry sky, that the new astronomer first fixes his eyes on the sisters.

banished

The sister whose turn it is to take the trash bins out into the alleyway for pickup has forgotten to complete her chore. But a mournful wailing in her dream wakes her. The room is still dark and only a dusty blue light comes in through the window. She rises from bed, pulls on a sweatshirt, and slips on her tennis shoes. It is early yet and the warm glow outlining the closed bathroom door tells her that Mother is getting ready for work. She steps gingerly through the house and carefully opens and shuts the door to the backyard. The gate to the alley opens with a grumble. In the dis-tance, she hears the beeping and clunking of the garbage trucks. She pulls the two bins up, one at a time, over the grass and the gravel, and parks them next to the neighbor's bins. A piercing

howl fixes her to her spot. She looks left and right down the alleyway. All is still. Another wail, this one longer, more distant, more
humanlike, draws her attention to the right. But a crash to her
left, and a few houses down, makes her jump and turn to face
that direction as she backs up against Father's car. A willowy form
emerges from behind a knocked-over trash bin. It is a silhouette in
the early dim dawn, yet it is lighter than all around it. It seems to
shift without moving, not gliding, but flickering in and out of her
vision—though she has not blinked—and each time appearing
inches from where it was. And all the while, it keeps its gleaming
eyes steady on her as well. The upright ears, the pointy snout, the
full tail, the long legs tell her it is a dog. But the way the animal
stands motionless-moving and familiarly gazes at her, and the
wails still echoing in her ears, assures the sister the creature is not
a dog. Finding her courage, she backs up into the yard, closes the
gate and stands inside for several minutes. She hears the more
distant howl again, and hears a rustle, then a rush outside the gate.
Answering its mate's call, the jackal streaks down the alleyway.
The sky in the east has a pink tinge to it now. She walks back to
the house. Through the neighbor's chainlink fence, she sees the
neighbor's dog curled up and soundly asleep on its blanket.

correspondence

The sisters scanned the sky and the sisters dug as deeply as they
could into the earth. The earth let in fingers and bodies but denied
the eyes their faculty. What it hid, it hid deeply, covetously from
the eyes. The well-watered lawn beneath their feet teased the

sisters, promising them a return to the internal, promising a peek into the mysteries that lie deep. But their digging in the valley floor yielded, at best, seashells that told of an ancient receding tide, which captivated their imaginations, but did not sate their longing. They dug up old nails, washers, buttons, marbles, and occasionally a small bone, and used these finds to make dolls, instruments, and jewelry. Still they longed. They used the stiff, slippery mud to shape beads and urns, and still longed. They painted their faces with the brown slip, dressed their hair in leaves and berries, but could not erase enough history to return to the beginning.

Unlike the earth, the sky was amenable to the eye (and other lenses). So, longing for a return back to the vast internal, the sisters looked up to the boundless sky. While the tender earth kissed and warmed the soles of their feet, provided them with minerals, flora, and fauna to satisfy their busy hands and feed their imaginations and hearts, it would not quench the longing. So, practicing the gesture, scanning the sky from horizon to zenith, they began to see patterns. Across the many nights, they saw the sky repeating. The fixed stars became familiar, the restless planets spoke to the restless girls, the plummeting meteors flashed, then faded, then flashed again across the domes of their minds, thrilling them. There in the sky, they sensed harmony and order. They nodded. The sisters used no charts, tallied no integers, kept no records, but they found correspondence in the sky. What was above was also within.

recollection

And the eyes, when they alight on the stars, locate in the sky the harmony lost through exile.

tomb = tome

And will you judge the sisters when they rise in the deepest hours of the night, file out of doors in flip-flops and pajamas to collect Father's shovels and picks from the garage, and, by the dim, orange light of the streetlamp, dig the graves into which they might transfer the dead from their own small casings? Would not the manicured suburban yard—rather than the child's busy, grimy, gawky form—be a more suitable home for the weary war dead? Will the warm earth not be a more restful bed? Do you not see that the dead are made nauseous by the sisters' twirling and skipping, their climbing and swinging, their laughter and their fickleness, day in and out? They need to rest, the dead. And these new beds the sisters dig will sprout grass over them again; they will be daily watered and weekly mowed by the industrious girls. Father, unknowingly, will plant more roses, more fruit trees over the graves, and these roses and fruit trees will produce as never before. Mother will be delighted! The neighbors will share in the bounty. Is this not a solution for all—the sisters, the dead, Father, Mother, the birds and insects who will no doubt arrive from near and far to partake of the cornucopia? No? Reader, you say no? This is too uncanny, too morbid for your palate?

No, say the dead, whose bodies lie elsewhere, already. It is the dead who counter. (My dear reader, I have misjudged your sensitivity again. I asked the question and heard a clear answer, firmly in the negative, and, looking up, mistook the shadow for you.) It is the dead who say no. They will put up with the twirling and the climbing yet, the dead who occupy the living. They have mastered equanimity and patience. In time, they will lie in the pages of books, and there will find the restful sleep. This is what the dead dream of when the sisters close their eyes at night. The promising dream is what they await the day through. And the sisters, like narrow, teetering tenement houses, conscious/unconscious of the restless occupants within their slight frames, are themselves eager to assume the horizontal position at night. After the girls have completed the last of their homework, washed the dishes, swept the kitchen floor, finished watching the game show and the news, brushed their teeth, braided or unbraided their hair, let out or let in the cat, kissed Mother and Father goodnight, slipped into bed, and immediately or by-and-by fallen asleep, the war dead will follow suit. They will turn out the lights, lie prostrate, and dream about the still tomb, the quiet and the final sleep, the dark between the pages of the book on the library shelf.

irreducible

Their longing led them to search. Their searching, which grew
out of a need, became in time a vocation for the girls: a systematic
study of the nature of the world about them.

And the aim of their science was to locate what is irreducible:
The earth
The sky
The story (*born of earth and sky but no more divisible than its parents*)

Having discovered these, they drew their lids closed.

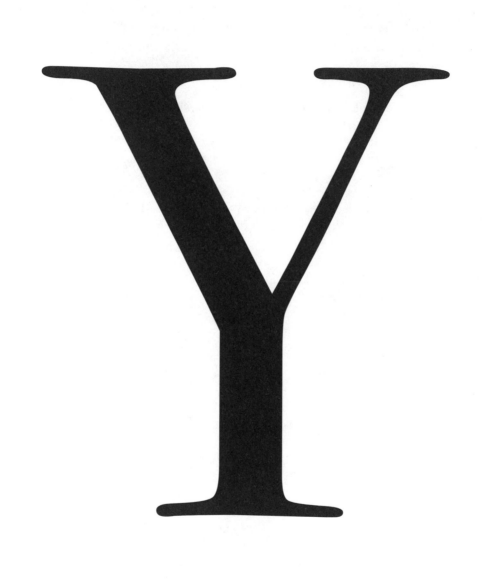

Yesterday, and all it holds in its deep pockets.

in the beginning

In the beginning: tanks, soldiers. Fire in the sky, limbs in the trees, blood in the streets.

No, in the beginning, before the visitors: silence. A silence born of nothing, arriving from nowhere. Though perhaps it descended from above, for it reached the adults first and cleared the world of talk. Then suddenly, how crisp the birds' chitter, how full the chorus of turning leaves, fluttering wings, scuttling feet! And the full song of nature in the city brought all of the children out of doors. How bright, lovely, and lively the world became for a brief moment in the middle of winter. Until the hum of the tanks, the beat of the soldiers' boots, the sigh of the rockets, silenced the animals too. And then, the children.

No, in the beginning, before the silence: a dream. A god's plan folded into a child's dream. Not one child but many children dreaming the god's mind, seeing: where he would plant which tank, on what street, beneath what tree; from what house, which humble village, which sparkling city in the distant land he would cull the soldiers; from which mountain he would extract the minerals to fabricate the weapons to place in the sleepwalking soldiers' hands; from what heights he would drop the many bombs; into whose beating temple he would fire the bullet; in which patch of earth he would hide the bodies. For a year, the children shivered and turned in their sleep, woke weary.

In the beginning: the gods. Gods who would plant the future in the fertile soil of the child's dream. Not to ready her but to steal and lock her gaze: for all theater needs an audience. And the gods who fashioned the eyeball prefer its silent steady gaze to the noisy clapping of the hands, which learned the awkward motion through fumbling, while the world was still dark.

In the beginning: the eyelid. In the pact made between god and child, the one fashioned the firm wet orb, the other answered with the soft dark curtain—to protect the eye, to clear the stage, to open and close the ages.

birth

Mother says to Father, it is a girl again. Father picks up the small bundle—warm, burbling—and whispers a welcome and a prayer into her ear.

kaleidoscope

So the sister is once again in the dream that takes the veil from the face of the cosmos and shows the stars for what they are: mortal. Here they are, the stars, wild and acute entities, monumental forces acutely gathered into pulsing points of light. But they are not light, not mineral, not human, not animal, not plant, not god. In these dreams, the stars are vastly brighter, more colorful, beautiful, terrible, mischievous, gleeful, breathtaking!—markedly keener than what they affect at night in the waking world.

And what is it that has allowed the stars to reveal themselves in the girl's dream? She guesses it is her old playmate/adversary: Time. Here in these dreams, Time has wound two clocks—the earthly one and the cosmic one. And it lets the earthly clock unwind at the normal rate while it makes the other clock fly so that eons pass in the sky as seconds tick on earth. And the earthbound child looks up and sees that the stars too coil, breathe, hunger, dream, hurtle, and expire.

And over her head, in the dream, all the stars come together in formation to try to speak in a language the sister might understand. The girl's eyes, whether she is in a field, or by the ocean, or at an airport, or in a grocery parking lot, whether she is alone or surrounded by few or hordes of people, her eyes are drawn in the ascendant direction, as if raised by two strong magnets deep in the sky. And here they are again, the true stars, the stars unmasked! And in the dream, each pulsing point of light and color is a separate and ardent being who wants avidly to speak in a language the child will understand, but who knows that without a tongue, all it can do is line up with its sibling stars in formation to create first one, then another, then another picture against the inky backdrop. *Do you not see?*, each and all of the stars seem to ask the sister. She nods, I do, I do! I see you have something to say. They realign themselves, some moving closer, some receding, creating disks and lines, spirals and triangles, all the while pulsing intensely, able to communicate to her no more than *Look! Look!*

And the dreaming sister tries just as earnestly to understand them, feels the endeavor in her toes, her gut, the palms of her hands. She tries to read the stars, but she cannot. She goes to those around her, commands them Look! Look! But they are too absorbed in kicking and chasing a ball about a field or tuning the radio in their car or cutting a cake or pushing a grocery cart. Look up! Look up! she begs of the people all about. *Do you not see?* the stars pulse down at her. And all she can do is wonder at their beauty, their splendor, their ferocity. In some of the stars, she senses a warmth and a joyfulness, in others a crafty playfulness and, in others still, a gaping hunger. Though they are light, they are dark. Though they are playful, they are cruel; though loving, hungry.

And the sister dreaming understands that all that is dark is not wicked and what is bright might also feed the destructive appetite. She knows that good and evil are not unrelated; they are two parts of the same egg; they both feed the same mouth, both advance the same coiling apparatus: Life. She admires the cause of Creation and fears the appetite of Chaos. And what is this order/disorder in the universe? What is its source? It is a beautiful and a magnetic thing. It is a churning, chaotic thing. It fuels and extinguishes. It swells and contracts. It collects and packs the dust into hot twinkling nuclei or sends it hurtling lifeless-rudderless across the cold dark spaces. It is a beautiful and fathomless cosmos. It steals the gaze and palpitates the heart. She cannot turn away.

so, life

And in time, the horror and the banal—the distant war's incessant clawing at their young hearts and the repetition of life's small diurnal doings—came to rest one next to the other, and soon merged one into another, so that the two were one. And was a sister not capable of crying into the kitchen sink as she rinsed a basket of strawberries and swayed to her favorite new song on the radio? Was she not able to draw the snow-covered mountain peak while listening to Mother plan her nephew's funeral over the telephone? The sisters were whole and wholeness was a blend of guilt and glee, humor and remembrance, great losses and small achievements, slumber and nightmare. And the sister who studies for the history exam looks at the text on the page in the book and thinks, no, that is not correct. That is not how they do it. There is no need for the blindfold on the prisoner, and the weight of his body alone is sufficient to produce the desired effect. The sister sent to call her sibling in to dinner calls out a name long-unused and now misshapen on her tongue and strange to her own ear, the name of a favorite cousin already a widow in the first land. The sisters wrestling on the floor writhe and roll, pant, screech and giggle, scramble and plead, and come to rest panting-giggling on a small pile of bills, advertisements, and a thin, creased blue envelope addressed to Father by an awkward hand in the letters of the new alphabet.

And the sister brushing her teeth finds in the mirror two new gray hairs at her temple. She nods and the mirror returns a foamy grin.

So Mother says to her girls: Life, you cannot unravel it. It is not the ball of yarn, not the braid on your head, not the living room rug. It grows in on itself, coils, collects, flourishes, fuels, warps, rasps, bleeds, brims, pulses, and empties; it enters even as it exits, sighs even as it howls, bruises even as it sweetens. This. This is life.

message

And though the sister who dreams does not grasp, or is unable to pull through that diaphanous yet impervious veil—not the eyelid but the dreamlid—the vital dream message of the birds, or of the stars, or of the moon, or of the living and the dead left behind in the first land, she, nonetheless and unwittingly, delivers their communications to any who might be playing or reading or cleaning beside her, when, on a random date, at an arbitrary hour, in the bright middle of day, beneath a cloudless, sun-drenched sky, she opens her mouth to speak the words that are not her words in the ecstatic voice of the child momentarily unmoored from custom and from consciousness. And afterward, all within hearing, including the girl, burst out in laughter and writhe with giddiness at the rare absurdity she has delivered into their midst.

above

Dear reader, come, look! Place your eye here. Just here over the lens. Look at the cloud, that dense shifting mantle in the sky. Keep watching. Do you see it spiral? Look again, it begins to evaporate. And the radiance at its center: a star, at inception.

in the beginning:

a star

flowers

In the land of the sun, summer reigned but briefly disguised itself as the year went round, donning the mask of each season for days at a time, and puckishly throwing it off lest the inhabitants of the land doubt where it was they lived. During the long winter break, when Mother and Father were at work, when neighbors and shop owners went off to distant destinations on holiday, and the sisters had endless days to practice not-doing, they left the house, one after another, and entered the deserted streets with a faint intention in the backs of their minds of heading somewhere—to school or store or library or friend's house. They walked from block to block, passing school, shut up and shrunken, or the dark and cool library, with its door half-open in invitation, or the friend's house, which may or may not contain within its festively decorated exterior and shuttered windows the friend. The crape myrtles bloomed red, pink, and white and dusted the sidewalks with their tiny crinkled petals. Neighborhood pets lay against fences and car tires, across driveways and rooftops, imbibing the sun. The sisters aimlessly marched to the hum of pool motors and the spray of lawn sprinklers, their eyes always on something just down the next block, around the next corner. The dream called. The sun soothed and drew them round and round the neighborhood. Unconsciously, they stepped over cracks and lines while their arms lifted to pet the trunks of trees, or thrum the chains of fences. Here they plucked a rose, there a fern frond, at this corner a sprig of rosemary, from the friend's yard a daylily. They wandered and collected under the sun's spell. The school gates were locked but the purple asters growing along its fence begged to be picked. Birds and butterflies visited honeysuckle, hibiscus, lavender, and lantana, and the sisters followed, and plucked. From lawns and deserted parking lots, they collected golden poppies. Jasmine and clematis reached out to them through overburdened trellises. The sisters obliged. They picked and gathered. They meandered. And each in her time found her way back out of the dream, retreated into the cool house, kicked off tennis shoes or flip-flops, and headed toward the kitchen. Arms filled with color and light, each was eager to find the right vase or pot, eager to put up her feet and busy her hands composing her bouquet.

in the beginning: a flower

See the rose, it opens and it opens and it opens. It is all petal. All color. All fragrance. All light and mineral, captured, coded, presented. Adored reader, a flower.

in the beginning: a story

And if you search for the sisters, you will not find them. They are movable and have moved again. The house they lived in is that one there. See how the guava tree still blocks the kitchen window? Although, that is not the lawn on which they practiced somersaults and backbends, and that isn't the garage in which they tinkered. No, the house is this one here, the yellow one with the white trim. The sycamore has lost its vigor, though the screen door still squeaks. But their house did not have an attic—what adventures an attic would have afforded them! No, they did not live on this street; this is not their neighborhood. Perhaps they lived in another city. Maybe they have not yet arrived. Still, it is a good story: five sisters, a mother, a father, a tree, a cat.

the characters

A B C D E F G H I J K L M N O P Q R S T U V W X Y Z

Exit

My dear reader, it is late. Please switch off the light. Turn over the page. Sleep.

dream

And when you look up at the stars, do you not feel a sensation as of falling forward, turning in? Are you not like the dry seedpod dispersing seed, the wave crashing onto the beach, the wrist turning to present the watch face? Is not all of life a turning in? Do you not see your own shadow cast across the dome of the cosmos as the warm sphere beneath you spins? Can you not sift the stars with your fingers? And the sky is beautiful. It gleams. And your eyes are closed, not open. Dream.

the sisters, outside

The sisters are called on from both directions. They are pulled at from below and from above. Tonight, they step outside after Mother and Father have gone to bed to sleep the unenchanted sleep of the toiling wage earner in the new country, tucked beneath their new-life comforters, which make Father's feet tingle and swell with false heat, and Mother's bladder fill too early in the night with the same false heat, and cause husband and wife to toss and turn under a barrage of false dreams, dreams like many supermarket apples. And the girls, unable to sleep, small and wafery, step outside and onto the lawn, wet with dew. They gather beneath the grandfather tree, now wakeful and watchful in the night, as he is not by day when he is more tree than memory. The sky is clear. And the sisters are pulled on from below and they sense the earthworm, warm and moist and not-forgotten beneath the skin of the earth under their feet. And the worm, which writhes and works tirelessly, turns the earth in all places and with equal force, minuscule, in all places minute, but proportionate in all places, so that the earth is tilled and the earth turns and is made to rotate on its tilted pin. And while the earthworm wiggles and turns the earth, the earth draws and draws its offspring to itself and pins them to her surfaces, holds there their many feet, many and multiplying, feet crooked and clawed, hoofed and horned, feet spread and flat. And the sisters, with their soft, arched feet bound to the earth and kissed by filaments of dewy grass, walk out onto the lawn to stand bound, drawn by earth and earthworm. But their eyes are called to the sky. Above them, the Milky Way writhes and pulses.

The sisters are not asleep. They are tugged at from below and from above and it is neither the earth nor the sky that makes them girls, flesh and living. It is the draw, calling them up and pulling them down, that makes their blood circuit through their small bodies and makes their breath leave and return, exit and return, and makes them stand upright. But how is it possible we should be standing upright, like reeds, we are animal and yet we stand upright and the blood circulates, is drawn down and then fights this pull to rise up only to fall again and rush upward again and plummet again. And standing upright, the girls are not gods, and they are not of the gods, and the gods were conceited to think so. It is not god who speaks through the child, the child born of two opposing forces, forever bringing these two colossal forces into equilibrium, at every second breathing them into balance, at every moment knowing that she has little choice if she is to stand upright, if she is to feel the star's light upon her cheek and the earth's moisture between her toes. It is a strength the gods cannot fathom and can therefore not claim as their own. It was an illusion. Theirs. From the beginning. When the gods passed over the earth and saw the upright children, they could not help but smile and could not help but weep and this weeping, new to them, kept them gazing down with parental pride. And with the pride of parents new, they took to dancing, putting on their best theater to entertain the earthbound child, all the while their own gazes set and bound upon the child. But the child has parents elsewhere and, like all orphans, senses these parents but does not know them, senses them and yearns for them, comes out nightly in search of them. The mysteries of the world lie deep. The child, bound, upright, yearns but does not know that the writhing worm, the spinning earth, and the spiraling arms of the galaxy are the forces that move her blood, and fill, then relieve, her lungs.

Zenith. The point on the celestial sphere directly above the observer. The point that drew and drew the sisters' eyes.

Zenith. The highest point reached in the sky by a celestial body. The point where nightly the sisters' forms, drawn crudely with the light of passing stars, linger momentarily.

Christian Fagerlund

Fowzia Karimi was born in Kabul, Afghanistan and grew up in Southern California. She immigrated to United States in 1980 after the Soviet invasion of Afghanistan. Karimi has a background in Studio Art and Biology, and received her MFA in Creative Writing from Mills College in Oakland, California. Her work explores the correspondence on the page between the written and the visual arts. She is a recipient of the Rona Jaffe Foundation Writers' Award, and has illustrated *The Brick House* by Micheline Aharonian Marcom (Awst Press) and *Vagrants and Uncommon Visitors* by A. Kendra Greene (Anomalous Press).

Thank you all
for your support.
We do this for you,
and could not do
it without you.

DEEP
VELLUM

PARTNERS

pixel ||| texel

EMBREY FAMILY
FOUNDATION

ALLRED
CAPITAL MANAGEMENT
of
RAYMOND JAMES®

AVAILABLE NOW FROM DEEP VELLUM

MICHÈLE AUDIN · *One Hundred Twenty-One Days*
translated by Christiana Hills · FRANCE

BAE SUAH · *Recitation*
translated by Deborah Smith · SOUTH KOREA

EDUARDO BERTI · *The Imagined Land*
translated by Charlotte Coombe · ARGENTINA

CARMEN BOULLOSA · *Texas: The Great Theft* · *Before* · *Heavens on Earth*
translated by Samantha Schnee · Peter Bush · Shelby Vincent · MEXICO

LEILA S. CHUDORI · *Home*
translated by John H. McGlynn · INDONESIA

SARAH CLEAVE, ed. · *Banthology: Stories from Banned Nations* ·
IRAN, IRAQ, LIBYA, SOMALIA, SUDAN, SYRIA & YEMEN

ANANDA DEVI · *Eve Out of Her Ruins*
translated by Jeffrey Zuckerman · MAURITIUS

ALISA GANIEVA · *Bride and Groom* · *The Mountain and the Wall*
translated by Carol Apollonio · RUSSIA

ANNE GARRÉTA · *Sphinx* · *Not One Day*
translated by Emma Ramadan · FRANCE

JÓN GNARR · *The Indian* · *The Pirate* · *The Outlaw*
translated by Lytton Smith · ICELAND

GOETHE · *The Golden Goblet: Selected Poems*
translated by Zsuzsanna Ozsváth and Frederick Turner · GERMANY

NOEMI JAFFE · *What are the Blind Men Dreaming?*
translated by Julia Sanches & Ellen Elias-Bursac · BRAZIL

CLAUDIA SALAZAR JIMÉNEZ · *Blood of the Dawn*
translated by Elizabeth Bryer · PERU

JUNG YOUNG MOON · *Seven Samurai Swept Away in a River* · *Vaseline Buddha*
translated by Yewon Jung · SOUTH KOREA

KIM YIDEUM · *Blood Sisters*
translated by Ji yoon Lee · SOUTH KOREA

JOSEFINE KLOUGART · *Of Darkness*
translated by Martin Aitken · DENMARK

YANICK LAHENS · *Moonbath*
translated by Emily Gogolak · HAITI

FOUAD LAROUI · *The Curious Case of Dassoukine's Trousers*
translated by Emma Ramadan · MOROCCO

FORTHCOMING FROM DEEP VELLUM

MARIO BELLATIN · *Mrs. Murakami's Garden*
translated by Heather Cleary · MEXICO

MAGDA CARNECI · *FEM*
translated by Sean Cotter · ROMANIA

MIRCEA CĂRTĂRESCU · *Solenoid*
translated by Sean Cotter · ROMANIA

MATHILDE CLARK · *Lone Star*
translated by Martin Aitken · DENMARK

LEYLÂ ERBIL · *A Strange Woman*
translated by Nermin Menemencioğlu · TURKEY

ANNE GARRÉTA · *In/concrete*
translated by Emma Ramadan · FRANCE

GOETHE · *Faust*
translated by Zsuzsanna Ozsváth and Frederick Turner · GERMANY

PERGENTINO JOSÉ · *Red Ants: Stories*
translated by Tom Bunstead and the author · MEXICO

FOWZIA KARIMI · *Above Us the Milky Way: An Illuminated Alphabet* · USA

TAISIA KITAISKAIA · *The Nightgown & Other Poems* · USA

DMITRY LIPSKEROV · *The Tool and the Butterflies*
translated by Reilly Costigan-Humes & Isaac Stackhouse Wheeler · RUSSIA

GORAN PETROVIĆ · *At the Lucky Hand, aka The Sixty-Nine Drawers*
translated by Peter Agnone · SERBIA

C.F. RAMUZ · *Jean-Luc Persecuted*
translated by Olivia Baes · SWITZERLAND

TATIANA RYCKMAN · *The Ancestry of Objects* · USA

JESSICA SCHIEFAUER · *Girls Lost*
translated by Saskia Vogel · SWEDEN

MIKE SOTO · *A Grave Is Given Supper: Poems* · USA

MÄRTA TIKKANEN · *The Love Story of the Century*
translated by Stina Katchadourian · FINLAND